---

# GAME ON

---

JUNO CHASE

ISBN: 978-1-947234-09-3

ISBN: 978-1-947234-24-6

Change the game, don't let the game change you.

--

Macklemore

Cheyenne LeFleur dried the largest fry-pan her mother owned and handed it to Dallas to put away. As many Friday nights as not, Cheyenne spent a couple of hours in her mom's kitchen with her siblings cleaning up after their family dinner. It wasn't the sudsy fun that drew her to the chaotic family meal so much as the time she spent with her older brother and sister afterward. They caught up on each other's lives without little ears listening in while they worked. And, this week, Cheyenne had quite a few things she couldn't share in front of the kids.

Sky washed, Cheyenne rinsed and dried, and Dallas put things away. Cheyenne was itching to share her latest adventure with Sky, but not necessarily in front of her brother. As soon as Dallas took a bathroom break, Cheyenne leaned in close to her sister.

"I checked off a *major* bucket list item this week."

"Awesome. Dish it out. I live vicariously through you." Sky shoved her arm into the gigantic stock-pot their mom used for boiling pasta, the appendage disappearing into bubbles elbow deep. "You know that, right?"

"Ha," Cheyenne said, tossing a scrubbie at her.

Sky caught it mid-air. "Seriously. I'm an old married woman these days. I hardly get to do anything fun anymore."

"Love, marriage and the baby carriage getting you down?" Cheyenne bumped her hips against Sky's to emphasize the teasing sing-song to her voice. Sky was one of the happiest people she knew.

"Ugh. Mom needs to use some oil next time," she said, still scrubbing at the pot. "Nah. I love it. Wouldn't change it for the world. I got all the wild stuff out of me before getting married."

Cheyenne winced and closed her eyes as her hands stilled on the pot she was drying.

Sky stopped scrubbing and put a dripping hand on Cheyenne's. "I'm sorry. I didn't mean anything by that."

Cheyenne swallowed away the lump in her throat. "It's all right. If I had it to do over again, I would have listened to you. I would never have married Alberto."

"Don't stress it. You thought it was love." Sky

plunged her hand back into her washing. "Bucket list, Cheyenne. Spill it."

The bucket list was one they had made when they had gotten together a couple days before Sky's wedding. Cheyenne's list was filled with things like skydiving, going to a Bowie concert, and drinking tea in a Japanese tea ceremony. Both lists were filled with travel, adventures, and sexual conquests—and they kept track of everything. Cheyenne's list was way longer than Sky's, but Sky was nearly ten years older than Cheyenne and was way more experienced.

"Bucket list?" Sky nudged her back into reality, handing the clean pot over to Cheyenne to rinse and dry.

"Right. There's this Bingo game thing we're playing at the office. It's a fun way to decide who gets to go to a meeting with the boss." She couldn't tell her sister anything about the super secret meeting in Las Vegas that initiated the Bingo game in the first place. Congressman Pierce and been very clear that this meeting —with the code name Sunflower— was critical to upcoming legislation and had to be handled carefully from the outset to get bi-partisan support. Mentioning the game to her sister in the first place was probably a mistake. *Dang.* "Hey. I need you to promise me you won't tell anyone about this game, okay?"

Sky snorted as she drained the sink and swished it

clean. "No worries. Who'd I tell, anyway? Not like the kids would get it. And Robert? You know his head is at work. He's probably reading email right now instead of watching the movie."

"Point taken. Okay. So, it's called Monument Bingo. We have to kiss five different guys at monuments around DC to fill out a Bingo line. Whoever gets their Bingo first, goes on this trip with Congressman Pierce."

Sky wiped her hands dry and relaxed against the counter. "I hope Congressman Pierce didn't come up with the game."

"Oh, God, no. It was Madeline, one of the women I work with."

"How long do you have to wrangle up these five guys?" Her expression had changed from one of shock to one of amusement.

Cheyenne shrugged. "By next Friday."

"I can't even imagine five dates in a month, let alone two weeks. Wow. Continue, please. Bucket list? Bingo? Connect the dots here."

"I'm getting there. Let me tell my story, will ya? As part of the game, I got two of the kisses on Wednesday night. *And*, we didn't stop with kisses. I took them both to the same monument and kissed them, one right after the other." She had posted the Instagram link right away, but without the selfies of the two guys on either side of her; she'd kept that one to herself.

"Both of them? At the same time?" Sky asked, fanning herself.

"Yep. At the same time." It had been one of the most exciting evenings of her life, a fantasy turned reality. "I made out with one while leaning into the other. They took turns. And then, after the kisses? We went to a hotel." Cheyenne didn't want to admit that there were some fuzzy details about the guys' relationship. She was pretty sure they were friends before they'd met her at the bar. She'd asked if they were friends but they'd been kind of vague in their answer. "At any rate, by the end of the evening, they were bosom buddies." Cheyenne giggled.

Sky's mouth dropped open and moved soundlessly for a few seconds. "Oh. My. God. Cheyenne...you actually had a *three-way?*" She looked past Cheyenne toward the living room and dropped her voice. "Was it as hot as you'd imagined?"

"Totally. We were just the right amount of tipsy. You know, enough to get us over the initial weirdness of it all. But we weren't drunk, so that helped the... technical aspects and all that consent stuff."

"Holy hell. I can't believe you did it. You really went through with it? I thought that was going to be one thing that never got checked off either of our lists."

Sky twisted the towel she holding and snapped at Cheyenne's butt. "Totally daring, kiddo."

Cheyenne used to hate the age gap between her and Dallas and Sky—nine years for him, seven for her. As Cheyenne neared thirty, they were more like good friends than siblings. It was possible that if Sky and she were closer in age there might have been a lot more competition between them.

"Wanna share the details?" Sky asked, pulling out two wine glasses from the cupboard. "Well, not the exact details. But how are you feeling about it? It's not something everyone is going to approve of."

Cheyenne finished drying the giant pot and set it on the stove top for Dallas to put away. She cracked the door to the family room. She wanted to make sure no little ears were pressed against the door spying on them. The older kids were piled on top of each other and engrossed in the movie—a safe distance away from their conversation.

Caden, Sky's youngest and the baby of the group, was splayed out across Robert's lap. He had that adorable trusting face toddlers get when they sleep. And, as Sky had guessed, Robert was focused on the phone in his hand rather than the television or his child.

Cheyenne's heart ached, but she managed to stem the flow of tears that used to come whenever she looked at a baby. The pain from three failed pregnancies during her short marriage was something she hid better these days.

*Therapy must be working.* She rounded her shoulders and sluffed off the blues that burbled at the edges. She had exciting things to talk about with Sky. *Shift to the fun stuff.*

Cheyenne closed the kitchen door, convinced they had time to continue their very adult conversation.

"They'll be another hour at least," Cheyenne said.

Sky poured a rich merlot into their glasses. "I'm patiently waiting for details, Cheyenne."

Cheyenne slipped into the booth that served as a kitchen table and held up her glass for a toast. "To Bucket List items."

Sky clinked her glass against Cheyenne's and took a modest sip. Cheyenne rolled the wine over her tongue to get the full flavor profile. The Argentinian wine had a fruit-forward presentation that made it a perfect substitute for dessert.

"Was this three-way as awesome as it sounds? Any regrets?"

"It was better than awesome. They both...how do I say this? They totally catered to my needs and desires. They got my consent on everything. There was a lot of talking, making sure I was happy. I don't think I've ever said 'yes, more,' or 'keep going' that many times in my life."

Cheyenne squirmed in her seat with the memory. Had it only been a few days ago? Four hands roaming over her body. Two mouths. Two hot and hard bodies writhing against her in every position imaginable. She was going to use this for fantasy fodder for a long, long time.

"Did you..." Sky leaned in close and glanced at the door between them and the rest of their family. "Did you, you know, actually...have both inside...at the same time?"

"You can't even say it, can you?" Cheyenne back-handed Sky's shoulder gently. "Come on, say it. Then I'll tell you."

Sky rolled the stem of her glass between her fingers. "You are so cruel."

"Hey, if you want the deets, you need to earn the rights."

"Fine. Did you...have. Nope. I can't. I can't even say it."

"You're thinking about it, though. Your face is bright red."

Sky covered her face with both hands and dropped her voice to the lowest of possible whispers. "Did you do the double entry thing?"

"The *double entry* thing? Is that what the kids call

it these days?" Cheyenne giggled again. "Yes. Sky, I did the double deed. And it was maybe the most intense sexual experience I've ever had in my life."

Sky's jaw slung open. "Holy hell, Cheyenne. I can hardly believe it. You really did? Wasn't it...painful?"

"By the time we got around to that, I was well primed." Cheyenne held up her glass of wine in emphasis, and Sky clinked against it with hers.

"And it wasn't weird? Really?"

Cheyenne considered this. "No, the guys knew each other. It was like they'd done it before."

"Lucky, lucky girl. I can't even imagine Robert sharing me and not getting all bent out of shape. Nope. Never gonna happen. Not now, anyway. I wish I would have done that before getting married." Sky's eyes glazed over briefly as she stared into the depths of her nearly-full glass of wine.

Was Sky actually jealous of Cheyenne? That would be a first. Cheyenne finally had done something her bigger sister hadn't.

"These guys didn't bicker or squabble. I would suggest something, and they would eagerly hop to it. They weren't afraid of accidentally touching each other, and they were both totally into me."

"Being the center of attention of two men," Sky said dreamily. "I don't think I could actually go through with it. At least, not now. Robert wouldn't stand for another man in our bed. And I'm pretty sure I couldn't do it without him. My days of crazy are long over."

Cheyenne opened the photo of the three of them at the monument to show her sister. "Both are kinda cute, eh?"

Sky swiped to make the photo larger to examine the men. "Wow. One of them is a doppelgänger for Lincoln Pierce. Wasn't that kinda incestuous?"

Cheyenne snatched the phone away and examined the photo closely. "Huh. I guess, maybe. In the picture he might barely resemble Link. In real life, though, he's nothing like him. He doesn't move or sound like him. This guy had a super sexy British accent. Oh, man."

Cheyenne didn't add that she'd seen Lincoln in a swimsuit at a pool party. The Honorable Congressman Lincoln Pierce was muscled and toned, but not ripped like the guy from the other night. Also, Link did not have any visible tattoos. The guy who vaguely looked like Link had a tat on his torso of a griffin. Cheyenne had traced the delicate lines of ink along the man's firm chest and sides.

"Still crushing on the honorable congressman?" Sky asked.

Cheyenne tilted her head back and laughed. "No. No. No. Not anymore. I mean, he's hot and all, but he's...not the right guy. He's always reading and thinking and super serious. Besides, I don't like to think of him *that way*."

"He's absolutely dreamy. If I worked there, I'd never get anything done."

"I think he'll be president someday. And the last thing I want is to be scrutinized by the press. My photo all over the net? Everyone prying into my personal life? Ugh. You just know people wouldn't understand things like this." She held up the phone and wiggled it in demonstration.

Sky rocked her head from shoulder to shoulder, considering. "You're right. I'm sort of shocked you actually went through with it. And, yeah, that kind of media scrutiny would totally suck. But, you know, Dad's dying on 9/11 would play well as part of the whole political rah-rah story."

"Yeah, not wanting to go there, thanks." Cheyenne swirled the wine around in her glass to give it a little more air. "Thanks for not being all judgy about the guys."

"Why would I be? That was on my bucket list, too." Sky squeezed Cheyenne's hand. "Though, honestly, I knew I'd never get around to that one. But you have nothing to be ashamed about if you had fun and no one got hurt, right?"

"Honestly? I had a great time. It was a bucket list

item, but...I'm not keen on doing it again. Once was enough."

"Even though it was super intense?"

"It was physically fabulous. But emotionally? I didn't have a real connection with either of them. It was...*only* physical. I'd like more than that."

Cheyenne poured herself another glass of wine and held the bottle over Sky's glass in question even though she'd hardly had any.

Sky put her hand over the top of her glass. "I only wanted a little taste."

"Suit yourself. This stuff is divine," Cheyenne said. She crept to the kitchen door and cracked it open quietly to check the movie status. Her mom leaned back in her custom swivel rocker, her head tilted up to the ceiling and jaw hanging down. At least she wasn't snoring.

"Mom's asleep. Caden's still adorable, and Isabella is about to drift off any moment."

Sky leaned back against the kitchen booth. "Why don't you tell me more about this game you're playing at work. What exactly, is the prize?"

"Game, what game?" asked Dallas as he stepped into the kitchen.

## Chapter 2

*D*allas grabbed a beer from the fridge and scooted into the booth next to Cheyenne, squeezing her in between the two of them. "I always knew you guys talked about the juicy stuff when I go off for a few minutes."

"Oh, Dallas, stop whining and sit down. You've got to hear what our baby sister has been up to this week. You know you never miss out on anything that goes on in this family," Sky said.

Dallas laughed and took a swig from his beer. "Right. So, what gives?"

"Sky has the gist already. It's a Bingo kissing game and whoever wins gets to go to Vegas to attend an important meeting..."

"Sounds like a sex game," Dallas said, grinning.

Cheyenne punched him playfully on his bicep.

"Not necessarily. Only a kiss is needed to get a Bingo stamp. Sex is optional."

"This super important meeting is something you're all willing to play with?" Dallas asked. He sat up straighter, his fingers gripping his bottle of beer a little too firmly.

"Chill, Dallas. It's not that big a deal."

Dallas frowned, his eyes narrowing. "Let me get this straight. You have to drag a guy around and kiss him at five different monuments?"

"Close, but no cigar," Cheyenne said, wiggling her eyebrows like Groucho Marx. "It's a little bit harder than that. Our Bingo cards are marked with guys in different professions and different monuments. So, five guys, five monuments. You get the idea. But all I have left is to find a guy from the CIA to kiss at the Lincoln Memorial, and..." Cheyenne closed her eyes so she could picture the card from memory. "Oh, right. A scientist at the Smithsonian Castle."

Cheyenne had started out playing the game thinking she'd just fill the whole card in as some sort of super challenge. Twenty-five dates in two weeks. Not all would be real, full evening dates. Most would would be short—coffee, breakfast, lunch, drinks— ending in chaste kisses at a monument. It would be a hoot. She'd only slept with the two guys in her ménage. But she was meeting a lot of interesting men.

She'd kissed the two guys from her ménage a trois at the same memorial. It had earned her two stamps, but not in the same row. She thought of it more like hedging her bets. It was only five days into the game and she'd already kissed ten men. Unfortunately, they were scattered all over her card. She needed to focus on one line now in order to win.

"That last one should be easy," Sky said. "Weren't you just blathering on about that guy you're meeting tomorrow? Isn't he a scientist who works for the Smithsonian?"

A blush crept along Cheyenne's neck and flared brightly on her cheeks. "Alexander Moore? He goes by Xander. I honestly hadn't considered him for the game."

"Why, because you might actually like him? Glad to see you have *some* morals." Dallas' lips pursed together. "Honestly, Cheyenne, I don't see how playing these kinds of games is good for anyone."

"Have I really talked about him that much?" Cheyenne asked.

Sky's jaw dropped. "You've mentioned him maybe a bajillion times over the last couple of months."

Dallas put his hands against his cheeks, batted his lashes and raised his voice into a high falsetto. "Xander said...Xander told me...Xander is going to...Xander, Xander, Xander."

Cheyenne swatted at Dallas and he laughed.

"Seriously, Cheyenne," Dallas said, dropping all mockery. His big dopey eyes met hers with nothing but concern. "You talk about him all the time. Like you've been dating him for months."

"It's funny," Cheyenne said, "I honestly didn't think of Xander as a *scientist*. He's not at all boring on the phone. It didn't occur to me I could use him for the game."

The very thought of kissing him to score on her Bingo game bothered her. She couldn't use him like that. *Not Xander. Calm yourself, girl. You are blowing this out of proportion. You haven't met him yet.*

They were treading in dangerous waters now. Cheyenne's raging crush on the enigmatic Alexander Moore was something she thought she'd kept to herself, and yet, here Dallas and Sky were, both teasing her about him.

Xander had contacted her via the cooking school where she taught pastry arts on the weekend. He had described himself as a curator at the Smithsonian and that he was putting together a new exhibit. He wanted her help converting some ancient recipes into something usable with modern foods and cooking techniques. Together they'd designed a class, blending history and cooking to go with the exhibit. But they'd done it all over the phone and via email.

He worked at the Smithsonian and taught at George Washington, so he was not far from where she worked in the Cannon Congressional Building, but neither had suggested they meet in person to work on the project together. Every time she spent ten minutes on the phone with Xander, she was left with a warm, fuzzy feeling. She could listen to him talk forever; his voice was warm. Sweet. Calming.

One day, he had called to discuss a translation he was working on that was completely unrelated to the cooking project. He'd just wanted her opinion of a poem he'd translated from Ancient Sumerian into English for a class he was teaching. It was about spring and flowers and sweet smells and love. He read it first in what he described as their 'best guess' at original and then in English. It had left her in a dazed fantasy about him.

In her last session with her therapist she worked it out. She had built Xander up into something unrealistic in her mind and had unconsciously kept them apart physically so as to not tear down her fantasy. He was perfect on the telephone. There was bound to be something wrong with him in person, and, as her therapist had pointed out, some subconscious part of her wanted the fantasy to last as long as possible.

Dallas crossed his muscular arms over his chest and leaned back, giving her his big brotherly disapproving glare. "You actually like him, don't you? Maybe it's not the best idea to play games with someone you're attracted to."

"I don't know how I feel, actually." Saying it aloud was a relief. "I haven't even met him in person yet. I know nothing about him other than what his professional LinkedIn profile shows, and it doesn't even include a picture."

Xander didn't do Facebook, or she couldn't find him there, and even his LinkedIn profile showed a photo of an old clay tablet instead of a photograph of him. He was an archaeologist, so, technically he was a scientist. Xander might be someone different than the guy on their phone calls. They got a little flirty but had never gone over the top. For all she knew, he could be married. Or gay. Or fifty.

"I'm meeting him for the first time at my pie-making class tomorrow morning. He's coming to that and staying afterward to finalize the details for the class we're co-teaching," Cheyenne said. "In the evening, we're going to the exhibit opening. At the Smithsonian."

It would be the perfect opportunity to get a kiss for the game. But the very notion of it set her on edge. Kissing Xander just for the game was...wrong. Other guys? Guys she didn't care about? Sure. But not Xander.

She was mooning over a man she hadn't met yet. The fantasy of what he might be. She'd built him up into perfection, and she doubted he could possibly live up to the image of him she'd dreamed up.

Dallas leaned in close. "So, tell the truth Cheyenne, is this Xander guy real, or did you dream him up?"

Cheyenne punched him in the shoulder and scowled. "Of course he's real. I'm meeting him tomorrow. You want me to send you a selfie to prove it?"

Dallas put up his hands in surrender. "I'm teasing, Cheyenne. You really have been talking about him like you've been dating a while. You going to kiss him for that silly game of yours?"

"You play plenty of games yourself, Dallas," Sky said. "Just because your games have to do with national security doesn't mean they aren't still games..."

"My point is, Cheyenne, your life is kinda crazy. Like you've gone wild the last few years. I don't understand it."

"Leave her be, Dallas," Sky said.

Dallas tilted his head back as he took a slow swig of his beer. It was his way of getting some time; drinking meant you didn't have to say anything.

Cheyenne took it as her personal duty to shock her older brother. He could be quite the old-fashioned prude some days. He was often so stoic nothing seemed to bother him.

Maybe it was the wine breaking down her inhibitions, but Cheyenne couldn't help herself. And she had to get the topic off of Xander. "You wanna hear about *wild*, Dallas? I got it on with two guys in one night this week. How's that for *wild* and crazy?" Cheyenne blurted it out knowing it would drive him bonkers.

*Push. Push. Push.*

Dallas coughed, catching a few splatters of beer against the back of his hand. "Two guys, one night? Holy moly, Cheyenne! I know you're a modern woman, but...are you at least staying safe?"

"Oh, please, Dallas. You think we didn't use condoms?" Cheyenne rolled her eyes.

"No. Not that kind of safe. I mean...you're a woman, and I know you're a strong woman, don't get me wrong. But going off with two men? Did you know them? Did you at least send GPS info to a friend or share your location?"

The buttons she pushed hadn't been the ones she'd intended. She had expected righteous indignation or disgust over a sexual tryst he didn't approve of. Instead of flipping out over the nature of it, he'd gone straight to her safety.

Maybe she shouldn't have goaded him. The

concern and fear on his face tugged at her heart. She wrapped her arms around herself, making herself as small as possible. Disappointing Dallas was not something she liked to do.

The night she met Kyle and Shane had been pretty wild. The three of them hit it off at a bar, and, she'd taken the opportunity to get kisses from each of them for the Bingo game. After the monument kissing, things got really crazy.

"I got their business cards, what's the big deal?"

Dallas grasped one of her hands in his. "I'm your big brother, and I hate that you could be putting yourself at risk out there. Bad things happen to women in this world. Trust me. I've seen how cruel men can be."

Instead of all the remonstrations she'd expected, he dug deeper into his worry. His eyes were gentle and compassionate as always. Dallas had a huge heart, and it always went where it should. She blinked her eyes to fight off the waterworks that were building with the emotion. Dallas always had her back.

*Or, as he would often say, "I've got your six, sis."*

"Thanks. Dallas, it was a one-time thing. I'm fine." Disappointing Dallas in any way made her feel like a two-year-old, and she hated it when she failed him.

He wasn't quite done yet, though. He pulled a couple of business cards out of his wallet. "Do these look real to you?"

Cheyenne examined them. "They're just like any business card."

"Am I Tom Sloane or Jefferson Thompson? Do I work for Genesis Realty or Parkland Trust? If I handed these to you and told you I was either of these guys, how would you know who I was?"

"Who spends money to make fake business cards? And for that matter, why do you have them?" Cheyenne handed the cards back. "It doesn't matter anyway, what am I supposed to do, Dallas? Ask for a driver's license or passport and send you a photo so you can do a background check before I leave the bar with someone?"

Dallas' lips tightened. "That's a pretty good idea. It would only take about ten minutes. You could delay leaving for that long, couldn't you?"

*Was he serious? Really?*

Cheyenne rolled her eyes at him again. "I was *joking.* I am not about to ask for ID. I'm fine. I think I'd know if someone was a total creeper. Lay off."

"What does your shrink think about all this?" Dallas asked.

Cheyenne scowled and crossed her arms over her chest. He always ended contentious discussions with asking her what her therapist thought.

Sky coughed. "Change of topic, shall we? I have something I want to tell you two."

Sky's eyes shifted from amusement to the one she always wore when she was worried about hurting Cheyenne's feelings.

*What now?* Cheyenne's stomach twisted, knowing Sky was about to drop a bomb of some sort. Dallas and Cheyenne eyed each other warily, suddenly compatriots again, before turning their full attention to Sky.

"I'm pregnant again," Sky said.

Cheyenne's stomach clenched and she avoided her sister's over-earnest eyes. Sky was always so worried about her, how she'd feel or respond to this kind of news.

"Sky, that's...wonderful." She hid her shock by throwing her arms around her sister and hugging her tight. Three kids in five years. Sky was as fertile as Cheyenne was barren.

Biting back tears of jealousy, she met Dallas' eyes over Sky's shoulder. He mouthed *I'm sorry* at Cheyenne as she hugged her sister. It was no secret amongst them that Cheyenne wanted children.

"When are you due?" Dallas asked, breaking the silence that had fallen over them.

"In October."

"Oh, I hope they're born on Halloween, that would be cool," Cheyenne said, dragging herself off her sister. She pretended to focus on her wine as she forced the sting away. She was happy for Sky and miserable for herself at the same time.

*Why was this so hard?*

After the hours she'd spent in the therapist's office, she didn't think hearing about a new pregnancy wouldn't bother her so much anymore.

*When would that pang go away?*

It had been four years since she'd lost the last baby and Alberto had divorced her, annulling their short marriage. The church granted the annulment due to her inability to bear children so he'd be free to get remarried in the eye of his church. His mama had pushed hard for it so she could have her grandbabies. It had been four years since she'd moved back to DC and rebooted her life with new roommates and new goals.

It had been four very long years, but she was over him and mostly over grieving the losses. She'd always have some sadness around the miscarriages. Her therapist had told her it got easier with time, that the grief shifted and changed. She'd finally accepted Alberto's love had come with expectations. When she couldn't have a baby to meet those expectations, his love for her had sputtered and died.

"Are you okay, Cheyenne?" asked Sky.

"Oh, Sky. Sure, I'm jealous of your easy reproductive system. Sad that I can't have children—or at least four years ago I couldn't. The doctor said new technology comes along every day, right? But I am really happy for you. You're such a good mom. Maybe you can have my babies for me one day, you seem to pop them out so easily."

Sky sat stock-still for a moment before slowly putting a hand on Cheyenne's. "Hey. You know what? I would totally do that for you, right? Have your babies for you if you still can't when you're ready. When you decide you want to go there. I'm serious, Chey." She squeezed Cheyenne's hand for emphasis. "I love being pregnant, and three kids will be plenty for us."

They'd never spoken about surrogacy before. Maybe it was because Sky hadn't had her own kids yet. She was still traipsing all over Europe when Cheyenne and Alberto had gotten married.

"Really?" Cheyenne asked, meeting her sister's eyes. It was easy to offer something big and grand up in the moment, to make someone feel better, but it wasn't always so easy to follow through with it.

"Really. Well, not for a year or two." She patted her belly which was barely beginning to round out. "I need to get this one out and heal up, but yeah. My body. My eggs, your eggs...someone's sperm."

"Would Robert agree?" Cheyenne asked, a spark of excitement, of possibility, coursing through her.

Sky considered the question a moment before

answering. "Maybe not at first, but he'll come around. I can see to that."

Cheyenne loved her sister for offering, but no babies were coming without the crucial other half being involved. She tried to lighten the mood. "And...if I *ever* find the right sperm, I'll let you know," Cheyenne said, laughing. It had been a long time since she'd dated anyone she'd considered long term. Maybe it just wasn't in the cards for her.

Dallas stood and tossed his empty beer in the recycling bin. "When *you two* start talking about sperm, I know it's time for me to leave."

"Oh, come on, Dallas, I can't believe we're scaring you away now," Sky said, "not after everything else we've talked about tonight."

He opened the door to the family room and paused, turning back to face them.

"Cheyenne, it's part of my nature to worry about you. You know that, right?"

Cheyenne held up her wine glass in a toast to him. "To the best big brother on the planet. I know you have my back."

"Absolutely."

Once the door swung shut behind him, Cheyenne dropped her head back and groaned.

"He means well, Chey. I didn't even think about

going off with two guys as being particularly scary. He thinks differently than we do."

"It's just kind of a buzz kill. I really had fun the other night. But now, I'm having a hard time not thinking about how things could have gone wrong."

Sky wrapped her arms around her. "You're here, safe and sound, aren't you? You didn't do anything wrong and nothing bad came out of it. So, ignore him."

"You're right. I'm an adult woman in the twenty first century. I had a good time. End of story."

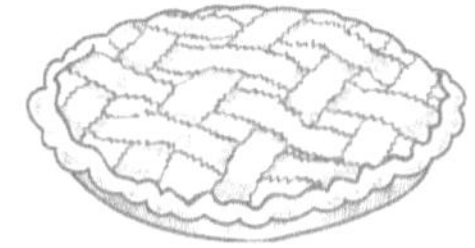

## Chapter 3

Cheyenne was finally meeting Alexander Moore—Xander—in person. She rolled his name around on her tongue. It sounded exotic, like he could be the hero in an adventure movie. Over the last couple of months, they had spoken on the phone, emailed, and texted. Ostensibly, the calls were for them to prepare for the class they would be teaching together. But she had no idea what he looked like and knew almost nothing about his personal life.

Come to think of it, she hadn't shared much about her personal life with him, either. She had told him about getting her BA in Communications followed by the Culinary Arts degree in California while leaving out the details of her failed marriage and subsequent return to DC.

Of course, she'd told him all about her desire to

own a restaurant with her roommates, Zach, Tiffany, and Chelsea. One of the most exciting things she'd ever done was audition for a cooking competition with them a few months before. But she'd not mentioned anything about that to Xander or anyone else because of a strict nondisclosure agreement. Not as if it mattered. They hadn't heard a peep from the show since the audition.

Their conversations began with predictable discussions for the class. At first, he was business like, but over time he relaxed and the conversations turned a little flirty. She'd kept the flirting at a minimum because she didn't want him to get the wrong idea. Business and pleasure didn't always mix well. Besides, he could be in his late fifties and married for all she knew. Or not her type. Or...something that would make it all wrong.

When Xander asked what she did outside the Culinary School, she'd told him that she worked for Congressman Pierce, but gave no details. Certainly not anything about how she worked for the money and got little satisfaction out of her job or how she resented going to work as it interfered with her real goals in life. Why admit to anyone she was becoming a slacker and showing up late to work and daydreaming about quitting? No. Instead, she focused on what she was going to do with her life. It was only a matter of time.

Xander was a curator at the Smithsonian and an adjunct archeology professor at George Washington University. He was in charge of a new exhibit at the museum featuring ancient Sumerian cooking. After discovering stone tablets in a store room of the museum—placed there nearly a hundred years ago and long forgotten—he'd become enamored of the idea of creating an interactive exhibit and experience after translating them. Instead of the usual inventory of basic supplies he was used to finding on such things, there had been a dozen recipes describing three distinct cooking techniques.

Xander had called the culinary school and asked for someone who had practical knowledge to recreate the recipes using modern ingredients and techniques, the ability to teach a class with him, and deliver a presentation at the Smithsonian. The director had suggested Cheyenne and connected them through email.

The email exchanges started with Xander requesting Cheyenne's help with a complicated recipe involving a dough wrapped around a meat filling. He couldn't figure out how to make it work with the flours that were known during the time period. Cheyenne talked him out of trying to find flours that were specific to the region of the time, and, instead, to adapt the recipes for the modern kitchen. It would be tricky enough to substitute some of the spices with modern ones, why make it harder than it needed to be?

The opening of the gallery exhibit was in the evening and the classes were the following three Saturday afternoons. It cut into her socializing a good deal, but the project was so exciting she wanted to do it. *No regrets.*

Xander had signed up for her pie-making class before their scheduled afternoon meeting. They needed to go over some final details for the opening at the Smithsonian that evening. She was excited to be teaching a class that was half history and half hands-on cooking. While Cheyenne focused primarily on pastry as her passion, she could cook anything. Besides, her awesome roommates—chefs all—had stepped in to help whenever she had questions.

She spent an hour getting her classroom ready. Each station had all the ingredients and utensils needed for the class. Bowls, measuring spoons, the flour and butter for the crust, pastry cloths and rolling pins were all laid out in a particular order. She had set up a separate counter for various fillings so students could make their favorite kind of pie to take home.

As people trickled into the class, she checked them off her roster and memorized their names. Five minutes before class and two people hadn't shown— Xander and some lady named Carroll.

Cheyenne stifled her disappointment as an old man in his seventies shuffled into the room. His hair was pure white and fanned around his head like Albert Einstein. Several decades ago, he might have been a hottie. Great. Xander was an old guy, nothing like the guy she'd imagined. *Just her luck.*

His eyes twinkled with the air of an absent-minded professor. He wasn't awful or anything, just...not her type and way too old to match the fantasies she'd dared not admit to. Fantasies that were now flitting away like the tendrils of a dream. She was definitely not going to flirt with him anymore.

She offered her hand, trying to hide the disillusionment welling within her. Her brother had been right. All the denials the previous night with Sky and Dallas had been cover for her fantasy. Maybe she was crushing after the guy she'd gotten to know over email. There wasn't going to be much kissing this guy. Except maybe on the cheek. *Would that count for the game?* She smiled brightly, deciding that she could deal with a kiss on the cheek for the game's sake. Even if it was as exciting as kissing her grandfather. "Hello, Xander. It's so nice to finally meet you."

"Finally meet me? Xander? I'm not Xander," he said, tapping a bent finger on her clipboard. "I'm Carroll. Carroll Fielding. I should be on your list."

Cheyenne blinked as she followed his finger. "Oh,

I'm sorry, Mr. Fielding. Carroll. I...I'm glad you made it, then." Relief flooded through her. She helped him to one of the two empty stations. Hope fluttered in her tummy.

Fifteen minutes later, just as she was launching into her discussion about the virtues of butter as the fat of choice for pastry, a man rushed into the room—this had to be Xander Moore.

He was almost exactly as she had imagined him. He was taller than she was by a good six inches. His dark curly hair was framed by a sexy set of white wings at each temple, giving him a distinguished professor air. With a name like Alexander she had expected something akin to a Greek god walking through the door, and he delivered admirably well. He was movie star gorgeous.

After slinging off a messenger bag and sliding it under the only free station in the room, he shrugged off a well-worn leather coat and wrapped it over the top of his chair. His button down shirt was open to the collarbone, and masses of dark thick curls peeked over the top.

Xander's eyes were the big surprise: bright hazel, almost green, contrasting against his darker skin with a fierce intensity. As their eyes met, a calmness descended upon her. The light in the room shifted into a tunnel focusing on him.

*She could lose herself in the sweet, sweet depths of this man. Why was she always so drawn to tall, dark, and handsome men?* Lightly bronzed skin. Leather jacket cut perfectly over his shoulders. Early stubble along his strong jawline.

Cheyenne's knees wobbled. She focused on the food in front of her. She couldn't dive deeper into the sensation—not with fifteen other people in the room. It wasn't love at first sight, so much as a deep knowing from within. There was definitely something about this man that made the rest of the world fade around him.

"Pardon me for being late. I didn't think there'd be such traffic on the weekend."

"No worries. I assume you're Xander Moore?"

He smiled, and she thought she was going to faint. It wasn't just the bright white smile, but the way his eyes crinkled at the corners and a deep happiness welled out from within.

*And what confidence. God. Alpha male all the way. Calm down, girl. He's definitely a little bit older. He could be married or otherwise unavailable. Stop jumping ahead. You just met the man.*

"Yes. That would be me."

"Nice to meet you. I was just discussing the various attributes of butter versus shortening versus lard in a pie crust." She tapped the various fats as she spoke. "I can catch you up with what you missed later."

Xander unbuttoned his sleeves and rolled them up to his elbows, revealing well developed arm muscles fringed with jet black hair.

Cheyenne wished he'd just take his whole shirt off, but that wouldn't be practical in a cooking class. She shook her head, refocusing her efforts to teaching. "I actually prefer lard for most crusts, particularly savory ones. People with delicate palettes and super-tasters can taste the difference as lard has a very particular flavor."

Cheyenne uncovered a tray she had prepared before class. "The blue plate is a butter crust, the red plate is a lard crust, the yellow plate is a shortening crust, and on the last plate, the orange plate, is the crust we shall not name."

This last got a few laughs, but more people were confused by her lame attempt at humor. Cheyenne hated it when a joke fell flat like that. She held up a piece of the crust between two fingers.

"The crust on the orange plate uses both butter *and* shortening. I made it to demonstrate something *not* to do. Other than the fat, the crusts were each made with the exact same technique. Oh, and one of my secrets is to use a combination of chilled vodka and ice water in the pastry. The vodka reduces the amount of moisture in the crust and helps create a divine texture. Pass the crusts around and examine them. Some are flaky, others are crumbly. You'll find you might like the taste of some better than others."

After sending the tray on its way around the class, she continued her lecture. She held up the butter. "For this class, I've chosen an all-butter crust recipe you'll find on the first sheet of your packet. The techniques I will show you will work the same regardless to which fat you choose. The temperature is critical to good pastry. The butter must be chilled—frozen, even. Does anyone know why?"

She and Xander had talked about this over the phone as part of their recipe development. Ancient Sumerians didn't have refrigerators, but they did have access to ice and cold streams. He politely kept his hand down as someone else answered. As she fell into the details, teacher mode took over, putting *girl falling for hot guy mode* on pause.

As the tray of crusts moved around the room, she watched people's reactions. Some took only a single bite of each crust. Others made faces as they tried them, some even spat out a couple. When the tray landed at Xander's station, he examined the structure of each sample first. He tasted all of the crusts except the lard crust. He didn't even pick that one up to examine it.

As she continued the class, Xander made a few comments without being disruptive. But it was clear, even to her, that they interacted like old friends.

Cheyenne couldn't believe her luck.

*Handsome. Funny. Into cooking.*

After her demonstration, Cheyenne made a circuit of the room as everyone rolled out their crusts. Xander's was even and flattened smoothly under his pin. Cheyenne snuck a peek at his muscular forearms, the white sleeves of his shirt a perfect frame for his dark skin.

He managed the dough with a practiced efficiency.

"You've done this a few times, I take it?" she asked.

"I love pie," he said, his eyes locking on hers. "It's my favorite dessert."

"What's your favorite filling?" she asked, her lips twitching upward into a smile. Those gorgeous eyes. And his dark lashes contrasted beautifully with his skin.

"Cherry, apple, and peach. In that order."

Cheyenne swallowed. She sucked in her lower lip, wanting to believe he wasn't talking about fruit. Xander's mere presence made it almost impossible to stay focused on what she was doing. He appeared to be paying close attention to every word she said, which made it even worse. She made it through the next couple of hours, helping students roll out their dough, teaching them how to crimp the edges, figuring out what they'd done wrong and starting over.

Finally, the class was over. She handed out evaluations and hoped no one noticed how scattered she had been during this class. People left with their finished pies, a ceramic pie plate provided by the school as part of their class fees.

As soon as everyone else was gone, Xander helped her clean up the kitchen. Most people had been pretty good about tidying their own work-stations, but it still took them an hour to finish up. They chatted amiably as they cleaned, as if they'd known each other forever and not just met a few hours ago. Their emails had ben fully focused on work, and their telephone conversations had been a little flirty and centered around the Sumerian project.

Now was a perfect opportunity to get a little closer to the man behind all those calls. Find out if he was just being friendly.

Cheyenne handed Xander the dustbin while she swept the floor. "What do you do when you're not deciphering ancient Sumerian tablets and cooking pie?"

Xander dropped to his haunches as she filled the dustbin with scraps of dough and flour.

"This and that. I read. Watch movies. Sailing. The usual stuff."

*Reading?* Check. *Movies?* Check. *Sailing?* That was new, but something that had always intrigued her. She'd have to delve a bit deeper to figure out whatever he meant by *the usual stuff*. Cheyenne had dated enough men to know that could mean just about anything. One man she had dated spent ten hours a weekend on model railroads. Another played Dungeons & Dragons every Saturday morning with a group of geeky friends. Yet another brewed beer every Sunday with a buddy. She liked men who had interests beyond her own as long as they managed time together.

"Oooh," Cheyenne said. "What are you reading right now?"

"I'm on the last *Master and Commander*."

Cheyenne could picture the series on Dallas' shelf. The books all had a prow or two of an old sailing ship on the front with dramatic waves splashing all around. "I tried reading those once. My brother has the whole series at his place. But I couldn't get into it."

"I had so many sailing buddies tell me I had to read it, I decided I couldn't continue hanging out at the club anymore without having read them. Too much of a poser otherwise. I loved them from word one. So, what are you reading right now?"

"I'm going through a bit of an Ann Radcliffe phase. I'm reading *The Mysteries of Udulpho* at the moment."

Xander stood and dumped the contents of the dustbin into the garbage. "I've never heard of her."

"I hadn't until recently. I was going through a Jane Austen phase. Read all her books. Watched the movies —every version I could find. Saw plays. Listened to them all on Audible. It was a movie about Austen that mentions Radcliffe as one of Austen's influences."

"Can I ask you something?" he asked.

"You just did," she said, laughing.

"Seriously. What is it about Jane Austen?"

"What do you mean?"

"Don't take this the wrong way, but a lot of women I know are really into her. Can you explain the attraction?"

"A lot of women you know?" she pushed him playfully on the shoulder. "You mean women you date?"

"Dated, anyway," he said, his eyelids dropping to half-mast. "I am not dating anyone at the moment. But yeah, women I dated, *in the past*, seem infatuated with her."

Cheyenne rolled her eyes at him. "We're not infatuated with Jane Austen. We're infatuated with the way she presents love. Romance. Darcy."

"Darcy. Why does everyone bring him up? Who is this Darcy, anyway? Why are you all so gaga over him?"

"Watch *Pride and Prejudice*, the one with Colin

Firth, and you will totally understand what I'm talking about."

"I'll give it a go. Sometime soon. Is there anything else you read, other than Austen and romance novels? Do you always immerse yourself in one author like that?"

Cheyenne made another pile with the broom. "I go back and forth, actually. I'll read a mystery, then a romance, then something classic, something more literary. I have yet to meet a book I didn't like."

He held the bin in place for her again. "Except *Master and Commander*? Didn't you just say you couldn't get into it?"

"Point to Xander. You're right. I guess I'm not particularly fond of science fiction or fantasy, either. I love contemporary romance, chic-lit that makes me laugh. Huge dramas like Wuthering Heights. Mysteries are probably my favorite, though. I always will pick up a good mystery."

"Me too. I love mysteries," Xander said. "There are quite a few authors I follow."

Cheyenne bobbed up on her toes. "Have you read the latest Bosch?"

Xander grinned and went off on a delicious ten-minute rant about his love for that series.

After they had exhausted their lists, discussed their favorite series, compared books to the television versions of their favorites, they were done cleaning. They had an amazing crossover in tastes.

They moved on to the final wipe down of the counters. Each took a bottle of disinfectant and several fresh cleaning towels and started at opposite ends of one counter, working toward the center.

"When do you find time to read?" he asked.

"In between this and that." She paused and met his eyes. "Mostly before I go to sleep." Did she dare mention she never brought boyfriends home to her apartment? Sharing with three other people meant little privacy, plus it was her safe space.

"And movies? What do you watch?" she asked before he could comment.

"I'm partial to heist movies. Thrillers. And an occasional rom-com. But I've been known to enjoy 'films' and I love Hitchcock."

"He was amazing, wasn't he?" Cheyenne asked. "So, how often do you get out sailing?"

"Not as often as I'd like. In the summer it's maybe once or twice a month. This month we have our Saturday classes which will cut into sailing time."

"I've never been sailing," Cheyenne said. "It's not something that's ever come up. No one I've ever dated has been into boats."

Their hands met in the middle of the counter, each having finished their side. Cheyenne playfully brushed his off and swiped once down the center in a finishing flourish, her eyes never leaving his.

"We'll have to remedy that. I'm a member of the Central Marina and can get a boat for us sometime. I'd be happy to show you the ropes."

They both laughed. Even Cheyenne understood that pun.

As they continued the clean-up, they shifted in and out of topics, mining each a little more deeply at every pass. By the time the kitchen sparkled, Cheyenne knew more about Xander than she did most of the men she'd ever dated for months.

The only thing they didn't agree on was where to find the best burger in DC. After a heated debate, they laughingly agreed to a burger-duel sometime in the near future.

After the kitchen was clean, Xander took off his apron and rolled down his shirt-sleeves. He grabbed his coat and held up his messenger bag. "The power-point presentation for tonight...do you want to go over it again?"

"Sure. It'll help to run through it in person."

Xander set his computer up on the counter they'd just finished cleaning.

"Want some pie?" Cheyenne asked.

"Absolutely. I've been looking forward to tasting your treats for months," Xander said.

A frisson of excitement danced along her neck. She cut into the lattice-topped cherry pie she'd made as her demo. Red cherry juice oozed out into the pan as she removed the first piece. "Well, that's what happens when you don't let things cool completely."

"I like my pie fresh and hot," he said, waggling his eyebrows, taking the double entendre to a ridiculous level.

Cheyenne laughed as she handed him his slice.

He took a forkful and closed his eyes as he ate the first bite. "Mmmmm...this is the best cherry pie I've ever had."

Cheyenne tasted it and decided it was pretty good, but lacking something. It needed a hint of almond and maybe a little more sugar for perfection. But her crust was perfect; she could make that blindfolded. "You know how to flatter a girl."

"No flattery involved. Pure truth."

Tiny smile lines crinkled around his eyes, and the spark in those gorgeous hazel eyes of his was friendly and open as if he was inviting her to reach into his soul and find the real him. The familiar warmth of a blush creeping up her cheeks made her focus on her pie.

*Mutual attraction achievement unlocked. Slow down girl, this one might be a keeper.* Cheyenne took another bite of her pie so she wouldn't have to respond right away and pointed at his computer with her fork.

He shoved the last bite of his pie into his mouth and opened up his computer. He popped up the slideshow, and she sat next to him to see the screen. They'd planned a fifteen-minute presentation for the big gala opening that evening. After going through the presentation, it took them twenty-five minutes.

"People won't want to stand around this long. They don't need these," she said, removing three slides.

"But that's half your presentation. And its great information. Let's keep it."

"These specifics will be more interesting during the cooking classes next week. It fits better there."

They reworked their spiel for another hour until it flowed smoothly. By the time they were done, half the pie was gone and they'd honed down their talk to fifteen minutes.

Xander stood up and stretched. Cheyenne had to resist the urge to poke him in the stomach as his arms went up overhead.

*Where had that come from?*

Not that this was all business. But maybe she didn't want whatever this was to be all business. They were already flirting with each other, first on email and now in person.

Xander slung his leather jacket back on, and a

sweet wisp of cardamom mixed with rosewater wafted over her.

"So, tonight?" she asked. "I show up at the front door and they'll let me in?"

"You'll need to bring ID. It's a pretty high-brow event, but yeah, that's basically it. Your name is on the list. I'm sorry I forgot to ask you about a plus one, I don't know if I can add it to the list this late, but I can make it happen...if you want."

"That's okay," she said, smiling up at him, "I'm not seeing anyone right now."

His lips pursed and then quirked up into a smile. "Does that mean you'd be interested in going out after the gala? On a date. Maybe dancing or a late night dinner somewhere? Or maybe a movie?"

"A movie sounds perfect, actually. After today, and the gala tonight, I'll be ready for something more low key."

"I don't have a television at home. You okay watching something on my laptop?" he asked.

"We've got a huge screen and a comfy couch. I can ask the roomies to go to their rooms if we want to be alone," she said.

Was he disappointed? It wasn't until after she offered her apartment that she realized watching a movie on a laptop would be way more conducive to cuddling than at her apartment.

"Sounds like a plan, then," he said. He paused before leaning in close and kissing her lightly on her cheek.

She watched as he walked out the door. He was exactly everything she had always wanted. Everything about him was perfection. He read the same books and watched the same movies. He even enjoyed cooking. He was smart. Funny. Handsome. His job made him happy. Was anyone really that perfect? What was wrong with him? Why hadn't someone already snatched him up?

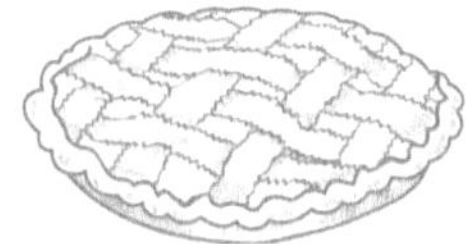

## Chapter 4

For the first time since moving to DC, Cheyenne wished she had more than one party dress. She never had a reason to own more than one. She wasn't invited to the fancy parties.

Madeline Asher, the PR guru in the office, would take her to parties when she didn't have a 'real' date or was post break-up. Madeline owned expensive shoes like Leboutins and wore only couture designs. Madeline had all this thanks to her family's money. Cheyenne got her shoes at Payless and tried to ignore the fact she felt like the second-handed step child.

She only had one fantastic dress because she only needed one. Fancy didn't pay for dreams, and Cheyenne had more important things to do with her money. She was saving every penny she could to open a restaurant with her roommates. Spending money on things like clothes was on the bottom of her priority list.

The single black dress in her closet was versatile enough to hide the fact she wore it to everything. She could wear the dress with a high neck in front or turn it around so that the neckline showed off her cleavage. The thing that saved it was how simple and boring it was. Dressing it up with various bits of jewelry or scarves disguised the basic canvas.

Tiffany sauntered into her room without knocking as Cheyenne slid the dress on so that the front aligned with her lacy black bra. "What do you think, Tiff?"

"Turn it around. You're going to a museum gallery opening, not a bar."

Cheyenne shifted the dress around so that the back became a simple boat neck across her front, and paired it with jewelry her brother had brought back from Spain. The intricate gold patterns reminded her of Islamic tiles, and she thought they would fit right into the theme of the new gallery exhibit.

"Who's the guy, anyway?" Tiffany asked.

"What makes you think there's a guy? This is for work."

"Hah. Right. You're wearing sexy underwear. No one wears lace like that for work shit."

Cheyenne ignored her and fussed with her long, blond hair. She tried to do something different, quickly braiding it and wrapping it around on top of her head. She let it down. Shook it straight and tried to wrap it into a French bun. The result was messy, but not stylish messy.

Tiffany rolled her eyes. "Sit on the bed. Let me deal with your hair. I have three younger sisters and a lot of practice." She pinned Cheyenne's hair into a classic, elegant chignon. "Come clean about the guy."

"I finally got to meet Xander today." Cheyenne said.

Their eyes met in the mirror and Tiffany's lit up. "I knew it. Chey, girl, I told you there was something up with him. All your talk about him. Did the face match the voice? Is he half as cute as you thought he might be?"

"He's even better than my fantasy. We spent an hour cleaning up the kitchen today, and we talked about books and movies and cooking. And sailing. He's into sailing. But, we clicked, Tiffany. He's gorgeous. Dark. Intense. Broody. But then, when he smiles, it's like..." She closed her eyes and breathed in deeply. "He's everything I imagined he'd be."

"Girl, you really are into him, aren't you?" Tiffany asked through a mouthful of bobby pins. "Never seen you like this about a guy before. Are you wishing you'd met with him earlier?"

"Can't change the past, can we? All I know is

when he walked into the room, everything else blurred out and he popped into focus. Like in a movie."

"I was right. Admit it." Tiffany said, adding an extra bobby pin.

"Before meeting him, I was worried that I'd misread things. I was sure we'd meet today and it would be all business."

Tiffany placed her hands on her shoulders and squeezed. "All done, what do you think?"

Tiff had braided and twisted Cheyenne's hair into an elegance she'd never be able to manage on her own.

"I love it," Cheyenne said, jumping up and hugging Tiffany. "Thank you."

"So tell me, girl, I want details from the beginning. He came to class and...then what?" Tiffany dropped stomach down on the bed, propping herself up on her elbows.

"Well, I got all set up for class like usual. Every time someone walked into the room, I was like, *'is this Xander?'* It was excruciating. We get to five minutes before class and there're only two people left on the list. Some lady named Caroll and Xander. Then, this really, really old guy walked in. With a cane! I was totally crushed."

"Noooo." Tiffany dropped her head. "Wait. So, it wasn't love at first sight? Don't tell me you fell for Gramps. Why are you getting all hottied up?"

"Haha. Gotcha. The old dude's name was Carroll. You know, C-a-r-r-o-l-l. But I missed the spelling and was certain that only Xander and some lady were missing from class."

Tiffany tossed a pillow at Cheyenne. "Lordy, girl-friend, you are so mean. Xander came in last, then? Well? Out with it."

"Seriously, Xander is a babe. Total hot alpha male babe. His eyes are this incredible green. Luscious skin. Thick hair. I can't wait to run my fingers through that hair of his."

"But...Was he all business-like? Or did he get into flirting mode right away?"

"Well, he didn't make out with me on the spot, Tiffany." Cheyenne turned back to the mirror and carefully applied eyeliner. "Of course he was a professional, but... Have you ever had that moment? Where the world slows down and...anyway, all I could see was Xander. Everything else got blurry. Like tunnel vision. There was nothing else in the world other than the two of us for a moment."

Tiffany leaned back against the headboard and crossed her arms. "That stuff never happens. Come on. Quit pulling my leg."

"I'm not. I swear. The world slowed down around us," Cheyenne said. "He stayed to clean up and go over the presentation for tonight." Cheyenne dropped on the bed next to Tiffany and hugged a pillow close. "He reads. He's smart. He likes cooking. We talked the whole time we cleaned up and never ran out of things to say."

Tiffany gave her a pitying stare. "Haven't you learned anything?"

"What do you mean?" Cheyenne straightened her shoulders.

"You fall in and out of love way too easy. I'm worried your picker might be broken. And you read too many romance novels. That whole *time slowing down* thing? It doesn't really happen."

"Hey. I don't claim to have *really* fallen in love with anyone for years. Not like this. Can't you be happy for me?"

Tiffany shook her head and tossed her hands up in surrender. "You go out with a lot of guys, Cheyenne. Like, way more than anyone else I know. You get in deep really fast, and then you have some excuse why it's not working. Just...be careful with your heart, okay?"

*Tiffany. Dallas. Sky. Her therapist.* Everyone was ganging up on her.

"It won't matter anyway. With my luck, it won't go anywhere."

Her *picker* was fine. It was her *keeper* that was broken.

CHEYENNE BRUSHED off Tiffany's warning as she walked out the door. She was fine. She could handle herself. Her *picker* wasn't broken. Four years of therapy had given her the skills she needed. She wasn't whole again, she hadn't been since she lost the last baby, but that had nothing to do with her *god damned picker* being broken. Even the divorce didn't hurt her as much as losing the babies.

The cab stopped short of the Smithsonian Castle on Jefferson. She had never spent time at the Freer Gallery, and its somewhat boring exterior didn't do much to beckon her inside. She hung back on the wide circle in front of the Freer, considering the Castle next door. Its arched windows, framed in a rich red brick, and its front turrets were as romantic as ever.

As of twenty-four hours ago, her only goal had been to kiss Xander at the Smithsonian Castle and that would've been that. His asking her out on a real date had changed everything. It would still be possible for her to get a kiss for the game as part of their date. She'd have to re-evaluate her Bingo game plan if things went well between them. After all, they could kiss and there would be no spark—end of story. Cheyenne had to have spark and sizzle physically for a relationship to work.

She had worried it might be a little awkward going to the gallery by herself, but several people ahead of her in line were flying solo. Besides, she was meeting Xander here. It wasn't like she had just met him. All those emails and telephone conversations had added up to many hours. Several dates worth of talking. Not that they were dates. As a matter of fact, this didn't feel like a first date at all.

The line of people threading their way through to the exhibit laid a path before her to follow. The exhibit was visually stunning. The entire Islamic section had been transformed for this specific exhibit. Cheyenne scanned the crowd, recognizing a few DC notables—a senator here, a lobbyist there—but no one else from Congressman Pierce's office.

Xander stood in a corner near a glass display case filled with crockery surrounded by a circle of younger women paying him rapt attention. Why would he ever choose her when he had this crop to pick from? She was a divorced woman who couldn't have kids. Facts were facts, no matter what her therapist said.

*Get over yourself and move along. Kiss him for the game. Date him for a few weeks until he learns that you're not a viable mate. Have some fun with this hottie while you can.*

Cheyenne couldn't take her eyes off him as she maneuvered her way through the crowd, like a moth to a flame. He used his hands a lot when he spoke, waving them around and drawing with them in the air. They were elegant and masculine at the same time—wide palms, elegant piano playing fingers. She imagined them in a glissando against her naked skin and stumbled. She caught herself before falling flat on her face.

A waiter tried to hide his smile as he paused in front of her with a tray of wine. She gathered herself together, pretending nothing had happened as she took a glass of white wine.

She tipped the glass toward the waiter. "Wish me luck."

He dipped his head almost imperceptibly and turned toward other guests.

"I'm going to need it," she said to herself while taking a sip. It was sweeter than she liked, but she wasn't expecting much from a gallery opening at the Smithsonian. She sidled up next to Xander, feeling a little self-conscious of the fact that he was surrounded by women.

Xander paused in his story, then opened his arm to let her into the circle. A couple of the girls threw dagger-like stares at Cheyenne. If looks could kill, she'd be bleeding on the floor with a dozen stab wounds.

"This is Cheyenne LeFleur, my colleague at the

Culinary Arts Institute. We're collaborating on the three-week long class beginning next Saturday."

Cheyenne smiled kindly at them but none of them made eye contact with her.

A red-head with pasty white skin giggled oddly. She actually raised her hand.

"We're not in class, Mandy," Xander said, his tone weary and somewhat annoyed. "What is it?"

"Professor Moore, when will you be returning to Syria to continue your research? It seems so dangerous." Her voice was breathy with admiration.

"Unfortunately, the catastrophic damage the war is causing may make some relics completely unattainable. My current plans are to finish up the work I've begun with these tablets, and then reassess in the fall. I'll be in DC for the next year, at least."

The relief that Mandy showed on her face, along with the other women, was more than Cheyenne would have expected.

Mandy leaned toward him. Her puppy dog eyes spelled out her crush on Xander in front of every one. "So, Xanderrrrr..." drawing his name out as if she'd called him that forever as some sort of special right, "you told me earlier that the spice blend you devised for tonight's meat pies should taste super close to the food they actually ate in Sumer five thousand years ago. How do you know for sure?"

Xander took a step back, clearly distancing himself from this girl.

Xander slipped an arm around Cheyenne's waist and it was all she could do to not flinch in surprise. Not that she didn't mind having his arm around her—it was just so unexpected, particularly after the 'my colleague' comment a few seconds before.

Maybe this was a date, after all. Maybe all he was doing was protecting himself from this younger woman's obvious advances, doing the 'I'm claimed' thing Cheyenne had done in bars since she'd learned the trick.

This whole situation was amusing. It was pretty rare for a guy to rely on Cheyenne to get out of a sticky situation like this. She saw a waitress carrying a tray of the small pies and waved her down. Xander's hand fell away, and she missed the warmth of it.

"I'm excited to see what the caterer did with our recipe," Cheyenne said.

"Oh my god. I can't wait to try one," Mandy said rubbing her hands together and bouncing up on her toes.

"Cheyenne and I formulated the crust recipe after some trial and error. They would have ground their grains on stones, and their flour was never as refined as ours is. It would be more like a very course whole wheat or corn meal, even. Small pebbles made their way in, too. This was all very damaging to the teeth."

"Let's be glad we used modern flour," Cheyenne said. She paused while the waitress served everyone. "Go ahead and take a bite. Can anyone guess what the spices are?"

Everyone in the circle took their first bite. A couple closed their eyes, concentrating on what they might be tasting.

"Cinnamon?"

"Pepper."

"Cardamom."

"Garlic."

"That's right," replied Xander. "Anyone else?"

A dark haired woman who had been silent up until now tilted her her head to the side. "There's something different here. I get all these other flavors. But there's a smoky, piney thing going on."

"Can you guess what it is?" Cheyenne asked, excited that someone had picked out the mystery ingredient.

The other woman made a face. "It's familiar but I know I've never tasted it before. What is it?"

"Myrrh," Cheyenne said. "Just a tiny bit of it."

"Whatever. I don't care if they have gold in them. They are so good," Mandy said after a large bite. "I want to eat them all." She went after the waiter.

Xander made eye contact with Cheyenne and smiled as if they had shared an inside joke. He held up the hand pie and closed his eyes as he bit into the crust. He chewed it thoughtfully for a moment. "It's even better than I thought it would be. You did a great job translating the recipe, Cheyenne."

She didn't think it was perfection. They could use a tad more salt...roll the crust a little thinner, add a tiny bit more filling. The catering staff hadn't asked her questions, and she'd not been asked to taste test their interpretation of her recipes.

The small group discussed historic variations and applications of meats and spices and bitter greens for quite a while as the waiters continued to pass food and wine through the gathering. In addition to the meat pies, Cheyenne and Xander had developed four other appetizers based on the tablets to round out the evening. The bulk of the recipes on the tablets had been for stews and vegetable dishes that would not work as finger food.

A loud gong interrupted the general hubbub of the evening. Xander led Cheyenne to the front of the room for their presentation.

She hadn't known what to expect, but she was suddenly shy. Her work with the congressman kept her in the wings. Speaking in front of a couple hundred people wearing tuxedos and evening gowns was a whole new level of adrenaline rush. Her usual classroom audience was small, never more than ten or fifteen people. Her heart rate picked up a notch, and her knees were all wobbly.

Xander stood next to her, no longer with his sustaining arm around her, but close enough that their arms pressed against each other as they stood side by side at the podium. He squeezed her forearm. Assured by his presence, she leaned into him a little and exhaled long and slow. Her heart slowed from beating frantically to a manageable pace.

He began the presentation with a map of Mesopotamia and where the artifacts for the exhibit had originated. Xander gave a brief description of the overall exhibit and some special details to find throughout the exhibit before telling the story of how he had found the tablets with the recipes languishing in corner of the museum for years.

"Once I'd translated them, I realized what a treasure they were. Nearly every other similar piece from the same era is an inventory. It's quite rare to get a glimpse into the way they prepared their foods. However, bringing these recipes alive is a lot trickier than you'd think. You won't find myrrh on the grocery spice aisle. I turned to Cheyenne LeFleur for some help."

With a calming breath, she delved into their exploration of the herbs and spices prevalent in the area thousands of years ago. The words came easy to her once she got going, and her speech was invigorated by the rush of adrenaline. As planned ahead of time, waiters mingled around the guests with several more sample dishes. With less than two slides into the presentation, all of her jitters tumbled away. She loved talking about food, and with Xander at her side, she was confident. The animated faces of the guests put Cheyenne at ease.

Cheyenne and Xander interwove the story of how some plants went extinct and evolved into modern plants over time, how exotics fell out of favor—due to expense or availability—or were replaced by local and cheaper substitutes. All their practicing earlier in the day paid off. They traded off like pros and, as a result, the presentation was interesting and lively. When it ended, the audience clapped enthusiastically. Behind the cover of the podium, Xander's hand reached out and squeezed hers in gentle triumph.

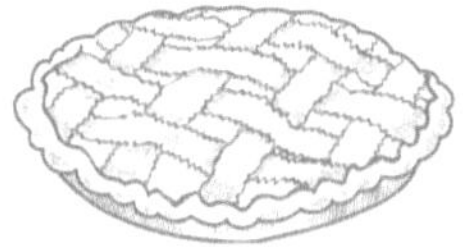

## Chapter 5

After their presentation, Cheyenne and Xander were whisked off into different circles of sudden admirers who had dozens of questions. Cheyenne was approached by several individuals interested in more information about her regular cooking classes. She handed out business cards she had stashed in her purse. It was as close to celebrity as anything she'd ever experienced before.

She lost track of Xander in the hubbub. By the time the event was winding down, Cheyenne's voice was raw from talking above the din. After extricating herself from the last group of admirers, she perused the exhibit, reading every label as if she were studying for an exam. Xander had sent her photos but seeing the all the ancient relics in real life—especially after tasting the recipes—was an intense experience.

In particular, she found a series of bread forms particularly intriguing. They were shaped like modern pie plates—shallow with rims that leaned out a few degrees, but there were indentations in the bottom that formed distinctive patterns that would show on the top of the baked bread once it was turned out. The resulting loaves would have been lovely.

Xander appeared at her elbow as she took photos of the forms.

"Cool, aren't they?" he asked.

"Oh, man," Cheyenne said. "My roommate is going to blow a gasket on this. We've been trying to come up with some interesting and unique items for our restaurant, and this is awesome. I have a friend who is going to art school. Maybe she could make me one in her pottery class."

"I bet the museum might be interested in carrying them in the store. Especially if we get all of this stuff we're doing into a cookbook."

"Are you kidding? I'd love to write a cookbook." She snapped a photo and put her phone back into her purse. "But I just don't know how I'd fit it in. Between work and the school. Maybe after this class is over, I'll have some free time."

"It would be a fun project. You're right, let's assess where we are after this class." He said.

*Where we are after this class?* That would be in

another month. Cheyenne hadn't had a relationship last that long since Alberto. Cheyenne's heart thumped against her chest. She didn't trust her voice at the moment so she only nodded.

"Things are winding down. I need to grab some things from my office before we go out. Come with me?"

It wasn't even eleven yet. Cheyenne had high hopes for the rest of the evening. Maybe she'd get Xander to go on a walk after they were done. The castle wasn't that far away. He led her through the back hallways of the Freer Gallery. Outside one of the classic oak doors with opaque glass on top half, he paused and pulled out keys. Pushing the door wide, he invited her in with a sweep of his hand.

"This is where I spend most of my time," he said. The interior was about twelve foot square. His desk was up flush against the wall closest the door so that he would be facing the door when seated. Two of the other three walls housed floor to ceiling bookshelves. Scattered across the shelves were piles of books. Art books intermingled with text books along with some in other languages she couldn't even identify.

"Don't you have an office at GW?" she asked. Against the third wall was a narrow stainless-steel table. On top were several clay tablets out in the open.

"I'm an adjunct professor, so no office over there."

The tablets drew her in like a magnet. She reached out to run her finger along the base of one, an automatic gesture. Xander's grabbed her wrist before she actually touched it. Gentle, but firm. "Oh no. No touching. You have to put on gloves if you're going to do that. But I'd rather you use your eyes only, please."

He released the grip slowly, his fingers skimming deliciously across the top of her hand. The gentle touch was warm and intimate without being invasive.

"I'm sorry. They're so fascinating. It's like they called to me." She clasped her hands behind her back to remind herself to not touch and leaned over the largest of the three tablets. "And you can read all this? It's cuneiform, right?"

Xander used a finger to follow the line of text, hovering above the tablet at a safe distance and read, "Set forth for the marking of Dumuzi: one hundred small stone Dumuzi statutes, seventy small stone Innana, fifty large stone Geshtinana." He paused and caught Cheyenne's eyes. "I suppose an inventory list is as exciting as reading a phonebook."

"Actually, I find it pretty interesting. Is it an inventory for an idol shop?" Cheyenne asked. "And what is Dumuzi? Some sort of festival?"

"The Sumerians mourned the waning of the summer sun by throwing a funeral for Damuzi every year. Innana was Damuzi's goddess/wife and Geshtinana was his sister. They both play prominently in his life story and their figurines would have been set up on altars and used to re-enact their stories."

"Interesting. I've never heard of any of them. I guess I'm not really up on ancient Sumerian myths and gods."

"Well, if you've heard of Persephone and her descent to the underworld, Innana and Damuzi had a compatible marriage and descent. Same general story and themes set in a different land."

"Oh. I remember that one," Cheyenne said. "I guess it makes sense. The same myths and stories get retold across time and different peoples."

She pointed at the tablet. "So this shop only sold figurines?"

Xander scrolled his finger down the marks on the tablet and paused half-way down. "Down to here it's all various gods and figurines. Here, the list switches to fabrics. Fourteen lengths dark brown sheep course spun, twenty-three lengths white sheep soft spun. And here, we have beads. And some more ceramics."

Cheyenne pictured the shop as it might have been —half the shelves filled with figurines and the other half piled high with fabrics and ceramics, beads, notions. "No more recipes?"

"Nope. My next exhibit is focusing on the arts and crafts. Textiles. Beads. Glassware. Ceramics."

Xander's eyes sparkled in the dim light of the office. "These figurines are well known and documented. The rest not so much. I've uncovered a text about how the Sumerian upper classes sewed their hair into elaborate braids to hold them."

Cheyenne had struggled with bobby pins plenty of enough times to wonder if sewing her hair together might not be such a bad solution. It might be easier than all those pins.

"I find it all fascinating," Cheyenne said. Was he going to collaborate with someone else on that exhibit?

She brushed aside the sudden twinge of jealousy. *First date, girl. You don't own the man.*

"You spend your days in here?" she asked, changing the subject. It was close, but not entirely claustrophobic in spite of the fact there were no windows.

"Here and in the lab where I date things."

She pointed to a print on the wall. The jewel-toned colors were stunning, lined with gold patterns mirroring the necklace she was wearing. In the center was a calligraphic script but definitely not in English.

"What's this say?" she asked.

"It says 'Do What is Beautiful' in Arabic."

"It's lovely," she said, her throat tightening a little bit. *Arabic?*

"It's a quote from the Koran."

*The Koran?* Xander was Muslim? Cheyenne recalibrated her thinking. That's why he'd skipped tasting the lard crust. How many times had she recommended they try using pork in their recipes as a substitute? Or lard in their crusts? Had she offended him? He *had* suggested they stick to lamb and goat instead of using any pork whenever she brought it up. And the wine for the gala? He'd taken her suggestions for what to order without comment. Had he had any to drink? She didn't think so. He'd eaten her pie crusts, all of which she had made with vodka instead of water. Had she told the class she'd made them with vodka?

"I didn't realize you were Muslim," she said quietly. "I hope I haven't accidentally offended you with all my pork and wine talk. And vodka in pie crusts."

Cheyenne recalibrated a couple of family favorites in her head. Meatballs could work with just beef and veal. Charcuterie was mostly out of the picture, but there was some decent substitutes for salami out there. She'd get Tiffany to work up some non-pork salami substitutes. There had to be a halal store somewhere in DC.

"America loves bacon—almost to an irrational level," Xander said. "Believe me, you become immune to it after a while. I've been known to taste alcohol now and again. Mostly out of curiousity. But, the vodka cooks out, and I don't really care what other people drink or eat."

"I guess I just never considered religion during our discussions."

"Is my being Muslim a problem for you?"

Cheyenne blinked, trying to weigh the implications of the question. The last few months had been free of any and all religious discussion other than how it might affect Sumerian culinary habits. Was he asking if she couldn't handle working with him because he was Muslim or was he asking about their budding personal relationship?

Religion had never been a big part of her family life. Having Alberto use it against her had simply made her more resentful of all religion. She considered herself vaguely American Secular Christian by celebrating Christmas with a tree and gifts and Easter with chocolate and egg hunts. Dating a Muslim guy would only be a problem if he tried to convert her because she didn't want to be beholden to any religion, it didn't matter what variety.

"No," she said. "It is complicated, in some ways, but it's...I've learned a lot about Islam in the last few years. I had to...in order to get over some old anger."

Xander didn't say anything but waited in silence for her to continue. How did she explain things without coming across as racists or phobic? There was a time when she was probably a little bit of both, but she had changed a lot over the years.

"My dad died on 9/11. It really affected all our lives. And, yes, for a while, I bought into a mantra of hate. But, my brother? Dallas? I'm sure I've mentioned him to you. He spent ten years over in the Middle East. When he came back, he taught me so much about my own worries and prejudices. He made very close friends with several Muslims. People who saved his life and welcomed him into their homes. He helped me see the difference between the religion and terrorists."

"So you're saying dating me isn't out of the question?"

"As long as I don't have to convert," she said, only half-joking to see where he might go with it.

"I'm not that kind of guy," he said.

Cheyenne looked away, suddenly overcome with a shyness she didn't usually feel. *Please. Please let him be real. Let* this *be real.*

Xander turned their attention back toward the print.

"My mother gave this to me. She was born in Pakistan. She moved to the States with her parents when she was young. Part of the war with India. Lots of people came over at the same time." Xander straightened the frame. "She met my father in college. My dad is this white dude who loved my mom so much he converted so she could stay Muslim. My last name isn't particularly Pakistani. Believe me, I'm used to people asking questions all the time. I'll be honest, people aren't always nice. Sometimes the attitude is harsh, but most of the time people are just curious, they want to understand."

"I've come along way. Well, I think I have anyway," she said. "I just feel bad about all the times I've suggested we use pork or whatever, and you've been so nice about ignoring it."

"It's really no big deal." He stood behind his desk and shuffled papers around. "Anyway. Our class is full, and we have ten on the wait list." He offered her a thin sheaf of papers to look at. "By the way, I want to thank you for saving my butt earlier this evening."

She took the papers and scanned the list. A couple of names were familiar, but the vast majority were strangers. She handed them back to him. "What are you talking about? Saving your butt?"

"At the gala. When I was surrounded by my students from Arch 201, and I put my arm around your waist without asking. I shouldn't have done that, but...thank you for not slapping me away."

He was thanking her and apologizing at the same time. It was amazing and awesome and sexy. And so sweet. And she'd having his arm around her had been the most natural thing in the world.

"Mandy would be all over you if she could," she teased.

"She's an English major. In my class to fulfill one of her requirements," he said wryly. "I'm used to it, but it's sometimes tiring to constantly be saying *no*."

"Do you *always* say 'no'?"

He raised an eyebrow playfully as his lips curled into a smile. "Depends on who's asking."

*In for a penny...* She closed the small space between them and tugged at the tails of his loosened bowtie. "I feel like we have a connection. I mean, ever since we first talked on the phone. Am I wrong?"

His warm hands were suddenly wrapped over her fingers. "I wake up in the mornings thinking about you. Hoping we'll have time to chat during the day so I can hear your voice."

Cheyenne's heart skipped a beat. She'd been right. They'd each found excuses to talk to each other nearly every day—it wasn't just her. "Me too."

They stood there, inches apart, gazing into each others eyes. The slamming of a door somewhere down the hallway made her jump, and his steady hands squeezed against hers, calming her. Reassuring her.

"So," he said, breaking into the silence. "Still up for a movie?"

"If you're still willing to come over."

"Why wouldn't I be?" he asked.

She pointed to her mouth. "Pork loving lips. Don't know if that will ever change."

He dropped one of her hands and lifted it to cup her cheek while tracing her lips with his thumb. "I don't see anything but lips that need kissing."

Cheyenne turned her mouth into his palm and kissed it.

"Oh, man," he said, his other hand lifting to her face so that he held her between his palms. Leaning in close, he circled her nose with his, their eyes meeting again. Tiny gold flecks were only visible this close.

Cheyenne had never been comfortable with someone observing her so brazenly, so hungrily before. Her right hand slid along his chest, along his neck and up to his thick curly hair.

Xander's warm lips brushed against hers. Tentative. Testing. Tasting.

She tilted her head, angling for that perfect fit. Their lips met again, this time with energy and desire zinging between them. Cheyenne stumbled backward toward the door for support, breaking their kiss. Xander caught her at the elbows and held her steady.

"We should probably go," she said.

Xander grabbed Cheyenne's hand and led her through the staff hallways of the Freer Gallery. Functional and hidden hallways like this always held an allure for her. The same held true for the tunnels connecting the various government buildings. Maybe it was being part of the underpinnings, the hidden backstage she found so fascinating. But tonight, all she wanted was to get Xander home. If she was lucky everyone else was out or asleep. She didn't bring men to her apartment often, but Xander was special.

The smell was something between hospital sterile and musty library. She wanted to explore the various workrooms—to see the work that went on behind the scenes of the more elaborate and well-put together exhibits—but Xander walked at such an efficient pace she could barely keep up with in her high heels. A few people were in offices working, even this late on a Saturday night. Most didn't bother acknowledging them as they passed. When they did, Xander waved at them and reminded them of the leftovers in the staff kitchen.

An elderly janitor paused his mopping to let them pass near the exit.

"Jeff," Xander said, "there's some really tasty things from this evening's gala in the kitchen. You won't want to miss them before the vultures set in."

"Already had some, thanks, Xander," Jeff said. "I had four of those little empanada-like pie things. Tasty for sure. Oh, and, you were right. The missus loved the book. I'll put it on your desk before I leave tonight."

Xander gave the man a thumbs up as he pushed the exterior door open. They emerged onto Independence Ave, opposite of where she had entered the building early in the evening. This was the backside of the building and the one she was used to seeing. It wasn't much different from the front of the building.

"I lucked out with parking," he said. "Usually, I take the Metro in for work, but I like driving when I can."

He held out his arm for her and they walked down the street, crossing over to the line of parallel parked cars. The evening air was cool and crisp. The sweet scent of the blossoming cherry trees wafted down from above. DC was at its prettiest in the late spring.

He paused next to a red Tesla. "This is me."

Cheyenne had never ridden in a Tesla before. She wasn't a car person; she believed a vehicle was to get you from point A to point B. But a Tesla? Something about this car made her giddy. Pretending like this was an everyday thing and faking a coolness she did not feel, she climbed into the car with all the tentativeness she would have had climbing into an airplane cockpit or a space shuttle, for that matter. The car door shut and sealed them inside.

The silent and powerful acceleration pinned her to her seat. Her hand landed on his thigh for balance—an automatic gesture, but once there, she kept it where it was. "You did that on purpose, didn't you?" she asked as he slowed into a legal range.

"I suppose," he said, grinning.

While he drove them to her apartment, she stole a few glances at him, trying not to stare. She had always thought tuxedos were a turn off for her, until tonight. Other men she'd dated had been uptight and unnatural in the constricting clothing—fidgeting with their ties and their cuffs, tugging and pulling at them. Like they were wearing a costume. But Xander wore his like he owned it. He was as comfortable in the formal wear as he had been that morning in an apron while cooking. He had loosened the bowtie and the top buttons of the shirt, and the bit of dark curly hair peeking out over the top beckoned to her.

He slid the car into a spot in front of her building. He was out of the car and opening her door before she had her seatbelt off, hand in front of her in an offer to help her out of the car.

She placed her hand in his and he guided her out of the Tesla. He kept hold of her even once she was free of the car. Lights were on in all three of her apartment windows that faced the street. So much for privacy.

"I should warn you, my roommates are probably around," she said as they reached the door to the building.

"It would be great to meet them and put faces to all their names," he said. "You've told me so much about them."

Tiffany had helped with the spices on the meat pies and Chelsea had helped with the vegetarian meat balls. Zach had helped with the flour mixes on the pies. Cheyenne had probably blathered on and on about them on the phone too much, but Xander had never stopped her or changed the subject.

A little spark of happiness tingled along the back of her neck. Maybe they *could* have something special. If it ended up being a short term romance, at least she could soak up as much of him as she could for as long as he'd let her.

At the first landing, Xander paused. "Before we go all the way up," he said, "I want another moment with you alone."

He put a hand on either cheek and held her face still, studying her intently.

"Are you for real, Cheyenne LeFleur?" he asked.

"Are you?" she asked, covering one of his hands with her own. Time stopped like it had when he'd walked into class earlier in the day. She delved into it, soaked up the sensation and stayed with it. It was as if she could see into him, through him, become part of him and that she'd become transparent to him.

Was this really happening?

He kissed her again, but this time with raw hunger. She parted her lips slightly, answering him by inviting him in for more. He slid his hands to her waist, then along her lower back, bringing her in close to him as he kissed her again, this time with a forceful and hungry passion.

It only took them a few moments, a couple of minor adjustments, until they found their rhythm. Their tongues darted in and out, dancing and playing with each other. Cheyenne linked her arms lightly around his neck and stepped backward, taking him with her, until she could lean against the wall for support.

Cheyenne had no idea how much time passed before Xander broke the kiss, guiding her up to the next landing where they kissed again. She pressed herself in close, wanting to feel as much of his body against hers as possible.

They made it the rest of the way up to her apartment two or three steps at a time, stopping for long, uninhibited kisses. As they finally reached her door, she turned toward the door, body pressed against her back, and his lips on her neck as she worked the key in the lock.

She opened the door to her apartment and stopped dead in her tracks. A vase of fresh flowers took center stage on the coffee table instead of the usual mishmash of magazines, books and empty take-out containers. The shoes that normally crowded the rack by the front door had been neatened and culled down to a spare four pairs. Was she even in the right apartment? The sofa cushions were neatly plumped and arranged at jaunty angles. The artwork that had been leaning against the fireplace was now hanging. Even the cobwebs in the corner had been taken care of.

Xander must have sensed something was wrong. He moved quickly to stand in front of her, blocking any potential threats. "Cheyenne, what's the matter?"

He was scanning the interior of the apartment like a soldier on watch.

He'd gone from cuddly lover to protector man in seconds.

"My roommates changed things around, is all. Things are where they belong, which makes every-thing all weird. It's nothing, really."

"You sure?"

"Yeah. Honestly? They cleaned up, and I hardly recognize my own apartment. Zach? Tiff? Chelsea? Helloooo?" Maybe someone had spirited them all away and replaced them with replicas—a modern day version of *The Body Snatchers.*

A crash from the kitchen was followed shortly by Zach's creaky tenor. "Bam, shazam, Cheyenne is finally home! Thank Goddess, you gallivanting rogue, you. It's about time, girl." The raw excitement in his voice was way more than her getting home from a date warranted.

Cheyenne couldn't hide Xander now. He was here, he might as well get the full treatment. When Zach was excited, things could get a little weird. The curve on Xander's lips told her he was ready to be amused.

Zach bounded out of the kitchen, arms flapping on either side in his best Tigger impersonation, a large white envelope in his hand. "Oh my god, oh my god, oh my god. You're finally home."

Tiffany was close on his heels, skipping behind him with equal enthusiasm. Their bright smiles froze on their faces and they stopped mid-bounce when they saw she was not alone. Zach thrust the arm holding the envelope behind his back, and they both donned fake smiles to recover from their exuberance.

"Ohhhh. Didn't realize you had someone with you," Zach said in a calmer, almost dignified voice. "Sorry about that."

Tiffany's eyes widened at Cheyenne with her personal 'what the heck is going on' face. Cheyenne rarely brought anyone home to the apartment, and it was clear neither Tiffany or Zach expected her to return with company.

"What is going on? You two are acting weird." Cheyenne said.

Tiffany waved her flour-caked arms toward the kitchen. "It's nothing. Just excited about this...erm... challah. You will *never* believe the bread we just made. It's really very exciting, but maybe not so much for other people."

Cheyenne led Xander to the kitchen. As she went past Tiffany, she tried to get a better read from the other woman. There was no way Tiffany or Zach would get this excited over a loaf of bread.

Zach and Tiffany moved quickly back to the counter. They had just finished braiding a loaf of challah on steroids. Seven strands of dough criss-crossed and twisted around each other in an amazing pattern.

"Whoa," Xander said as he leaned in to examine the bread. "This is gorgeous."

Zach kept his hands behind his back as he focused on Xander. "I'm Zach. And you'd be?"

"Xander."

As far as Cheyenne could tell, Xander was unfazed by the remarkable rudeness Zach and Tiffany had displayed thus far. She kept trying to get their silent attention, but they were both doing a damned fine job of avoiding eye contact with her.

Xander examined the challah, his finger tracing the design in mid-air.

"What's with the giant challah?" asked Cheyenne with a pointed glare. "Why is everything so...clean? And why are you acting so freaky?"

"Never mind." Zach whispered with a meaningful nod towards Xander. "I can't say until it's just *us*." He hurtled the emphasis on the last word straight at Xander. Luckily, he didn't see the rude gesture because he was focused on the challah.

Cheyenne pursed her lips and opened her eyes wide over Xander's shoulder. "Be nice," she mouthed at him while throwing him the best *'what-the-fuck-is-going-on'* look.

"Hey man, you gotta move." Zach said to Xander.

Xander backed away to the opposite corner of the kitchen, his hands up on either side of his head as if he was being held up at gun point. "No worries."

Cheyenne followed him and leaned in close. "I don't know what's going on. They don't usually get so weird over bread. I promise, they don't always act like jerks."

Xander chuckled under his breath. "Maybe I should go and let you have some alone time with your roomies and their monster challah."

"Oh, please, do not leave me alone with these freaks. I'm kinda scared." She leaned into him and they pretended to huddle in the corner.

"Very funny," Zach said. He turned back to Tiffany. "On the count of three. One, two, three..."

Each lifted two corners of the parchment paper the loaf had been built on and carried it to to a metal baking tray. Zach sprayed the top lightly with oil and covered it with a giant plastic bag. "This is going to be a slow over-night rise."

Tiffany held the refrigerator open for him as he adjusted the tray on a shelf inside and barely fit it in. The contents of the fridge had been entirely re-arranged to accommodate the bread.

Cheyenne caught the fridge door before Tiffany could close it and found a bottle of unopened chardonnay.

"Xander, you've already sort of met Zach. And this is Tiffany." Cheyenne pointed the bottle in her direction. "Chelsea still at work?"

Tiffany finally threw Xander one of her genuine smiles. "Nice to meet you, Xander. Sorry if we were distracted just now."

"Chefs throughout the centuries have made elaborate breads, amongst other novelties of course, for royals," Xander said. "Your challah would impress anyone. It was worth the exuberance."

Zach's expression underwent a change: annoyed to inquisitive and then impressed in a matter of five seconds. "I'd like to cook for royalty some day," Zach said. "Do up one of those amazing medieval feasts with peacock feathers sticking up out of things. I've read about some pretty wild dishes that practically require a degree in architecture."

Zach took the bottle from Cheyenne and grabbed a wine opener. He uncorked it with the practiced ease of a sommelier and poured glasses all around. Xander held up a hand to indicate he didn't want any when offered.

A frisson of panic passed through Cheyenne. She couldn't remember seeing Xander with a glass of wine earlier in the evening. Did he drink at all? Would her drinking wine be a problem for him?

Zach handed a glass to Tiffany.

Tiffany chugged the glass in moments before holding it out to him for seconds. "You didn't pour me a *full* glass." After Zach refilled her glass, she said, "Come on, y'all, let's finish the train station so we can clear the table for dinner tomorrow."

"Dinner tomorrow?" Cheyenne asked. "We have plans? What is going on?"

Tiffany and Zach exchanged a furtive glance. "We'll tell you about it later."

Whatever was going on with them was totally annoying. Did they have to act like that the first time she brought someone home with her? Were they behaving weird only because Xander was there, or because of something else? Was it obvious to them that he was Muslim and was this wigging them out? She had already made the mistake of being racist in his office, she wasn't going to stand for it to happen twice in one night. Add in the general state of the apartment —so organized and clean shouldn't make her on edge, but it was clear Zach and Tiffany had spent the entire evening cleaning. And overnight challah at midnight? *Why?*

"Now. You need to tell me now," she said.

Zach dropped his voice to a whisper and leaned in close."Ecretsay ingthay."

"Really, Zach? Xander probably speaks pig Latin as well as he does English and Arabic."

Xander laughed and put his hands up. "It's okay. Maybe I should leave so you all can do...whatever."

"No. Chelsea isn't here. Whatever these two are going on about can wait until she gets back," Cheyenne said, leading the way to the dining table that was rarely used for anything other than jigsaw puzzles.

*Dinner. Who would be coming over for dinner?* They all worked in restaurants and mostly ate at work. Sit down meals were reserved for special occasions and parties. Cheyenne was pretty sure no one she knew had a birthday coming up.

"A puzzle?" Xander pointed to one that occupied most of the dining table. "You do get up to some pretty wild stuff in your spare time, don't you?" He tilted his head to the side, scanning the pieces that were left and popping one into place.

Zach's clapped his hands together and bounced up a bit off his seat. "I've looked for that piece a thousand times. I'm gonna hate taking this off and putting it back in the box. We'll need the space."

"For that secret dinner we're having tomorrow night?" Cheyenne asked.

"Shh," said Zach.

Cheyenne scrunched up her face at Zach and stuck out her tongue.

"We're usually done with a puzzle in a few days, but this one has been out for ages," said Tiffany. "Oh, I found one!" She picked up a piece and snapped it in.

Xander gathered three pieces in a row, silently fitting them where they belonged.

"You're good at puzzles," Cheyenne said.

"It's a little bit like work. Pieces of pottery. Shards of this and that. You get good at it."

Cheyenne sipped at her wine. Tiffany's second glass was still topped off. At least she had slowed down. After that first chug, Cheyenne had thought Tiffany was going to go off on a bender. This evening was one roller coaster after another.

There was a single knock at the front door, and it swung open. Her brother came in; he had a habit of making himself at home. All her roommates liked him, and he treated them like younger siblings.

"Hey everyone, how's it going?" He paused when his eyes landed on Xander and a smooth poker face slid over his features. As much as Cheyenne dated, she rarely brought men back to her apartment. It was much easier to ghost a guy when they didn't know where you lived. Was Dallas reacting to the fact that there was a man with her or that the man was dark and Pakistani?

He kissed Cheyenne on the cheek. "Do you happen to have any syrah? I'd love a glass."

Tiffany jumped up and gave Dallas a hug. "We just opened a chardonnay. Want some of that instead?"

"Sure, that'd be great. Thanks, Tiffany." Dallas took the chair next to Xander's and held out his hand. "You must be the archeologist food guy?"

Xander met Cheyenne's eyes briefly before taking the proffered hand. "I am. Alexander Moore. I prefer Xander. And you are?"

"Dallas," Cheyenne said, jumping in before Dallas could say anything, "my older brother."

"Her very protective older brother." Dallas made that smile he made when he was sizing up other guys.

Dallas applied a tight, appraising grip. Cheyenne pursed her lips and gave Dallas her fiercest stinky-eye, willing him to chill out.

Dallas' eyes narrowed and he released his grasp.

"He can be a little over-protective," she said to Xander. "Can't you, Dallas?"

Xander laughed and shook his hand. "I get that. I have a younger sister, and there are times I think the guys she dates needs to be tossed out the window."

"I know, right?" Dallas said. "The things

Cheyenne gets herself into sometimes...it drives me nuts."

They were bonding, but not in a way that could possibly bode well for her. "Did you just stop by to say hello?" Cheyenne asked hoping he would take the hint and leave.

"I was working late tonight and didn't want to drive home right away. Thought I'd drop by and unwind a bit. You know."

Cheyenne never doubted that her brother cared about her even when he was spying on her. Had he assumed she'd bring Xander home and wanted to check him out? There was definitely something in the air. First, Zach and Tiffany were all eager and excited to tell her something, then clammed up when they saw Xander. Then, Dallas had shown up—but it couldn't just be to do a general check-in.

Xander leaned over the puzzle and fit a piece into place. "My sister is dating a man who thinks McDonald's serves the quintessential burger."

Everyone at the table gasped except Dallas. He laughed like it was the funniest joke he'd heard in a long time.

Tiffany placed a fresh glass of wine in front of Dallas, and he took a sip. "So how'd your stuff go, anyway—you know, the pie class and the exhibit?"

Cheyenne hadn't thought Dallas was listening the

previous night at dinner. He'd asked her about her *real job* when she'd brought up the Smithsonian gig and had only teased her about crushing on Xander. Following Dallas and Sky into public service had been the natural thing to do, but she wished Dallas would be more open to her baking instead. Whenever she brought up pastry, he asked about her work with the Congressman. It was as if he was reminding her where she really belonged by changing the subject.

"She is the best pie-baker on the planet," Xander said. "And a good teacher. Did you know iced vodka makes the perfect crust?"

"Vodka in a pie crust? I had no idea," Dallas said. "Maybe I should take your class sometime."

"Wait, you used vodka in the crust? I thought you decided water was fine," said Zach.

"So did I, until I did a blind tasting in class," Cheyenne said. "I prepared a bunch of crusts ahead of time. Butter, shortening, lard, shortening and butter. Butter won, of course."

Dallas raised his wine-glass in a toast. "To vodka and butter...two of the world's best things. Where's Chelsea? She's usually around by this time."

As if on cue, Zach's phone chimed. He read the text. "Well, she's going to be late because boss-man insisted she deal with some shit at the restaurant."

Tiffany set her glass on the table hard enough that

a little wave of wine lapped over the edge. She caught the drip with a finger. "That jerk. This is getting old."

"Jerk? Getting old?" Dallas and Xander both said at the same time.

"Jinx," Dallas shouted, laughing. "You're okay, man. You're okay. Sorry, Cheyenne. What's up with Chelsea?"

"So," Cheyenne said, "Chelsea works at the Mongoose Bistro, you know the one run by Gerald Kinney? Anyway, she's getting a bunch of experience, but Kinney is just a douche bag. He yells at people, cusses them out, then has the audacity to make them stay late to do bullshit work."

"A total asshole," Zach said. He crossed his arms and jut out his lower lip. "He demands more and more of her, doesn't give her time off, pays her crap wages."

"And, lately, he's been hinting at worse," Tiffany said.

"So, why does she work for him?" Dallas asked.

"Because he's a genius," Zach said, almost spitting it out. "A good reference from him could make a career."

"Yeah, he's brilliant, but it's not worth it. If she pisses him off, he'll blacklist her. No one will hire her if it ends badly with them. She's afraid to quit, and she's afraid to not do whatever it is he asks her to do."

"Is there some sort of harassment going on here?" Xander asked.

"Nothing provable. No groping, no touching. He just says things that are inappropriate. He insists she stay late with an excuse like working up a sauce, organizing the storage, or some special project. All the while he lingers around and nitpicks at what she's doing and makes lewd comments."

"That's still harassment," Xander said.

"Not in the restaurant business. We work long weird hours and it's expected."

"Fuck that shit," Cheyenne said with a vehemence she hadn't expected. "She needs to speak up. We all do. This is the twenty-first century and all that crap has to change."

Tiffany huffed. "Bless your heart. Can't happen overnight. And you know if she quit out of principle some new little thang would be take up her job quick as spit no matter how much an ass Kinney is. Besides, he's being a jerkwad, but as far as I know, he's never put his hand on her or asked anything sexual of her. It's not like she wouldn't slap him upside the head for that kind of shit."

"Not gonna happen in our place," Cheyenne said. "We'll manage things without the drama, thank you very much."

"Our restaurant is definitely going to be different," Zach said nodding.

"Absolutely," Tiffany said.

"I don't get your attraction to the whole food business thing," Dallas said, shaking his head. "The hours are insane. And this crap with Kinney is...well...crap."

Cheyenne snorted. "The best revenge is success. I...we...are going to prove you can be successful in this biz without being grade-A jerks. Besides," she said, tapping her watch, "your hours are normal? Most people are at home on a Saturday night. Late?"

Dallas rubbed at his face. "Yeah. Well. Shit happens. But, you're right, I better get moving."

He shoved his hand at Xander again who took it and stood up at the same time. "I should be going, too."

"No," Cheyenne said, almost squeaking in her surprise. She didn't want Xander to leave yet, let alone have him walk out of here with her brother. "I have a recipe we need to go over."

Dallas laughed. "Yeah. I'm out of here." He kissed Cheyenne on the cheek and whispered in her ear. "I'm doing a complete background check on him tomorrow."

## Chapter 7

Cheyenne had to get Dallas to drop the security check. Maybe reminding him that—technically—he wasn't allowed to run backgrounds on a man his sister was dating would be enough. She gave up trying to do anything about it now. Besides, once Dallas got something in his head there was nothing she could do to stop him. He'd do whatever he was going to do. She'd deal with his reaction when it came.

Tiffany yawned and feigned sleepiness as she left the room, winking at Cheyenne. Zach gave her the double gun salute just as he declared how insanely tired he was before exiting the living room.

"Sorry about that. My roommates aren't always so strange."

"But you love them," Xander said. "It sounds like something exciting is happening, anyway."

*Nothing could be as exciting as being alone with you.*

Just as she was about to suggest they skip their earlier plans of watching a movie and invite him to her bedroom, Xander pointed at the television. "So, how about that movie?"

Disappointment at the switch in mood flooded through her. It wasn't quite midnight yet. There would still be time for more later.

"What should we watch?" she asked as they settled into the sofa together. "I have an app on my phone that decides for you..."

"Whatever you're in the mood for. I just want to spend the time with you."

She opened Movie Roulette and held it up for him. "My co-worker, Eleanor? She's this super techie guru. She wrote this app for fun. It takes all the angst out of deciding. It's connected to databases that crawl over all the streaming services. You choose the genre, hit spin, and it suggests a movie. Anyway, the idea is to watch whatever movie comes up. You can spin again or accept. It even tracks what you've watched."

"What about the Pride and Prejudice you suggested earlier?" he asked.

"Well, you'd have to spend the night for that one," she said, teasing him through her long eyelashes.

His eyes widened even further.

*Had she gone too far? Was that too brazen?* Cheyenne tried to backpedal. "It's six hours long. That's all I meant," she said.

"Oh. Maybe something shorter, then," he said. "I have early plans tomorrow." He wiggled his fingers in a gimme gesture toward her phone. He selected romance and tapped the spinner icon.

The screen flashed and whirled and displayed "Becoming Jane Austen" on the screen along with where to find the movie for streaming.

"Isn't that another one you mentioned earlier today? Says here you've already seen it...three times? We can spin again."

"No, it's fun. I'll watch it again. It'll give you a good primer on Austen, too."

She found the movie online and they settled in together. He moved into the corner of the sofa so she could slide in between his legs and he could wrap his arms around her. The simple act of watching television while cuddling with Xander was singularly more romantic than anything she'd experienced in the last six months. And all they were doing was sitting on a sofa—his broad chest against her back, his firm arms around her waist, her head supported by his shoulder.

He sighed and held his breath at all the right parts

and kissed her on the neck whenever Anne Hathaway, the actress playing Jane Austen in the movie, looked particularly fetching. When it was over, they stood, each stretching from having sat for so long.

"You're right. That was a pleasurable introduction to Jane Austen," he said.

Cheyenne playfully grabbed the edges of Xander's bowtie and drew him into a deep kiss.

"That was fun," he said when they parted for a moment.

"The kiss or the movie?"

"Both." He kissed her again. "I can see why Austen is so popular. She puts you in the mood for romance."

"Definitely," Cheyenne said.

"I should be going," he said. But he made no move to get away. Instead, his lips found hers again.

"Would you like to spend the night?" she asked when they came up for air. She wanted to know how those lips would caress her body, what he would taste like.

"Would I *like* to? Yes. But... I shouldn't."

She dropped her hands from his tie. He captured them in his, focusing at a spot on the floor in the space between them, pressing his forehead against hers.

"Yes, but no?" she asked. "I thought..." her voice trailed off.

*She'd thought they'd hit it off.* Why did a man saying *no* to her make her want him all the more? She wasn't used to anyone turning her down, but she could tell Xander wanted her as much as she wanted him.

A lock of his dark hair fell over his forehead in thick round curls. He squeezed her hands with warm fingers, intertwining them together. Such a simple gesture, and yet it was warm, intoxicating.

"I haven't always treated women the way they ought to be treated. I'm currently working on becoming a better man."

A shiver ran through her. Was he about to confess to some atrocious crime?

"You're good enough for me as you are," she said. *Probably better than I deserve.*

His gaze remained fixed on the floor. "I've had enough one night stands and short term relationships. I have hurt a lot of feelings. And, I don't want to be *that guy* any more. I'm not *that guy,* not really. But, I had to put a few rules in place to stay on track and not fall into old habits. I can't right all the wrongs of my past, but I can move forward with integrity."

His thumb skimmed the inside of her palm, sending shimmers of desire through her body.

"Rules?" She didn't want him to leave, not now. "Please tell me you're not anti-sex."

"Don't get me wrong, Cheyenne. I want to stay.

And...*Trust me,* I am not anti-sex." His voice had gone husky with desire. He nipped at her lips, catching them in his for a moment and breathed out heavily.

"Stay, then."

"I need to leave before it's too late."

And yet, he *still* didn't move. He remained close.

"You're not saving yourself for marriage, are you?" she asked, inhaling the warm cardamom, cinnamon, scent that was him.

He let out a sharp, hawkish laugh. "Way too late for that. And that's the problem. I've been too cavalier with my affections. Throwing myself at women. Using them. That whole thing with my students? I almost ruined my career last fall. Not saying 'no' when I should've. I needed to pull back, make sure what I'm doing with people...with you...is right for me and for you." Xander kissed her forehead. "I'm thirty-six years old, and I want to go beyond *just sex*. I'm looking for meaningful."

Isn't that what she wanted too? Wished for? Longed for? The problem was, she'd been there once before. Promised herself, all of her—the best and worst of herself—to Alberto. He'd left her when her body had failed them both. More fake promises would crush her.

In spite of the grumble of fear in her belly,

Cheyenne clung to this man who said he wanted more. "Tell me then, what are these rules of yours?"

"They're designed to help me catch my breath and not get totally caught up. Like now. Because, believe me, a year ago, we'd already be naked."

Cheyenne leaned into him, dropped her head against his shoulder, memorizing all his musky undertones. "Sounds good to me."

He groaned. "Believe me, this is not easy. I have to slow things down. No sex on the first date. No more one-night stands."

"Okay, so no sex tonight," she said. "What about tomorrow morning? You could spend the night..."

She grinned up at him as she left the sentence unfinished.

"And," he said firmly, rolling his eyes at her immediate workaround. "We have to share a meal."

"Easy," she said. "We had pie earlier today."

"You are incorrigible." He said it with a smile, but even Cheyenne was picking up on an earnest underlying need. "I need a little time. That's all I'm asking for. I want to get to know you and you to know me."

The guy was asking for time. How rare was that? And something about the way he said it got through to her. She needed to accept his needs, acknowledge them, and move on. "Okay. I think I got it. We can kiss and make out, right?"

"Oh yeah, that's the best part of slowing things down."

They kissed again. Cheyenne relaxed into it as if it were the main course of a fine meal, understanding for the first time that evening that kisses were it for the night and savoring each little nip of his lips, each movement of his tongue, the way their breaths moved into sync with each other. Knowing the kiss was the goal made it sweeter and memorable.

When they broke the deep kiss, she was physically shattered. She wanted more from him. And yet she was content knowing that would be it.

"How long have you been following these rules?" she asked.

"Six months."

"How many women have you slept with since you started following these rules?" she asked.

"None."

*None.* And not a breath of hesitation.

"It sounds like a very long six months," she said.

"It was worth the wait," he said, practically purring.

"So no sex for now."

He laughed. "We need to have a date and a meal then see where it leads us."

"Tonight was a date, wasn't it?"

"Doesn't count." He laughed and kissed the tip of her nose. He pulled away from her, held their hands up to his lips, kissing her fingers. "Cheyenne, we've spent hours on the phone. I feel like I know you. Because of that, I'm even more determined to not rush things."

All those hours on the phone talking connected them in a deeper way than purely physical. "You're right. We have known each other for weeks now, just not face to face."

His unrelenting smile sent her heart skittering again.

"I can wait. So...you want to come over tomorrow?" she asked. "Like around lunchtime? We can hide in my bedroom and neck if that's all you're ready for."

That smile again. She traced his lips with her finger. He turned her palm toward her mouth and kissed her. "What about that mysterious dinner and challah thing? Won't a mid-day tryst be a problem?"

"Nah. Whatever is driving Zach and Tiffany to distraction can't be that big a deal."

"You don't have much patience, do you?" he asked. His chest heaved with the effort of breathing. He was holding back, too. "You are making it very hard for me to leave right now."

"Good."

"Cheyenne, you are going to be trouble."

"You can count on it."

"Okay then. Lunch. Tomorrow. But at my place so we can be alone." Xander kissed her on the lips—simple, chaste, and quick—and walked out the door.

Once he was gone, the room was suddenly devoid of life. Cheyenne touched her lips. Were they actually hot, or was she imagining things? She closed her eyes and inhaled the lingering scent he left in his wake, savoring the spicy undertones and rich, heady manliness of him.

Something about Xander had wakened a strong urge and craving within her. She had not been overwhelmed by desire like this in a very long time. Not since Alberto. Sure, she'd been dating and having a good time, but no one she'd been out with since her divorce had given her pause, had cared about making sure she was meaningful.

*Longing? Need? Lust?* A combination of all three. *Addlepated.* That was the word her mom would use.

With the men she'd dated for the game, it had been a simple conquest. Go out, kiss 'em, leave. She had gotten used to dismissing any long term relationships. For so long, she'd told herself she didn't want marriage and everything else that went with it. She'd had it and lost it. She wasn't ready to go through the pain again.

Or was she? For the first time she doubted her assertions to stay single.

She had spent so much time telling herself all she wanted was to satisfy her desire. Period. That was it. Anything more had been too painful. Where had four years of therapy gotten her? She had been warned it would be difficult putting herself out there into the real world.

The evening had ended up completely different than she'd expected. She plopped onto her bed, grabbing her extra pillow and wrapping her arms around it, pretending it was Xander instead of goose down.

She tossed and turned, trying to get past simply pretending to be in his arms, but try as she might, she couldn't do it. After a while, she dug through her bedside table for her vibrator. It had been a couple weeks since she'd needed it. She revved it up to high. She wanted quick relief.

But nothing. Even on full power, her body didn't respond like it should. There was definitely something wrong. She conjured up the feeling of Xander sliding his arm casually around her waist, claiming her. That brought forth a tiny twinge of interest. Then her hands tingled at the memory of his grasping hers and his thumb skimming across her palm.

She tried to picture him naked, but she couldn't see beyond the tangle of hair at his throat in her fantasy. Why was she having such a hard time going further than that? And analyzing it sure as hell wasn't helping. She turned off the vibrator and slammed it back into the drawer. The aching hunger pounding between her legs was not going to be sated by anything short of Xander's touch.

Chapter 8

Cheyenne woke to the smell of fresh coffee and fresh bread. The heady yeast smell from the oven filled the entire apartment.

A loud pounding on her door brought her fully awake.

"Cheyenne, wake up. You cannot sleep in today," Tiffany said as she thrust the door open.

It was time for a lock on her door.

The clock read eight o'clock. "Go away. It's Sunday." Cheyenne pulled her spare pillow over her head, determined to ignore Tiffany.

"Seriously, Cheyenne, get out of bed. Now. This is an emergency."

Cheyenne peeked out from behind the pillow. "Emergency?"

Tiffany dropped her head back and thrust her

arms out to the sides. "Yeah. Get dressed and get your ass into the kitchen. We'll explain everything then. But move it."

"Okay, okay. Give me a few. Gee whiz," Cheyenne said.

Cheyenne stretched and threw on her sweats and an old Capitals jersey she had confiscated from one of their players she had dated a year or two ago. She tried conjuring up his face, but she couldn't remember what he looked like. His name as Paul, but his features escaped her. She sniffed at the jersey as if it might contain a lingering image from the past. Nope. Well... *That* had never happened before.

Cheyenne liked men. She liked sex. She had lots of sex with lots of men, but she remembered every single one of them. She could list and name them if she wanted to. But the names and the faces, they had just disappeared from her mind. She couldn't picture any of the men she'd slept with since Alberto. The only man she could picture was Xander.

*Damn.* There was no denying it. All she wanted was to get to lunch. She paused for a moment, remembering their conversation. If he was willing to take the time to make sure that whatever sex they had was meaningful, shouldn't she do the same for him? She was already genuinely curious about him, his past, but wanted to make knowing him a priority over sex.

A retro Wilson Phillips song about saying goodbye played in the living room. Tiffany had a penchant for all things '80's. The lyrics whispered across her lips; words like changing and that things would go her way.

Cheyenne stumbled into the shared living space, wanting to get coffee first. She stopped midway to the kitchen. The apartment was even more immaculate than it had been the evening before. The puzzle was off the table. Fresh flowers in a vase had taken its place.

The table was set for six in the best dishes they had with linens she'd never seen before. Four forks to the left of each plate were balanced with a large soup spoon, a fish knife, a regular dinner knife and a steak knife on the right side of each plate. At the top of each was a dessert spoon and fork. Four glasses for wine plus one for water finished each place setting. They didn't own this much cutlery between them.

"What in the world?" Cheyenne asked. "Where did this all come from? What is going on?"

"We're in the kitchen!" Chelsea said.

Tiffany was slicing up a baguette into perfect crostini. Zach had returned from work, but 8 o'clock was too early for his shift to be over. He must have cut out early. The challah lay on a cooling rack. The largest pot they owned was filled with something simmering away. Bits of celery leaves and onion dotted the surface of an already darkening stock. The rich beef and vegetables vied for her attention against the warm, yeasty smell of the bread and the fancy table setting.

Chelsea held a knife in her hand, and she was bouncing on the balls of her feet.

"Holy hell. Put that knife down before you hurt someone. No one should be that excited in the morning. Spill it guys. What's going on?"

Cheyenne slathered butter onto a slice of the baguette and bit into it. It tasted sweet and just the right amount of airy lightness. Comforting. There was nothing better than warm bread with salty butter. Tiffany waved the envelope Zach had hidden behind his back the evening before in front of Cheyenne. "You guys, we need to get Cheyenne up to speed."

"Easy, Tiffany, not in my face, okay?" Cheyenne backed away from the letter.

"We got in."

Cheyenne had never seen Tiffany so wide-eyed excited. She was positively buoyant.

Cheyenne poured herself a cup of coffee. "Got in? To what?"

"*Kitchen Wars!* The show? The contest? Cheyenne, are you fucking kidding me? We are in. Well, almost, anyway."

Comprehension slid over Cheyenne like a glacier. She shivered at the implication.

"Wait. What? We got in?" she asked, grabbing at the envelope and pulling the acceptance letter out.

Three months before, the four of them had auditioned for *Kitchen Wars*—the latest hot franchise from Tricia and Llewelyn Branton's restaurant kingdom. The famous couple had hundreds of restaurants throughout the world and ran four different cooking show competitions. Cheyenne had given up hope on ever hearing back from them, let alone being considered as finalists.

In *Kitchen Wars*, twelve teams of four chefs worked to create the perfect restaurant over a ten-week long competition. They had all signed Non-Disclosure Agreements about their involvement. They weren't even allowed to tell anyone they had auditioned until they were told yes or no.

If accepted, they would have to move to Los Angeles for twelve weeks to film the show. They would live in the competition apartments, leave their phones behind, and would have limited access to the internet. No email was allowed, but they would get one ten-minute phone call per week to the outside world. All four had agreed that they would be available to be on the show as it was taped over twelve weeks.

Everyone in the apartment had agreed to the terms, including Cheyenne. She had decided getting in was a long shot and had signed without thinking that she'd ever have to live by the rules. She'd managed to keep her mouth shut about it, even though she wanted to tell her family. To keep herself from talking about it, she'd shoved it aside as a 'never really gonna happen' thing in her mind.

The winners of the competition won the restaurant they designed for the show. The Brantons would build it out and hand it over to the winners with an added bonus of a six months operating expenses and all the free publicity the show would generate.

While they were planning and scrimping and saving to open their restaurant, they'd jumped at the audition when it came up because...well, why not? It would take them another five years of hard work to save up enough money to build their restaurant on their own. Winning the show would provide them with their own, completed, restaurant. They could use their savings as a cushion for operation for a year or two.

The best case scenario would be for them to go on the show and end up with a completed restaurant. The worst case was they'd be passed over and they'd have to come up with the money for the restaurant on their own as they had been planning to all along.

Between them, they had almost two hundred thousand dollars saved up, not nearly enough. They needed at least a million to get through the six-month start-up slump most restaurants experience upon opening.

Cheyenne had saved nearly seventy thousand on her own over the last four years since her divorce. The congressman paid pretty well, her food bill was practically nil between all the free lobbyist happy hours and restaurant leftovers, and she lived cheaply. Having only one dress had been worth it.

Cheyenne held the letter with shaking hands. "Why didn't you say anything last night?"

Zach held his hands up. "The NDA? Remember? We weren't even allowed to tell anyone we auditioned."

"*That's* why you were so annoyed when Xander came home with me. You wanted to talk about this."

"Yeah. And then he hung out and wouldn't leave."

"We figured it would be fine to tell you this morning," Tiffany said.

"Right. Sorry about that."

Chelsea tapped the letter. "You've got to read it!"

"All right, Chelsea." We made it past the initial evaluation... There were twenty-four teams left to be evaluated. Only twelve teams will be chosen. The Brantons were planning various tastings and interviews to decide which of those teams would continue onto the show. Cheyenne pursed her lips. "So we still have to get into the finals?"

"Keep reading, Cheyenne. And don't be such a Debbie-Downer," Zach said.

Cheyenne re-read the letter three times to make sure it was real and absorb it all. "They're coming with a camera crew for dinner? Tonight?"

"That's why the apartment is so clean. The producer contacted Zach yesterday to let him know it was happening tonight!" Tiffany rolled her head back and huffed at Cheyenne. "You knew this would happen. They told us those making it into the next round would be notified of a private elimination round with only twenty-four hours notice. It came by courier right after you left for the opening last night."

Chelsea rubbed her hands together and chortled with glee. "We gave them this address for their private home tasting when we did the audition. At least we'll be cooking on our own turf for them. There won't be any surprises with the equipment."

"I thought we were good, but the chances of making it are so slim, I guess I didn't think it'd actually happen." Cheyenne said. "And six at the table? Are we supposed to cook and share the meal?"

"Yep. We'll each cook our own courses and serve it to the whole table," Chelsea said. "You've watched the show, you know how it works."

"You could have texted me." Cheyenne had the sudden impulse to run. How was this even happening?

She'd agreed, believing they'd never get onto the show. Not with the thousands of people entering the contest. How was she supposed to uproot her life and move to LA? "We have less than ten hours to prepare the most important meal of our lives. I'm not sure we can do this."

"Look at us," Zach said proudly, "we are their dream team. Chelsea and Tiffany are killers at the grill and everything savory, you are an amazing pastry chef. Between us we've got a full-service restaurant covered."

"We got what they need in every way," Tiffany said, patting the back of her head.

Half of the show was all about representation, and their little group had a bit of everything. Zach was handsome and friendly and oozed almost every gay stereotype on the planet. Chelsea was Korean, her parents first generation immigrants. Tiffany was as dark as midnight. Cheyenne was white and blond. Together, they looked like the cast of a racially balanced sitcom.

The four of them were all hot, in their twenties, and awesome chefs. Together, they had all the skills needed to create winning menus. This audition was everything Cheyenne had dreamed of for years. Why, then, were her hands suddenly icy and her heart racing like she'd just run a 10K? The ground didn't feel solid and everything spun around her as though she were on a merry-go-round. Her body became gelatinous. Her sight went all blurry and then, everything went black.

SHE WOKE to a strong ammonia biting at her nose. Zach was holding a wedge of blue cheese just inches away from her and grinning like an idiot. She pushed his hand away. "God, get rid of it. That's gone bad."

"Nah. It's just super ripe," he said, tossing it in his mouth.

"Don't scare us like that," said Chelsea, fanning her.

"I knew the blue cheese would work," said Tiffany, who helped her stand up. "It's delicious, but it smells bad enough to gag a maggot."

"I got a glass of water for you," Chelsea said.

Cheyenne took a slow drink. "Was I dreaming when you said we made it onto *Kitchen Wars?*"

"Nope. It's real," said Tiffany. "And we're gonna kick ass. Get your shit together. We're doing this."

Zach handed Cheyenne a hand written menu. "All you have to do is one of the starters and the dessert, of course. Sorry, but we decided for you and got the ingredients while you were out with Mr. Dark and Handsome last night."

The menu was impressive while being doable. They'd chosen well without her, though she might have pushed for something less fussy for a couple of the courses. But no risk, no reward. Nothing on the list was impossible, but everything had something that could go wrong.

Cheyenne excused herself to get dressed. If she was going to cook for the Bartons, she was going to do so in professional gear with her hair up and her shoes on. As she stepped out of her super short shower, she caught her breath.

Damn. She would have to cancel her lunch date with Xander. There was no doubt that the competition trumped her personal desire to hook up with him. She couldn't tell him why she was canceling, though. That would break her NDA with the show. Would he understand? At the least, she'd get to see how he handled himself when she turned him down.

She gathered her towel around her and texted him the simplest explanation.

**Cheyenne:** I'm so sorry. Something of an emergency popped up and I can't see you today.
Lunch tomorrow instead?

He didn't text back right away, but she didn't even expect him to be awake this early.

Cheyenne threw on her checkered pants and white top she reserved for special catering events. *Might as well look like a chef.* She put her phone in her back pocket and set it to silent buzz mode.

Zach, Tiffany, and Chelsea were all in the kitchen prepping their individual courses. In spite of the size of the kitchen, they had managed to delineate separate work stations for each of them. It was tight, but they knew each others' moves well and rarely got in each others' way. The four worked in companionable silence as they prepared their own parts of a gourmet dinner intended to impress one of the country's top celebrity chefs.

Llewelyn Barton was known for his years-long run as the host of several popular cooking shows. To people in the business, he was a restaurant gold mine, known for his successful fifty-eight restaurants scattered across the country.

He had two restaurants in DC. Both were award winners with the highest rankings by Michelin and Zagat. *The Wide Table* was a gourmand's delight and was the fancier of the two. Focusing on farm-to-table dishes, it served only food grown within two hundred miles of DC. Cheyenne couldn't imagine a restaurant that didn't serve coffee or chocolate, but she hadn't been able to score a dinner there yet to see exactly how Barton did it. *The Wide Table* was booking reservations a year out and wasn't slowing down.

The second DC restaurant was more of a pub, drawing influence from Llewelyn's Welsh heritage. It didn't take reservations and Cheyenne had eaten there twice. Each time there had been a two hour wait—but totally worth it. She'd had the most amazing shepherd's pie ever.

Cheyenne had been tasked to make a molded chocolate dessert for this evening's meal, and it usually required a couple of hours to make, build, and set for perfection. Plating it was super fussy, but the layers of chocolate—from white to dark—with hand painted gold on chocolate disks was a show-stopper for sure.

She gathered all the ingredients and prepared five different *mise en places*. She needed to make five layers of mousse, dark to light, letting the previous layer firm up a bit before adding the next. She usually layered the mousses in parfait glasses, but that wouldn't work for this evening. Plating them so that the layers were even and beautifully delineated would be way more impressive. She would need specifically designed dessert molds to get this right.

She put her trays in the fridge, wondering if the restaurant supply shop was open. "Guys, I need taller molds for this thing. I can't use parfait glasses tonight."

Zach spun around from his station. "You missed

the whole part about all this stuff we rented yesterday, didn't you?"

Cheyenne had no idea what he was talking about. Maybe fainting had messed with her head. She followed his long finger to a box in the corner of the kitchen. Inside were perfect spring form dessert molds made precisely for what she was doing. She crossed the kitchen and kissed his cheek.

"Brilliant."

They really would make a great team. She rinsed the molds and prepped them for the mousse. And what if they did get on the show? Would it all work out for them in the long run? They had lived together for three years and knew each other's quirks. They'd subbed at work for each other on occasion as well. Cheyenne had taken a couple of evening shifts for them, loving the work even though it made her late to her day job. For some reason, they'd never offered to sub for her at the Congressman's office—their love for her only ran so deep. She didn't blame them. But so far, their talk about running a restaurant together had been all talk.

The plan had been for them all to save for another three years before jumping into anything concrete. Cheyenne had planned on three more years of stability as a staffer at Congressman Pierce's office. She pulled out the double boiler and filled the bottom pan with water.

As she organized the various chocolates, she decided to make the bottom layer a baked flourless chocolate cake—a dense fudgy layer that would act as a structural and visual support to the rest of the layers.

"Anyone need the oven?" she asked and filled the others in on her plan.

"Are you sure?" Tiffany asked. "It seems like overkill."

"The fluffy texture of five mousses will bore the Bartons. He's always talking about mouthfeel and wanting a variety."

"You're the expert," Chelsea said. "We don't need the oven for another hour, so have at it."

Cheyenne could make this particular cake with her eyes closed—butter, tempered eggs, melted chocolate, low oven.

Her phone buzzed and she pulled it out to see if Xander had replied to her text. Instead, it was an alert from Eleanor. She'd gotten another kiss for the Bingo game. Cheyenne stared at the screen for a second, gob smacked that she had completely forgotten about all of that. Sure, she'd thought about it a couple of times the day before, but it had flown out of her mind completely with the news she might be going on *Kitchen Wars*.

With four kisses under her belt (more, really, but four in *one* row), all she needed was one more—her scientist at the Smithsonian. *Xander.* If things went well in Vegas, and she continued climbing the work ladder, she was guaranteed success in the Pierce political machine.

And, now, suddenly, that might all be over. If they got on the show, she'd have to be in LA for three months to tape it. Did winning Bingo even matter anymore? Did it *ever* really matter to her? Working for Congressman Pierce was a way to make money and keep her family happy. Serving her country somehow had always been important to her, even though she wasn't sure she was accomplishing much in her current job.

Her real goal was owning a restaurant and being her own boss. Winning *Kitchen Wars* would get her there faster than working while scrimping and saving. Building a restaurant was expensive, and the prizes from *Kitchen Wars* would save them all years of work.

Cheyenne broke up the chocolate for her first ganache, a bittersweet dark chocolate, and put it in a glass bowl over water in a pan. She stirred it to melting over the simmering water until it was smooth and set it aside to cool.

She'd have to quit her job if they made it past tonight's round. There was no way the congressman would hold her job for her in case things didn't work out. Would he? What would happen if she quit her job to go on the show and they lost? She'd have to return to DC with her tail between her legs and find something else to do.

After chopping the milk chocolate for the next layer, Cheyenne popped a piece in her mouth to check the flavor. It had gone off.

"Crap, this chocolate is rancid," she said.

Chelsea spun around. "No way! We just got it yesterday."

"I told you we should have sampled that."

"I sniffed it. It smelled okay. I'm so sorry, Cheyenne."

Cheyenne opened the fridge and pulled out a spare carton of whipping cream. "This is extra, right? I'll lighten some darker ganache with more cream. Don't worry about it."

Cheyenne tossed the rancid chocolate and prepped more of the dark chocolate.

Failing at the competition could set her back months on saving if she didn't get a new job right away. The last thing she wanted to do was fail at something. Her whole life was a failure, her marriage, her babies. She didn't want this to turn into a bad dream. If she jumped ship, she might end up in an ocean she couldn't navigate, she'd probably lose the friendship of her roommates and the one shot she had of achieving her dream. Pierce's office was a known quantity. If they didn't get on the show, they would stick to their long-term plans.

Cheyenne pulled the mini-cakes out of the oven and set them aside to cool. Once they were room temp, she could add the darkest layer of ganache. She dissolved some gelatin in water to stabilize the whipping cream she'd use for all the mousses.

What would she tell Xander? The show wasn't set to tape for another six weeks. It wasn't like they were *together*. Maybe in six weeks, though, they would be. She could definitely finish her class with him, but getting into a relationship now would suck. Maybe she could put him on hold until she got back. The plan was definitely to have a restaurant in the DC area. She'd only be in LA for three months. Of course, if they didn't even get onto the show, then none of her worries would even matter.

"Earth to Cheyenne..." Chelsea was singing in her ear.

"What?" Cheyenne snuck a glance at Chelsea while whisking a continuous stream of sugar into steaming cream.

"I was asking you if you could do something with this yuzu? I was thinking it would be cool to tie the dessert to the main dish with the same flavors, and I got some extra."

Cheyenne continued whisking with one hand as she took the cut fruit from Chelsea and sniffed it. She generally associated yuzu with Asian foods, not chocolate. The tart orangey fragrance was bright and perky.

"Cut me a sliver, will you?" she asked.

Chelsea peeled off a bit of the fruit and Cheyenne opened her mouth, accepting it like a baby bird. The orangy-grapefruity flavor burst across her tongue. She dipped a spoon in the tempered dark chocolate and meshed the two flavors together. Perfection! The tartness of the fruit was an excellent foil to the sweetness of the chocolate. She pictured the layers of the dish and ran through a bunch of options.

"I know," Cheyenne said, "I can use it in the white chocolate layer. I'll add a bit of the grated rind and some of the juice to flavor it. The Bartons love it when people use the same ingredient in multiple courses, so I should definitely try it. My only concern is the citrus could curdle the dairy."

"I trust you, darling," Chelsea said, leaving the fruit at Cheyenne's station.

The four chefs continued their preparations in silence. Cheyenne made the yuzu infused white chocolate mousse as the top layer of the dessert. The final dessert was white chocolate with tiny flecks of color from the yuzu peel, milk chocolate, semi-sweet chocolate, dark chocolate and the fudgy cake layer. Five layers from light to dark.

While each layer set in the fridge, Cheyenne turned the thin tendrils of yuzu peel into sparkling shreds of sugared candy. She twisted them around a chopstick to make them into spirals with a stem for support. When they were hardened, she would be able to poke three into the top of each dessert as garnish. The crystalized sugar would sparkle nicely.

"Those are beautiful," Chelsea said. "Are you going to use the gold with that? It might be elegant sprinkled across the top."

Cheyenne considered the creamy white surface and shook her head. "I don't like the contrast of the gold with the orange of the Yuzu. The colors are too close and we'll lose the contrast."

"That totally makes sense. You're the dessert queen."

They had been told the set-up crew would arrive at three o'clock and the Bartons would arrive at six o'clock. The hours slipped away. Cheyenne finished the top layer as the doorbell rang.

## Chapter 9

"Okay everybody," Chelsea said, "it's show time."

Zach, Tiffany, and Cheyenne all lined up next to the door as Chelsea flung it open, a big grin on her face.

There were twenty people crammed into their tiny hallway. They all wore black jackets with "Barton Productions" in bright green and yellow letters and were laden with various black boxes, camera equipment, and oddities Cheyenne didn't recognize.

People poured into their apartment, passing the four stunned cooks. The crew made themselves at home, setting up their gear to get shots of them in the kitchen as they prepped. A short red-headed guy with a pasty-white face directed people around and told them where to set up their cameras, lights, huge microphones, and reflectors. The crew moved furniture and re-arranged their whole setup.

"Whoa," Cheyenne said. "What are you doing?"

"We need to maneuver the cameras around the table to get the best shots. Don't worry, we'll put things back the way we found them. I'm Jason Hopkins, the producer." He shook the hands of each of them before pointing two people toward the bedrooms. "Patricia and Damon will take two of you at a time for makeup while we set up."

Jason basically took over everything, managing and telling everyone what to do. The next couple of hours were a whirlwind, and it was all Cheyenne could do to breathe, let alone think clearly. She needed a moment to herself and went to her room and closed the door to shut out the hubbub from the camera crew. If this was what it would be like to be on the competition, she wasn't sure she could handle it. Within a minute, someone was knocking.

The makeup artist sat her down and put a plastic apron around her. She got out pots and tins, holding them up to her face.

"Your skin is fabulous. I'm going to have fun with you. Is that okay?"

"Sure," Cheyenne replied. "Can I check my phone before we get started?"

"Make it quick," she said rolling her eyes. "I have to get all of you picture perfect for the camera."

Xander had texted back a while ago, and she'd been so busy with her cooking she had missed it.

**Xander**: No problem. Hope all is well. Rose Garden Cafe at the castle for lunch work for you?
**Cheyenne**: Perfect. See you there. 1:00 tomorrow?

This was all so surreal. She wanted to tell him why she'd bailed, but she had to pretend like nothing out of the ordinary was happening while a camera crew was in her apartment and two of the most important restauranteurs in the world were about to eat her food. And she couldn't tell anyone. Not Dallas, or Sky, or Xander. This was going to be its own kind of hell.

The crew had managed to re-arrange all the furniture so that they could shoot a living room scene, a dining room scene and a kitchen scene. Her entire apartment had been transformed into a television set with different stages—all of them faked to perfection.

Jason gathered them together all together in the living room and gave them the low-down on the entire evening. First, everyone would be interviewed individually regarding their hopes and dreams in relation to the show. He continued with rules about how to interact on camera and with the host, giving them tips and tricks to help them do their best and win that coveted spot on the show. *Do this. Don't do that.* Do this, and no matter what you do, don't ask Llewelyn about his name. Apparently he was touchy about people trying to pronounce it in Welsh and failing.

*Whatever.* Cheyenne could relate to having the wrong name. People always expected her to be Native American and from Wyoming. No one seemed to notice her last name, which was French in origin. And, she wasn't even French so much as an American mongrel with parents from two different parts of the country and a penchant for naming their children after their places of conception. She didn't want to think about where her parents had sex.

Jason pulled Zach aside. "We'll start with you."

HER INTERVIEW HADN'T scared her so much as caught her off guard. Cheyenne hadn't really thought through it ahead of time, exactly, and she hoped it didn't sound too fake or worse, sappy. Even though she had known the format for the show included these personal introductions, she hadn't *planned* for it. She'd watched Madeline prepping others in the congressman's office for press releases, giving them pertinent talking points and asking practice questions. If she'd had that beforehand, she might not have droned on about her family or her dad dying on 9/11.

Jason clapped loudly three times.

"Five minutes, everyone. Five minutes. The Bartons are parked and are on their way." One of the windows was above the main street below the apartment. Someone had marked off the street with tape and city approved A-frames so that parking would be a breeze.

She wished they had an elevator and hoped walking up three flights of stairs wouldn't tire the Bartons out. Maybe the exercise would make them hungrier.

A production assistant opened the door and Tricia and Llewelyn Barton entered as if they owned the place. Both appeared older in person than they did on television in spite of their perfectly quaffed hair and makeup. They'd come ready for the cameras.

"I can't wait to see what you'll be making for us," Tricia said as she sniffed the air. "Something smells divine."

Jason made formal introductions all around. Cheyenne was surprised at how short both the Bartons were. On television, Tricia and Llewelyn were larger than life, big personalities and taking up the television screen. In reality, Llewelyn was a good three inches shorter than Cheyenne, and Tricia was maybe five feet —with heels on. Come to think of it, they were often standing on a stage a bit taller than the competitors. However, her diminutive stature did nothing to make Tricia Barton seem anything less than the food giant she was.

"Let's start with an aperitif, shall we?" Tiffany waved everyone over to the living room. She'd placed an impressive charcuterie platter on the coffee table. Layers of locally made salami, specialty cheeses, pickles, olives, fruits and other things that paired well with them were arranged in an artful way.

Llewelyn and Tricia settled onto the sofa. Zach brought a tray from the kitchen laden with cocktails. The classic martini glasses were frosty from being chilled in the freezer before being dipped in a special blend of salt and sugar.

Tricia eyed the glass before taking a sip. She closed her eyes and inhaled deeply before taking another sip. "Let's see...Pisco, drambuie, campari, and lime juice?"

Llewelyn took a sip, his signature eyebrow raise sending a shiver of anticipation through Cheyenne. That particular left eyebrow lift was one of his positive 'tells.' "And egg white."

Zach clapped his hands together. "You guys are amazing. You only missed one ingredient."

Llewelyn eyed the glass and took another sip. "Clever, young man. Bitters."

"Lime bitters," Zach said.

"Good choice, it adds that perfect ending note to the drink," Llewelyn said.

Tricia held up her glass to make a toast. "To young chefs and their endless and boundless enthusiasm."

Cheyenne wasn't sure it was a compliment, but everyone lifted their glasses and clinked them together. Tricia was older than Llewelyn by a few years. It was only obvious to Cheyenne now that she was here in person, that the older woman was worn. Her makeup hid the fatigue remarkably well.

Llewelyn put together a plate for Tricia, pairing the cheeses and fruits with an expert eye. An uncomfortable silence descended on the group as everyone sipped at their aperitif and ate the charcuterie.

"This salami, did you get it at Bordeccio's?" Tricia asked.

She was referring to Carmen Bordeccio's charcuterie. The tiny shop was considered the best in DC. Tiffany was an apprentice with Bordeccio's chief rival—Giovanni Sambuco. Sambuco's kept their business small to retain their artisanal quality and sold mostly to local restaurants and savvy DC area gourmands.

"Not exactly. It's one I made. I'm an apprentice at

Sambuco's, but this is my own twist on one of the classics," Tiffany said.

Tricia's lips twitched as she suppressed a smile. "Now, don't tell her I said this, but it's better than Carmen's. We need to consider sourcing our charcuterie from Samubuco's, Llewelyn."

He tried the salami for himself. "Tiffany, you said this was one of your adaptations, not one of Sambuco's recipes?"

"It's my own." Tiffany beamed. She couldn't get any more puffed up than she already was. There was going to be no living this one down, but it gave them high marks as a team. To have Llewelyn and Tricia gaga over anything you made was a new chef's dream.

"Thank you. I'm glad you like it. I wanted to make something with a more front-forward profile than the standard salami we make there. He's thinking of adding this recipe to his regular production."

"He should. It's delicious," Tricia said. "Now. What is on the menu tonight?"

Chelsea stood up and took on a waiter-like stance, her hands clasped in front of her.

"The first dish of the evening is a salad of grilled Treviso with pear, saba, Fourme d'Ambert blue cheese, and sweet and salty walnuts."

Cheyenne sipped at her drink. The salad sounded over complicated to her, but it would be delicious.

"After our home-made yuzu and rosemary sorbet palate cleanser, Zach will provide a tagliatelle with a bright sauce. Tiffany will prepare the main course, a pan-seared duck breast on a bed of greens with yuzu and crispy fried grits. We'll have a separate cheese course, followed by Cheyenne's amazing layered chocolate mousses."

Llewelyn drained the rest of his drink and added three more slices of salami to Tricia's plate. "So far so good. You're definitely impressing us."

Cheyenne's tummy did a little flip. They were definitely on the right course, so why was she feeling so nauseous? Shouldn't she be excited? One more step toward the road to their restaurant.

Chelsea disappeared into the kitchen to plate the salad.

"Tell me about your histories, then. Where did you all study? Work?" Llewelyn lounged back against the sofa like he owned the place, his arm outstretched across the back behind Tricia. Cheyenne had never noticed just how much gray was in the man's hair before. Maybe he colored it while taping a show to cover it up. His dark brown eyes moved constantly, taking in his surroundings. On television, he came across as large, booming, and a little scary. Here, sitting across from Cheyenne on her sofa, he reminded her of a young Ben Kingsley. Spry. Almost elven.

Cheyenne tried to ignore the giant camera that suddenly loomed over her. "I studied at the International Culinary Center in San Diego," Cheyenne said. "In pastry arts."

A lot of famous chefs had come out of that school, and Cheyenne wanted to be one of them, right up there next to Bobby Flay and Christina Tosi. They were over the top famous, and Cheyenne could only hope to get there done day.

"And where do you work now?" Tricia asked.

"I teach at the Culinary Institute in Virginia, along with everyone else here."

Tricia cocked her head. "I don't recall seeing your name on their faculty listing."

"Cheyenne teaches on the weekends," Zach said. "She's working full time as a staffer at a congressman's office."

Cheyenne's cheeks flooded with warmth. It was such a pathetic excuse for not working a 'real' industry job. "I needed some stability. It pays well, and I've saved every bit of extra money to start our own restaurant."

Llewelyn and Tricia exchanged a look. Cheyenne knew the meaning behind it. She wasn't real, and they saw right through her. She was a poser. A complete imposter. Someone who played at cooking and not a real contender. She had never put in the time with midnight clean-ups or four-am wake-ups.

Tricia wiped imaginary crumbs from her thighs. "You are aware that *everyone* else in the competition are full time in the profession?"

Cheyenne's cheeks burned. "I could be full time if I wanted to be. I've held onto my day job to earn the money we need for our restaurant. After all, winning this competition isn't guaranteed."

Llewelyn rubbed his hands together and tipped his chin toward Jason. "You think that's a useful angle? Playing Cheyenne's position as weaker and possibly not so good for her team?"

Jason bobbed his head side to side. "We could use it as a way to play the members of the team against each other when one of the challenges goes south."

Tiffany's eyes had gone round at this blatant discussion. They hadn't really considered the drama around the show and how it might affect them. This was how it started though, wasn't it? The show's producers picking up on possible weaknesses and mining them for conflict to make the show entertaining.

Tiffany took a deep breath. "We've lived together for years now. We're like siblings—we yell and scream at each other a lot, but we always come back to loving each other. We'll make great TV."

Chelsea swore loudly from the kitchen. Through the doorway, Chelsea could be seen handling a pan with flames licking the bottom. She elegantly flipped the Treviso and set it back on the stove.

Zach waved his hand around his head as if he were batting away a fly. "Oh, she really meant grilled, didn't she?"

Llewelyn clapped his hands together. "Jason, be sure you have good shots of whatever is going on in the kitchen."

"Should be, we have a camera in there."

Chelsea poked her head out of the kitchen. "I'm about ready here, so please take your seats. Zach, get the pinot grigio out of the fridge and pour it, will you?"

Cheyenne ended up next sitting between to Llewelyn and Zach at the table. The salads were plated beautifully. All the elements were equally distributed, and a thin line of saba circled the outer edge of the plate. The purple grape syrup was strong, and a little went a long way. It was headier and sweeter than balsamic and would balance the bitterness of the radicchio nicely. The blue cheese added some creaminess and its musty flavor hit the top of the nose just right as a finish. Cooking was about seduction as much as romance was.

Llewelyn and Tricia, with fork and knife in hand, examined their plates before digging in. Llewelyn studied the salad as if it were a work of art at the National Gallery.

*What was he thinking about?* Was it just the presentation? Was he counting the bits of cheese and walnut on the plate? Measuring the overall dimensions in his head? Cheyenne had a sudden wave of panic. As contestants on the television program, everything they did for three months would be examined under this particular microscope.

She squeezed her fork and clenched her jaw, steeling herself against the fuzzy feeling. Cheyenne wanted to win. She wanted her dream to come true. Her dream of being a wife and mother had fizzled, but she had an incredible chance here to realize the chance of owning a restaurant and bringing to life her passion. She wanted to quit her job with the congressman and be a success in the restaurant world. Nothing else mattered. Not the Bingo game at work, not her failed relationship with Alberto. Even the tingles of hope she had for Xander were set on the back burner.

Tricia and Llewelyn were taking this salad very seriously. Tricia cut into the radicchio like a surgeon, swiped up a bit of the saba against the wilted greens, and tipped a bit of the cheese, pear, and walnuts onto the bite, ensuring every element on the plate into one taste. Cheyenne held her breath as Tricia wrapped her lips around the fork. So much relied on that one taste.

If she spat it out—which she had done before on her shows—the audition was over.

Tricia chewed, her face falling into a perfect poker face. They had passed one hurdle, the food was still in her mouth.

"Well, let's see, shall we?" Llewelyn took a similar bite to his wife's. His left eyebrow quirked upward for a second, and Cheyenne breathed easier. The signature arched eyebrow sent relief flooding through her.

If they did pass the audition, she had no idea how her brother would react. He'd never considered her passion for cooking as anything other than a hobby. He rarely asked about it, and she wanted him to acknowledge it. While he eagerly devoured any treats she brought to Friday night suppers, he had never said anything to suggest her being a pastry chef would be anything remotely honorable as a profession. Family duty prevailed.

Dallas was so protective of her. Even the discussion around Xander had been more about his possibility as a date than anything else. Her heart beat a little fast at the thought of Xander. And what hell would break loose when he learned the truth about Xander's religion? Tomorrow. She could think about Xander and her brother's reaction to all this tomorrow. She needed all her wherewithal to get through this meal.

It was so weird having a crew of people watching her every move. One of the cameras zoomed in on Zach as he finished his salad. Tiffany ate in silence, wolfing down the salad as if she were at the table by herself. Chelsea feigned a casual nonchalance as she fidgeted with her salad, but the worry lines on her forehead got deeper with each passing moment. Tricia was only on her third bite, and there was no way of telling what she thought about the salad. The two celebrity chefs remained silent as they ate every last bite of their salad.

Llewelyn put his knife and fork down on his plate, indicating he was done. "Before we move on to the next course, I want to know exactly what you did to this."

The cameraman panned the camera around the table, startling Zach. Chelsea handled it like a champ. She broke down all her techniques, every seasoning, every movement to make the dish. Cheyenne thought it was pretty straight forward, but the combination had certainly been more than the sum of its parts.

Llewelyn held up his hand to stop and grill Chelsea several times while she spoke. And yet, he never pronounced judgment on the dish. After a while, he turned his attention toward Tiffany.

"Go ahead and prepare the next course," Llewelyn said. "I believe you said tagliatelle?"

Zach jumped up and ran for the kitchen.

Cheyenne followed him in."Are you okay, Zach? You seem kind of pale to me."

"This is worse than being on their show. It's...like... I don't know...a...a...final exam that I showed up for without a pencil and no underwear on." His eyes went wide as he realized a camera operator stood at the door, with the lens zoomed in on him.

"You're going to rock this. Totally. Do you need any help?"

Zach salted and oiled the water in the large pot. Chelsea had set it on to heat up while they ate their salad, so it was already near boiling. "No. We need to show them I can plate six dishes at once on my own. That's part of their thing, I think. If we can't handle this, there's no way we can handle twelve weeks of it."

Cheyenne eyed the camera in the corner of the kitchen. It was hard to think with someone watching you like that. She put a hand on Zach's shoulder, trying to comfort him. "You know, in a real kitchen you'd have four sous chefs."

"I know, I know. This is just pasta, anyway."

"There's the spirit. I'll help you serve when you're ready," she said. "Be glad you're not dealing with a tower of mousse. Which, given the changes I made at the last minute..."

Cheyenne opened the fridge and pulled out one of

the extra desserts to check on it. The top was wobbly as hell. The white chocolate mousse hadn't set right. *What in the world?*

Cheyenne put the mold on a plate and released the ring holding it all together. The top layer of mousse oozed out over the top of the rest. Her dessert was a mess.

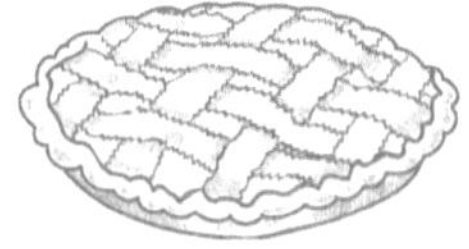

heyenne tried to hide the blob of chocolate goo from the camera, but the woman operating it was too well trained to not spot a great moment for television. She moved in close over Cheyenne's shoulder, and, all of a sudden, Jason was right there, too. How did he know to move in so fast?

"What are you going to do?" he asked. "Is your dessert hosed?"

"It should have set better," Cheyenne said. She found the small glass bowl of dissolved gelatin that must have been shunted aside earlier—she'd never added it to the whipped cream. She held it up for the camera. "When you add gelatin to whipped cream, it helps everything set more firmly and last longer. This mess, however, is a problem."

There was less than an hour left before she would

have to serve this. She had to fix what she had somehow.

"What are you going to do?" Zach asked.

"The only thing I can do at this point," Cheyenne said, trying to not break down into tears in front of the camera. "Fix it."

"But how?" asked Jason. "For the camera, Cheyenne. If your team gets onto the show, this will be a great clip for us to use in the teasers."

"My falling apart, or the messed up dessert?" she asked.

Jason grinned. "Both."

The man was like a shark, circling around them hoping to catch them while they were bleeding so he could gobble it up on camera.

Cheyenne tilted the plate and examined the dessert. She grabbed a fork and slid it through the layers, testing them. The only part that had failed was the top layer. She swirled the pool of white chocolate yuzu up with the other layers and tasted. It was amazing. Okay. So the mouth would be happy. Now she had to figure out the presentation.

"Well. Damn. Good luck with that." Zach turned away and dumped the cooked noodles into a colander, the steam curling upward toward the ceiling in a great warm cloud. "I'll take care of this so you can concentrate."

He tossed the pasta in the pesto he'd made earlier, twisting the noodles expertly around a fork and forming a neat wreath in the center of each plate. After adding droplets of basil oil along the outer rim, he shaved on thick slices of parmesan as a final garnish.

Cheyenne closed her eyes and imagined various ways to fix this mess. She removed all the desserts from the fridge and carefully dumped the top layer out into a pitcher. Carefully wiping the inside rim, she released a second cake from its mold. The top other layers were pristine and nicely delineated just as she had expected, though the top layer had a film of the white chocolate left.

Cheyenne had an idea. She grabbed the leftover yuzu and tossed it into a small pot with water and brought it to a boil. While she worked, she listened in to the conversation at the table. Zach's pasta was a hit. Excellent. She had the sherbet course, the main course, and the cheese course to fix this.

Tiffany and Chelsea finished cooking the rest of the dinner. Each course was finished and served with plenty of breaks for the camera to get in their way. Zach presented the challah with the main course to Tricia and Llewelyn's appreciative *oohs* and *ahhs*.

When it was finally time to present her revamped dessert, Cheyenne was convinced she'd ended up with a better presentation than planned.

She put the finished plates in front of Tricia and Llewelyn first, then served the rest.

"Explain your dish," Llewelyn said, eyeing it. "This is different than Chelsea described it before dinner."

Centered on each plate, the chocolate mousse tower was topped with the planned yuzu twists, but she had added a thin layer of yuzu jelly on the top to hide the missing white chocolate. She had cut out smaller circles of the yuzu jelly to float delicately on top of the failed mousse-turned sauce.

"Yes, sir," Cheyenne said. "I made some last minute changes. You have a flourless chocolate cake and layered chocolate mousses in a pool of white chocolate yuzu, crowned with yuzu jelly and sugar spears."

Llewelyn lifted one of the yuzu circles and held it up to the light. It glistened and glowed a beautiful golden yellow. He might as well be holding a squashed bug. His frown drew his lips down as far as she'd ever seen them go. "You used food coloring?" he asked.

"No sir. I used the entire yuzu to make the juice for the jelly," she said.

"I should be able to cut down the length of this cake and see each layer individually. They shouldn't mesh together, is that right?"

Cameras were trained on the cake, on Llewelyn

and Cheyenne. "Yes."

He cut down the middle of the cake with his knife and spread it open for the cameras. All four layers showed clean and elegant. "Beautiful," he said, his accent adding to the breathiness of the word. "Now let's see if you balanced the flavors. Too much citrus will ruin the chocolate. Not enough, and you won't even notice it."

Cheyenne held her breath as he slid the forkful of chocolate into his mouth. His eyes closed as he ate it with a poker expression. Their eyes met, but she couldn't read his expression or see any meaning in them at all. Three months of all this mind and expression reading was going to be a *long* three months.

Then it was Tricia's turn. She waited for the camera to focus on her before she plunged into the dessert. Unlike her husband, Tricia let everyone know exactly what she was thinking. She tilted her head back, eyes closed as if her entire consciousness was focused on the food in her mouth. "Divine. Absolutely delicious."

As far as Tricia was concerned anyway, Cheyenne had nailed it.

Llewelyn stood up, stretched. "Tricia and I need a few minutes to discuss whether or not you will move onto the next stage of the competition. May we have a room for privacy?"

"You can use mine," Zach said, leading them away.

Zach returned and they cleared the dishes from the table and Jason asked them to line up near the sink and discuss how they thought things had gone.

"As you know, reality TV has some staging behind the scenes. One of the things we do is talk to people between the tastings and the actual pronouncements. We cut things together to make it seem they are giving you feedback in the moment to add drama. But, what we really want is your response before you know what the judge is going to say."

"The skin on the duck was perfect," Zach said, tipping his head to Chelsea.

"And the pasta was toothsome, rich, and perky," Chelsea said.

"Cheyenne, I thought your dessert was going to be a disaster," Jason said. "How could you forget adding the gelatin? That seems to be a pretty basic thing."

"It was better than it would have been. A serendipitous mistake, I say. That yuzu jelly was unbelievable with the chocolate."

"Meh," Zach said. "I actually didn't like it. I'm not a huge citrus and chocolate fan in general. But Tricia seemed to like it well enough."

Tiffany laughed. "You think?"

"But you guys are being nice. The duck was barely cooked. I almost ruined it on that bit."

Cheyenne eyed all the cameras trained on them, waiting to catch every little moment and cut it into dramatic footage. Three months of this? The alternative was another three years of working hard and scrimping and saving. It would be worth it if they won. And the only way they could win is they could prove they were not only cooks, but also good television. And good television meant drama. As much as she hated real conflict, she understood politics and how playing along with some level of crazy shit could get you far in life.

Jason jumped into the discussion, pushing some buttons. "Zach, why didn't you speak up about the yuzu chocolate combo when Cheyenne was working on the dish initially?"

"Yuzu wasn't even discussed. She just added it kind of spur of the moment." Zach pushed his lower lip out in his over-the-top pouty face.

Laughing right now would be a problem, but it was hard for Cheyenne to contain herself when she recognized Zach's acting for what it was. He had also caught onto the need for good drama to help them win.

"I handed Cheyenne the yuzu when I realized I had more than I needed for the duck," Chelsea said. "I like the combo. And think Cheyenne's dessert killed it."

"Zach, how do you think you all will handle team

assignments on the show? Do you think these ladies will always run rough-shod over you like this?" Jason asked.

Zach's jaw dropped. "They did not mow me over, we never discussed it. I was surprised. That's all."

"I'm sorry, Zach," Cheyenne said. "I just kind of went with it."

Zach bobbed his neck side to side and mimed throwing down a mike. "And that is exactly what you had to do, girlfriend. You made it work."

Cheyenne tossed a towel onto the counter. "Do you guys think three months of this is going to be a good idea?"

Zach opened a bottle of wine and poured them each a glass. "If we win, yeah. It will totally be worth it."

Chelsea crossed her arms, lips tightening into a straight line for a moment. "You don't think it will destroy our friendship?"

Tiffany threw her head back. "Honestly? I can't believe y'all are actually talking about it like this. If we get in, we are going. And we are going to win. We made a pact."

"That was before I knew how tough it might be on our friendship," Cheyenne said. She hated conflict. "As much as I want to win this and get our own restaurant, the last thing I want is to ruin our friendship."

Jason clapped his hands together when they dropped into a silence. "That was perfect, you guys! Perfect. We can't script things better than that. You're worried about your relationship, and that makes this all golden TV. Perfect drama for the show."

Cheyenne's stomach twisted at the comment. Did she want to be out there like that? The show was watched by millions of people. And they loved the drama as much as the cooking content. There was no doubt that Jason would mine their relationship for weak points and find a way to exploit them for content.

"We'll make it work," Zach said after a brief pause. "I love you all, and nothing is going to ruin this for us. If we don't get on the show, we'll just be that much more determined to do it without them. At least we can bank on free publicity, good or bad."

"Let's make a pact that no matter what, no matter what crap they drag us into, we'll forgive each other by the end of the show," Tiffany said.

"I love you all," Chelsea said.

They fell into a group hug without any prompting. They swayed back and forth before breaking apart with a renewed energy toward their success.

JASON USHERED everyone into the living room and

made sure a camera was trained on each of them by the time Llewelyn and Tricia reappeared. The four cooks held hands as Llewelyn and Tricia gave point by point critiques of everything they'd done wrong with their dinner.

Llewelyn always went first, followed by Tricia. The salad was close to perfection, but he'd have liked a few more walnuts. She'd have liked more of the blue cheese and saba. Llewelyn lambasted Chelsea for the almost-too-rare duck, but gave her points for her flavor profile and plating skills. According to Llewelyn, Zach's pasta was perfectly done, but Tricia thought it needed more cooking. He loved the intricacies of the challah, but questioned it being there at all. They didn't need bread, and if they were going to serve bread, why pick challah and not a sourdough baguette?

"You made it to impress us, am I right?" Llewelyn asked.

"Did it work?" Zach asked.

"Well enough. It was perfectly cooked, a beautiful braid, and impressive. But it didn't go with the meal."

"Challah is as close to cake as a bread can get. It was a perfect example of challah, but Llewelyn is right. It did not belong on that table," Tricia said, adding to Llewelyn's condemnation. "Don't get me wrong, I like challah, but keep it to Shabbat or save it for the next day's French toast breakfast."

"Now, young lady. You and your dessert," Llewelyn said, clasping his hands in front of him.

Cheyenne braced herself for impact.

"You set out to make one dessert. You failed, and then you did something quite amazing. You fixed the mistake best you could and managed to pull off an astounding recovery by creating something you couldn't have planned."

Tricia broke in. "You need to be more precise with the layers. I didn't like that they were not perfectly even, but each and every layer was distinctly flavored and delicious."

"I'm not a big fan of desserts," Llewelyn said. "You all know that. But, I will say that this was quick thinking and excellent execution."

"When we learned you were the only one who was not already a full time chef, we were skeptical of your team as a whole. After all, if your team is picked for the show, you would be the only person we've ever had on the show who is not a full time professional chef. Did you know that?" Tricia asked.

Cheyenne shook her head. "No, I had no idea."

Llewelyn held up his hands. "You've proven that just because you're not working at it full time doesn't mean that you don't belong in the kitchen. The dessert was, in short, the best part of the meal."

Cheyenne released her breath.

"My biggest question for your team is how are you all going to come up to Cheyenne's level? Will you all be able to react quickly when problems arise and come together as a team?"

*And there it was.* Llewelyn was pitting her against her friends.

Cheyenne met Zach's, then Tiffany's, then Chelsea's eyes. She only found love and support. Mutual respect. Any jealousy or anger over Llewelyn's words were invisible.

Chelsea broke the silence that had dropped onto the group. "Yes, sir. If Cheyenne is our weakest link, I can guarantee you we can win this."

Tiffany and Zach echoed Chelsea's words. The four linked hands even tighter.

Tricia and Llewelyn were a married couple working together, sharing their days and their nights. There were times when Cheyenne would swear they were reading each others minds. This was one of them. Their eyes met and held. Tricia's chin dropped just a fraction of an inch, and Llewelyn's left lip curled upward ever so slightly. They must have their own secret language.

Tricia tilted her head to the side, giving Llewelyn the floor again. "And...we have decided..." pause... pause...pause... "You're in!"

The four jumped up and down and hugged each other.

"Yes!"

As the camera came in close Cheyenne put on her fakest, most confident smile. "I knew we'd make it in."

AFTER THE BRANTONS LEFT, Jason explained that the film would be cut together with a commercial in the first episode of the new season. The crew had stayed to help put the furniture back as planned, but it still took them another two hours to get the kitchen clean and back into working order. A pro chef never left dishes unattended overnight. One great thing about rooming with three other pros was their kitchen was always sparkling.

As they cleaned, they planned how to not let the show tear them apart as friends.

"Y'all know that every one of the winning teams has had lots of drama," Tiffany said. "I bet you a dollar to donuts that we would win if it were just the food prep."

"Whatever it takes," Chelsea said. "If we win, we get to open our restaurant this year or next. No more waiting."

The last thing she wanted was for them to fall

apart as a group because of the show. Every season, at least one team fell apart completely either directly on the show in some huge dramatic falderal, or afterward.

"I have an idea," Cheyenne said. "What we need to do is plan our own drama ahead of time. Discuss what we can live with and how we can poke fun at each other in ways that we will get through this."

"You mean we need to manipulate reality TV? Who ever heard of such a thing?" Zach asked.

They all laughed and fell into silence.

"You're right, Cheyenne," Chelsea said. "We need to plan for this so that whatever they throw at us doesn't drive a wedge between us."

Over the years she'd lived with Chelsea, Tiffany, and Zach, they'd spent hours and hours talking about the overall concept of their restaurant. But now, with the excitement of the competition fresh, they went over it all again. One of the biggest components of the competition was selling the judges on their particular restaurant design.

Theirs would feature a coffee and breakfast bar walk-up service in the morning and full-service sit down lunch and dinner. Tiffany, Chelsea and Zach would handle the main menu, Cheyenne the breakfast pastries and desserts. Since she had the best business background, she would also be the general manager of the restaurant.

Almost everything would be farm to table, but they would also rotate through a different region of the world so they could explore the variety of spices and flavors.

Cheyenne put the last dried pot on its hook above the stove and spun around. "We should consider time periods, too. We can have an ancient food item featured each month."

"Your work with Xander is getting to you, but I kind of like it," Zach said. "I don't think there are any restaurants out there that attempt ancient food preparation."

They all agreed it could be fun to add that into the mix, but that it would be in its own little box as a special offering with each menu change. Foodies and gourmands in the area likely would pick up on it and come in at least once a month to try the latest gimmick. It was sure to pull people in.

The collective mood in the apartment was one of general joy. Even if they didn't win the competition, they had a clearer vision of their restaurant. It was definitely going to happen one way or another.

As Cheyenne finally collapsed into bed, she realized she hadn't thought of Xander since before the pasta dish was served. She had been so involved in prepping for the audition, that she had put him completely out of mind.

She checked her phone before falling asleep. Xander had texted her just a few minutes before saying he could hardly wait until their lunch date the next day and wished her sweet dreams. She touched her finger to the phone, caressing the words as if they were his cheek. She sent him a giant kiss emoji. Cheyenne was afraid of words at the moment. What could she say to him?

One of the most exciting moments in her life and the one person she wished she could tell was off limits. She sat up in bed as the weight of the quandary hit her full force. She wasn't allowed to tell him about the competition. The NDA was very clear about who she could tell and when. Guys you haven't even been on a date with did not come into the picture. She opened her bedside table and withdrew the NDA contract. She was only allowed to tell the people on the form that she had been accepted onto the show and that she would be gone for three months. During the show's taping, she would only get a few minutes each week to talk over the telephone, and she was bound to not divulge anything that had happened during the taping.

She had filled it out before meeting Xander. Before she knew he existed. The only people she'd named were her mom, Dallas, Sky and Katherine O'Malley—her direct superior at work. Xander wasn't anywhere on the page.

## Chapter 11

*C*heyenne woke up Monday morning, the heady scent of cinnamon and cardamom filling the apartment. Images from her dreams stuck with her in snippets and flashes. They had been a strange conglomeration of real life and fantasy. Xander featured prominently in them, but every time they were about to kiss, Llewelyn Barton's beaky nose and piercing eyes replaced Xander's.

Cheyenne stood in front of her closet for a long time trying to decide what to wear. Soon, this entire wardrobe would be rendered moot and replaced with checkers and whites. Whites with "Chef LeFleur" embroidered in a royal blue script. Or maybe purple. They hadn't gone so far as to design their restaurant-wear yet, but she was partial to a deep aubergine script on crisp white chef's uniforms. No silly hats, but she would be fine with individualized hair caps. One restaurant she went to as a little kid allowed their entire staff some fun with that, and everyone from head chef to busboy had customized fabrics ranging from cartoon characters to leafy batiks.

She put on what she would normally wear to the office—a pencil skirt, a tucked in silk blouse, and a slim line jacket. The clothing weighed against her skin like handcuffs. Knowing it was a short time made the constriction more bearable.

And any attempt on her part to seduce Xander at this point would lead her to grief. She had decided not to play the Bingo game anymore; it hardly mattered. Besides, she didn't want to kiss Xander under the pretext of a game, and she was heading LA soon.

The NDA did allow for her to tell an immediate supervisor, Katherine O'Malley, about why she was really leaving. She would pretend to still be playing Bingo even though she had no desire to win. Why take up a spot at the meeting when someone else who wanted to continue their career with the Congressman could go instead? If she suddenly declared she wasn't playing, it would raise plenty of questions from the others. All she had to do was say she was stuck and hadn't had any luck with finding that last kiss.

Jason, the producer from the show, had assured them that most employers were very understanding and allowed people to take extended leaves of absence. After all, only four people went on to win the game and everyone else generally went back to their previous jobs. For most people having been on the show was something their employers use for promotion. You couldn't get on the show if you weren't already a decent chef and restaurants loved bragging rights.

The fact that all their housing and food would be provided for three months, plus their healthcare, helped reduce the financial strain. The pay from the show wasn't as good as any of their jobs, but it was decent especially given the room and board was extra.

Would Katherine give her a three month leave of absence needed for filming or would she give Cheyenne her allotted vacation and make her quit? Dallas would be proud of her. If she could get away with a leave of absence instead of quitting, she'd come across as responsible. And, if they won, she'd have to quit permanently.

When Cheyenne got to the Cannon Building, the line for security was longer than usual. She checked her watch and realized she was going to be to work early. It had been a while since she'd managed that.

No wonder she wasn't used to the lines. Too late to fix all that. She'd have to power through the guilt that bubbled up within and move on.

The inside of the building rang with hammers and buzzed with power equipment. The scent of freshly sawn wood mingled with the acridness of new paint. Remodeling the old place was taking forever. After all these years serving in the decrepit part of the building, she would never see the finished remodel. Unless she blew it in the competition and had to come crawling back for her old job. Did she even want that? Wouldn't it be better to cut ties now, go to LA and pray she won or move on to the right thing for her if she didn't?

Opal sat at her desk as Cheyenne entered Congressman Pierce's office, otherwise the rest of the open part of the plan was empty. Katherine O'Malley's office was dark so she'd have to wait a while before approaching her with the news. Cheyenne settled into her desk and organized her things for the day. Coffee cup to the right of the terminal. Notepad to the right of her mouse. Phone next to that. NDA neatly hidden in her purse hanging off her chair.

"Cheyenne, are you okay?" Someone tapped her shoulder. "Hello?"

Cheyenne shook her head to clear it. Chloe was standing right next to her, a folder in one hand under her crossed arms. Chloe was the newest intern to join the Pierce team. Cheyenne had a love-hate relationship with interns. Most of them stayed for three months, barely got trained and moved on. Cheyenne didn't put a lot of emotional investment into them.

Chloe glanced over her shoulder. "You are going to be Katherine's aide at the hearings this week, right?" she asked.

"Yes. I'm basically there to help her find things as they come up." Cheyenne pointed to the piles of binders she'd been compiling over the last couple months. "I have all the case law organized. Why?"

Chloe leaned in closer, eyes wide. "Did you hear anything about what happened with Liz this weekend?"

Liz's cubicle was just as she had left it, sans Liz herself. It had been untouched since...when? Last Wednesday? That was weird. "Maybe she is just taking the day off after having to work so much last week. She was managing the Chinese delegation through the weekend."

Chloe dropped her voice to a whisper. "I over-heard something between the congressman and Carleen. It was about Liz and having some PR fixer coming in over the weekend. Something hush, hush. I couldn't catch the details because they were whispering. I thought maybe Katherine was filling you in on it." She tilted her head toward Katherine's office.

Cheyenne's jaw clenched. Who was this intern to pump her for information? "I'm sure we'll find out when we find out," Cheyenne said. "But, honestly, Chloe, idle speculation on a potential scandal is not something we should engage in. And admitting you were listening in on a private conversation? You have a lot to learn."

Chloe gave her a three-second silent glare without responding directly to her. "How'd your pie-making class go on Saturday?"

The tone Chloe used was one of pure condescension, as if Cheyenne teaching a pie making class was a cute or novel idea. A game. Not worthy or special in anyway. It was the same tone men used when they asked women about their careers—to fill time and not gain knowledge. Here, it was a dig from a younger up and coming law student to an older, unmarried, and low ranking worker bee. Chloe, like Dallas, saw pie-making as less than worthy.

Cheyenne's watch beeped, reminding her to find Katherine so they could discuss her leaving.

"Duty calls," she said, ignoring Chloe's question. She grabbed her purse and stalked over to Katherine's office.

The Non-Disclosure Agreement she'd been given for her employers included a cover letter of introduction from the show explaining the process. Some contestants returned to work within the first two weeks of filming and the show asked employers to keep an open mind about the nebulous nature of the process.

Katherine was at her desk, her left hand wrapped around a cup of coffee, her right scrolling on her trackpad, and her eyes glued to her screen.

Cheyenne knocked lightly on the doorframe to get Katherine's attention. She held the NDA papers at her side and stepped lightly into the office. "Can I bug you for a minute?"

Katherine broke contact with the monitor and pointed at the seat opposite with her chin.

Cheyenne closed the door behind her and took the seat, shifting around in it without entirely settling in.

"What's up?" Katherine asked. "Everything okay with Chloe and all that?"

The question threw Cheyenne. It took her a moment to figure out what Katherine was asking about. The prior week, their newest intern, Chloe Cassell, had fallen one of their consulting attorneys and he'd fallen for her. As far as anyone knew, they were ready to elope—or whatever. Harrison and a lobbyist had even gotten into a fight over Chloe at a bar one night. So much had happened in the past six days, Cheyenne could barely keep track of everything.

"Oh, sure. I think that will all sort itself out. I'm here about something else."

Katherine leaned back in her deluxe black leather chair and sipped at her coffee, eyeing Cheyenne expectantly. One nice thing about Katherine was how she was able to give you her full attention. Many people would still be eyeing their screens while pretending to listen—not Katherine. On the other hand, her intense scrutiny sometimes felt like she had x-ray vision.

"Can I ask you something in complete confidence? Like attorney client confidence?"

Katherine narrowed her eyes and leaned forward. "Is everything okay, Cheyenne?"

"Yeah, it's great, actually. But, I have this non-disclosure agreement I've signed. And I am only allowed to talk to you about it as my direct supervisor. I need you to agree to keep what we've discussed here in complete confidence."

Katherine tipped her head and narrowed her eyes. She set her coffee aside and clasped her hands together. "I'm all ears, Cheyenne."

Cheyenne clasped her hands in front of her over her knee to keep herself steady. "Okay, so here's what's going on." Everything tumbled out—how she'd been saving for the restaurant, her roommates, the super-secret audition, the dinner the previous day, their acceptance to the competition, their vision for the eventual restaurant. As she went on, Cheyenne relaxed as she spoke her truth—one that she'd hardly ever admitted to at work. She ended with a request for a leave of absence for the competition.

Katherine listened with her usual attentive, piercing gaze. "This is amazing, Cheyenne. I love that show." She shook her head and laughed. "I can't believe I'm going to know someone on it."

"You can't tell anyone, though. Not until after the show airs on TV. I can't even tell anyone if we won; the show wants total control over information flow...but if I quit when I come back it'll be kind of obvious."

"Oh, I understand. That's going to be hard, but you're well practiced in keeping secrets. This job is great training for that."

"This is a little different, but yeah, I suppose it has been. I'm so excited to tell everyone about it. But, I can only tell you, not even the whole office. And my family? They're good at keeping secrets, but I don't think they'll approve."

"You've always wanted to be a chef, haven't you? I mean, ever since we met, you've spent as much time in the kitchen as at work. You're always bringing in amazing treats."

"It's my dream. But it's not exactly serving my country, now, is it?"

"Why would you care about...oh. Right. Your whole family thing. I'm sorry, Cheyenne, I totally forgot about your dad."

Cheyenne's joy flipped and skidded to a sudden halt. Dallas was not going to think this was a good idea, even if she behaved responsibly around it. Ever since she could remember, Dallas had always done more than talked about making personal sacrifices to serve the country—he lived it. He'd served his time overseas, and he still served every day. "Don't worry about it, Katherine. Most people don't go around living it."

"You know, Cheyenne, you owe yourself some professional and personal happiness. Doing something you're passionate about is important."

"I'm passionate about Congressman Pierce," Cheyenne said. But, it sounded false—a little tinny and not entirely accurate. She loved him the way most people loved him—honored him and wanted to see him succeed. But Katherine was right—Cheyenne spent the majority of her head time thinking about cooking, not shaping Congressman Pierce into a president.

"Cheyenne," Katherine said, getting up and coming around her desk to grab her hands. "I like you, a lot. I love the treats you bring in. You're also good at your job. You keep people organized. You have work flow and process down. But your eyes light up when you talk about your restaurant dreams. Your passion comes through when you describe how you came up with some new flavor profile."

"Am I that obvious?"

"You don't come across as hating your job." A kind smile spread across her face. "It's more that you're distracted. Your head isn't always in the game."

Working for Congressman Pierce was her contingency plan, not her calling. Even Kat could see that. Cheyenne twitched a little at the word *game*. Katherine was talking about the political game, not Bingo. But it made Cheyenne think about the Bingo game. She had been pursuing Bingo hard, almost recklessly, and for what? Giving up her job to pursue her dream?

"Work sabbaticals are not entirely uncommon. I don't see a problem with it, but in order for Carleen to approve a long term absence, she'll need to know why. The approval is up to her."

Relief flooded through Cheyenne. Carleen Bigalow was the actual office manager with overall hiring and firing authority. They'd always gotten along well and Carleen came across as more than fair.

"I don't know if I can. I put you down as my supervisor at work on my competition application so I'll call the producer to see what to do." If all the pieces fell into place, and Carleen approved a work sabbatical, Cheyenne could tell Dallas she had a backup plan if they lose the competition.

"That sounds reasonable. Do it today if you can—the red tape around all this could take time."

"If we lose, I'll be back in a week or two. They send home a team a week. We could be the first to go."

Katherine squeezed her hands and released them. "I don't believe that for a second. You are going to win. I'm certain of it."

They hammered out some details and dates before Cheyenne returned to her desk.

Xander texted mid-morning to confirm their lunch plans. They would meet halfway between her office and his, right at the Smithsonian's rose garden cafe—at the castle. It had been a serendipitous moment when he suggested it—a scientist at the castle and another mark off her Bingo card. And now? What did it matter? As a matter of fact, if she checked in on Instagram, she'd probably win the game. She didn't want that. Not anymore.

It was such an irony. She wasn't going to break her date with Xander a second time, but she would need to cool it between them. Tamp it back into just a professional level.

They had a class to teach over the next few weeks,

but then she'd be leaving for LA and the competition. He'd said he wanted to settle down and find real connections. She had nothing meaningful to offer him other than a short term fling. And the NDA meant she couldn't tell him why she was cooling it.

What was she going to tell him?

# Chapter 12

It had warmed up into a perfect late spring day. The air was cool without being chill, and the cherry blossoms still clung to their branches. Cheyenne walked at a brisk pace and breathed in the fresh air. Katherine had been as positive and graceful about the news as humanly possible. Encouraging. Maybe too encouraging? It was almost as if the other woman had been relieved.

The rose garden behind the castle was blossoming, though it was early in the season and only half a dozen of the plants had flowered. Cheyenne stopped by a particularly beautiful yellow rose to sniff its sweet scent. It smelled just the way a rose was supposed to smell—none of that waxy refrigerated grocery store staleness in these bushes. By the time she got to the restaurant, she'd restored her sense of calm. Roses and fresh air could do wonders.

Xander was sitting at a table when she arrived. He'd already ordered an iced tea and was emptying a couple of packets of sugar into the glass and stirring it vigorously to make it melt.

He half-stood but she waved him back into his seat.

"I wish they'd pre-sweeten tea up here," he said as she sat.

"Or serve sugar syrup at the table."

"Even better. I hate having the crystals at the bottom of the glass."

"So, up here? I take it you're from someplace in the south?" she asked. Sweet tea was such a southern thing. Tiffany liked hers achingly sweet.

"Outside Atlanta. Originally anyway."

"You don't sound southern." Cheyenne winced. Hadn't she already told him he didn't sound Muslim? She had to stop making assumptions about people.

"Ah. Well. I went to private boarding school up north, starting in eighth grade. Plenty of training me out of the southern slur. I rarely say 'y'all' anymore, either. It comes out when I go home for a visit."

"Did you miss your parents?"

"My mom mostly. I grew up pretty fast." Xander's eyes focused on the swirling bits of ice in his glass.

"You could say the south was beaten out of me. But I still like my tea sweet. Nothing is going to change that." He held up his glass and took a long drink and smacked his lips in appreciation.

The waitress came by to take their orders. Cheyenne ordered herself a plain glass of iced tea instead of her usual glass of wine. Did it matter if he didn't drink or why he didn't drink? The only thing that mattered was if it was a problem for her to drink while with him, and he'd said nothing the other night. He'd hung out with them working on the puzzle even though they all had wine and he didn't.

He'd been the one to make the arrangements for the catering at the opening on Saturday night. It must not be a problem for him to provide wine to other people even if he didn't drink himself. It didn't really matter to her, anyway, did it?

"Is everything all right, with the emergency thing I mean?"

"Pretty much." That damned NDA made it so she couldn't tell him about *Kitchen Wars*. Being vague was one thing, outright lying was another. "It's complicated. I can't really talk about it. Confidentiality issues."

Xander held up his hands. "I didn't mean to press. It's just that I've come to like you very much. Whatever is going on, I'm happy to be of service in any way I can. I hope you don't think less of me for not spending the night Saturday night." He lifted one of her hands to his lips and kissed it, sending delicate ripples of desire through her entire body. "It was hard. Not staying. I wanted to, but…"

"You would have felt like a jerk. Like you were using me."

His smooth fingers over hers were gentle and firm at the same time. His hand against hers was such a simple gesture, yet it was so much more. Maybe the fact that they had restrained themselves made the touch more intimate. With him in front of her, all she could think about was his lips. Kissing her, nibbling at her bare skin.

"I don't want to ever make a woman feel used, not ever again, Cheyenne. Especially not you. Is that so strange?"

"No. Not at all. I was disappointed, but I *get* it." At least she *mostly* got it. Having someone show that kind of concern for her was new and a little disconcerting. "I haven't dated seriously in a long time, so forgive me if I seem a little impatient."

Xander squeezed her hand before removing his. "It's not that I have been a horrible man, but I have been…callous or cavalier. I won't lie to you, Cheyenne. I've had my share of one night stands. But that kind of connection no longer works for me."

"I feel like I know you better than a lot of guys I've slept with." She stared into her tea. Keeping Xander at a distance was going to be hard. He'd made it clear he wanted a long-term relationship, and she should make it clear she couldn't offer that right now.

"I'm glad you're willing to give us some time to get to know each other. It's not like I'm asking you to wait until our wedding night, right?"

Cheyenne's breath caught in her throat. Had he just mentioned the "W" word? *Really?* Most guys wouldn't come near that one in any form of conversation unless it they were serious. And she was leaving LA just as soon as their class was over and couldn't tell him why. She liked him too much to just blow him off or to outright lie about things not working between them. The honest truth was that everything *was* working for them—so far, anyway.

The waitress brought their food, saving her from needing to reply to the wedding comment—a Cobb salad for her and a salmon dish for him. Cheyenne scooped up a piece of bacon and held it over her plate.

"Does it bother you that I eat bacon?" she asked.

He shrugged. "I've had it a couple of times. By accident, of course, but I don't personally see the appeal of it. I suppose the lack of pork-love is pretty ingrained in me. Some people seem particularly obsessed with bacon."

What would Friday nights be like without pork? She pictured her mom trying to find things to make that had no bacon, no *lardon*, no prosciutto. That was if he made it past Dallas's security check. That was if he made it past any misgivings he might have about her.

*Slow down, Cheyenne, you can't go there with this guy! You're leaving in a month.*

She brushed the thoughts away, reminding herself they were only on their first official date. It was hard not to jump ahead when the guy she was having lunch with had just said "our wedding night."

"I'm not exactly obsessed with bacon, but pork plays a huge role in my family's cooking and in my professional life. Like lard? There are some things I *have* to use it for."

He smiled, his eyes lighting. "Pork is something that I simply don't eat, but I don't care if *you* eat it. And, if I were on a desert island with only wild boar as food, I would eat it to save my life. So...eat all you want. I'll even kiss you once you have had some. But do me the courtesy and let me know when you've used it in something so I can avoid it."

That was easy enough. It was hardly any different than a vegan or vegetarian request coming in. "What about wine?"

"I have had a couple of drinks over the years, but

never to get drunk. The problem is with the state of mind and the wastefulness. An occasional bit of alcohol to enhance a meal or boost flavor is not a problem for me. But honestly, I don't care for it much. I don't understand the general appeal of wine with food. Or alcohol in general." He met her eyes. "I'm willing to learn from a master, though. My friends believe three bucks is enough to spend on a bottle of wine."

"I drink wine. Hard liquor not so much." She tapped her iced tea. "Sometimes at lunch—it all depends on the meal. With good food? Wine for sure."

"Why do you drink?"

"Wine? To enhance the flavor of the food."

"What about hard alcohol?" he asked. "Do you go out to bars to get drunk?"

Would that be one of *his* deal breakers? "Occasionally. Sometimes I go out to bars to be with friends. But I've been saving money so I hardly do that much. Happy hours. Hanging out." Cheyenne stirred her salad. Something deep inside her was gnawing at her to be as honest with this man as possible. She put down her fork and clasped her hands together under the table, screwing up a little more courage for the rest. "And, of course, to meet men."

How much would her recent history bother him? She'd obviously been ready to hop into bed after their first evening together, and yet, he was here now. What would it take to drive him away?

"So getting drunk isn't your prime reason for going to bars?"

Her mention of meeting other men didn't seem to faze him. Did she want him to act jealous about that? He had mentioned being cavalier and callous with women. Maybe he was just acting cool about it because he was the other end of the same equation.

"Actually, no. It isn't. It's more social. If I get drunk, it's just part of it." That was something she could easily give up if he asked her to. "Never again if it bothers you."

"I would never ask you to give up your friends. Do you do other things with them besides bar hopping?"

"I play on a softball team, go hiking, go to movies. But of course, most of my free time is taken up at the cooking school and working on restaurant planning." If only she could explain *Kitchen Wars* and what that meant to her time going forward. They'd talked about the restaurant plan during one of their conversations early on, but now everything could change.

"Right. Restaurant. That's still three or four years out?" he asked.

"Maybe," she said. "You never know. Tiffany's aunt is really old and might leave her enough money for us to move faster. One of us could win the lottery."

*Or we could actually win Kitchen Wars, and my whole life will go topsy-turvy in less than a year.*

"How many children do you want to have?" he asked.

Cheyenne felt the color drain from her face. *I can't have kids.* Would that be the ultimate deal breaker? *Another one bites the dust.* She wasn't ready to go there. Not yet.

"I...I'm not sure," she said. It was too soon to tell him the whole truth about her past. "I honestly think that's a leap ahead of where we are...I mean...we haven't even...and..."

He put down his fork and studied her closely. "I must apologize. I hit a raw nerve with that question. Maybe it was too soon. But it felt like we were doing some general discussions around relationship compatibility."

Cheyenne gripped her fork tighter. "I just think... some things are best left 'til we know each other better. This is our first real date, right?"

He gazed intently into her eyes. "Ah. I can't quite believe it's our first date. Can you? Just reassure me you don't want ten or twelve kids, and we'll be good for now."

She shuddered visibly. "Well, ten is definitely not happening."

He laughed. "Got it."

Cheyenne searched for another topic. "Are both your folks alive?" she asked.

Xander blinked a couple of times at the abrupt switch and his lip twitched upward. He picked up his fork and took a bite of his salmon before answering. "Yep. My dad is a neurosurgeon. My mom is an electrical engineer. They moved to DC two years ago when I finally convinced them I'd be living here permanently. I have two younger sisters. One followed us all up to DC, the other is in college. I expect she'll move here, too, when she's done."

"So you're close to them?"

"Yes. Maybe closer than I'd like to be, but, family is family, right?"

"Oh, I know how that is," Cheyenne said.

"You already told me about your dad. Is your mom still around? Where are you from?" he asked.

Most of their phone conversations and emails had been focused on food and history. She tilted her head in the general direction of Maryland. "My mom still lives in the house she and Dad bought when they were newlyweds. I grew up there, and my family gets together for dinner every Friday night."

Xander laughed. "Dallas made it clear you're all pretty tight. What does your mom do for a living?"

"My mom stayed home to raise us. She has a degree in English. Probably why I love to read so much. There was an insurance policy that kicked in after Dad died so she never had to go to work. I was only nine when he died."

"So, your brother. Dallas? He's a lot older than you, isn't he? He probably has a different take on things."

"He's nine years older than me. Sky is seven years older. So, yeah. Dad's death hit him hard. He was a senior in high school, and he went straight into the military. Decided he had to dedicate himself to serving the country after Dad died."

"He served in Iraq?"

"Yep."

"He's got a good poker face," Xander said. "Polite on the surface. But I wouldn't want to get on his bad side. The overt racists? The ones who call me names and spit at me directly aren't as scary."

Cheyenne knew what Xander was getting at. Dallas was, once you get to know him, a huge teddy bear, but he could scare the bajesus out of people without saying a word. "Don't let him fool you. He's really just a bunch of fluff inside. And you should know, he is doing a background check on you as we speak." Admitting this to him could hardly be a surprise.

"Great. That's so incredibly soothing."

She put her hand on his and raised an eyebrow to

tease him. "If you don't have anything to hide, you should be fine."

"Oh, trust me, I would never do anything to cross that brother of yours."

"Like I said," Cheyenne said, pointing her fork at him for emphasis, "he's all fluff inside."

"Yeah, right," Xander said, but he didn't meet her eyes.

Did he know something about Dallas she didn't know? How could he? They'd only met for the first time on Saturday. Guys could be so territorial and weird sometimes.

By the time they were done eating, it was as if they had known each other for years. And every minute that went by the guilt over not telling him about the competition mounted. She had to get permission from Jason, the producer-guy, before telling anyone they hadn't listed as "important people" on their original application. She had already left a couple of messages, but he hadn't gotten back to her.

XANDER OFFERED to walk her back to work after they finished lunch. Any excuse to spend more time with him. They wound through the rose garden arm in arm.

"I've always loved roses," Cheyenne said, "but I'd

never really thought much about them before reading your lecture outline for our dessert class."

He cupped a white rose and held it for her. She bent over it and breathed in deeply.

"The lovely, poor rose. The flower with the most baggage in the history of flowers," he said.

"Baggage?" she asked. "You feel sorry for roses?"

"Yes. Think about it. If I were to send you a dozen roses tomorrow, what would you think?"

"It would depend on what color you sent me."

"See? My point exactly. You wouldn't think, '*Oh, what a bunch of pretty flowers, what a sweet man.*' You would be trying to decipher the message based on the color of the flower."

"Not if you wrote something on the card to make your intent clear," she said.

"And if I sent you a mixed bouquet? White, yellow, red, purple, all mixed together?"

Cheyenne grinned. "That you are schizophrenic or have no sense of aesthetics."

"Ah, here we are," he said pausing as they reached the botanical gardens. "Do you have a few more minutes? There are some amazing orchids inside."

"I don't know much about orchids," she said. Cheyenne half-turned toward the Cannon Building as he opened the door. She was already late getting back from lunch, but she didn't think extending it a few more minutes would harm anything.

"They are the most prized of all flowers, even above roses," he said. They stopped in front of a prolific flowering bunch of yellow orchids. He gently lifted one flower with his index finger so she could see inside.

"It's almost like a little face staring at me," she said.

"Did you know vanilla comes from orchids?" he asked.

"Mmmm...vanilla," Cheyenne said. "My favorite flavor."

"In all things?" Xander asked, his voice dropping just a smidge with an extra layer of meaning.

Cheyenne caught the twinkle in his eye, the quirk of his lips and considered the question. "You'll have to wait to find out, won't you?"

"Will I?" he asked.

What exactly did he have in mind? There weren't that many people inside. With each corner, she felt more and more like they were in their own secret garden, surrounded by intoxicating scents.

Xander led her through the exhibit. It was obvious that he knew his way around.

"You come here a lot?" she asked.

"Yes, but never with anyone else. I find it a lovely place to meditate. To think things through."

After a few twists and turns, they found themselves in a fairly secluded corner. Layers of greens and plants hid them from view. Cheyenne couldn't hear other voices or footsteps.

"Let me guess, you want me to meditate with you for a bit?" she asked leaning against the one wall nearby for support.

"Cheyenne," he said, "the last thing I want to do is meditate."

She linked her arms around his neck at the same time telling herself she shouldn't let this happen. She should tell him she was a short timer. That she was moving to LA. She didn't have to tell him *why* she was moving. It wouldn't be that hard to make up some little lie about why. This was DC, after all; people had to keep all kinds of secrets around here.

They were in the shadows of a large collection of droopy plants. Their musty warm wetness did nothing to mask Xander's heady clove and patchouli scent.

It was *just* a kiss. What harm could another kiss between them do? It wasn't like she was promising more of herself.

Cheyenne opened her mouth, inviting him in. Her tongue swirled around his, darting in and out of his mouth, lapping at his lips.

Their tongues swirled around each other, darting around, trying to find the perfect dance. She broke the kiss and let her head fall backward, opening her neck to him.

He kissed her, nibbling and licking his way toward her shoulder.

"Xander," Cheyenne said, unable to tell him to stop. Unable to warn him away from her.

His hands slid up her body and into her hair. He supported her head as he kissed her deeply for a second time. She wanted more. Needed more. She needed Alexander *Moore*. The words tippled around in her mind. She was giddy with desire for him.

She pressed her hips toward him, her body begging for more. He responded by scooping her up and lifting her against the wall, guiding her legs around his waist. She opened up to him as her skirt rose up above her hips, baring her skin to him.

His erection pressed against her through his pants. He wanted her as much as she wanted him. Here? Now? She broke the kiss to rest her chin on her shoulder. No one was around, dare they go further in such a public place?

Xander pressed against her, pinning her between the wall and his body to hold her up. He cupped her breasts through the silk of her blouse and lace of her bra—pinching, pulling at her nipples through the fabric until they were hard and erect.

Someone laughing broke through the greenery,

and the sound of footsteps coming nearby made them both become statues. Xander helped her to her feet, and pulled her skirt down around her thighs, his hands smoothing away any rumples.

"Guess we'll have to try later," he said, circling her nose with his.

By the time a cheery family of four came into view, they were both bending over a plaque pretending to be in a deep discussion about the orchid in front of them. The two adults in the group were smirking as they passed. At least they hadn't been caught totally en flagrante.

"Well, that was exciting," Cheyenne said. "But I really need to get back to work. Can I take a rain check on whatever was going to happen next?"

He kissed her lightly on the lips. "What do you think that might be?"

"You are a tease."

"Only to a certain point," he said, wrapping his arm over her shoulders. They walked along, side-by-side, their bodies fitting together like two peas in a pod. Xander guided them out of the maze of a garden and accompanied her all the way back to the Cannon Building.

"Tonight work for you?" Xander asked as they approached the security line. She was on the tail end of the lunch crowd, but there were still twenty people ahead of her.

"I can come over later. I have something until eight."

He tilted his head, but she wasn't ready to answer his silent question. She'd tell him she was seeing a therapist some other time.

## Chapter 13

When Cheyenne got back to her desk, there were two sticky notes on her computer monitor—one each from Opal and Carleen. Opal was the least intimidating of the two women, so Cheyenne would visit her first.

Opal tore herself away from whatever she was concentrating on as Cheyenne approached. As busy as Opal was, she was always on top of things and aware of her surroundings.

"Cheyenne. You're back from lunch *already?* What is it, almost two?" The sarcasm in her voice was sickly sweet and annoying.

"I saw your note. What can I do for you?" Cheyenne leaned against the cubicle divider, crossing her arms over her chest and one foot over the other.

Opal sniffed and swiveled in her desk chair to a

pile of binders stacked against the wall. "There's new information for Wednesday's hearing. Different precedents around the country, from similar court cases." She lifted four of the thickest binders and thrust them at Cheyenne. "Chloe and Harrison put together these for you. They're tabulated and organized."

"At least the hard work is done already," Cheyenne said. She added the new binders to the pile already stacked on her desk. She'd review them later so she'd know what was in them, but a part of her was excited to know there would only be another month of this kind of work before she headed to LA.

Cheyenne thumbed the note from Carleen asking her to drop by. Maybe Kat had already mentioned the show to her? But Cheyenne had asked Kat to wait until she'd talked to the producer about adjusting the NDA. She made a mental note to call Jason as soon as they were done. He hadn't responded to any of her texts. Carleen must want to talk to her about something else.

Carleen's office was right next to Congressman Pierce's office, and they shared a private door so Carleen could go in and out of his office without going around and through the receptionists. It was a hodgepodge of furnishings. The bookshelves were crammed with binders and leather-bound legal volumes. A dead fern collected dust in the corner by the window. Every time Cheyenne was in Carleen's office, she itched to grab the fern and toss it in the garbage. How Carleen could live with it sitting there like that was beyond her.

"Cheyenne, there you are." Carleen pointed to a seat across from her. "Close the door and sit."

Cheyenne perched on the edge of the chair. She'd never been particularly comfortable in Carleen's presence. The older woman was hard to read. She never went out with the rest of the staff.

"Do you have any idea why I asked you in here?"

Cheyenne shook her head.

Carleen leaned forward, an earnest expression on her face and clasped her hands together on top of her desk. "Are you happy working here?"

Cheyenne's stomach flipped and twisted. "Why would you ask that?"

Carleen tapped her watch with her index finger. "Today is not the first time you've been back late from lunch, or just late into work. Last week, you didn't show up until nearly eleven in the morning. Twice."

*Last week.* Cheyenne blushed at the thought of her crazy three-way in the hotel room. The other time was innocent enough, she'd stayed up too late the night before re-working an ancient recipe with Xander. They'd talked until two in the morning, and she had forgotten to set her alarm.

"I'm sorry. Today's lunch. I met someone last week, and we had a date. I lost track of time."

Carleen held up her hand. "I don't want your excuses. I'm simply telling you what I'm seeing. Late. Inconsistent. These traits are not going to keep you employed here."

Cheyenne didn't want to lose her back-up plan of working in Link's office. "I'm sorry, Carleen. I promise, I won't be late again. I just...have been preoccupied."

"I know this is not your career choice. You'd rather be out there baking things, but as an employee in this office, you are expected to work as much as everyone else does."

"Yes, ma'am. I know that."

"And, if you want to go further here, you'll need to put in more consistent hours and show up on time."

Every part of Cheyenne's being wanted to escape. She grasped the chair on either side of her to prevent her from bolting out of Carleen's office, running down the hall and out the building.

The room was suddenly so claustrophobic that Cheyenne couldn't find any words. She dipped her head and avoided eye contact with Carleen.

"Okay then. Consider yourself on probation here, Cheyenne. I expect good things out of you." She relaxed a bit and added, "You can totally redeem yourself at the hearings this week and by getting to work regularly and on time."

Cheyenne couldn't get away from Carleen fast enough, but she dared not draw attention to herself by running out of the office. She walked as calmly as she could back to her desk and buried her head in the binders.

Dallas could not find out about this. Ever. He'd be mortified that she was on thin ice here. It wasn't like she had a high-level job, either. She was not nearly as highly educated as most of her co-workers, and she only earned as much as she did because she'd been there a few years. Even Chloe, their new intern, had a higher education than she did. A bachelor's degree in communications was what got Cheyenne this job. Her degree from the cooking school hadn't even been discussed during her interview.

How on earth would Carleen take her request for a sabbatical now?

heyenne spent the rest of the day in a daze. On the one hand, she could just quit. She was moving on to better things. On the other hand, she'd been raised to finish what she had begun—to be a good girl, to treat her employers with respect. And, if she cut ties with Congressman Pierce's office in a bad light, it would screw up her back-up plan. And worse, Dallas would be disappointed in her. He'd always treated her cooking like a hobby, not her calling.

Had she ever had the same passion about working for Congressman Pierce that she had for cooking? It wasn't that she was miserable with her current job. It was just...not her dream.

She used the Metro ride to her therapist's office to go through everything that happened since her last session. It was hard to keep track—the Bingo game, the three-way bucket list, meeting Xander, the *Kitchen Wars* competition. No wonder she was getting panicky. Cheyenne wasn't sure they could cover everything in her regular hour-long session.

Nia William's office was calming, bright, and cheery all at the same time. The furniture was comfortable without being Freudian. She had her choice of a deep arm chair or a sofa. Nia always sat in her leather swivel chair next to a side table with her water glass. Between them was a coffee table with a water pitcher and glasses lip-down on a tray and a box of soft tissues.

The moment Cheyenne had first entered it, she had felt at ease—in the space and with the older woman. The office had two doors so clients could wait in the outer office before their appointments, and an escape hatch out the back for privacy while leaving. Cheyenne had never seen anyone else at the office either coming or going. While she was open with her family about her visits to the therapist, she didn't broadcast it to the world.

Nia poured herself more water as Cheyenne settled into her usual seat—the deep arm chair. She nestled against the back and pulled the side pillow across her tummy to hug it like a big square teddy bear.

Nia crossed her ankles. "How're things going, Cheyenne?"

"Oh. My. God. You are not going to believe the shit storm of crazy that hit my life this week." Cheyenne paused before delving into things. "Nia, I just want to make sure of something. If I signed a Non-Disclosure Agreement about something and I want to talk to you about it..."

Nia held up a hand. "I know what you're getting at. I am bound to confidentiality. Unless you admit to planning on injuring yourself or others, I'm not going to break that oath."

"In that case..."

Nia jotted down a few notes as Cheyenne laid it all out—the Bingo game, the menáge a trois, Sky's offering to be a surrogate, meeting Xander, the cooking competition, Carleen's warning her about being late.

"Wow, you are right. That's a lot of different things, plenty of stress," Nia said. "What would you like to address first?"

Cheyenne took a breath. "Well. We can skip talking about Sky's offer. That's not even on my list of real worries right now. I just thought it was amazing. And super sweet. And...I can totally put that on the back burner."

"It must be a relief, though, to know you have options."

"Yes. Exactly."

"You've been talking about Xander for a couple of

months now. How did meeting him in real life compare to your fantasies about it?"

"Better. I could not have dreamed up the reality. He's gorgeous. Smart. Funny. He reads, he's into cooking..."

"I sense a but coming in to play here."

"But, the competition. And he wants kids."

Nia tilted her head to the side. "Explain the problem to me as you see it."

"Well, the competition takes me away from DC for three months. And he wants kids. So, here we are, just getting to know each other. We have a few cooking classes together over the next month, and then, poof! I have to move away. And the competition is really strict about outside communication. We get one ten-minute window to make phone calls each week."

Nia wrote something down and peered at Cheyenne over the rims of her glasses. "And?"

"I can't imagine holding onto a relationship without seeing each other for three months."

"So you think you want to end things before they get too far? Nip it in the bud, so to speak?"

"Exactly."

Nia flipped to the front of her steno pad. "I've been keeping track of all the men you've talked about to me. Whenever you bring up an encounter with a man, I make a note of it." She held up the pad for

Cheyenne to see. Even across the coffee table, she could see the list filled out one column and almost a second. "These are all the men you've dated. You see the little check marks to the right? Those are how many times you've mentioned the person."

Cheyenne leaned forward to examine the page, but she already knew there would only be one name with more than a couple of marks next to it—Xander's. Nia's neat handwriting cemented something she had felt but not really wanted to acknowledge.

"Obviously, you just told me about several more names to add, but none of them are going to get another mark now, are they? You've already written them off as one-night-stands and moved on." She drew a bracket around the names below Xander's—everyone she had met in real life since she'd started talking to him on the phone. "All of these men? You have been comparing all of them to the mental image of Xander you created without having met him."

"You're saying I'd already fallen for Xander before I went out with the others?"

Nia bobbed her head from shoulder-to-shoulder. "Is that what you think?"

"He can't possibly want to stay with me forever. Once he learns that I can't have kids, he'll run away. I haven't even told him about being married to Alberto."

"Why not?"

"We've been out on one real date. Two, if you count lunch. It's kind of fast and sudden."

"Are you afraid he'll drop you as soon as he finds out?"

"Wouldn't you? If you know you want kids, why even date someone who's infertile?"

"So, you tell him you can't have kids and he says he's not interested. It's what you expect, so why not get it over with?"

"I..." Cheyenne paused. "I want to...I like...I need...I...can't imagine not talking to him." She blinked in confusion. "I want to keep exploring what we have. I'm not ready to be all in or not with him. I don't know him well enough to jump in with two feet."

"So, you're willing to string him along and not give him important bits of information about you that might possibly send him packing?"

"Is it stringing him along?"

"He told you Saturday," Nia said, flipping through her steno pad, "that he wasn't interested in any more one-night-stands and that he was wants a long-term relationship. To settle down. At lunch, today, what, six hours ago or less, he said he wanted to have children. In what way is not telling him you're not sure what you want or that you might not be able to have kids is not stringing him along? Have you considered what it will take for you to tell him?"

"There are so many reasons for Xander to run screaming from me," Cheyenne said.

"And what would happen if he didn't actually run screaming from you at all?"

"What do you mean?" Cheyenne pulled the pillow up higher, until it was against her chest.

"The entire time you have been seeing me, you've used excuses about why you can't be with certain men. You say they won't want you because you can't have kids, that you are damaged goods. What would happen if you tell Xander every bad thing about yourself and he didn't run?"

"Of course he'd run. That's why I can't tell him. I don't want him to run. Not yet."

"You're being selfish, Cheyenne. Consider his position for a moment. He's been honest with you. He wants to explore real, long term possibilities with you. How long can you wait to tell him about your history? When would it stop being awkward. A month? Six months? *'Oh, by the way, I know we're engaged, but I might not be able to have children. Just thought you should know.'*"

"But it can't last very long anyway."

"And you're willing to play him for the few weeks you have left and just disappear to LA? Is that what you really want?"

"Of course not."

"What do you want, Cheyenne?"

Cheyenne covered her face with the pillow and closed her eyes. What did she want? To run away and hide and make all the difficult decisions go away. Nia's chair squeaked, and Cheyenne assumed Nia was leaning forward, trying to close the distance between them.

"You have to overcome this fear of people leaving you. Until you do, you'll keep putting up roadblocks so you don't allow yourself to get attached. You've done this with all these men by putting them in sex-toy categories. Now that you've met a man who's not letting you do that to him. You want him desperately, and you're terrified he'll leave you."

Cheyenne peeked over the edge of the pillow, still pressing it close against her mouth.

Nia sat on the edge of the coffee table, directly across from her, her large brown eyes earnest and compassionate. "Your dad did not leave you on purpose. He was taken from you, and there's nothing you could have done to prevent that. This thing with Xander? It's different. I can see it from the way you light up when you talk about him. You are terrified of what he could mean to you. And you are even more terrified that once he's part of your life he could be taken away."

Cheyenne ran Nia's words through her head half a

dozen times in the ensuing silence, trying to understand them and their implication.

"You're wrong. I got through all that grief stuff with a counselor years ago, when I was a kid. My feelings about Xander have nothing to do with that. I'm just not ready for a commitment, and Xander is. I need to get to know him more before I can figure it all out."

Nia returned to her seat. "I have a suggestion for you, Cheyenne. One of the things we've talked about before is changing patterns. Why don't you try proving me wrong, then? I believe you deserve a man who loves you and accepts you for who you are. All of you, faults and foibles. This perfect man won't care that you can't have kids. He will take every excuse you throw at him and reflect back his love for you."

Cheyenne shrank back into her seat. "What do you mean prove you wrong?"

"I want you to take every fear you have, every excuse for why relationships don't work out, why you think it won't work out with Xander and tell him about them. One by one. If you are so sure he's going to reject you, then prove it to yourself by giving him the opportunity to do the rejecting."

"But, if I tell him why he shouldn't want to be with me...he'll be justified in dumping me."

"I'm going to say this one more time. If he's small-minded enough to leave you for any of the reasons you've ever given me, he doesn't deserve you. It's not a good match. You need someone who's okay with you being infertile—willing to work through whatever that means because he loves you. You need someone who can handle what is going to be a very strange schedule while you work in a restaurant. You need someone who will love your nosy brother and your bossy sister."

"He's a different religion."

"And he knows that already, right? Was that a deal breaker for him? Obviously not. Is it for you? Ultimately? Do you already know you can't handle that?"

Cheyenne leaned back, dropping the pillow to her lap with her hands on top. "No. It's kind of weird, more like I'm not sure how to deal with a few things, but he's already told me I can eat all the bacon I want."

"And your family?"

"Dallas is doing a background check on him," Cheyenne said, laughing through sudden tears. Where had *those* come from? She grabbed a tissue out of the box. "It will be your fault if I tell him something that makes him drop me like a hot potato."

Nia held up a hand palm up. "It will be your fault if you lose him for not being open and honest with him. And it will be to your credit if you actually work through all the shit it will take to open up to him."

"You want me to make a list of all the things that I think are deal-breakers?"

"That's a good start," Nia said.

"Infertility. I need to tell him about Alberto. The divorce and annulment."

"And?"

"And what?" Cheyenne asked. "That'll be all it takes to send him scurrying."

"Are you going to tell him about the three-way you had four days before the gala? What about the Bingo game?"

"Why would I need to tell him about all that? They have nothing to do with him."

"You don't think it's important?"

"Why would it be?"

Nia flipped back through her notebook. "You first mentioned Xander in the context of work. That shifted over time. Six weeks ago you said, and I quote, '*Xander has the sexiest voice I've ever heard.*' That same session you described a song he sang to you over the phone."

Unable to meet Nia's intense gaze, Cheyenne picked at the cuticles on her fingernails.

"Cheyenne...sexiest voice? Singing over the phone? I believe you said it was a lullaby? Is there some small part of you that knows you and Xander were making a deep connection at the same time you were out dating other guys? Some small part of you that thinks, maybe, he'd be upset about this?"

"How could he? We had never even met in person."

"You were on the phone an awful lot." Nia closed her book and crossed her legs. "Then, there was the gala on Saturday. Followed by a movie late Saturday night with the discussion about going slow, lunch today, hot make-out-almost-sex-in-public? How is that *not dating?*"

Nia was right, of course. Even Dallas and Sky had teased her about liking Xander long before Cheyenne was willing to admit it.

"But...I hadn't really met him before Saturday. How was I supposed to think it was real?"

Nia dropped her chin and stared over the rim of her glasses at Cheyenne with a genuine come to Jesus moment glare.

Cheyenne lowered her eyes, bent over, dropping her face in her hands, groaning. "Fine. Fine. I'll prove you wrong. I'll tell him about *everything*. I will go through every issue one at a time until he breaks. Next time I see you, I'll tell you exactly which one made him run screaming away from me."

## Chapter 15

*A*ll the way over to Xander's apartment, Cheyenne rehearsed what she would say to him like an actor going over lines. She and Nia had spent the last fifteen minutes of her session figuring out how to approach all the various issues she was dealing with. Even Nia agreed that Cheyenne shouldn't spill everything out in one long monologue. It would be too much for Xander to address, let alone take in all the details. Instead, she would pick the scariest feeling issue first. She'd work through them one at a time by doling them out over their next few dates.

They had a six weeks before she had to leave for LA, and Nia had agreed to see her every week before she left. Nia had long ago given her permission to text her in order to avoid a panic attack. But, Cheyenne had always felt self-conscious about it and never texted Nia for anything other than schedule changes.

Xander had sent Cheyenne his address, but the number and street didn't mean anything to her. It wasn't until she stepped out of the cab that she understood where he lived. She contemplated the facade of one of DC's most famous buildings before approaching the front door.

Xander lived in *The Cairo*. When Cheyenne had first moved back to the city, she'd taken several walking tours to get a better sense of the city. One of them was an architecture tour that featured places like The Cairo. Once a hotel, it had been converted into condominiums a long time ago. It was mostly due to this building that there weren't any skyscrapers in DC. It's height had enraged the neighbors so much that they lobbied congress to pass some really funky laws regarding building heights in in the city. She didn't remember the details, but buildings were restricted by the width of the streets that they were on. It explained why the city streets were so open and roomy. The wide streets and low buildings made the city open and welcoming—at least physically.

*The Cairo* was a beautiful building. And it perfectly fit Xander's personality to live there. Geometric patterns lined the arched entry. Small carved elephants flanked each windowsill. The front of the building declared its name in giant art-deco letters. An exotic building for an exotic man.

After taking in the details on the front of the building, Cheyenne forced herself to focus on reality again. Xander had invited her for dinner, not knowing she was coming over after a major therapy session where her therapist had challenged her to scare Xander away with authenticity. Why hadn't she stuck with her original plan of dating him until she had to go to LA and ignore all the crap running around in her head?

*Because, if you did that, you'd have no chance at keeping him in your life, you silly git.*

Cheyenne could linger in the renovated lobby forever, even before she had a good reason to hang back. It was beautiful inside. The arched doorways and restored tile were true to the original design of the hotel. The old-world feel transported her to another time and place. It felt safe.

After texting Xander she'd arrived, she made her way to the elevators. She couldn't procrastinate any longer. He opened the door before she could knock. He wore a button-down shirt and black jeans and an apron that said 'lie to the cook.'

She stared at it for a long time. *Was this a sign?* Maybe Nia was wrong about everything and Cheyenne should keep up all her pretenses. It wasn't as if she had promised to blurt out her whole truth the second she saw Xander again.

Maybe dinner first. Some wine would help. Would Xander even have wine at his apartment? Cheyenne paused in the doorway, trying to gather her senses and thoughts. The apartment was beautiful. Breathtaking. Xander knew it, too.

Deep brown leather chairs were offset by complex Persian carpets. There were three picture windows built into the brick framework of the building, all with rounded half domes at their tops. While the apartment was physically small, its furnishings were grand and poetic. Romantic. Plus, whatever Xander was cooking smelled divine.

She followed him into the kitchen. He had a small table in the corner of the apartment by one of the three windows. It was set for two with elegantly simple dishes, wine glasses, and candles. He must have just lit them for ambience.

A bubbling pot of something on the stove drew her in right away. A frying pan was filled with slices of onion sizzling into crispy brown bits.

She waved the steam from the stew toward her and inhaled. "This is intoxicating. What is it?"

"It's a Pakistani stew. Haleem."

"I've never heard of it."

"You won't find it in many restaurants around here

because it's kind of a pain to make. Comfort food more than fancy."

On the counter next to the stove was a plate with finely chopped cilantro, sliced peppers, quartered lemon, and shredded ginger. "I am guessing these go on top, with the frizzled onions?"

Xander stirred the haleem. "You got it."

He pulled her into his arms and kissed her. "I'm so glad you're here."

Cheyenne wrapped her arms around his waist and buried her nose against his neck. It all felt so perfect. So natural. She never wanted to leave.

He released her all too soon to scrape the onion onto the plate. "I got a bottle of wine on the way home tonight," he said, tilting his head toward the fridge. "I asked the guy at the store what he thought would work with the haleem and trusted he'd steer me right."

Cheyenne opened the fridge and found the single bottle of wine, a riesling. "Are you having some, too?"

"I'll have a taste so you can educate me."

"Are you sure?" she asked. She unscrewed the bottle, skeptical of it already since it didn't have a cork. She poured a splash into one of the glasses and sniffed at it before tasting it.

"Is it okay?" he asked, putting an earthenware bowl filled with the steaming stew on the table.

"It's good. A little on the dry side depending on

how spicy those peppers are, but I like it," she said. She poured them each a glass and sat across from him.

The haleem was rich and earthy and unlike anything she'd ever had before. The brightness of the shredded ginger, cilantro, and peppers cut through the very rich stew while bringing out the undertones.

"I think I need to learn how to cook this."

"Nope. I'm not going to teach you. I need to have at least one thing to impress you with."

"I'm betting you've got a few other things you can cook."

"Maybe." He grinned and took a sip of the wine. He pulled a face. "That's supposed to be good, eh?"

"You don't like it?"

"Meh. I'm willing to give wine a few sips here and there. Have a glass in front of me so you don't feel weird or whatever."

"I don't have to drink wine at every meal," she said. "It's not mandatory. And you don't have to pretend to drink for me."

He caught her hand in his and pulled it to his lips. "I'll make this for you anytime."

She could see him making this for her when she was tired or sick or feeling down. An image of her sitting up in bed, gray haired and her face lined with age, with Xander spooning haleem into her popped into her head. She was so startled she choked on the last bit of her wine. *Where had that come from?* As surprising as it was, it was an equally comforting image.

When they were done eating, Xander stood up to clear the table. When she did the same, he waived her away. "I want to put this away and toss the dishes in the dishwasher. Give me a minute."

While Xander worked in the kitchen, Cheyenne perused his book shelf. They were ordered by subject and then alphabetically within the subject. One shelf was filled with the twenty volumes of the *Master and Commander* series in hardbound leather. A collector's edition. He *really* was into them.

Next to the sofa was an end table with three books stacked on top. One was a book on medieval Persian food. She was pretty sure he'd talked about it when they were working up their spice profile. On top of that was the final volume of the *Master and Commander* series. A bookmark hung out near the very end of the book. On top of this was the same version paperback of *The Mysteries of Udulpho* she owned with a slip of paper stuck out of it halfway.

She picked it up and flipped through. The paper was a sales receipt from the day before. He'd gone out and purchased the book while she was cooking up a storm for the show audition. The receipt also listed a used DVD version of the Pride and Prejudice she had recommended.

Xander emerged from the kitchen as she closed the book. "Spent most of yesterday afternoon reading that."

"I thought you'd stuck the receipt in at random. You're actually that far along?"

"It's gripping in an odd way."

"You're further along than I am," Cheyenne said fingering the bookmark. "I'm impressed."

Her eyes caught his, and she saw in them a reflection of her own desire for him. For *them*. For *this*. Suddenly, Cheyenne hoped Nia was right and she was wrong—that Cheyenne would throw every messed up aspect of her life on the table for Xander to examine and he'd swipe it all aside and declare his love for her.

Xander took the book from her and set it back on the table. "I've had a hard time concentrating this afternoon. All I could think about was kissing you in the orchid house. The way our bodies responded to each other."

Cheyenne's cheeks warmed at the memory. "That wasn't exactly taking it super slow, was it?"

"Slow is relative." He wrapped his arms around her, closing the distance between them.

"So, if one-night stands are your usual, a couple days…" She left the question unfinished.

"*Is* slow," he said. "But we have our whole lives ahead of us, Cheyenne. I want to keep things slow, but not *completely* chaste, if you get my drift."

His erection pressed into her—teasing. Taunting. Tantalizing. She wanted him inside her—now. Fast and hard and hungry.

*But no. Can't go there yet.* She had promised herself she would do this right. She dredged out one of the questions she'd practiced earlier with Nia to get the ball rolling.

"What are you hoping for in a relationship, Xander?" In spite of all his words about the future, a hook-up with her would be enough. Maybe all her angst over losing him for long-term issues would be a waste of energy.

"You." He said it with a sudden firmness that brooked no confusion. His fingers dug into her for emphasis, and his eyes burned bright hot with unmitigated desire. "I've been waiting for you my whole life, Cheyenne. Now that I've found you, I don't want to ever let go. But I am a realist. And I know you've had other relationships. You have expectations, and I am happy to take whatever time it takes to convince you that we were meant for each other." His hands moved up her back and into her hair, his fingers spreading out across her head.

There it was—a promise of a long term commitment. *Could this be real?* It was so fast. Cheyenne stuffed the hope that surged inside her to the side for the moment.

"The thing is, Xander, I'm not sure what I want right now," she said. His simple honesty was surprising and refreshing, she reached deep for her own truth. "I don't know if I can make a good..."

"Lover? Wife? Partner?" Xander filled in all the blanks her unfinished statement left between them. "I must come across as some weird stalker guy. Ready to jump into this with both feet. But I've been with enough women to know I've found what I've been waiting for."

"But we've only known each other three days," she said. "There's so much about me you don't know."

He closed his eyes and breathed in before answering. "Okay. Let's sit down and talk, then. Talk it out. Tell me everything you think I need to know."

She dropped onto the sofa, steeling herself. *Everything?* Cheyenne suddenly wasn't sure if she could keep her dinner down. Calming herself with a few deep breaths, she started and stopped a couple of times, terrified that she would blurt everything out all at once and sound like a complete lunatic.

"Wow. This is serious." Xander sat close to her, turning to face her and holding his hands out for her to hold them.

"You're wanting a long-term relationship. I need to make sure some things are out on the table before I'm in too deep. I can't fall in love with you and then have you reject me over...things in my past. Things I can't control. It doesn't seem right for me to not...disclose... I don't know if they'll matter to you or not, but...I can't... string you along for what I'm sure is going to be awesome sex."

"I appreciate that. I honestly can't think of anything that you could say that would freak me out enough to make me not want to love you."

*Love?* That word had never been said so fast or early in any of her relationships. Either Xander was nuts or he was determined. Determined felt a little better to her than nuts.

"You say that now," she said, silently cursing Nia and her challenge to be so completely honest. The first bit was already out. She'd admitted to Xander she wasn't sure what she wanted, the easiest of her scary truths, and the world hadn't come crashing down around her. Time to put it out there for him. "I'm divorced. Annulled marriage. It's been four years."

As far as Cheyenne could tell, Xander's only reaction was confusion. "Divorced and annulled? What does that even mean?"

*The annulment. Ugh.* It was a perfect segue into

the most shameful and traumatic part of her history. *Out with it, Cheyenne.*

"The annulment was religious. Alberto, my ex, is very Catholic. *Italian* Catholic, actually from Italy. He had our marriage annulled based on the fact I couldn't *bear him children.* In the Catholic church, divorce isn't enough for him to remarry. So he had our relationship annulled—something about *a defect of capacity.* This allows him to get married again according to his church."

Xander's eyes narrowed as she spoke. He didn't say anything right away, but dropped his eyes from hers to their hands clasped together in the space between them. "Thank you for telling me. How did you find out you can't have children?"

Cheyenne trained her gaze on their hands now, too. "I had three miscarriages. The Catholic church doesn't allow for any infertility treatments. That would be interfering with God's will and all that."

"Wait. You're telling me he divorced you rather than go through IVF or whatever other treatments there might be?" Xander asked. "Are you serious?"

"He categorically refused any medical intervention."

Xander's eyes rounded and sparked, his nose flared and his lips tightened. "Son of a bitch. What a complete asshole. He didn't deserve you."

"Children were important to him. And to his mama. His beliefs were stronger than his love for me." A calmness settled onto her and the last little chink in her heart connecting her to Alberto released itself. The angst and anger that usually came when she spoke of Alberto was gone. The lingering sadness over her losses were dulled, though not entirely gone.

"Did you consider adoption?"

"Alberto insisted on wanting his own child. Genetically his own. He couldn't stand the idea of adopting."

"Wow," Xander said. "Alberto sounds like an ass."

What a perfect description. "You know what? I just realized how lucky I am. If I'd stayed in California and had those babies, my whole life would be totally different now."

"And you wouldn't be here with me. Maybe I should be thanking this guy instead of wanting to bash his head in with a shovel."

As touching as his anger at Alberto was, Cheyenne pressed the subject a little harder. "I honestly don't know if I can have kids. You need to know that about me going in."

Xander nodded thoughtfully. "The more important part of that discussion is whether or not you want them. I would love to have my own biological children, if you'd consider medical intervention to try some day —like years in the future? I want them, but not tomorrow, you know? And, if we can't have our own, I'm okay adopting. If you don't want any children at all, that would be a very different discussion."

"I'll be running a restaurant. That's the long term plan, anyway. I'm not sure how that will work out with kids," she said, slipping another worry out on the table. "But, yes, I've always *wanted* them. I love my niece and nephew."

"Nannies. Babysitters. Me as dad..." Xander kissed her gently on the lips. "The details of how will resolve themselves if we put our minds to it."

"You have an answer for everything, don't you?"

"I have a confession to make."

"Your turn now?" Cheyenne hoped Xander had some of his own skeletons in the closet to share. It was hard being the subject of so much magnanimity.

"When I first emailed you?" he asked, tilting his head to the side. His eyes were on her, watching her intently.

"Yes?"

"I contacted the school for help, and they gave me a few different names to contact. The director? Anthony Baldwin? He didn't really know who would enjoy working with me. So, I went to the school website. He gave me about six names, not just yours. I was trying to figure out who might be most receptive to this project."

*Where was this going?* Cheyenne circled her hand around in the air, urging him to continue.

"So, I saw your photo...and you took my breath away. Shallow? Maybe, but you are so beautiful. Then, I read your bio, and decided I would contact you. I actually prayed you'd say yes to the project that night. I don't do that very often."

"Are you saying you contacted me because you thought I was hot?"

"That sounds a lot worse than it was. Yes. The initial moment when I first saw your photo...I was blown away. Immediately, I wanted to get to know you better. I read your bio. Went on all your social media and followed every post I could see for a couple of days. I liked what I saw. You're so much more than a pretty face. You're stunning on the inside, too."

And then he'd emailed her, eventually asked for a phone call, and, finally, after all the warming up to it, they met on Saturday.

"You've had a lot longer time being attracted to me than I have to you. Longer to think about where this could all go."

"I feel a little bit like a stalker. But there was something about your name, and then your photo, and all the food photos."

Cheyenne had the habit of posting a photo of everything she baked. It was as much for her own record as it was about showing off her talent, but it would also help build her chef 'platform' to have hundreds of pictures of tantalizing treats.

"You totally stalked me," she said punching him lightly in the shoulder. "I'm trying really hard to not be creeped out."

"You look *soooooo* scared," he said, his eyelids half closing as he circled the tip of his nose around hers.

"And you have no photos on the internet. Not even the GW staff page has anything other than a Sumerian tablet for your photo."

"Ah, hah! So, you admit to stalking me a little bit, too? Pot meet kettle." He grinned broadly with those kissable lips of his.

"I tried, but I honestly thought the old dude in the pie class was you when he walked in. It was quite disappointing."

"Were you relieved when I finally showed up?"

"Immensely. I admit it. I found you quite compelling over the phone," Cheyenne said. "I was hoping there would be a spark in person, but I wouldn't let myself count on it."

Xander stood up, holding a hand out to her. "Come with me to my bed?" he asked.

"What do you have in mind?" she asked. "Are we still taking it slow or..."

His lips curled up as he tugged at her blouse to

free it from her skirt. He slid his hands along her back, and up to her neck. His fingers dug gently into her muscles.

"God, that feels good," she said, groaning with pleasure at each movement.

"Slow doesn't mean not any touching. Remember what you used to do as a teenager? Everything but?"

Cheyenne laughed. "I think your teenage years were different than my teenage years."

"Were you a wanton young woman?" he asked. His eyes twinkled. "I wouldn't care. You should know I don't care when you lost your virginity or how many men you've slept with in the past."

*Great.* A perfect opening to mention her trio from less than a week ago. Nia had been right. None of this would matter to Xander, would it? She could tell him anything and he'd stay by her side.

Just as she was about to admit she had more to share, he kissed her. A deep, forceful, hungry kiss. He cupped her ass with his hands. Her pussy throbbed with an aching need, one stronger than she'd had in years. She pressed her thighs together hoping to stem the tide of warm, wet desire.

Xander loosened her skirt and pulled it down over her hips. His thumbs caught in the top of her panties. Cheyenne made no move to stop him. She lifted her arms so he could free her of her blouse. With a swiftness she hadn't expected, Xander had whipped off her bra. She leaned into him, wholly naked.

"Not fair. You too," she said.

Cheyenne tugged at his belt and opened the top of his pants. She thrust her hand into his pants, palming the cotton of his briefs against his erection. He groaned and broke the kiss. Lifting her off her feet, he carried her the fifteen feet across the apartment to his bedroom.

She barely noticed the surroundings as he ripped off the covers to reveal rich scarlet satin sheets. The coolness of the fabric sent little thrills up her back as he guided her onto her back. He stood over her as he removed his shirt and dropped his pants.

Cheyenne watched intently as he removed his briefs.

"Ground rules?" she asked, unable to take her eyes off him. He was muscular without being bulky. His dark hair covered his chest, drawing a deep triangle like an arrow down to his erect cock. She didn't need a tape measure to know he would fill her perfectly.

Xander growled in response and dropped to his knees next to the bed. Grabbing her gently by the ankles, he slid her across the satin surface, spreading her open before him until her legs dangled over his shoulders. She lay on her back, spread wide for his inspection. His lips danced across her inner thigh, up to her warm, hungry mound and across to the other thigh.

Cheyenne sat up on her elbows so she could meet his eyes as he paused. "Okay, then," she said. "Only if I get to return the favor next."

"Deal."

Cheyenne dropped back onto the bed, her arms spread out to either side.

He lingered, kissing her thighs, teasing her with his tongue everywhere but the one spot she needed it most. She writhed under him, hoping to guide his tongue to her throbbing, aching clit. It took her a while to realize he was intentionally avoiding it.

Xander slid fingers inside her, twisting to catch at her g-spot. He paused, fingers deep within. "You want more?"

"Xander," she breathed. "Please, I'm so close."

He laughed against her pussy, the deep rolling buzz nearly sending her over the edge. "How close?"

Cheyenne thrust her hips upward, trying to gain traction. "Seconds. If...you'd..."

Groaning against her now, Xander circled her clit before going all out. Inside, his fingers pulsed against her g-spot in unison with his tongue. The wave of blissful pain shot through her as her hips writhed against him, both wanting more and overwhelmed. Her upper body jerked upward and she grabbed at his head, not sure if she meant to hold him against her or pull him away. His free arm pressed against her stomach, pinning her to the bed. He didn't let up, but kept his tongue and fingers moving. Pulsing. Thrusting.

Finally, after what seemed like hours, Xander slowed, pressing the flat of his tongue against her, soothing and calming as she came out of the orgasm. Or had it been more like ten orgasms?

Once her breathing had calmed, Xander leaned his head against her thigh and removed his fingers.

"All right, I'm ready," she said sitting up and lifting one leg over his head. "Switch."

"You want to be on your knees?"

"Tonight, anyway," she said, grinning.

Xander settled onto the bed, seated near the edge. Cheyenne straddled his lap, pushing his cock between them against her belly, and kissed him, his lips still hot and wet with her own juices. He caught her hair with his hands as she settled in between his legs and nuzzled her nose against his thigh. She nibbled, licked, kissed, and teased him.

His cock twitched as she breathed on it without touching it, and he groaned with frustration.

"Cheyenne," he begged, his voice low and husky with desire and fell onto his back, though his hands remain locked in her hair. "Please."

Only after hearing that magic word did she place

her tongue fully flat against the base of his cock before running it up to the very tip and engulfing it in her mouth. She grasped the base of his cock with her hand to cover him entirely. He tasted salty. A little sweet. Her tongue darted around the tip, flitting in and around as her fingers squeezed and slid to take him over the edge.

Cheyenne kept her lips around him until he spasmed and his hips thrust upward. He came into her mouth in delicious threads of hot come. She swallowed each spurt down, hungrily hoping for more.

After a few moments of quiet relief, they climbed into bed together. Xander lifted the covers over them. Cheyenne snuggled in close against his shoulder and he wrapped his arms around her.

"That was perfect," Cheyenne said, "but I need to leave soon."

"No. Stay."

"I can't."

"I'm driving you home, then," he said. "It's late. Give me ten minutes of cuddling, then we'll go."

Cheyenne was afraid of breaking the perfect mood if she brought up any of her other reasons for him to dump her. Nia had suggested she dole them out over the next few days, and now, more than ever, that seemed like a great plan.

## Chapter 16

Xander drove Cheyenne home and walked her up to her apartment. After a long, lingering kiss at the door, he finally left. Cheyenne almost changed her mind and asked him to stay, but decided against it. She'd already told him the biggest reason for him to leave her, and she didn't want to jinx her luck by piling it all on.

Xander texted her when he got back to his apartment, wishing her sweet dreams. She wrapped her arms around her spare pillow and held it close, pretending it was Xander as she fell asleep. When Zach's early alarm woke her, she rolled out of bed and threw on some sweats instead of covering her head and going back to sleep. She had been dreaming about a pastry and had to see if she could make something that came close to the fantasy. As usual, she took a plate of her creation to share at the office.

Her first stop was Carleen's office. Was it wrong to want to prove she was in early and offer a bribe at the same time? Carleen had a steaming cup of coffee in front of her and peered over her glasses at Cheyenne as she knocked on her door.

"You like cinnamon, don't you, Carleen?"

"Looks delicious, as usual. Thank you for thinking of me." Carleen's eyes drifted over to her wall clock as she took her first bite. Her eyes widened and then closed as she chewed. "Wow," she said at last, "this? You need to patent it or something."

"Glad you like it," Cheyenne said as she spun away toward Katherine's office.

She chatted with Katherine for a while about the Bingo game. So much had changed in the last few days. Only a week ago Cheyenne had been determined to win, setting up dates willy-nilly and kissing guys at every chance. She wiped at her mouth. *No one else would kiss these lips again but Xander.* Not if she could help it. And just last night, she'd told him she wasn't sure what she wanted. It wasn't exactly a lie, but it had been a prevarication. She knew damn well what she wanted, but she fully expected things to fall apart as usual. Even if Xander hadn't fled at her revelations from last night, he might do so on any moment. She still had a list of things that could scare him off.

Katherine's enthusiasm for playing Bingo had waned as well after meeting someone during her girls' weekend in New York. *Go figure.* Chloe was glowing, Lizbeth was gone—who knew where—and Katherine was not interested in the gorgeous CIA dude a friend had set her up with. Even Eleanor was chipper and friendly.

Everyone stopped Cheyenne as she passed to grab a pastry from the plate. Sounds of delight followed her path through the office. By the time she got back to her desk, there was only one lonely pastry left. She snapped a photo and texted it to Xander.

**Cheyenne**: Dreamed of you last night. This came to me just before I woke up. I think my mind took your wish for 'sweet dreams' literally.

She hit send, took the plate to the coffee room and poured herself a fresh cup before cutting the pastry in half and examining it and taking a big bite out of one side. After an hour of cooling and travel, it had held up pretty well. While it had been fabulous warm from the oven, she would downgrade it to *merely delicious*. After finishing off the pastry, she washed her hands and returned to her desk. Xander had texted during her brief absence.

> **Xander**: Save it for me. I'll be right over.
> **Cheyenne**: LOL.
> **Xander**: No really. It looks amazing.
> **Cheyenne**: Too late. I ate it.
> **Xander**: What? You tease! Then let me come over and kiss the remaining sweetness off your lips.
> **Cheyenne**: Tempting. Need to focus on work ATM.
> **Xander**: Ok. Dinner tonight?
> **Cheyenne**: Let me check with roomies. They were planning a test night tonight.
> **Xander**: I'd love to see you all working. And, of course, taste things…You need tasters, right?
> **Cheyenne**: I'll let you know later. XOXOX
> **Xander**: XOXOXXXXOOOOOXO

Cheyenne turned her phone over to do not disturb and concentrated on the hearing prep. She would do her best at work until she left. No more shirking, no more avoiding things. Enjoying her job was suddenly easier knowing it would be over soon.

A hand on her shoulder made her jump. Cheyenne had been so lost in her work that she'd completely lost track of time. The clock on her computer said it was almost four o'clock. She blinked and spun around to find Chloe hovering at her side.

"Sorry. Didn't mean to startle you, but you didn't answer to your name."

"I don't even have headphones on," Cheyenne said shaking her head. It was kind of cool to be so into things again. "What's up, Chloe?"

"I can't find Eleanor, and I don't know how to do the security check on this." She held up a disc with no markings on it.

"What is it?" Cheyenne asked.

"It's supposed to be a case study that Harrison and I want to add to our report, but I know I can't put it straight into my computer. I forgot how I'm supposed to make sure it's okay. The whole security protocol thing Eleanor went over is kind wobbly in my head."

"No worries." Cheyenne stood and stretched. Sitting for so long was hard on her body and she needed to work out some kinks anyway. "Let's go to Eleanor's desk. At least you remembered the rule about checking everything before you use it."

"Eleanor scares me," Chloe said in a low voice. "I was so caught up in her rules, I spaced out on what she told me I was supposed to do."

"No worries. This is the security protocol here," Cheyenne said, lifting a laminated card that was attached by string to a computer. "This computer is here for one purpose, and one purpose only. To check incoming media for viruses and spyware. Eleanor makes sure this machine is updated daily and then removed from any internet connection. You'll know if it's in the middle of the update immediately when the screen says 'Please wait, I'm updating' in big flashy letters when you wake it."

Cheyenne moved the cursor and the screen shifted to a huge icon that said 'insert media now.'

"Well, this is embarrassing," Chloe said, inserting the disc into the drive. "I guess I could have figured it out on my own with a little more poking around."

"It's free of viruses and spyware, anyway. That's all that matters," Cheyenne said and left Chloe to it. It was tempting to add that she had been terrified of Eleanor when they first met and that her standoffishness was actually some sort of safety mechanism or professionalism that made Eleanor so strict and stiff. She was definitely someone who kept new people at a distance.

Cheyenne texted Chelsea asking her about their plans for the evening. Chelsea replied that they would all be home for dinner and that Cheyenne should plan on bringing her A game to menu planning. Chelsea followed with another text giving her a list of different ingredients she'd need to pick up.

The competition was all about building a firm foundation for a real restaurant. Previous winners of the competition won largely based on how their overall restaurant concept was likely to succeed in the real world. Part of the research would include things like actual resources they would need to make their restaurant idea a success—including realistic budgets and actual connections with vendors. It would be pretty impossible for them to design a locally sourced restaurant that included pineapple on the menu. The time between now and going to LA should be spent practicing recipes thoroughly so they were ingrained. Apparently, being filmed made a lot of people go blank.

They were each going to cook a few dishes and see what they could do about organizing their ideal menu. They needed some no-brainers to pull out of their sleeves for many of the show's challenges.

They had no way of knowing if there would be all new challenges or if some would be repeats. They'd watch every episode over the next couple of weeks to see what kinds of things were repeated and make sure they could nail them almost blindfolded. Ironically, one of Cheyenne's favorite challenges had to do with special diet customers. It was usually either a vegan or a gluten-free dessert challenge, but once they had combined them. Cheyenne had a lot of good ideas for both. Other allergies might require more effort on her part.

She texted Tiffany, Chelsea, and Zach all in one text so no one would be surprised.

> **Cheyenne**: Do you mind if Xander joins us tonight? We can tell him we're planning our restaurant and keep the conversation away from the competition. He knows about our original plan to open one.
>
> **Tiffany**: As long as he can add to the conversation or stay out of it. BTW, he's cute, but not your typical guy.
>
> **Chelsea**: Fine. Agreed with Tiff.
>
> **Zach**: He can taste my dishes anytime. Woof!

Bolstered by Xander's non-reaction to her revelation about Alberto and her infertility, she was beginning to believe Nia was right about everything. Jason had yet to send her a new Non-Disclosure Agreement, so Cheyenne couldn't tell Xander about the months long separation looming over them. Her next biggest reveal would be the three-way the previous week. He'd hinted at having a wild sex life in the past, so she doubted that would send him packing. She did the required shopping while practicing ways of telling him about her bucket list. She couldn't just bring it up in the middle of dinner.

Xander was parking his car down the street from the apartment as Cheyenne passed him, her arms laden with groceries. He took the heaviest of the bags and they walked the rest of the way together.

"We're going to eat well tonight. This is a lot of food."

"It's only part of it. Menu testing can be intense. I hope you don't mind a working dinner."

"Sounds awesome to me. I'm happy to be your guinea pig."

Walking up the stairs took less time than it had the last time they'd done it. Instead of stopping to kiss every third or fourth step, they plodded their way up under the weight of the groceries.

When they reached the top of the stairs, they found Zach pounding on the apartment door. "Tiffany. Chelsea. Come on. I left my keys."

"Zach, keep it down. The neighbors will complain." Cheyenne handed her bag to him and dug through her purse for her keys.

"I'm glad you came along. Tiff and Chels are like, totally ignoring me. How could they not hear me knocking?"

As Cheyenne slipped the key in the lock, Chelsea opened the door. She was wearing an apron and holding one hand up and away. It was covered in a shiny mixture of oil, herbs and something sort of grainy. Bulgar? Cheyenne wasn't quite sure.

"Sorry, was kinda in the middle of mixing." She held up the paper towel she'd used to touch the door. It stuck to her fingers.

The apartment smelled of a rich blend herbs and spices. Garlic and chopped parsley, mint, oregano, mingled with the rich scent of duck fat and caramelized onions.

Xander carried the bags into the kitchen and closed his eyes, sniffing. "Oh, man. I think I'm here to stay."

"You can help out." Chelsea tossed him an apron and pointed to the bags. "Unload those. Then, cube the potatoes—about one-quarter inch."

As Cheyenne was about to protest, Xander hopped to it. "Happy to help."

The group worked around each other, talking about the various elements of the dishes they were cooking, tasting things, adding more spices and vinegars to balance the flavors. They were focusing on a couple of traditional French techniques to make sure they had them down. Chelsea had already rendered a big pan of duck fat. They'd be cooking the potatoes twice. Once on a slow temp to make sure the interiors were rich and creamy and a second time at a high temp to insure a golden brown and crisp exterior.

The main dishes were two entrees all of them needed to have down without any chance of error. One of the show challenges included switching the teams up and have the pastry chef cook the meat dishes, so Cheyenne had to get this right. She always overcooked steak, so tonight she got to practice her pan seared steak with caramelized onions, mushrooms, and an herb butter plated with the duck fat fried potatoes and steamed green beans. Of course, it had to be plated beautifully to wow the judges.

Zach, as the bread chef, would probably be asked to cook fish without turning it to dry mush. So he would be working with halibut. As a team, they'd have to all be able to fill in the sides.

Cheyenne and her roommates managed to not mention the competition as they worked. After all, they spent many evenings working on recipes and techniques—the competition had done little to change that. After an hour and a half, they sat down to the table with the steak, the halibut, the potatoes and four vegetable side dishes. No need to practice plating right then.

It was an unusual evening in that Cheyenne hadn't made any dessert. They'd do another round of practicing with Chelsea in charge of pastry. The last time they'd tried it, Chelsea left out the sugar in the crème patisserie.

They made comments as Chelsea took notes. Then they cleaned their kitchen to sparkling again.

THE OTHERS MADE their excuses and left Cheyenne and Xander alone. He dropped onto the sofa and Cheyenne followed.

"I'm beat," she said. "Maybe my day job isn't so bad after all. Every night in a kitchen is going to be hard work."

Xander shifted so that he could lift her feet onto his lap. He took off her shoes and massaged her toes, then the balls of her feet and then her heels. The warm firm touch instantly relaxed her. "I loved watching you cook. You are so relaxed and happy in the kitchen."

"I am. Usually. Did you really like the steak?"

"Honestly? It was overdone—not by a lot—just enough to notice. But the flavors were as good as anything I've had elsewhere."

"Blargh. I knew it as I was cooking, but once it gets over you can't go back. Next time," she said.

He lifted her foot with one hand and ran the other up her calf, squeezing it and releasing it all the way up to her thigh.

"That feels amazing," she said. "Are you sure you're not a trained massage therapist?"

He switched legs and repeated the delightful combination. By the time he was done, her feet no longer hurt and her entire body was relaxed. Her eyelids weighed about a ton and she fought the sleep that threatened to overtake her. She yawned broadly.

"I'm so much fun right now, aren't I?" she asked sleepily.

Xander slid her feet off of his lap, stood up and scooped her off the sofa.

She buried her face against his shoulder as he carried her to her room. Once inside, he kicked the door shut and gently set her on the bed. She stretched out and held her hands out to him, beckoning him toward her.

"You can barely keep your eyes open."

"Spend the night?" she asked. "Not that I'm up for sex, but I would love the warmth of your body next to mine."

"What constitutes sex?"

She groaned as she imagined all the stages in between cuddling for warmth and actual sex. "I like to sleep naked. Will that be too hard for you to resist?" she asked.

"Whatever it takes for you to let me stay." He grinned and held up his hand with the fingers in the

Scout's honor salute. "No touching the naked lady in ways she doesn't ask to be touched."

It was kind of refreshing to have a man spend the night with her without having sex. Not that she was tired of sex, but this man might be worth waiting for. How long had she spent talking to him without even thinking much about him as a prospective lover?

Even Dallas had seen her attraction to the man before she had. Would the very new relationship survive three months of virtually no contact? Would he run right now if she told him about the competition?

He pulled his shirt off. "If you're going to be naked, then so am I."

"That is not fair," she said, her eyes locked onto his rich brown skin. His chest was broad and firm. He dropped his jeans but left his boxers on. They were a soft cotton plaid in green and black, simple and soft.

He turned in a circle for her inspection.

Her body tingled all over in a newly awakened hunger. Would they be able to keep the no sex bargain? Given the erection he was sporting, she didn't think it would be hard to coax him out of his self-induced celibacy if she really wanted to. Cheyenne's tiredness from the day nudged at her, and she brushed it aside best she could. This was different than the usual rush to throw off clothes, get naked, and get busy. This was intimate, but in a playful way.

"Tempting. But you're wearing shorts, that's not naked. Apparently, you need instruction, Professor." She rolled off the bed. Her back screamed and sharp spasms ran up her calves. She hadn't worked so long in a kitchen for a while. Getting back into restaurant-shape would take some effort.

She breathed through the aches and pains that came with the territory and peeled her clothing off one layer at a time. She had always been comfortable with her body and loved having his eyes on her.

When she was done she ran her hands along her sides. "This is naked."

"All right. Eyes only, eh?" He stripped out of his boxers.

His rigid and ready cock indicated he was ready for way more than sleep. She reached out to stroke him but pulled her hand back before she actually touched him. There was no way she could carry through on the action. It would be cruel to lead him on like that when her body screamed at her to rest.

He pulled the covers back on the bed and climbed in, holding them up for her. "Cuddle time?"

"If you insist," she said. She snuggled into his shoulder, draping her arm casually over his firm chest.

His nipples poked up out of thick curly hair. She caught a few strands and swirled it around a finger.

"This is a good deal harder for me than it appears, you know. I am spending every ounce of my will on not flipping you over onto your back and pouncing on you."

"I kind of wish you would," she said, leaning into him. "Change the subject to dead kittens or something. That should help."

His chest rumbled underneath her ear as he laughed. Everything fit perfectly. Her head into his shoulder, his arm around her body. She was certain, when the time came, he'd be perfect inside her, too.

"You up for some talking or do you want me to leave you alone and let you sleep?" he asked.

"I don't want you to leave me alone, but I might fall asleep mid-sentence."

"We've talked so much I feel like I know you so well. Cooking. History. Other things, but there are some things I don't know about you."

"Is there something you want to know about me?" Cheyenne asked. "Go ahead. Ask me anything."

"Anything?"

"Do your worst," she said.

Nia would be so proud of her right now. Cheyenne cuddled in closer against Xander, wondering where he would go. What scared him the most? She held her breath until he spoke again.

"Hmm. Okay. How many men have you slept with?"

She was surprised by the question. No one had ever asked her that before. Was it that no one had ever cared enough about her before? Maybe it was just the nature of one-night stands to not ask directly. "Why do you want to know?"

"Oh, mostly curious. I'm assuming you've been with a few. I've slept with thirty-nine women."

"I would be number forty?"

"Yes. Is that horrific?"

Cheyenne had slept with more than that number in the last two years alone. Of course, before that, she hadn't been so wild and crazy. Her total count was fifty-two men. And, until the other night, she could still name and conjure up the faces of every one of them.

Telling Xander her detailed sexual history was going to be important. What would he think about the threesome from the other night? Would he be appalled? Turned on? Nia had urged her to tell him everything, but not dump it all on him at once. Cheyenne buried her face against his skin. She wasn't sure she could watch him as she told him.

"Just a number, Cheyenne. No judgment. Mostly curious."

She hesitated. Fifty-two sounded like a lot more to her when she considered it like this. None of them seemed as important to her as they once had. They had been learning experiences and about everything she didn't want or convenient lovers.

"Okay, Miss Hesitant. This is my round-about way of asking if you're a healthy partner. I just got back my latest blood work last week. I'm totally clean."

*Oh.* That's what this was about. Cheyenne hadn't been tested recently. It had been months and at least ten guys. At least she didn't need to worry about being all hot and bothered. She appreciated the frankness, but it wasn't going to make her perk up and jump his bones.

"Dang. I haven't thought about testing for months," Cheyenne said. "I should do it every few months, but...I just trust the people I end up with."

"Well, I guess it's a little late, after last night, anyway. So, I told you how many. What about you?"

Smooth fingers tilted her chin upward gently until his beautiful green eyes bored into hers. Open, kind, questioning. No judgment there.

She yanked at some hair on his chest and he grabbed at her hand, laughing. "Fifty-two. My first was in college when I was eighteen."

"About six a year then?"

"That would be averaging them out, yep." No need to go into the four years of solo time with Alberto. Ten a year average was just a guy a month. She knew other women who went out with two or three times that amount.

"You know," he said, pressing his fingers into her neck, massaging gently. "This might sound weird, but I think prior experience is a good thing. Personally, I know what I'm looking for. I already know we're a good match outside the bedroom. All we need to do is confirm we fit together in bed. Beyond what we did last night."

*All we need? All we need before what?*

He turned so they were facing each other, their bodies no longer touching. Xander dropped his gaze for a moment before turning his face up to the ceiling as if searching for words from on high. It was his turn to fess up to something bugging him. There was something *he* needed to tell *her?*

"I've had some crazy times. I got caught up in some things that got weirder and weirder and scarier and scarier."

"Scary sex?" she asked. Maybe there was more to his short-term celibacy thing of his than what was on the surface.

"Once you cross a certain line it's hard going back to being normal. I want to get back to being normal."

What was he talking about? Normal could mean so many things. "Can you give me an example?"

"How about I ask you if you've ever done something and you tell me if you have or haven't."

"And I get to ask you the same?"

"Yeah. A way to get to know each other's sexual preferences."

Cheyenne had never talked much with the men she had sex with. Sure, most asked if they could do x or y, but usually it was in the heat of the moment.

"Okay. You first." Cheyenne propped herself onto her elbow so she'd get a better read on him.

"Have you ever had sex outside where people can see you?" he asked.

"Well, not that anyone probably saw us, but I did have sex on the beach once. It was pretty foggy. You?"

"Yes. And people did see us. There were about six couples at a campsite and we all agreed to have sex outside at the same time. So we could watch each other. On purpose. Your turn."

Cheyenne pictured a circle of couples around a campfire. Immediately, she shoved the image of Xander with another woman out of her head. She didn't want to imagine that. Not at all.

What she really wanted to know is, what did he

mean by weird? Maybe he'd gone all fifty shades crazy and gotten into tying women up and beating them. She hadn't actually ever read the book, but she'd heard lots about it. Being tied up was not her cuppa. But, then again, things had gotten pretty wild the other night with the two guys. There wasn't any tying up, or kinky sex toys, but it was beyond 'normal' wasn't it? That was why it was on the bucket list to begin with.

"Have you ever tied a woman up and had sex with her while she was tied up?" she asked, thinking it sounded a lot more mild when she said it like that.

"I have. More than once, but always with her permission. Have you ever been tied up and fucked?"

A hot, warm wetness blossomed between her legs. Why was it when he said it, she wanted it? She'd never wanted anything like that before, but with Xander? Maybe. "Nope. Have you?" she asked. "Been tied up, I mean?"

"Yes. It was pretty hot."

She pictured him spread wide on a bed, his arms and legs straining against silk scarves. Having him lie there, all hers to play with. She breathed in deeply, his cardamom and cinnamon scent sending waves of desire through her.

"What about more intense BDSM stuff? Like whippings, nipple clamps, that kind of thing?"

She blinked in surprise. Silk scarves were a long way

from nipple clamps. She wasn't even sure what nipple clamps were for, though the name of them made her clamp her arms over her chest. Mostly in jest. "Um. No. Not ever been interested in anything remotely painful."

He let out his breath, obviously relieved.

"I take it you're not into all the pain stuff?" she asked.

"Nope. Not anymore. I'll admit to playing with it, and I can never quite get all that excited about hurting someone else—even when they want it. A playful spanking here and there, maybe."

*Not anymore.*

"I guess that puts us on equal footing." Cheyenne shifted so that her thighs squeezed together tightly. His mention of a playful spanking had sparked a sudden flow of excited juices. Again, the notion was only exciting when Xander mentioned it.

"Your turn," he said.

"Hmmm...let's see. I think last night told us we both like oral sex. Do you have a preference? Giving or receiving?"

"Interesting," he said, eyeing her intensely. "It's complicated. I absolutely love both...Giving is big for me. Receiving is good, but maybe a little harder for me."

"You managed last night," she said.

"It's easy when I'm with the right person."

Cheyenne closed her eyes and relaxed back into him as she stifled a yawn. As interesting as this all was, she was still tired. "I didn't at first because I was embarrassed. But, there was this guy when I was in college? He totally showed me the way."

Xander waggled his eyebrows. "Actually, I'm really big into foreplay."

"I can tell. The last few days are amounting to be the longest foreplay *ever*."

He kissed her on each of her closed eyelids. "You need to go to sleep now?"

"Maybe in a few more minutes," she said, her words slurring just a little bit with exhaustion.

"I think I need another dead kitten topic. Worst sex experience?" he asked.

Cheyenne didn't need any time to think about that one. "First. Being a virgin with a guy who was a virgin made it awkward. Neither of us knew what we were doing. What about you?"

"The last time I had sex, actually. Probably why I changed my ways. The woman I was with hadn't been honest with me, and things went very badly—she's fine. But, it messed with my head."

"How?" she asked.

"Bad enough that I'm pretty sure the kinkiest I will

ever get again is silk scarves with a quick release tie. You okay with that?"

Cheyenne sucked in her lower lip and batted her lashes at him. "And maybe a spanking when I'm a bad girl?"

"Bad girl, eh?"

His smile made her heart thump hard in her chest. Lordy, he was gorgeous.

"Craziest ever sex activity?" she asked.

"Hey, it's my turn. What's your craziest ever sex activity?"

She pulled at his hair, stalling for time. This was the perfect opportunity for her to tell him about her ménage. Once she told him, she wouldn't be able to take it back. If he didn't run after finding out about this, he might not run at all.

Cheyenne swallowed a couple of times, girding up her courage to tell him.

"I had a three-way. Me and two men."

Xander stopped breathing for a moment as he absorbed her words. "I bet that was intense."

"Yes. And, I'll be honest with you, Xander. I loved every minute of it at the time. I had a ball."

"But?" he asked. "I feel like there's a but coming."

"I don't have buyers' remorse. I mean, it was a bucket list item. Something I've been wanting to do for years, but the timing of it makes me feel a little weird."

Xander stiffened under her. "When did this hot time happen?"

Cheyenne turned her face against his chest again. "Tuesday. Just last Tuesday."

Xander's fingers, which had been gently caressing her neck, stilled. He didn't speak. Cheyenne couldn't even tell if he was breathing.

After what felt like eons, his fingers pressed into her shoulders again. "So, after we had been talking for a while."

"But before we had met in person," she said.

"Wow. I don't know why I care," he said quietly. His lips brushed against her forehead. "I think it's surprising because, in my mind, we were already together. I knew, before we met in person, I wanted to be with you."

Cheyenne forced her eyes open again and sought his. "I had no idea."

"I know. And that's why I really can't be upset, now can I? It's my fault I didn't ask you out until after you'd had your...ménage a trois."

"It does sound better when you say it." Cheyenne dropped back down to the comfort of his broad chest. "And your crazy times?"

"I'm going with an orgy. There were at least thirty people in this huge room. It was at a BDSM club."

*An orgy with thirty people at a BDSM club?* "That

makes my trio sound like a tea party." She'd been worrying over nothing, then. If he'd been to an orgy, what could her trio be like in comparison?

"It was both exciting and tiring."

"Would you do it again?"

"No. I learned that I'm a one person at a time kind of guy." He tensed a little, his neck muscles twitching as his teeth clenched. "It's weird. I was fine in the woods with all the couples. But this…it was wild and crazy and free-form and somehow…I felt dirty afterward. Soiled. I didn't even know most of the people by name. It was too disconnected. Tawdry."

"Ah," Cheyenne said. The thing she'd liked most about her three-way was the lack of connection—the utter overwhelming physicality of it all. Exactly what he'd found tawdry during his orgy.

"There was something missing," he continued. "It was like…I could have been having sex with blow-up dolls. Realistic ones, but there wasn't any emotion. Just the act. Physical. Primal. Hedonistic."

That described her night with the two men last week exactly. There was no emotional connection, though both had displayed an astonishing amount of tenderness and caring, checking in with her every step of the way, ensuring she was having a great time with each moment.

Xander made her want to find that connection,

though. Maybe she already had. He hadn't said she was tawdry or slutty for having the three-way, but he was definitely hiding some disappointment. Had he really gotten over it that quickly? He hadn't run away, either. Not yet anyway. Was he really here to stay?

"Xander...I'm getting sleepy. I think it's time we say goodnight and try to get some sleep."

He kissed her deeply. "What are you wanting, a deep emotional connection? Just something physical?"

Two days ago, Cheyenne would have said physical. Now? She was terrified and excited by the possibilities having Xander in her life might mean. She still needed to tell him about the competition. That would be next.

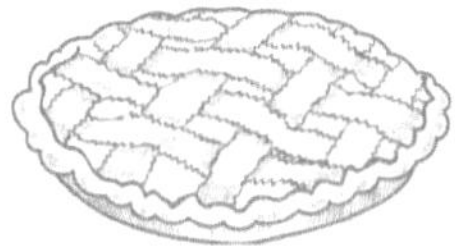

heyenne woke to Xander's gentle rumbling snore. It wasn't freight-train loud, but she might need to get ear-plugs if this was his normal. She kissed him on the lips to see if that would wake him.

His thick, dark, miraculous lashes parted to reveal his golden-brown eyes. "Good morning, Jaani."

There was something about the way he said this new word that sent shivers down her spine. *Jaani.* It wasn't the word itself as much as the way he said it—the familiarity in it with an intimacy that people gained over time—something she hadn't felt since she was married...since Alberto.

She had really loved Alberto in the beginning. Before everything had changed. Before his mother had moved in with them. Before the miscarriages. He never stood up for her, he always took Momma's side. He even left her because his mom had convinced him that she was no good because she couldn't reproduce.

Now, Xander was calling her something like Johnny but it sounded so much sweeter than that. "Hmmm... What does Jaani mean?"

He paused to wipe sleep away from his eyes. "It's an endearment...like darling."

He wasn't looking directly at her. Had he been mostly asleep when he said it? Had she caught him off guard? "Spell it for me."

He closed his eyes and swallowed. "J-a-a-n-i."

"Is it a common Pakistani thing?" she asked.

"Yeah. It's Urdu. My mom only spoke Urdu to us when we were growing up. She's absolutely fluent in English, but she wanted to make sure I had some of her heritage alive in me."

"Say it again?" she asked, propping herself up on her elbow.

"Jaani."

There was something extra intimate about the sound of it. Little shivers of hot desire coursed through her. She repeated it a couple of times to herself.

"I like it. Just so long as that's not something you'd say to your mom."

"How late can you be to work?" he asked. He kissed her before she could answer. "I was thinking breakfast?"

"I would love to, but I cannot be late today." She didn't want to be late for work again. She was ashamed that her job was in jeopardy. As a straight-A student, a rules-follower, and a generally 'good-girl,' she was not used to being in such hot water.

She rolled out of bed as if being naked with Xander were no big deal. There was no embarrassment or rush to cover herself up. They'd spent the entire night together, cuddling and naked, without actually having sex. And it had been more than just fine—it had been amazing. When was the last time she'd actually talked with a man like that? The openness. The honesty. It frightened her and buoyed her at the same time.

Cheyenne showered and did her hair before returning to her room. Xander was sitting up in bed, swiping his thumb across his phone, but he put it down as soon as she returned.

Putting on a show, she slowly but efficiently hooked her brand-new lace bra and shifted her breasts into place.

"Loving the demonstration here. I'll be thinking about *that* all day."

"That's the plan."

His eyes narrowed on her and he tilted his head to the side.

"What?" she asked.

"I could look at you forever."

Cheyenne spun around to give him a full view, aware only of his appreciation. "Would you like to take a picture? That way you could see me any time you want?"

Xander sat up and his face lightened several shades, a grave expression clouding his eyes. "No. I don't do that kind of thing." His voice had grown cold and far away.

Something twisted inside. She'd obviously said something that had hit a nerve with him. But what?

"Sure," she said, trying to keep her voice from quivering. "No problem."

Xander rolled his shoulders and shifted in the bed. "Uh...yeah. I'll just lock this moment in my memory." He tapped the side of his head and grinned, but the smile did not meet his eyes and there was a false joviality about the whole moment.

Xander was faking something. His eyes darkened into a deeper, murky green, as if a shutter had slammed shut against his inner light. The effect was slightly unnerving, and Cheyenne had no desire to see what he might look like if were ever truly angered.

Cheyenne turned around to hide the weird sensation as much as to give him the perfect view of her round hips and ass. After tossing him a playful look over her shoulder, she bent over and tipped each foot through the holes of her panties. She brought them slowly up over her legs and hips until they were in place. She turned and popped out her hip in full display. Finally, she put on a wraparound dress that came to just above her knees showing her legs to their fullest advantage.

"Man, you look amazing," he said. His features had returned to normal. "I'm not sure I can wait until this evening to get my hands on you."

"You'll have to." Cheyenne kissed Xander lightly on his lips. "Take your time getting up and help yourself to whatever is in the kitchen. Zach is already gone, and the other two sleep like rocks."

The truth was, leaving now gave her plenty of time to get to work. The evening had been intense—holding back her desire, sharing her thoughts, and wondering what she wanted from the relationship. She needed to clear her head. After stopping to get a latte, she paused at a park bench underneath an oak tree. The morning was warm enough to sit in the shade without being chilled, so she settled into the wood and sipped at her drink.

What had Xander called her as he woke up?

*Jaani.*

He had even spelled it for her. She typed it into the search engine to see what it meant. It was more than sweet or darling or sweetheart—it was a way more intense than that. The word Jaan meant 'life.' As an endearment, Jaan or Jaani, meant the other person completed one's own life. As she read the urban dictionary meaning of it, a warmness spread through her. This was what long term lovers called each other—not some light-hearted crush thing. Xander had fallen for her—fast and hard.

It had come out languidly, naturally, as if he had been thinking it for a while but not actually said it aloud. He'd barely been awake when he'd said it, so maybe it had slipped out.

Really, the only thing she had left to tell him that might scare him away entirely was that she was moving away for three months. How big a deal could that really be? All the married people in the army had to deal with way longer separations. Would he be okay with putting things on hold for a while so she could live her dream? She had to tell him about the competition before they had *real* sex. Xander obviously put a lot of emphasis on that level of intimacy as being important to him. How could she have sex with him without telling him this one last obstacle?

She didn't care that it was barely four-thirty on the west coast. She texted Jason again, telling him that she needed Alexander Moore and Carleen Bigalow added to her NDA and that she would be telling both people about the show later in the day. Maybe he'd done it already and forgotten to respond.

The day was turning out to be a bright one, early with great promise. Cheyenne didn't spend a lot of time on social media. The most she'd used it for recently was was the Bingo game. Idly wondering who was ahead on the game, she opened her Instagram account and scrolled through the images. Madeline was currently in the lead. Cheyenne hadn't added anything new since her encounter with the two men.

She thumbed through her feed and stopped short. Alberto had posted a photo for the first time in ages. It was of a newborn, all pink and fresh in his bare arms. Her heart skipped a beat, but it wasn't in sadness or sorrow. A bittersweet happiness filled her. For Alberto. For a man she had once loved but did not now.

Cheyenne hit the heart icon. Alberto finally had what he wanted, and Cheyenne felt nothing but joy for him.

Xander was all that mattered to her now.

# Chapter 18

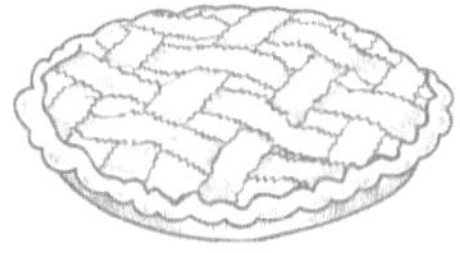

Cheyenne breezed through security and was in the office early. It was going to be a busy day.

Katherine called to her from her office before she had a chance to settle in. She held up a thin folder. "I got this last night. Our friends over at Ellis, Levin & Associates are poking around things. My guess is they have gotten word *something* is up, but I don't know whether it's about Sunflower. Just a heads up. I expect them to be at the hearings today."

Cheyenne checked her watch as she reached for the folder. Inside was a detailed report of the firm's activities for the last week. Congressman Pierce was paying a PI to follow the obnoxious lobbyist Gordy Carpenter. Gordy was sniffing around their newest intern, likely hoping to get info off of her. Cheyenne's limited interaction with Chloe wasn't much, but the younger woman didn't seem like a talker. Add in Katherine asking Harrison Auguste to keep an eye on Chloe, they probably didn't need to worry much about her.

Besides spending most of his time following Chloe around hoping for crumbs, Gordy spent an awful lot of time in half a dozen senators' and congressmen's offices. The only names that stood out to Cheyenne were Senator Wharton, Senator Markle, Congressman Talenti, and Congressman Sinclair. All of these men had been opponents to any legislation Congressman Pierce supported. Any one of them would love to have information on the big meeting in Vegas. Gordy could score major points with any of them for providing them with intel.

"You wanna head down there in about an hour and a half?"

Katherine took the report back and slid it into her desk drawer. "Sounds like a plan to me."

As she turned to go, Katherine stopped her. "Have you gotten your NDA figured out? I'd like to get Carleen in on things soon."

"No. Jason hasn't gotten back to me, but my last text to him was just a couple hours ago." Cheyenne checked her phone. "Still no response, but it's barely five there yet."

Katherine bobbed her head side to side as if considering the information and shrugged. "Not much we can do before the hearings today, anyway. I'd like her to know as soon as possible. I suspect we are going to need to replace you permanently—you are totally going to win this thing."

"Thanks for the vote of confidence," Cheyenne said.

Cheyenne grabbed a cup of coffee and made her way to her desk. On top was a padded manila envelope that hadn't been there the day before. It was addressed to her as 'private and confidential.' Her apartment was listed as the return address. The postmark indicated it was mailed yesterday from DC. She opened it. Inside was a second envelope with her name handwritten in a block print. Cheyenne slit it open with her sword-shaped letter opener to reveal a titanium thumb drive.

She peered inside the envelope. There was nothing else inside. *Interesting.* Maybe Dallas was pulling another of his incredibly elaborate practical jokes. But mailing her something was not in his known repertoire. She almost popped the drive into her computer, but Eleanor Winslow, the office Intel guru, had hammered in office safety protocols.

Cheyenne scanned the office, but didn't see Eleanor anywhere. It was rare for her to be late to work, but Cheyenne wasn't used to being to work quite so early, either. Cheyenne tapped on the computer used for scanning incoming media. The go ahead screen flashed on just as it had the day before when she had showed Chloe how to deal with security. She was pretty sure no one was watching her. Why would they? She wasn't doing anything unusual, not really.

Why was she so anxious about anyone seeing her checking this thumb drive? It wasn't unusual for anyone to be checking out stuff they'd gotten in the mail. There was just something weird about this.

The congressman received DVDs and CDs from people all the time. But something about the way the thumb drive was packaged and addressed to her sent alarm bells racing through her.

She stuck the thumb drive into one of the USB ports and waited while the computer scanned it. There was only one file on the drive. It had her name on it. Cheyenne LeFleur. And nothing else.

*Curiouser and curiouser.*

The scan came up virus free, so she ejected the drive from the system and took it back to her desk so she could view it in privacy. There would be a log of the scan on Eleanor's system, but nothing more.

The last time Dallas had sent her a video, it had been from a family wedding and she'd been pretty toasted. She'd geeked out to a few awful disco songs, doing a "Staying Alive" solo dance that had everyone laughing in the moment, but showed her lack of any dance training. It hadn't been all that bad, really, but she'd trashed the video and made her brother promise to destroy every copy in existence. As far as she knew, he'd done as she wished.

Back at her desk, Cheyenne rummaged in her purse for earbuds in case there was a sound track that would draw attention. Even as she fitted the drive into the USB slot, Cheyenne knew it wasn't from her brother. Her hands shook as she hit the play button.

At first, she wasn't quite sure what she was seeing. It wasn't until the video angle shifted and went wider that she recognized herself. She was kneeling on the bed with one man behind her and the other man right in front of her. The two guys from last week. Kyle. Shane. They were on either side of her. They had been captured in HDTV and stunningly clear audio. She reduced the video to the smallest size possible, but continued watching in spite of her rising nausea.

"Hey, Cheyenne," one of them said, "we're all good, right? You're wanting this, yeah?"

Cheyenne watched herself on the screen, horror building with each frame.

She was grinning up toward the man she was facing. "I'm loving this, boys. Keep it coming. Keep me coming."

They all laughed on the video. Cheyenne didn't now. She fast-forwarded through the rest. They'd taken clips of their six-hour sexual journey and put together the highlights. Cheyenne in every possible position available, having sex with both of them in every position imaginable, including the two of them inside her at the same time.

She watched in fascination. Part of her wanted to cheer—you go girl! Because it had been fun. And, frankly, the quality of the video was awesome. Better than any porn she'd caught on the internet, in more ways than one.

But she hadn't consented to the video. They had asked her if she was okay with everything else, but neither had said anything about them taping their play time. What was the point, anyway? To put up on x-tube? Or what?

Her confusion spun fully around to fury as she realized that everything she'd done that night had not been as private as she thought. And, even worse, Kyle, the man that Sky thought looked like Congressman Pierce, suddenly looked like Congressman Pierce to her when he hadn't before. She could tell it wasn't him, but only because of the tattoo on the side of his chest. And, in this video, it was only the other man talking. Kyle's sexy British accent had made him seem totally different from the congressman, and they'd cut it out of the video. Only a few groans of pleasure came from his lips on the video.

Her face was hot now as she forwarded to the end. Surely there would be a reason behind this intrusion. And, there it was. At the very end of the video was a website name. Nothing else.

She yanked the thumb drive from her computer and threw it in the trash.

She opened a new browser window and typed in the website name. "CongressmanLincolnPierceGetsIt-OnWithSexyYoungIntern.com"

What. The. Fuck. Her fingers hit the keyboard so loud it rattled. Cheyenne needed to punch someone. No, she wanted to punch two particular *someones*. Repeatedly. Or kick them where it hurt.

*Why would they do this?*

Cheyenne reduced the size of the window and made sure no one in the office was watching over her shoulder.

*What the fuck do they want?*

The website opened with a welcome screen and an arrow pointing down to the video. On the arrow, words said click below to see Congressman Lincoln Pierce get it on with his intern and another guy! Great. Anyone with this web address would be able to watch her. But that wasn't the congressman on the video.

And she wasn't an intern. But, who cared about the truth behind headlines anymore? Once this got out...

Underneath the video was a single demand: "What is really going on in Las Vegas? Upload all documents pertaining to the project to this site by this Friday at midnight, or we release this website link to the world with a viral social media storm to destroy Pierce." On the upper menu bar was a button labeled "upload here." She clicked on it and the 'choose file' option on her finder opened. Cheyenne automatically took a screen shot of the demands so she'd have it on her computer as proof of blackmail.

They wanted information. Their demands didn't specify or use the word SUNFLOWER—the secret meeting in Vegas they were all playing Bingo for. They, whoever *they* were, knew something was up and were fishing for information.

Who all had been at the bar on Tuesday night? Shane and Kyle had set her up, but they couldn't be behind this. Cheyenne had spent so much time in that bar, she couldn't remember who was there last week versus the week before or the one before that.

She exited her browser and closed her eyes to concentrate. She breathed deeply to calm herself. There was still a little over an hour to deal with this before she was stuck in the hearing room most of the day.

Bar. Who was at the bar? Eleanor and Daniel. She'd introduced them at the softball game. They'd left and Cheyenne had hung out with other people from her team for a while. The crowd shifted and morphed like any other night. Lobbyists, aides, lawyers, journalists... There were plenty of people who would be interested in SUNFLOWER for any number of reasons.

Kyle and Shane had approached her at the table where she'd been left alone after her teammates had left. Cheyenne had been standing there by herself for all of two minutes when Kyle said hello and asked if he could join her. Shane had come over a few moments later. They'd acted all along like they knew each other, but she couldn't recall if they had been with anyone else ahead of time.

She'd taken their business cards so she could figure out if they'd qualify for the Bingo game. Her brother had already shown what an idiot move that had been. And Cheyenne had thought she was lucky to get two kisses at once.

*Luck? Ha!*

Someone had planned this, but the congressman had only told them about SUNFLOWER on Monday morning. He, Opal and Carleen had probably known about it for a few days before that. It had been in the making for a while for sure. How long? Cheyenne wasn't privy to that information. And she hadn't paid that much attention to the other people coming to the meeting. Anyone planning the meeting or involved in it could have done some innocuous-seeming set of internet searches to tip someone off.

Cheyenne had to tell Eleanor. She would be the only one in the office who could figure who was running the website and who was behind this. That was the best place to start.

Cheyenne jumped out of her seat, angrier than a queen bee whose nest had just been poked. She didn't like being used. Or played. She fished the thumb drive out of her trash.

"Opal," she said, "Where is Eleanor? Is she here yet?"

"I think she's talking to Katherine, why?"

"It's a technical thing." She marched toward Kat's office but paused outside. Was bringing it up with Eleanor the wisest thing? She continued on past and headed to the copy room and shut the door. As much as she hated to admit she'd been duped to her brother, Dallas would know what to do. She hopped from foot to foot as she dialed, praying he'd pick up right away.

"Dallas?" Cheyenne couldn't keep the quaver out of her voice.

"Cheyenne? What's wrong? You sound upset."

She laid it out for him as briefly and as quickly as she could. "What should I do?"

"I'll come by to get the thumb drive from you in person. Make sure you save me the packaging as well, put it in a plastic bag now if you have it. Try not to touch it any more than you already have."

"Can you do this without watching the video?"

"Don't worry. I won't watch your amateur porn flick."

"You have to take this seriously, Dallas. It's not funny."

"You should have thought about that before going to a hotel with two strangers."

Cheyenne's fingers whitened around the phone. Maybe she should have gone to Eleanor first.

"They seemed like ordinary guys to me. How was I supposed to see this coming?"

"Sorry, Cheyenne. Not judging you so much as annoyed at the reckless behavior. You're my baby sister, and I worry about you. What was the website URL? I can do a lot with that info."

She gave him the information and held her breath. There was silence as he wrote it down. She could hear the video soundtrack over the phone as he opened the site.

"Well...I'm not watching, but it played automatically when the site came up." The sound disappeared and for a while she only heard the clicking of his keyboard.

"Well. Fuck," he said after what seemed like hours.

"What's wrong?"

"This site? It's bouncing around all over the world. I can't get a handle on it."

Cheyenne's heart suddenly pounded as hard as if she'd sprinted ten miles. "What are you talking about? People all over the world are watching it? They said it hadn't been released." Her voice rose in pitch as the implications freaked her out.

"No. Not that. The IP. The address where the site is being hosted. It's bouncing around. There's no static IP. This is going to be more difficult than I thought."

"IP?" Cheyenne had heard the term before but never really understood it.

"Never mind the details. Whoever put this up knew what they were doing and are tech savvy. They probably know you have an in-office IT person with skill and set it up so that they would be difficult as fuck to trace."

"So you won't be able to find them?"

"Not easily, and not right this second. Don't give up hope, Cheyenne. These fuckers may be smart, but I'm willing to bet they don't know *I'm* your brother. At least we have a few days to sort it out and catch these motherfuckers."

"That doesn't seem like much time to me." The fact that Dallas was swearing up a blue-streak made her feel better. When Dallas got angry, his mouth got foul.

"What all do you have on these sons of bitches? I mean, other than their fake business cards."

He'd already given her the riot act on them.

"You've already pointed out their business cards would be useless. Someone had to rent the hotel, right? That could give you something. And I took a group selfie at the Lincoln Memorial. Wait a second..."

"You were playing for that game of yours with these assholes?"

"You said you wouldn't get all judgy."

He let out an exasperated breath. "Not judging, Cheyenne. I need the whole picture. I don't need to see the video—don't want to, anyway—but am I right to assume there're no terrific shots of their faces?"

"No. Not really. Just profiles. Enough that Kyle vaguely resembles Congressman Pierce, especially from the side."

Cheyenne opened her photo app and scrolled back a week. The photos with Kyle and Shane were gone. Her throat tightened and she breathed slowly threw her nose. A panic attack right about now would not help things. Not one bit.

"They're not on my phone. The photo I took by myself, the one I checked in with? It's there, but not the photo of the three of us. I'm sure I took one."

"Calm yourself. Are you near your computer?"

"I'm hiding in the copy room, give me a minute." She kept the phone glued to her ear and faked a casualness she did not feel as she walked back to her desk.

Dallas talked her through finding her photo backups on the cloud. He'd originally helped her set up her phone to make wireless backups every few hours. After a couple minutes, she'd sent the file with both Kyle's and Shane's smiling faces to him for identification. It was a relief when he said he thought they could probably ID the guys.

"They got onto my phone, Dallas. How did they do that?"

"Did you go to sleep with them? I mean, actually sleep."

"Well, yeah. We all crashed about four in the morning. They woke up and left around seven. It was like any other, normal, party night."

"Normal?" The tone of his voice was weary.

It made her want to cry. Disappointing Dallas was the worst thing in the world.

"I'm sorry, Dallas. I really am." She held back tears. "I mean, I'm sorry about the tape, but I won't apologize for having fun. I'm not ashamed of what I did, I'm angry that they filmed it without permission. And now this. This? It is not my fault."

"Would you have said yes if they'd asked you? To the video, I mean?"

*How could he even ask that?* Why would she give permission to an all-out porn tape? No way. She might be willing to have fun, but she didn't want it out there on the cloud.

Cheyenne bit back an answer. Fighting with Dallas wasn't going to help. "Thanks, Dallas. I appreciate your help on this. I need to get back to work. I showed the photo to Sky the other night, though. How did they get it from my phone in between then and now? That was days after I saw them."

Dallas went silent for a moment. "That's weird. This *was* a week ago. Have you handed your phone to anyone since Friday? Given access to anyone?"

"I don't think so. Pretty sure not, but..." On Friday, she had been at their mom's, on Saturday at the Smithsonian, on Sunday at home, on Monday at work, Nia's, Xander's and home. Yesterday? Work and home. She'd not given the phone to anyone since then. Xander was the only person who could possibly have accessed it—and even then she would have had to be asleep or in the shower.

And, Cheyenne trusted Xander completely. He had no part in any of this. There was no way.

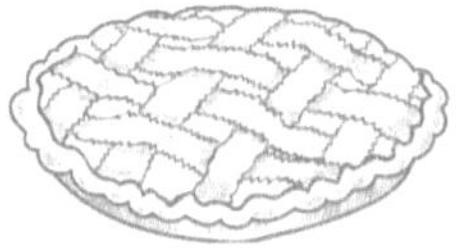

## Chapter 19

Cheyenne held the phone in her hand, and stared at it after her brother hung up. A full-blown panic attack bore down on her. Her vision blurred. But there was no way was she going to faint in the office. She ran to the bathroom, hid in a stall, and burst into tears buoyed by a mix of anger and despair. She furiously typed a message to send to Nia, telling her about the whole situation in one long text. Then, she deleted it when she remembered the text would be out in the cloud next. All she wanted was for the entire episode to disappear completely. How could she do that with a website already up and running?

Now that she had a chance to dry her tears and gather her wits, Cheyenne was pissed. All she wanted at the moment was to find Shane and Kyle and beat the crap out of them with a crowbar.

She hadn't felt violated by any of this until she saw the video. Even then, it wasn't the sex acts the three of them had committed that hurt. It was that they knew they were filming it without her permission. They had been acting the entire time, from the moment they met at the bar until the very end. She was sure of it. They had totally played her.

As she went through the details of that night, their requests for various positions had seemed natural. Spontaneous. Now she knew them for what they were. She hurled a roll of toilet paper at the mirror. It bounced off, ineffectual, but the act of throwing something made her feel good.

The business cards they had given her had appeared legit, but it was so easy to print something up these days—Dallas had been quick to point that out, hadn't he? It would have taken planning, though, and it was possible they had been trolling her way ahead of time. Why her? She wasn't anyone special in this office. She was just an everyday worker bee of no real consequence.

Cheyenne still had nearly an hour before the hearing. She had to address this now, and quickly. After taking some eye drops to reduce the red swelling of her eyes, Cheyenne approached Eleanor. Cheyenne didn't think she could go to Lincoln Pierce by herself. She didn't want to disappoint him any more than she wanted to disappoint Dallas.

"Eleanor, do you have a minute?" Cheyenne asked.

Her eyes remained on her screen as her fingers clacked against the keyboard. "What do you need? I'm very busy."

Eleanor's cool reception wasn't unusual, but it took Cheyenne everything she had to not burst out into tears again. She bit them back, unwilling to appear weak to this particular woman.

"I need to talk to you and Congressman Pierce alone in his office." She held up the thumb drive and leaned in close to whisper into Eleanor's ear. "I'm being blackmailed."

Eleanor's eyes locked on the drive as she rose from her seat. "Let's go."

Eleanor strode ahead of her without acknowledging the others at all. Cheyenne did her best to ignore the questioning looks, but it was hard. It was as if she was being marched off to the principal's office and everyone was watching. Eleanor could have been a bit more casual about it.

Link was in a meeting, but Eleanor pushed the door open anyway. Opal sat on a chair opposite Lincoln's desk, scribbling away on her ever-present notebook. She scowled as the two of them marched into the room.

"I'm sorry to interrupt, but we've got something urgent here."

Lincoln Pierce looked back and forth between Cheyenne and Eleanor. He blinked his eyes a couple of times and held up a hand, palm up. "Okay. Let's have it."

Cheyenne waited for Opal to get up and leave, but it was clear she wasn't going anywhere. Eleanor shut the door behind them and practically pushed Cheyenne into the seat next to Opal.

"Out with it, Cheyenne," Eleanor said. Her voice was even and firm. Annoyed.

"I..." Cheyenne closed her eyes and breathed deeply. "I am being blackmailed. I was told that if I don't hand over documents by Friday, a video would be made very public. They've edited it. One of the actors...well...sir...this video makes it look like you and me are...you know...with another man."

Lincoln Pierce would make an awesome poker player. He simply tilted his head to one side and laced his fingers together on top of his desk.

"Can you be a bit more specific, Cheyenne?"

Opal stiffened in the chair next to her. Her fingers whitened around the pen she was holding.

Cheyenne tilted her head back and drew in a long

breath. "The thumb drive is the video with directions to go to a particular website."

"What is it?" Link asked, his fingers poised over his keyboard.

"Stop there," Eleanor said before he could do anything. "Let me get you on the web via a proxy server so they don't see where the hits are coming from."

Cheyenne took in a deep breath. "I went to the website on my desk computer. If they can tell who is visiting, they know I've already clicked the link from my computer."

"That is too late to fix," Eleanor said. "I'll go through your machine when we are done here to make sure just going to the site doesn't trigger some malware or spyware. With the proxy and a strong firewall, this machine will be safe, and they won't know who is clicking on their links this time, only that someone is."

"My brother? He's already tried to see where the site is. He said he couldn't find their IP."

Eleanor flashed Cheyenne a look that told her she should just stop talking and clicked away before turning the machine back over to Link. It didn't take long for the video to load. Cheyenne's cheeks were hot with embarrassment. She had never wanted her boss to see her naked, let alone naked doing the things she was doing with these men.

Her moaning filled the room. Lincoln hit the mute button, but not until after they'd all heard more than enough. He leaned in close, eyes narrowing on the screen. "All right. I see the resemblance. He could be my older brother, maybe. But I have a mole on my right hip. This guy doesn't. Plus, that tat? Not like that could be erased very easily either. Anyone can tell this is a fake."

A glimmer of relief trilled through Cheyenne. The identifying markers could make a huge difference. Adding a mole to every bit of video, in the exact right place it belonged, would take a lot of work. "They could claim they erased it for the video?"

Opal jumped in for the first time. "As if that will matter. If this video gets out, no one is going to take time to fact check it before sharing it all over their social media. Your enemies have been waiting for some sort of indiscretion," Opal said. "No one will care about the missing mole, or that tattoo. People will read the headline and believe it's you because they are idiots."

Lincoln leaned back in his chair, fingers tapping at his chin. "I'm sure Madeline would put the right spin on it. *Congressman targeted for blackmail* or *Disgruntled staffer made a video to get back at her boss.*"

"Sir, I would never..." Cheyenne gaped at him, appalled by the idea.

He held up his hand to stop her. "I know, Cheyenne. I don't think we'll throw you under the bus on this."

Link clicked off the video. "They obviously know about SUNFLOWER. Or rather, enough about it to try this crazy stunt. When did this video get taken?"

"Tuesday night."

"We revealed it to staff on Monday morning." Lincoln turned toward Opal. "When did we first begin discussions with Donahue, Yukika, and August?"

Opal flipped through her notebook. The woman lived in the dark ages, but maybe she had a good reason to. No one could get to her notebook but her. It was worn, and used looking, but she never left it out of sight. And nothing she ever wrote on it would end up on the internet or in the cloud.

"Your first phone call with Donahue was four weeks ago, sir. You spoke to Yukika on the same day, just two hours later."

"So, someone on their staff could have leaked information anytime in the last four weeks, right?"

"We have been extremely careful about all this," Opal said, "but it's possible some of the other players are less concerned with secrecy. Renewable energy is the last big gold-rush, and they could be playing multiple angles. But honestly, I don't see Andrew being back-handed. I mean...Mr. Donahue. He's keen to be on Link's good side for the long run."

Cheyenne took in a sudden breath. She had forgotten to dial in Dallas.

"Eleanor, my brother, Dallas? You remember him?"

Eleanor shook her head but then changed to a nod. "Yes. What about him?"

"He's in Intelligence. I was supposed to conference him in."

"It's too late now," Eleanor said.

"Besides," Opal said, "We don't really need your brother listening to our strategy."

"My brother wouldn't leak anything to anyone, Opal. He knows how to keep a secret," Cheyenne said, puffing herself up a little bit, annoyed at the insinuation.

"I will run some of my own tests on this thumb drive," Eleanor said, ignoring them both as she snagged it. "I assume your brother has access to better tools, but I want to see if I can do anything with it. I'll be back with this soon. I don't need to be part of the control strategy."

Opal slammed her notebook down on the desk and paced the room.

"This is awful. Cheyenne, what in the world were you thinking?"

"I was thinking I was having fun. I had no idea that they were recording it. I feel violated."

"It was careless." Lincoln's voice cut through the tension between Opal and Cheyenne and sliced straight into heart.

Cheyenne turned from Opal and faced Lincoln directly. "I'm sorry, sir. I trust people too much, perhaps. I certainly didn't have a clue they were going to do this. That much is obvious, isn't it? I didn't even know they were taking video."

"Let me think on this a bit, will you? We have until Friday night to figure it all out. I'd like to get Madeline on it. Maybe Kenny, too. He could work with Cheyenne's brother on finding whoever is behind this."

Opal leaned against the desk. "Sir, with all due respect, I think you should demand Cheyenne's resignation. Immediately. Cut bait, and we can put a statement out before the tape is released so it will look like a retaliation."

"That's pretty draconian, Opal." Lincoln's eyebrows met in the center of his forehead.

"Maybe, but it's safe."

"We can't be safe forever."

Opal held Lincoln's gaze for so long Cheyenne got the impression the two were having some sort of telepathic conference. There was something silent going on that she did not understand.

"But, Link, this is going to spiral out in a very bad way." Opal's eyes shimmered with tears.

"Cheyenne has been a model employee. I refuse to fire her for her sexual proclivities."

"You'd be firing her for her lack of discretion." Opal's voice quivered with emotion. "Besides, there are plenty of people who would think everything in that video is depraved and immoral. I can see the headlines on the Enquirer, *Lincoln Likes to 'Pierce' Equally*. Or *Lincoln Pierces Everyone*. Or Lord knows what else."

Lincoln pushed the heels of his palms against his eyes and rubbed, something he always did when he was frustrated. After a moment of silence, he leveled his gaze on Opal. "We don't want the blackmailers to think they can just roll in here and demand information."

Opal held up her hands. "You're the boss."

"There is a contact link on the site in addition to the upload link," he said. "Cheyenne, go back to your desk and use that link. Tell them you'll try to have something for them in time. Make up a story about not knowing what they're asking for, and that it will take time for you to figure it out. Go ahead and say other people have been acting weird, but you don't really know what it's all about. Add in something about getting information when no one else is around. Beg them to not release the video until you figure things out."

Cheyenne didn't want to play that card. She didn't want to be a simpering victim. She wanted to smash their faces in—whoever *they* were, but maybe Lincoln's plan would still allow for that. She would do as he asked and bide her time. When they figured out who was behind all this, she'd find a way to get back at them. If she ever saw Shane or Kyle again, she'd personally whack them over the head with a barstool. No, not their heads. No. She would hit them where it mattered most and serve her sense of justice. She'd whack them squarely on their junk. They might just be tools in all this, but she didn't really care. They didn't deserve an out simply because they were the hired help.

"Also, tell them you need to meet in person. You can't let some things out onto the internet. Uploading documents directly would be too dangerous." Lincoln stood up, his hands moving as he spoke.

"And then what?" she asked.

"We'll prepare some documents that are legitimate but meaningless. Something that will get them off your back and send them in the wrong direction."

"And when they realize it's fake, then what? We're

back to square one. Sir, my concern is your reputation. Not mine. I can own the fact that I enjoy sex. I can righteously denounce them for not telling me about the video."

"The media shit-storm around its initial release will affect me, Cheyenne. There's no getting around that."

"Not if you release it first," Opal said.

They turned to stare at her.

Opal widened her eyes at them as if they were all a bit dim. "Here's the thing. People usually believe the story they are told first. So, you break the video, put it out there and talk about how someone abused a staff member and then tried to blackmail you. We get the video out there first, and put our context around it."

Lincoln's eyes narrowed on Opal for a long moment. "It is an option, Opal. But... I'd rather avoid it being in the public eye at all. If we catch the guys, we'll have good reason to get them arrested. Let's get Kenny in and Madeline in on this. Kenny was a genius last weekend."

Cheyenne had heard Kenny's name around the office. He was a fixer and a close friend to Katherine O'Malley, but Cheyenne had never met him. And she had no idea what might have happened the previous weekend, though there were rumors about Lizbeth and the Chinese Embassy making the rounds.

Opal scribbled in her book. "Of course. I'll get on it right away."

"Between Madeline, Kenny, and Dallas, they'll come up with a perfect solution," Link said. "Cheyenne, make sure Opal has your brother's information."

Link met Opal's eyes and tipped his head toward the door, silently telling her to leave. Opal grabbed her notebook from the desk and held it tight to her chest as she left Cheyenne alone with Link.

Once the door was closed, Lincoln got up from his chair and came around to the front of his desk. He settled back against it, half-sitting, half-leaning against it with his arms clasped in front of him. "Cheyenne, no matter how we play this, you have to face up to the fact you might still wind up all over the internet. Everyone you know is going to see you..."

*Xander. Dallas. Sky. Her whole family.* What would her mother think? They'd all been pretty open and positive about sex, but what she'd done had been wild. Unconventional. It was more about privacy and her ability to control who knew. It was one thing for her to choose to share this with Sky or Xander or whoever. It was something else to just have it out there for anyone to watch. She refused to be ashamed of the night. She was, however, disappointed and angry at herself for not considering this as a possible outcome.

Not that she had to worry about this in the future. She was done with three-ways. She was done with all other guys. The only man she wanted to be with was Xander. Just thinking about him calmed her nerves.

"I refuse to be embarrassed by the content, sir. Lots of people have ménages. Lots of people fantasize about them and do it. It's not illegal. I'm not married, I'm not seeing anyone."

*Or I wasn't at the time. Not really.*

What would Xander say about this? It had been less than two hours since she'd suggested Xander take a sexy picture of her. Would he think she'd offered to do the porn based on that? *Ugh.* It was one thing to tell him that she'd recently had a ménage, something else to show it to him. What would he think when he saw her with two other men blown up on the big screen?

"The truth is, sir, there are plenty of reasons why I don't want this to go public. I appreciate your willingness to help squash it before it gets that far."

Lincoln put a reassuring hand on her shoulder. "For now, go about your day as if this isn't happening, best you can. We will see what we can do to stop this hard and fast. Beyond the blackmail, there is some possibility the men might sell this somewhere, you know, for pornographic enjoyment."

Cheyenne had seen her share of porn with various boyfriends. Even without being an expert, she could tell that this video was as good as a lot of stuff out there. Being a porn star was not something she'd consented to, however.

"Sir, I'd really appreciate any help you're willing to give me to destroy every single frame of this."

Lincoln squeezed her shoulder and removed his hand. "Like I said. We'll do our best. But there are no guarantees. I just want you to be prepared. I've had a lot of bad things said about me, and I've gotten used to the flurry of fury over minutia. Unfortunately, you and I both know that the words they'll be slinging at you if this gets out are much more...offensive."

"Thank you, sir. I understand you can't control everything."

And then it hit her. *Kitchen Wars. Shit.* One of the clauses in the competition was that the contestants couldn't be famous by any other means. Contestants had to be unknowns without any sensationalistic history—and certainly nothing that denigrated the show. Being the star in a porn video would ruin everything for them all. Chelsea, Tiffany, and Zach would never forgive her.

Cheyenne smiled to cover her rising panic as she left his office. She had less than twenty minutes left to get herself together before the hearings began. There was no place for her to run.

Cheyenne walked back to her desk in a daze. If the video got out, she and her friends would be kicked out of *Kitchen Wars*. Xander had been cool about her ménage, but what would he think about her being plastered all over the internet with two other men?

Cheyenne sent a frantic text to Nia to see if she could see her later in the day or talk over the phone. She had no idea how to approach Xander. Was the possibility of the video leaking enough to tell him about it? If they were successful in destroying all traces of the damn thing, maybe Xander never needed to know it existed.

Nia texted back that she was in a conference the rest of the day and unavailable, but confirmed they were scheduled for Monday. Cheyenne wasn't sure she could last five days without help.

She didn't need the thumb drive to find the website. The download link let her send a message without a file, so she wrote out what Link had told her to—an excuse about why she couldn't hand them anything immediately and that the security on the system was so tight the only way she could give them any information would be the old fashioned way, on paper. She gave them her phone number and told them to contact her with a meeting location for ten o'clock Friday night. She'd have something to hand over by then.

Cheyenne followed Katherine down the corridor and into the hearing room in silence. She could sit behind Katherine and three aides from other offices who were there to help the people actually testifying at the hearing without interacting with anyone. Cheyenne spent the first hour of the hearings ignoring everything. She sat in her chair with a fake half-smile, pretending to pay attention while her mind raced in quiet circles over the situation.

At some point, she managed to calm herself down enough to keep from going into a panic attack. People were watching, after all. Nothing was certain yet, and she put all her hope and confidence in her brother and Kenny and the congressman at the forefront. They would help her out of this, and things would be fine. They had to be.

Cheyenne shifted her focus to the hearings and her current surroundings. The mostly male voices and general nature of the content made Cheyenne want to burst out of the room and go for a run. To scream at the top of her lungs. To do something. Anything other than to be in that room.

At some point, Cheyenne became aware that something was up with Katherine. Kat would occasionally turn around and glare at a man several rows behind them. She was usually a little more controlled than that, but there was something about the way the man first grinned at Kat, then, after a few hours of her glaring at him, finally glared back.

At lunch, Kat handed Cheyenne her stack of binders to take back to the office before disappearing with the stranger down the hall. There was an energy between Kat and the tall handsome man—sexual, romantic, explosive. As they disappeared into the construction zone, Cheyenne focused on keeping herself sane for the rest of the day. She only had to make it a few more hours.

After dropping the files back on her desk she checked her messages. Dallas had texted to confirm he was in contact with Kenny and Eleanor. They were working on things from their end. Relief flooded through her, but it was mitigated by the fact that everything that mattered to her was now up in the air. She had to trust in all of them to fix something she'd broken.

It was nine-thirty on the west coast, and she had yet to hear from Jason. All she wanted was to call Xander and tell him about the video, the blackmail, and the competition. If he didn't run after all of that, nothing would scare him away.

Cheyenne walked to the cafe at the Supreme Court. It was decent food and fast, and she needed to eat something. She chose meatloaf and mashed potatoes with a side of dark chocolate cake—comfort food. Her plan was to sit in a corner by herself and stuff herself into calmness.

As Cheyenne searched for a place to sit a woman's trilling laughter bounced around the room. It was light and joyous, exactly the opposite of how she felt.

At least someone was happy. Cheyenne scanned the crowded tables to see who it was, and stopped dead when she saw Xander at a table with another woman— the laughing woman.

She was a couple years younger than Cheyenne, and much prettier. The other woman reached her hand across the table and placed her hand on Xander's forearm, squeezing it. Her eyes were filled with tears, and Xander placed his hand over hers and kept it there. They sat there, gazing into each others eyes like long-lost lovers.

Cheyenne's world swam around her and threatened to swallow her up whole. She staggered toward the closest table and paused, leaning against it to gather herself.

She had spent so much time thinking about what would drive Xander away from her, she'd never considered what would drive her away from him. And now she knew, without a doubt, she would not tolerate another woman. That fact was suddenly abundantly clear.

Straightening up and rounding her shoulders, Cheyenne marched straight to the table where Xander sat with the beautiful blond, her bubbly laughter jabbing at Cheyenne with every trill.

"Hello, Xander," Cheyenne said, her voice level and cool. Detached. She slammed her tray onto the table.

His eyes met Cheyenne's as they widened into giant round saucers of surprise. They dropped to look at their intertwined hands before returning to Cheyenne.

"Chey...Cheyenne," he said, finally pulling his hands from the other woman, obviously guilty. "What a surprise."

"I bet," she said. Before he could get a lame excuse

out, she lifted her plate and flipped it onto his head. For extra measure, she pushed the plate with the palm of her hand against him. The sensation of meatloaf squashing into his hair gave her immense satisfaction.

Gravy oozed down his face and neck and onto his shirt. The blond had shoved herself away from the table and stared at Cheyenne with a gaping mouth and eyes wide and round. Beautiful big blue eyes, of course.

Cheyenne backed away a couple of steps before spinning on her toe and running from the cafeteria as fast as she could, leaving the mess and her dignity behind. While dumping a load of drippy food on him was freeing, it had been childish and rash. She didn't regret it doing it but hoped no one had caught it on video. It would do nothing to help her remain a contestant on *Kitchen Wars*.

Had everything Xander had said and done with her been an act? How many women were he stringing along?

For once, there was no one in the security line at the Cannon Building. Cheyenne charged through it and made straight for the staff bathroom. After locking herself into a stall, she forced herself to breathe. She had known it was too good to be true.

While she hadn't sent Xander running with any of her personal revelations, she wasn't going to let herself be taken advantage of by another man. He was like any other guy in DC—saying one thing while living a lie.

Cheyenne had to put herself back together and get back to the hearing. She wiped her face and added more drops to clear the red from her eyes. Just as she entered the hearing room, a text chimed from Jason. He'd gotten her messages and she was now free to tell Carleen and Xander about the competition.

Perfect timing.

## Chapter 21

Cheyenne had to get through a few more hours of work before she could escape and wallow alone in her personal agony. The video, the blackmail, Xander...it was all too much at once. And yet, she was going to do her best to buck up and do her job. She hadn't been fired, not yet anyway, and she wasn't going to shirk her duties. Now that there was a real chance she might be booted from the show, she had to keep her job as her back-up plan—continue working and saving.

Cheyenne slid into her seat next to Katherine with all her materials with a few minutes to spare. The hunky man Kat had gone off with at lunch was called to testify. He was a scientist named Gerard Porter, and he didn't take his eyes off Kat the entire time he was testifying. The longing in Gerard's eyes was unmistakable.

*Very subtle, dude.*

Watching this guy drool over Kat didn't make it easy for Cheyenne to not dwell on her own problems. Xander was a liar professing his love for her in the morning only to be off with another woman within hours. Cheyenne was being blackmailed by two assholes. And her best friends had no idea that their dream might be coming to a crashing end—all because of her. How was she going to tell them about the video and how it might get them booted from the competition? Cheyenne closed her eyes, wishing the world to go away while she covered herself in blankets to hide away from the world.

Near the end of the day, she was buzzed out of her reverie as Dallas texted her to meet him so she could hand over the thumb drive. Spending time with her big brother would help her figure things out. He was almost as good as Nia for advice, though his always came with a bit of an agenda.

She and Xander had made tentative plans for the evening, but she wasn't about to show up at his apartment now. He'd made his choice by staying silent and not following her out of the cafeteria. And he hadn't even texted her in the intervening four hours. That was telling in itself. Cheyenne fought back tears as she texted Dallas she'd be there with the thumb drive.

Dallas was waiting for her at Domingo's—a South American tapas bar. He had already ordered a couple of appetizers by the time she got there.

The lack of lunch was getting to her, so she picked up a skewer of beef and nibbled at it. Even her taste buds had gone numb. She dropped the flavorless meat back onto her plate.

Dallas held out his hand. "Give me the drive."

She fished it out of her pocket and handed it to him.

He examined it closely. "Nothing unusual about this. Probably bought at Target." He dropped it into his shirt pocket and buttoned it. "I'll delve into it asap."

Cheyenne ordered a martini.

"Cheyenne? What's going on?" Dallas asked as the waitress was out of ear shot. "You only drink the hard stuff when you're upset. You know we're going to take care of this, right?'

She tossed him her best fake smile. "Between you, Madeline's spin and Kenny's genius, I'm sure you'll fix everything."

"Kenny is awesome. Only heard about him before this, but he's fucking brilliant. We talked strategy for a while today. I'm betting we can make this disappear, but if not, Kenny will swing the spin around somehow."

"You should throw me under the bus to make sure Congressman Pierce comes out okay."

"What? You don't think your worth is as much as Link's? Don't sell yourself short, kid."

"I'm not a kid anymore, Dallas."

"Yeah, I kinda saw a bit of how not a kid you are today." He opened his eyes wide. "Are my eyes still red from all the bleach?"

She punched him in the shoulder. "Any idea who might be behind all this?"

"I'm tracking down some leads." Dallas clenched his jaw and put his hands out flat on the table. "Time for some straight talk Cheyenne."

"I thought we were talking straight."

"There are a couple of ways this could go. I do a lot of shit that isn't strictly legal. So does Kenny. We fix things, get things done and, sometimes, we break the law in order to preserve status quo. There are different kinds of justice. Putting away someone for a year or two might get you legal justice, but all that shit that goes into evidence has a way of getting out there. If you really want to hide this video, you might have to settle for something other than an arrest."

"Dallas? What are you suggesting?"

"I'm suggesting we do this all covertly. Get the

information we need, find out who did this, and squash it like a bug."

"But if we do that, they, whoever *they* are, won't go to jail."

"There are worse things than jail for some people."

Cheyenne knew Dallas lived his life in shades of grey, now she was experiencing it first hand. "Like what?" she asked.

"Depends on the situation. In this case, I suspect whoever is behind this will do just about anything to keep their involvement from getting out, and they'd let someone else take a fall for them. I can guarantee you the bit players in this will be easy to catch, but the person who benefits most will be impossible to convict."

"Let me see if I have this straight. If we catch someone and try to press charges, this video will end up everywhere anyway?"

"Basically."

"But, there is a chance we could...erm...exact some sort of personal revenge on them and destroy any chance it will see the light of day?"

"You've got it."

"I'll go for personal revenge and absolute squashing."

"I was hoping you would say that. I know it runs counter to taking the high road at some level, but..."

Dallas rubbed his hands together, "sometimes you gotta do what you gotta do. We're working on getting the information from the hotel. Not needing a warrant makes it easier."

Cheyenne sipped at her drink and sighed a big one.

"All right," he said. "Out with it."

"What?"

"Oh, come on. You just did the sighing thing."

"I don't know what you're talking about."

"Cheyenne, the big, breathy sigh thing you always do when you have a problem you don't know how to deal with, but you can't quite come out and ask for advice. You do it expecting one of us to ask you what's wrong. I'm asking. What's wrong? I mean, besides the fact you're being blackmailed."

"I...have a lot going on. The hearings at the office, the video. Xander." His name slid out with another sigh. Even she noticed it now. Telling Dallas she'd fallen hard for Xander and already lost him would be humiliating. If she told him she'd seen Xander with another woman, Dallas would probably go beat him up or hire a hit man or something equally testosterone driven.

At the mention of Xander, Dallas clapped his hands together. "By the way, his background came back clean enough. He travels a lot to some sketchy places—Syria, Pakistan, Iran—but he's on the up and up."

Cheyenne let her head drop for a second. "Of course he's on the...for crying out loud. Did you *actually* do a background check on him?" In spite of being distraught over Xander, she couldn't quite believe Dallas had *actually* done the promised background check. As far as she knew, he'd never gone through with his big-brother boasty threats.

"Duh. Told you I would. He's what he says he is. No prior marriages, no kids, and financially secure. He had a little thing at his job come close to blowing up in his face. Undergrads must be all wet in the panties in his class. He got too close to one, but it he didn't cross the line. There were some pretty damning allegations, but they eventually cleared him of some scary child porn charges." Dallas popped an olive in his mouth and followed it with a swig of his beer.

"Child porn?" No way. Not Xander. Even if he was a cheating liar, there was no way he'd be involved in anything like that.

"There was a student at GW who was only seventeen who sent him some selfies. Naked selfies. The good thing is he deleted them off his phone and dismissed her from class. Exactly what a good prof is supposed to do, but she brought some other charges against him. A retaliatory sort of thing, it turns out. But there were a few witnesses who swore that he led her on and welcomed her advances. It's hard to know for sure. He was eventually cleared and reinstated to his part time work at GW. In the meantime, he'd taken a full time gig at the Smithsonian."

"I knew he wouldn't be guilty of anything like that."

"It's pretty straightforward. He had a girl with a crush come after him, he flirted a little like a lot of profs do, not knowing she wasn't eighteen. She was a freshman in college. He made assumptions. He squashed the crush as soon as he found out she was two months shy of her eighteenth birthday, and she retaliated. Nothing happened between them. She eventually fessed up to making a big stink because she was embarrassed."

No wonder Xander had blanched when she suggested he take a photo of her. Anything to do with pictures would make him anxious. What would he say about the video of her with two men if a simple photo was that nerve-wracking to him? Not that it mattered anymore. What was she thinking? She'd dumped him in a very memorable way in public.

"Anyhoo. Xander was born in the US. Mom is Pakistani. Dad is American. His dad converted so his mom could stay Muslim. Xander's iffy on the religion thing. Doesn't attend a local mosque or hang out with any radical elements. No arrests. No speeding tickets. Perfect record."

"Radical elements?" In spite of her aching heart, she couldn't see Xander being part of anything other than academia. But she'd also thought he was telling her the truth when he had said he loved her. "Have you done background checks on all the guys I've dated?"

"Hell no. I'd be out of a job. This guy has been different from the beginning."

The familiar prickling of tears forming again made Cheyenne look away from him. She was going to be out of eye drops soon if she didn't get a grip on herself.

"Sorry. Why don't you tell me what's really bugging you. You know you want to," he said.

Cheyenne closed her eyes and shook her head to clear the jumble of thoughts tumbling around. It was time for a change in subject. It didn't appear as though anyone was paying them any attention, but she leaned in close to Dallas. She just hadn't taken the time to tell anyone in her family about the competition yet.

"Here's the big thing going on. I mean, other than the blackmail big thing. We auditioned for *Kitchen Wars* a few months ago—Chelsea, Tiffany, Zach and me. We signed all this paperwork that made it so we weren't allowed to tell anyone we had even auditioned. Sunday night we went through the last round of auditions in person and were chosen to be a team on the show. We're allowed to tell family, though, now that we're on the show. Just you, Mom and Sky. Not the kids. They won't understand keeping their mouths shut."

"Whoa, really? Cheyenne, that's awesome! Isn't that the one where you have to go live in LA for a few months?"

She tapped her finger to her nose and pointed at him. "That's the one."

"Wait. How is this making you miserable? This is the kind of thing that could totally launch your restaurant. Isn't that what you want?"

"Yes, but...this whole video thing? Part of our contract is we can't be famous by any other means and we have to all have a clean history. If this video makes it onto the internet, and I am connected with it? They'll boot us from the show before we even get to LA."

"Do the others know about the video?"

"No. I haven't even been home since I got the thumb drive." Had it only been ten hours since her life had been turned upside down the first of multiple times in one day?

"Shit. Well. I'll just work that much harder to convince whoever did this pays for it." Dallas's strong jaw worked back and forth.

His teeth clicked together and his chest heaved with a big breath. Her big brother was clearly wanting to kick someone's butt as much as she was.

"It also means quitting my job and leaving Congressman Pierce's office. Wouldn't that upset you?"

Dallas gaped at her as if she'd sprouted antennae and wings. "Why would it? You don't really belong in an office like you do a kitchen."

"But...running a restaurant? It's not serving my country."

"Uh, okay? Why would you care about that?"

Cheyenne stared at Dallas her mouth dropping open in disbelief. "In your valedictorian speech, you said we all have a duty to serve our country. That's why you enlisted instead of going to college."

Dallas scrunched up his face as he thought about it. "Don't remember the details. That was a long time ago."

Everything Cheyenne had done to get to the congressman's office had been because of Dallas' valedictorian speech. She had lived with the ideal of serving her country as being her goal because of it. And he didn't *remember it?*

Dallas grabbed both of Cheyenne's hands and squeezed them between his big thick fingers. His hands were rough and calloused even though he had a day job.

"Cheyenne, I really have no idea what my graduation speech has to do with this. I had assumed that your job, the one you get paid for, was *your* life's goal. That you had *settled* to let cooking be just a hobby. I always thought if I complimented you on your cooking or got to enthusiastic about it, you'd feel bad for not pursuing it."

Cheyenne had made a habit of giving away lots of food. She brought treats to the family dinners and handed over quantities of sweets at the office. Her office workers had always been enthusiastic, saying she could own a bakery. Dallas had always been less than enthusiastic, but not for the reason she had always assumed. Why had he held out on her for so long?

"I don't remember you ever saying you wanted to *own* a restaurant before. But that doesn't really matter. What I don't understand is what you said about serving the country. Why would you think that you had to do that?"

"I remember every word. You said, '*We may want to do a lot of things in our lives, but there is only one path for me to bring sense to the loss in my life. It will surprise no one that I have decided to put college aside for now so I might serve my country and bring my family some closure to the hurt and pain we're feeling.*

*Honor and country, it must be the mantra that fills my life.'"*

Dallas' jaw had gone slack and he held his palms up empty. "Why you are dredging that up right now?"

"Honor and country. How could I go off and be a chef, and have fun with my life every day, when honor and country is above all?"

"Cheyenne, I was talking about *myself*. What *I* needed to do. Why the hell would you think it applied to you?"

"You have spent your life devoted in service. How could I do any less?"

Dallas wiped at his face with his palms. "You were what, ten, when Dad was killed? Eleven when I graduated?"

"So?"

"You misunderstood my speech. That's all. It wasn't a charge to everyone in the room. It was a declaration of my desire to do something directly to honor Dad's memory. To combat what I saw as an evil in the world."

Cheyenne's stomach flipped. She tore apart Dallas' words from so many years ago, trying to see it from his point of view. Had he really only been talking about himself? It had felt like a rally cry to her, that everyone in the room should do something meaningful.

"Hold on, Dallas, later in that very same speech,

you said that everyone in that room should do something meaningful, to go beyond the basics and reach for the higher cause."

"Yeah, but I didn't mean for people to choose careers that would make them miserable. It was more about finding the higher purpose in what you love to do."

"So why did you treat my cooking like a hobby?"

Dallas shrugged and scrunched up his face at her. "Because you were treating it like a hobby instead of actively pursuing it."

"You aren't upset about me wanting to run a restaurant?"

"No. I had no idea you hated what you are doing so much. I want you to be happy, and, if cooking for other people makes you happy, then you should do it. You should outright quit, anyway. Now."

"Really? I'm not exactly miserable all the time."

"*Not exactly miserable all the time* is a pretty low bar."

Cheyenne took a sip of her drink. "Yeah, well... There's more, to all this. This competition means moving to LA."

Dallas leaned back with his arms over his chest, shaking his head. "Three months is not moving, Cheyenne. It's a deployment. A brief one at that. And dang cushy, to boot."

"Not that cushy," she said. The apartments were small and they had to share a room. She liked her privacy.

"If you're not sleeping on a cot and needing to check for scorpions in your boots every time you put them on, it's cushy." He tilted his glass at her in emphasis.

Leave it to a soldier to put things in perspective.

Dallas popped an olive in his mouth and chewed on it as she ordered new drinks.

"Hey," he said. "What does Xander think of this LA gig?"

"I haven't told him yet."

"Uh-oh. Are things already going south with you two?"

There was no use in trying to hide it from him. Dallas always had a way of ferreting out details from her. "I saw Xander at lunch today with another woman. He just sat there like a kid caught with his hand in the cookie jar who wasn't going to give up the cookie for anything. I dumped my plate of food on him. Ground the meatloaf and gravy into his hair."

Dallas didn't say anything at first. It was impossible to tell what he was thinking, but then, finally he laughed. "Holy hell. Where did this take place?"

"In the cafeteria." Cheyenne looked up at the ceiling, picturing the entire scene. "At the Supreme Court."

"Oh...now, that is hilarious. Lots of people around, too, I bet?"

"Yeah, well...the two of them were all but fucking on the table. Hands together, eyes all googly." The exaggeration made her actions sound more logical, justified. In hindsight, dumping food all over someone in public like that was not her most brilliant plan.

"Oh, man, Cheyenne..." Dallas said, his features hardening. "That's weird. He wasn't dating anyone else as of Saturday."

Cheyenne leaned forward. "Wait, your background checks are that detailed? Really?"

"We have access to data that will surprise you," Dallas said. "But, yeah. He hasn't been out on a date since before Christmas. Maybe he was with his sister? He has lunch with his sister once a week. Usually on Monday. He canceled this week, though." Dallas leveled his gaze at her and his smile went away. "I hear the orchid house is pretty amazing this time of year."

That level of knowledge was scarier than it was comforting. She eyed her brother for a moment, fully realizing what it was he did for a living, as the color drained from her face. How much did he *know*? How much was smart conjecture?

He waggled his eyebrows at her and grinned.

"Yeah, I get that look from a lot of people when they finally understand what's out there in the world. Your social media trail. Your credit card statements. Your email. Your texts. Most people have no idea."

"If you were really watching, you would know this woman was blonder than I am. Curly blond." She gave him a description of what she had seen. The way Xander had touched the other woman. His guilty 'oh' and lack of action afterward.

Dallas scrunched up his face. "Well, damn. Definitely not his sister. Amira is gorgeous, but she's almost the female twin to Xander. Dark, long hair down to her waist, but with brown eyes, not green. So, you saw him with this unidentified blond bombshell. Did you talk to him? I mean, after you covered him with meatloaf."

"No. I ran away."

"Of course you did."

"What do you mean by that?"

Dallas pursed his lips for a second. "*Nothing*. How about this? I'm going to go check out the thumb drive and see if there's anything I can get off it. You, my darling sister, need to stop jumping to conclusions and making assumptions. Go find Xander and ask him who the woman was." He dumped a bunch of cash out onto the table and kissed her on the cheek. "I'll check in with you later."

Dallas left her alone with the remainder of their

tapas. She closed her eyes and replayed the moment in the cafeteria over and over in her head. She wasn't jumping to wrong conclusions. The other woman was quite intimate with Xander. And he with her. The way she touched him. The way he covered her hand with his. They acted like lovers. What other reason could there be?

Besides, if it was all innocent, wouldn't Xander have said something when she approached? Why hadn't he texted her all afternoon since then? No. She wasn't wrong. Xander had been playing her.

## Chapter 22

Cheyenne ordered another drink and downed it in a couple of swallows. Soon enough, the pain and confusion would slip away or at least be obscured by a buzzing and pleasant nothingness. Things would sort themselves out one way or another, and she might as well get some relief where she could.

Three different men approached her to see if they could buy her a drink, and she declined each politely. They all looked like normal, nice guys. Much like Kyle and Shane had appeared to her. As a fourth stranger approached her table, she considered taking him up on his offer just so she could find some physical relief in a one-night stand. But she couldn't. There was no way. Even though things might be over with Xander, she couldn't let herself fall back into quick, meaningless sex with strangers. She'd come too close to perfection with Xander.

Cheyenne wandered aimlessly, letting her feet guide her. After a while, she found herself at the National Mall directly across from the Smithsonian Castle. The red brick building had always been so romantic to her. Had it only been five days ago that she'd considered kissing Xander there for the office Bingo game? Why had she decided not to play? What would she do now if *Kitchen Wars* didn't work out?

She should go home and crawl into bed with a pint of ice cream. And a big tall glass of whiskey. Cheyenne spun away from the building with fresh determination to go home and wallow in her misery and get completely blotto.

She didn't get more than twenty feet when Xander stepped in front of her.

"There you are," he said. "Your brother told me you were at Domingo's but I must have just missed you."

"My brother?"

"Yeah. He told me you were there with him over an hour ago."

Cheyenne took a moment to consider this. She couldn't tell if it made no sense because she had had too much to drink or if it made no sense because *why would Dallas have called Xander?* He may be her big brother, but he had no right to call Xander.

"Dallas?"

*Argh.* She didn't need her big brother always trying to fix things for her.

Xander's eyes widened in exasperation. "I thought we'd established that. Yes. Your brother, *Dallas*, unless you have another one I don't know about, told me you were at Domingo's. By the time I got there, you were already gone. I've spent the last hour looking for you. I gave up and was heading back to my car when I found you gaping up at the Castle."

"Why would he do that?" Cheyenne asked, still trying to piece everything together. Maybe that last drink had been a bad idea.

"I explained to him about our, erm, misunderstanding this afternoon. I couldn't chase after you covered..." he broke off abruptly. "Anyway, none of that matters right now."

"Right," Cheyenne said. "The gorgeous blond you were snuggling with at lunch...doesn't matter. Let me guess...she's your sister, right?" Alcohol had loosened her tongue and sharpened her voice into a nagging, braying tone.

Xander stepped back as if she had hit him. "I'm not sure what, exactly, you think you saw. Snuggling? Really?" He ran both hands through his hair as his mouth moved silently for a moment. His curls bunched together and straightened out into thick tufts on his head. "Snuggling? We were hardly snuggling. Your attitude isn't helping."

Cheyenne crossed her arms and frowned hard. "Whatever. Say what you have to say and leave me be."

Xander let out an exasperated groan. He grasped her shoulders, and his long fingers poked into her. When she eyed his hands with the coldest expression she could manage, he let go, holding both up in a gesture of surrender.

"Cheyenne, what I have to say to you has changed three times in the last thirty seconds. I'm not even sure who you are right now. Maybe we should leave this until later."

"That's just fine with me," she said, teetering toward him. Was he swaying or was that her? The whiskey she'd downed just before leaving the bar was hitting her hard all of a sudden.

"Are you drunk?" he asked, taking her by her shoulders more gently this time, his eyes shifting from annoyance to concern. He sniffed at her and shrank back, fanning a hand over his nose. "Oh, boy. You *have* been drinking."

"You said you didn't have a problem with me drinking," she said, challenging him on the point.

"Drinking wine at dinner is one thing, getting drunk is quite another. Let's get you home, shall we?" Xander tried to reach an arm around her waist, but she spun away from him.

"We? Is there a *we*, Xander? Was there ever a *we*?" she asked, trying to keep herself from turning into a blubbering idiot. "Or was it all a story? This whole, I need time thing? Did you need time with blondie? She was so all over you."

Xander's teeth clicked against each other as his jaw set. "You're embarrassing yourself, Cheyenne. My car is only a couple blocks away. Let me drive you home."

Hot prickles ran up her neck and cheeks. "I can walk. The Metro isn't far." She spun away from him, but the intended effect was lost when she tripped.

Xander caught her before she fell flat on her face and scooped her into his arms.

"Looks like walking isn't working out too well for you right now."

"Let me go, Xander. I can't handle this." Her fight was all in her words. Her body rebelled against her as it melted against him, seeking as much contact as possible.

"I'm not letting you go."

"Fine. But don't think I'm happy about it, buddy."

"Cheyenne," he said, kissing her lightly on the ear.

"Claire is no match for you. She's a sweet girl, but hardly my kind of woman."

"Claire, so that's her name? Claire?" Bright and pretty just like her name.

"Indeed. She's an old friend—a student from a while back—nothing more."

"Student, huh? Was she the one you almost lost your job over?"

Xander stopped for a moment, his entire body tensing and his fingers dug into her. "What do you know about that?"

"My brother did a very thorough background check on you, Alexander Moore. I know just about everything there is to know about you," Cheyenne said, the lie brazenly slipping out with the vapors of the whiskey.

"I see," he said, and started walking again.

"You can put me down. I can walk, you know."

Instead, he tightened his arms around her and hugged her closer.

"Claire was a student, but that is it. We met when I taught a summer program at her boarding school. I can't explain the details because there are some confidences involved, but you'll have to just trust me. If you can. She called on me to help her out. Professionally. That's it."

*Trust me. If you can.*

Cheyenne didn't have an easy answer for him or a quick one. "How could you not see what I was seeing?" she asked.

"I did. But I figured you'd understand when I explained it to you. You didn't give me a chance. It's not like I could do much after you dumped food all over me."

"Oh god. The gravy. What a mess. You were so shocked."

"I was stunned speechless. Literally. You were out of there so fast, I couldn't get my wits about me to stop you from running."

Cheyenne covered her face with her hands. "I've never done anything like that before. I was so sure..."

"And you were so wrong. Then when you didn't answer my texts, I was frantic trying to find you."

"What texts? I didn't get any texts from you this afternoon. Nothing."

"I sent you about twenty texts, and you didn't respond to any. That's why I called Dallas."

"Wait. You called Dallas? He didn't call you?"

"No. He didn't call me. I called him. I was frantic with worry when you didn't respond. I tried calling you, but I got a message that my number was blocked."

This was all so confusing. How would Xander have Dallas' number, anyway? "I didn't block you. I have no idea what's going on."

"You didn't? I thought maybe you were so angry you'd blocked me and I'd never get a chance to explain it to you."

"You don't have another girlfriend?" she asked, her lips buzzing against his neck.

"No. Claire is just a friend. I promise. She is in a terrible situation and needed my help. All you saw was me consoling her."

Cheyenne drew her head away from its comfortable perch on his shoulder to look for twitchy lips and droopy eyelids. His jaw was set and determined, but he wasn't lying. When they got to his car, he carefully set her on the passenger seat and buckled her in. The world swam around her.

"Remind me to not mix wine and whiskey in the future, 'kay?"

"No problem," he said, patting her cheek. He paused before closing the door. "You're not going to get sick are you?"

"Teslas are washable, aren't they?" she asked. The look on his face was pretty close to the one he'd had after dumping gravy all over him. She shooed him away from the door. "No, silly, I am not anywhere near that drunk."

While Xander had said he'd be cool with her having wine, getting wasted was not something he was down with. She would prove to him that she wasn't really that far gone. After a few minutes of silence, she opened her phone to look for his texts. There were none from Xander after the cafeteria incident.

"I didn't get any texts from you, erm, after lunch," she said.

"I sent them. Take a look for yourself." He handed her his phone and gave her his passcode.

Indeed, there was a long row of texts. The words clicked into hyper focus. The first was a simple request for her to calm down and contact him ASAP. This was followed by an explanation of his friendship with Claire, how he was helping her through a hard time.

The last couple of messages were simple pleas for her to contact him ASAP and imploring her to at least be willing to talk.

She compared the phones side by side. He'd sent the texts. But there was nothing on her phone. And she hadn't gotten a text from anyone other than Dallas the whole day.

"It's not just you," Cheyenne realized. "I usually get one or two texts from Tiff or Chelsea. This is... weird." Maybe there was an explanation for all of this, but she'd have to figure it out tomorrow when she was totally sober. "I'll have to call my carrier tomorrow and see what's happening. I've had miscellaneous texts go missing before, but this many? I don't know..." The timing of the glitch sucked big time. It was the number she'd given to the blackmailers. What if they'd been trying to text her and they couldn't get through? She wouldn't know where to meet them.

She hid her rising panic from Xander and stared out the window the rest of the ride home. She welcomed back the alcohol haze she'd been trying to push away. Xander found a spot right in front of the building. He helped her out of the car, but she insisted on walking. He supported her with his arm around her waist as they climbed the stairs together. No one answered his knock on the door.

"Everyone is at work," she said as she opened her purse and fished through it for her key.

"Great. Perfect timing."

"What's that supposed to mean?" She handed him her purse. "Find my keys, will you?"

"We're finally alone at your place and you're too drunk for sex." Xander riffled through her purse until he found her key ring.

Cheyenne took the keys from him and flipped to the right one and managed to fit it into the lock on the first try. "See? Not really drunk. Just a little bit tipsy."

She pushed the door open into the darkness of her empty apartment and stepped inside. She put her hand out to bar him from entering. "Thanks for getting me home, but I think you should leave."

"Let me tuck you in?"

"She really is just a friend?"

"Yes. I swear."

"I'm sorry about the meatloaf and gravy."

"It was pretty tasty, actually," he said, his lips twisting into a smile.

He had no idea how messed up she really was, did he? "Xander. I...honestly? This thing between us terrifies me. When I saw you with another woman, my world crashed around me."

"Let me help you build it back up. I'm not going anywhere, Cheyenne. Not unless you really want me to leave."

"I don't. I want you to come inside and never go away," she said, opening the door wide and allowing him to come in.

He kicked the door shut behind him and wrapped his arms around her. Cheyenne leaned into him, breathing in his scent again.

He kissed her neck.

"Forgive me? I was stupid. I should have wiped the gravy out of my eyes and chased after you."

"Forgive me for jumping to conclusions?"

He kissed her gently at first. It morphed into a genuine and mutual hunger between them. Cheyenne unbuttoned his shirt and shoved it off his shoulders.

"I want you, Xander. Spend the night."

Her head spun with the giddy excitement of it all.

Xander wasn't a liar. It wasn't all over between them. Not yet.

She had survived losing him for a few hours already, and it gave her courage to face the challenge Nia had given her. If he couldn't stand by her side with all the crazy things going on in her life, then she shouldn't want him anyway.

She had been ready to leave him because of another woman. She knew her limits even if she didn't yet know his.

*Shit.* She couldn't sleep with him without telling him everything.

Cheyenne broke their embrace and stepped back, her hands sliding down his arms and grabbing at his. "Xander. I have more things you need to know about me. Before we...finally have sex."

"More?" He blinked.

"Yeah. More stuff."

"Wow. Okay? You've already hit me with some pretty heavy stuff, Cheyenne." He laced his fingers with hers and pressed his forehead against hers. "Maybe this should wait until morning. You're still tipsy. I can hear it in your speech."

"Spend the night anyway? No drunk sex. Just cuddling." And another reprieve meant she'd have him in her arms at least one more night.

Cheyenne led him to her room. They stripped out

of their clothes, hungry eyes lapping up every detail. He lifted the covers and followed her into the bed, their naked bodies spooning together.

"Are you sure?" she asked. His erection pressing against her bottom only fueled her drunken desire for him.

His arms tightened around her. "You said you had something to tell me?"

Cheyenne raced through the options and picked the easiest. She described the initial audition for *Kitchen Wars*. The strict NDA. The Sunday dinner. She gave him the briefest description of their restaurant design. How the contest worked, and how she'd be gone for three months. When she was finished, he didn't talk for so long she was worried he'd fallen asleep and missed that crucial last element.

"Three months?" he asked, finally. "And you can only talk to someone once a week for ten minutes?"

"Yes."

Another long silence followed. Had she lost him? Was three months the deal breaker for him? She sucked in air, fending off panic. Why wasn't he saying anything? After what seemed like ages, he cleared his throat.

"You think your family would be willing to Skype with you? I mean, with us all together?"

Cheyenne's throat tightened as his words sunk in.

He was willing to share her with her family? And, the man was brilliant. She hadn't even considered a group call. He was loving. Kind. How could she have expected anything less from him? Why had she feared he would tell her there was no way he would wait three months for her?

He kissed her on the back of the neck. "Honestly, I don't want you to go away so soon after meeting you. Right as we are getting to know each other. But this is your dream. Jaani, if you have a dream, I must help you find it. If it means us being apart for a short time...then so be it."

Cheyenne had expected...what? That he would spring up from the bed and curse her? No. Deep down she'd known.

"Do you want to make love?" she asked quietly, offering it up in spite of knowing there was still more to tell but afraid she'd outrun her luck.

"Yes, but not now. I want you to be one hundred percent sober the first time we make love."

He wiggled in close against her, removing any space between them until his torso fit perfectly against hers. After slipping his arm in around her waist, he cupped her breast and rolled her nipple between thumb and forefinger.

"Um. You know... Getting mixed signals here," she said.

He released her nipple and smoothed his palm over it, finally bringing his hand to lay across her belly.

"Okay, my sweet. This, my gorgeous woman, is snuggling."

Cheyenne basked in the warmth of his arms and lay awake as he fell asleep holding her. Soon, his hand went lax though his arm was still draped over her side. His gentle snoring rifled across the back of her neck. She would have to get used to that.

She breathed in the scent of him, memorized the cadence of his snore—turning it into an endearing music—and savoring the time she had with him. She had a bad feeling about how he would respond to the video tapes and the blackmail threat. When she'd told him she had more to tell him, he'd shown some hesitancy. His silence between her telling him about the show and her three month absence had been a long and uncomfortable one—and it was pretty obvious to her that he'd struggled with coming to the answer he did. Her continuous barrage of issues was taking a toll on him.

Given how freaked out he had been over her offering to pose for him that morning and what Dallas had told her, she bet the video might be a bigger deal for him than her infertility. Possibly the big deal breaker she'd been terrified of handing over to him since her discussion with Nia.

She wanted to be wrong. One thing she knew for certain was she had to tell Xander about the video and the blackmail scheme before the deadline on Friday night. If that video went live, she would lose more than *Kitchen Wars*. It might very well be the one thing that made Xander run.

## Chapter 23

The dream Cheyenne was having poofed away from her, leaving only the general shape and none of the gooey details in her mind. Cheyenne rolled over to watch the gentle rise and fall of Xander's chest. She had finally fallen asleep in the wee hours of the morning. Racing thoughts and a near panic attack had threatened to keep her awake all night. Every time she had a plan all figured out, some other detail rushed in to squash it.

The sound of a hair dryer broke through the remnants of her sleepy brain and she twisted around to look at her clock. She had not set her alarm. Damn. It was a quarter past eight. She had forty-five minutes to get dressed and to the office. She'd have to jam in order to get to the hearing on time.

She kissed Xander on the cheek. Then, the lips.

Then the forehead. Back to the lips. Obviously, this guy was no Disney princess. Cheyenne slid out of bed and rushed through getting dressed, making as much noise as she could. And yet, Xander slept through it all.

Finally, as she was ready to go, she climbed back on top of the bed and straddled him. Placing both hands on either side of his face, she patted his cheeks gently. "Xander. Come on, sweetie. I need to say goodbye."

He made a little sound that got her thinking he might be coming around.

Finally, she leaned close again. "Jaani," she said in a sing-song voice and trying out the word on him for the first time. "My sweet, sweet Jaani, I have to go to work."

At long last, he showed real signs of waking. His lashes fluttered and he blinked several times before wiping at his eyes to remove the crusty bits of sleep that had formed in the corners.

"What? What time is it?" He yawned and stretched, the undulations of his body a gentle wave between her legs.

"I have to go to work. I'm sorry to leave you like this."

"Right now? Really?" Xander sat up, sliding her down onto his lap.

She could feel his morning wood through the thin

fabric of her trousers. "Yes. I forgot to set the alarm, and I need to be at this hearing in half an hour."

"I'll drive you. It will be faster than the Metro."

"No. You're groggy. You take your time. Get a shower. Zach is in the kitchen cooking something."

Xander breathed out and flopped onto his back. "Okay. What about tonight? Can you come to my place?"

"Yes. But I don't know if my phone will be working. Email me instead, or call on the landline," she said. "Tell Zach I told you about the competition. He'll be so relieved he doesn't have to keep it a secret from you anymore."

By the time she closed her bedroom door behind her, Xander was back asleep.

The morning was spent in a blurry haze of focus on work. The hearings ended at noon without anything exciting happening. Cheyenne never had to open one of the many binders she'd been charged with. Once the hearings were over, Cheyenne checked her phone. New texts. None of Xander's had come through yet, either. The phone company assured her everything was working normally and she should be sending and receiving texts.

She used her office landline to call Dallas. It took her a couple times to get through as he didn't answer the first two times.

"Sorry. I didn't recognize the number. Why aren't you using your phone?"

"I think it's weird that the only text I have gotten in the last twenty-four hours is from you. Xander said he texted me multiple times yesterday. He showed me his texts, but they didn't come through."

Dallas stayed quiet for a moment, but she could hear the clicking of his keyboard in the background.

"Hmmm...did you give your phone number out to anyone?"

Cheyenne didn't even have to think about it. "Um. This may have been supremely stupid of me. But I gave it to the blackmailers."

"What? Are you fucking serious? Please tell me this is your idea of a joke."

"No. Lincoln told me to ask them to meet in person instead of uploading files to them. I don't check my email every minute, but texts come through."

"Crap. It looks like someone blocked numbers from your phone yesterday. Mine...is a special number that you can't block. Heh."

"Wait. Why?"

"Intel, baby, intel. But, let's see. Someone got into your phone and blocked incoming texts and calls. Have you noticed you haven't gotten any calls either?"

"That's not unusual. I'm used to getting texts all the time."

"I'm restoring access, but...it might take a few minutes."

"How are you doing this, Dallas? I mean...does the government have the ability to do this with anyone?"

"Nope. We don't do this at all. The government, I mean. No idea what you're talking about. This is not happening, got that, kiddo?"

Cheyénne could take a hint. "Okay. Okay. Why, though? I don't see their point."

"I suspect they did it so it would be the only text you see. Intimidation. How did it make you feel knowing someone was messing with your phone? Blocking your friends? They're trying to freak you out. Make you think they are in control." More clicking in the background. "There. I just made it look like your in-office guru did the fix. That should freak the fuckers out of their minds."

Cheyenne's phone vibrated almost no-stop for a full minute as messages poured in. All the ones that Xander had sent the previous day plus a few more he'd written that morning while she was in the hearings. Half a dozen from Chelsea, a few from both Zach and Tiffany, and even Sky.

"We still have some time left," Dallas said.

"Yeah. Lincoln is preparing a packet of documents for me to hand straight over."

"Okay. I'll keep working on it from this end.

Kenny is doing some more digging from his side of things and coming up with a strategy to kill it with fire. We'll fix this, Cheyenne. I'm really hopeful."

They had until late Friday to deal with the blackmail, so she tried to keep calm and get work done. She spent the rest of the afternoon in a debriefing meeting about the hearings, and it was blessedly easy to ignore her personal life while focusing on real work.

Lincoln Pierce's passion around renewable energies was infectious. By the end of the meeting, Cheyenne was sad that she would be leaving soon. A tiny part of her would be happy if they didn't win the competition—if she managed to keep her place in it. Working for the congressman would be a big deal in the years to come. Sure, he wasn't top of the heap yet, but he was heading there.

Lincoln had that affect on people. He was charismatic, and when he got into his campaign mode—where he got all fired up about a topic—he was mesmerizing. Intoxicating. Inspiring. The end of the day came at a high-point and everyone gathered up their things with smiles on their faces.

Dallas texted asking her to meet at her apartment later. He and Kenny had an idea they wanted to try on her. Xander had texted twice to check in about the evening, and he'd emailed just in case she wasn't able to text. She told Xander that she would have to be at home this evening. She left the reasoning vague and let him think it had to do competition prep. She suggested he come by later to give her time to deal with whatever Dallas and Kenny had in store for her.

By the time she got home, Zach, Tiffany and Chelsea were already in the kitchen working. *Kitchen Wars* usually had one or two episodes featuring unusual diets. They were supposed to be practicing their all-vegan menu. Sometimes the show added further restrictions for fun—like vegan, *and* no soy or no coconut or no nuts. Cheyenne found vegan desserts to be the hardest, especially getting the taste right with alternative fats and leavenings. In the baking world, butter and eggs were her best friends.

The whole scene was a bit too much for her right then, though, oddly, she wasn't actually panicking over everything going on in her life. Her heart rate was normal. She hadn't fled to the bathroom to calm herself at all during the day. She stifled the sigh that nearly escaped her lips. After her brother's comments, she was suddenly very aware of this habit of hers. She poked a finger at the bag of chocolate chips on the counter.

"Cheyenne? Are you okay?" Tiffany asked as she slid a knife through an eggplant.

"No," she said, surprising herself along with everyone else in the kitchen. The expected answer was always to lie and tell everyone you were fine no matter your real situation. The others had a stake in this video not getting out, too, and Cheyenne had to make sure they understood what was going on so they weren't blind-sided if the video hit the internet the following evening.

The others turned toward her, hands not moving, their eyes filled with concern and surprise.

"So, you guys, there's something going on I need to tell you about. It could impact our place in the competition."

Zach rolled a pile of dough from a bowl out onto the counter and thrust his palms into it, kneading. "Sounds serious."

"I'm being blackmailed."

All three spoke at once.

*"Who would be blackmailing you?"*

*"Why would someone blackmail you?"*

*"What the hell?"*

Cheyenne crossed her arms over her chest. "Right. So...you might remember how I had that amazing three-way last week?"

The other three exchanged anxious glances, but they remained silent, waiting for the very unfunny punchline.

"The men I was with? They recorded the whole session. And now, they think that they are going to get me to divulge secrets from the congressman's office to keep it hidden."

Zach turned back to his dough, lifting it high and dropping it down onto the table before slamming into it with his fist in a deadening punch. "Fuck that."

"What are you going to do?" asked Chelsea as she too turned back to whatever she was sautéing on the stove before it burned.

"Yikes," Tiffany said, "they have no idea who they're messing with, do they?"

None of them were upset enough. Did they not understand the implications here?

"Uhm, *you guys?* There's that clause in our contract with *Kitchen Wars?* If I become an overnight porn sensation, they'll dump us from the competition for being famous or bringing disrepute to the show— one or the other."

That got through. Chelsea slammed her sauté pan onto the back burner and turned off the one she'd been cooking on.

"I didn't think about that," Chelsea said. "Shit."

Tiffany put her knife down and wiped her hands against her apron. "After everything we've been through to get here? *Shit* is right. How did this happen, Cheyenne? Who would do something like this?"

Zach redoubled his efforts at the dough, punching it with renewed vigor. "When does this thing go live?"

"Tomorrow night—late. We still have a day to figure things out. Lincoln hired a fixer to work it with Dallas," Cheyenne said. "They're both coming over soon. They're still trying to figure out who's behind all this."

"Can we see it?" asked Zach.

"You want to watch me in a porno tape?" Cheyenne asked, torn between confusion and disgust.

"You said there were two *guys*, right?"

"I didn't think you'd be interested in anything with a naked woman in it."

"It's mostly for solidarity purposes," Zach said laughing. "Besides, two thirds of that action is all male, right?"

"You're gross, Zach," Tiffany said as she swatted him with a towel. "She's our friend. Cheyenne, just for the record, I have no desire to watch you in bed."

It was good to laugh even in the bizarre circumstances.

The doorbell buzzed. It had to be Kenny and Dallas. Cheyenne sprung for the door, not sure what it was they were up to. Excitement over possibly ending this whole episode thrummed through her. The best case scenario would be for Kenny and Dallas to make it all go away before she ever needed to tell Xander about any of it. If they could disappear the video and the blackmail, she would never need to tell him.

She had never met Kenny Vaughn, but she had not expected the man that stood before her. He was not that much older than she was. Given his reputation, she had expected a wizened older man with sparkling eyes and maybe a wizard's cloak. In fact, she'd actually heard someone talk about him as if he waved his arms and chanted incantations to get things done. There were a few stories that sure made it seem like magic had to be involved. This man was clean-shaven, impeccably dressed, and exuded calm and confidence without the slimy feeling she was used to in DC.

"Good evening, Ms. LeFleur. It's so nice to finally meet you." His voice was a silky smooth tenor that could lull her into believing anything.

There was something about the way he said it that brought a hot flush to her cheeks. It was clear he'd seen the video. Probably watched it a few times to get all the details and to search it for any clues it might contain. Dallas ushered them both in and closed the door behind them.

Zach appeared with a tray of wine and snacks. "I'm trying out one of Cheyenne's museum recipes as an appetizer. Let me know what you think." He set it down on the coffee table as he scurried back to the kitchen, his eyes lingering on Kenny with undisguised desire.

Dallas and Kenny sat on the sofa as Cheyenne

perched on the chair across from them. "Well. You wouldn't be here if you didn't have a plan, would you?"

Dallas rubbed at his jaw and Cheyenne knew they were in trouble.

"You have no clue who they are, do you?" she asked.

Kenny reached for one of the appetizers Zach had brought out. Zach was watching from the kitchen like a puppy dog watching his owner dangling a treat out of reach.

Kenny took the first bite and chewed thoughtfully. Without saying anything, he took another. Then finished it with the third. "That is delicious. You could sell that."

Cheyenne raised an eyebrow at Dallas.

"No. I didn't tell him anything about your restaurant plans."

The edges of panic tickled at her, but she brushed it aside. Kenny was a professional fixer. He'd been hiding major scandals from the press for more than a decade, she could trust him whether he was on her NDA list or not.

"Kenny, I have to tell you something. I just need your word it never leaves this apartment."

Kenny's smile was immediate. Secrets and gossip were his manna. "Of course, Cheyenne. Anything you say to me is in complete confidence. Always." His voice washed over her with a calming sincerity. She had absolutely no doubt this man would keep her secrets to the grave.

"My roommates and I are going to be on *Kitchen Wars*," she said. "If this video gets out, I'm certain they'd boot us from the show."

Kenny leaned forward, legs crossed with his hands clasped across his knee. It was as if there were gears spinning behind his gray eyes. A spark of energy, wit, humor. She was drawn to him like a moth to a flame. Just being in the same room with him made her feel safe.

Dallas lounged back against the sofa, his feet on the table and sipped at the glass of wine Zach had brought out. "Well, I agree with Kenny. This empanada or whatever it is, is tasty as hell. I could eat the whole damn plate of them."

"The ancient Sumerians used a lot of oil and herbs in their cooking," Cheyenne said. She grinned at Dallas. "And, my sweet darling carnivorous brother, it is entirely vegan."

Dallas held the bit left between his fingers with sudden suspicion. He sniffed at it and popped it in his mouth. "Better than any MRE."

"Thanks, Dallas. That's quite the complement." Once again, Dallas put things in perspective.

Kenny did not take the glass of wine, but wiped his

fingers on a napkin and laced them together over his knee. "They are restaurant quality. If all your cooking is like this, you should be able to win at the show hands down."

"Well, if we don't kill this video, none of this other stuff is going to matter."

"Oh, come on, Cheyenne," Dallas said, "you know the restaurant will still happen. It just won't be as easy as winning the competition."

"You're right, of course, but we have a real chance at winning this competition, and what I did? It doesn't just affect me. It affects all my friends. My current boss. I just can't let it go."

Kenny rubbed his hands together. "The hotel room was the key. It was rented by a guy named Rick Cleeves. Turns out there is no Rick Cleeves that we can trace. Whatever ID he used at the hotel was a high quality fake."

"Rick? The two guys I was with were Shane and Kyle. So was the hotel a dead end?"

"Not necessarily," Dallas said. "So, the photos that you sent? We're running them through some state of the art facial recognition software. But the database is huge and it can take days to get through it. If either of them have a passport, we should be able to identify them. Just might be too late."

"Wouldn't this Rick guy have multiple passports?"

"We're not going to stop with just one ID. I'm keeping it running to find the multiples."

"I asked Dallas to bring me here because I want to see if we could work through the night you met them, and see if I could pull out any other details you might have picked up on subconsciously."

"How would you do that?"

"I want to hypnotize you. There are things your brain picked up on that you don't even know about."

"Hypnosis?" Cheyenne asked. "I thought that was just a parlor trick."

"Nope. And I'm good."

## Chapter 24

Cheyenne led Kenny and Dallas back to her bedroom so they could have quiet and privacy. Kenny told her to get comfortable on the bed. She slipped off her shoes and settled into the middle.

"Close your eyes," he said, in a softer, even warmer voice than his usual melodious tenor.

He led her through a series of deep breathing exercises and his voice melted into a gentle cooing, giving her directions she willingly followed. Soon, it was as if she was in the bar. The smell of old beer. A mingling of various aftershaves and wisps of end of day perfumes. Every detail was clearer than her memory of it. Kenny urged her to describe the bar from the moment she entered.

It was weird, but she could pause the video running in her head and focus on minutiae she would never have remembered if just asked to. She could see who was standing at the bar or at any of the tables. She knew almost everyone there.

"Do you see the guys you went off with later?"

She scanned the entire bar, but they weren't there yet. "They must have come in later."

He moved her through her conversation with Eleanor. Got her to turn toward the door every now and again. There were gaps. She couldn't tell him things that weren't hidden in the recesses of her mind, but her brain had recorded way more than she actively remembered. As they went through the exercise, she was stunned by the detail the popped up.

Halfway into her second drink, Gordy Carpenter ambled in and went straight to the bar. He was wearing work clothes and tugged at his tie to loosen it.

His wolfish grin made her want to heave, but she didn't show it when she nodded back with a fake smile of her own. Gordy tapped two fingers to his forehead in a simple salute to acknowledge she'd seen him before he scanned the rest of the bar.

"He was looking for someone," Cheyenne said, "When he saw me, he acknowledged me and moved on."

Gordy found his way to the bar. Shane and Kyle were there, but Cheyenne had not seen them come in. Each had a pint of beer in front of them. She couldn't tell if Gordy was looking for them or if he merely found the empty space next to Kyle convenient. Gordy pointed to the bowl of snack mix in front of the guys and said something. Kyle handed him the bowl and held out his hand.

In DC it wasn't unusual for strangers in a bar to introduce themselves. It was a place where connection meant everything, and people were determined to meet and greet everyone that crossed their paths. And yet, Cheyenne thought the way Gordy turned away from them but stayed at the bar even after his drink was placed in front of him was odd. Was there a connection, or was Gordy just getting the snack mix from strangers?

Cheyenne watched as Kyle and Shane finished their drinks, something she had not noticed when she was actually in the bar. They ordered a new round and turned around to face the general bar crowd. The oddest thing was, they didn't seem to scan the crowd so much as they honed straight onto Cheyenne and Eleanor.

"Cheyenne, I want you to go back to when Gordy walks up to the bar. Can you picture that?"

"Yes."

"When he says something to the other men, can you see his mouth? Is it visible?"

"No."

"Is it visible in the mirror behind the bar?"

Cheyenne found his reflection between the shelves holding rum and whiskey. He was looking at her in the reflection. How had she missed that?

"Watch his lips. You can read lips and see what he is saying. You can understand him. What is he saying?"

Cheyenne concentrated on his lips. The memory was from a peripheral view, but she could see them moving. "Two blonds. Table by the window."

"Good. Now, can you look at the tables around you? Are there any other tables by the windows with two blonds?"

"The one next to us has three people. Two Chinese women and a redhead. The only other table near the window has four guys crowded around it. They're laughing, already toasted."

"Good girl," Kenny said. He brought her out of her trance and helped her to sit up.

"I'm not exactly sure what that means," she said. She rotated her head around on her shoulders and yawned. Being hypnotized was kind of relaxing.

"This Gordy guy who came in and pointed you two out to the guys. You know him?"

"Yeah, he works for Ellis, Levin & Associates. He's a lobbyist who's also a pain in the ass. But...I can't see him doing this kind of setup. I didn't think he was that...skeevy. He was in the hallway pumping our intern for information the other day, so why would he do that if he knew this was coming?"

"He's playing multiple angles," Kenny said. "I think I've heard his name, but I refuse to do any work for Ellis, Levin & Associates. They're a shady group and they're always on the wrong side of everything I believe in."

Dallas clapped his hands together. "At least we know who is behind this—generally speaking. Between the face recognition and the lobbying firm being involved, we are going to crack this."

"It could be Gordy working alone. He might be trying to pull ahead," Cheyenne said.

"I don't give a flying fuck if he's working alone or if the entire company is helping him out. Seriously. He, and, if we're lucky, the entire fucking company will go down in gigantic flames."

Dallas was angry, but Cheyenne didn't want to point out any of the logical reasons she could come up with as to why it was unlikely Gordy's company was behind this. Cheyenne had met a number of the people working at Ellis, Levin & Associates over the years. While they represented all the wrong people, they weren't all totally skeevy. A couple of the women were actually pretty nice.

"The website they gave you has a link for

uploading documents, but Link told me you asked them to set up a physical meet so you can hand over paper. Have they contacted you yet?" Kenny asked.

"I gave them my phone number," Cheyenne said. "They hacked my phone and blocked all my contacts except Dallas."

"Sort of," Dallas interrupted. "They blocked all your contacts, but I have a phone that can't be blocked."

"I've never heard of that," Kenny said. "Must be a perk of a particular government branch?"

Dallas grinned like the Cheshire Cat.

"Anyway, I have yet to hear from them. I don't know if they are going to give me a place to meet, or if they are freaked out I got my phone fixed and we ruined it?"

Kenny shrugged. "As soon as you hear from them, call Dallas. We're putting together a team that will come in with you, but no one will notice, not even you."

"They probably have someone ready to upload the video the second anything goes wrong," Dallas said. "We still want to stop the video; our best means of doing that is to pretend to give them what they want and hope they don't upload the video anyway."

"What does that gain us?" Cheyenne asked.

"Time," both Kenny and Dallas said together.

"We give them papers. They won't know whether the information is good or not until later. They have to take the paper to someone. My guess is, they'll send a messenger who works for the company and has no clue what is going on anyway to pick up the package."

Cheyenne didn't see how that would achieve anything.

"Then we'll follow the package."

"Aren't you going to put some sort of chip in it so you can trace it?"

"Yes, of course."

Cheyenne flopped onto her back. "But it was already on the web. How can we get it off? You said it was bouncing around all over the world."

"The video itself is on a secure server somewhere. People have to know it exists to find it now, and, if we can take it off the server, it's unlikely it's been copied by anyone. We can still get rid of it."

Cheyenne covered her face with her hands. "Let me get this straight. Someone local took the video and put it on a server somewhere. It could be a server anywhere in the world, right?"

"Yes, but there's no access to the video without the right passcodes, so no one is watching it right now."

"And you need to find this server, wherever it might be and go to it, in person?"

"No. We need to either find the server it is stored on

and shut it down, or we need to find the person who set this all up and knock them around until they yank it off."

"Why don't we go after Gordy then? He's clearly involved."

"Gordy isn't that smart," Dallas said. "I've seen his file, and I think someone higher up the food chain is responsible for all this."

"Then we should go to Gordy and offer him a deal," Cheyenne said.

Dallas and Kenny looked at her hard then.

"What?"

"It could work," Kenny said. "It all depends on how self-serving he is."

Cheyenne laughed. "Believe me, Gordy is all about Gordy and making money. I don't think he gives a shit how he makes it, or who he steps on along the way. But, you know, I'm pretty sure he's just a cog in this. He's not smart enough to pull off the technical side of things. Someone else is doing that."

As they were leaving Dallas fished the thumb drive out of his pocket. "Here. I almost destroyed this and then thought maybe you'd want to do it yourself."

"Did you find anything on it?"

"Any helpful encoding had been wiped clean. Whoever is in charge is pretty good at covering their tracks."

She pulled the cover off the drive. It was amazing how something so small could wreak such havoc. "How do I destroy it?"

"Take it apart. Turn the chip inside into powder and then burn it."

"Toxic fumes, much?"

"That much won't hurt you. I figured you'd find the process satisfying."

"I won't be happy until every last remnant is removed from the planet. This is only the compilation. What happened to the raw footage?"

Dallas just stared at her for a long moment. Color warmed her cheeks as she realized the double entendre.

"Oh, gross, Dallas."

"You said it. We'll find it. Someone edited it, and we'll find that computer and let you destroy it too, if you want."

"And if these people have automatic backups? Dallas, I don't see how we can ever be sure this is really ever dead and gone for ever." The cloud was like a hall of mirrors—a never ending nightmare of duplicates.

"We've got some work to do," Kenny said. He helped Cheyenne up. "Don't worry too much. If this does get out, we will put a spin on it that will have the world crying for you and ready to tar and feather the people who did this to you."

Cheyenne tried to take comfort in his words but knew it wasn't true. There would always be people out there who would rather shame the victim than take down the attackers.

XANDER KNOCKED on her door about ten minutes after Dallas and Kenny had left. His smile lit up his entire face and she wanted to drown herself in it. If only she could. Cheyenne grabbed him by the hand before the others even noticed he was there.

Once down the hallway, she shut the door and asked Xander to sit on the bed. If she didn't get this over with soon, she'd go insane.

"Cheyenne? I take it you have some other huge thing about yourself you need to tell me."

He sounded tired. Uneasy.

"Yes. I'm sorry that it's been one thing after another, Xander, but this is it. I am falling for you hard, and I don't want there to be any secrets or things that could pop up later between us."

"I'm all ears."

The thumb drive was burning a hole in her pocket.

She pulled it out and handed it to him. "Remember that three-way I told you about?"

"Hard to forget that. What about it?"

"The guys I was with videotaped it. They're using the footage of the ménage to blackmail Congressman Pierce."

Even as she said it, she knew it had come out all wrong and jumbled.

Xander stood up, hands on hips, his fingers wrapping around the drive. "I don't understand."

"The guys in the ménage set me up. They were part of some elaborate sting and they taped us having sex. There was even one guy who looks a little like my boss, and they're using the video tape to get Congressman Pierce to hand over some secret information."

Xander turned away from her then, his head drooping to his chest.

Cheyenne held her breath. It was all out there. "If it helps, that's it. I don't have any more revelations about myself. Nothing else to hold back."

"When did you first learn of the blackmail?"

"Yesterday morning."

"And you chose to tell me about the cooking competition instead of your pornographic blackmail tape?" He rounded on her, his eyes sparking in fury.

"I thought my being gone for three months might

be a big deal."

"Bigger than...than...this?" He held the thumb drive up. He closed his eyes and shook his head, fists clenched on either side by his ears. "Did the congressman pay the price to save your honor?"

It was her turn to be flummoxed. "Honor? I'm upset about the video because they never asked my permission to make it. I'm not upset about what I did with these men. I wasn't in a relationship with you. I was a free agent. I had a great time that night."

Xander's lips flattened into a thin line. "Maybe I should see just how much fun you had, Cheyenne. Is the whole world going to see this? Is my mother? Is my sister going to be able to see this online and know that you did these things? It's one thing to have a private affair, quite another to throw it out there for the whole world to see."

"You're worried about your family seeing me fuck other guys? I'm worried about my chances with *Kitchen Wars* being ruined because two men took advantage of me. They had no right to film me. That's the problem here. Not that I had sex with two guys."

Xander stormed past her and out of the apartment.

Cheyenne let him go. She had expected this, after all. Nia had said a man who couldn't handle Cheyenne and all her foibles wasn't worthy of her. She had hoped of more from Xander.

heyenne tossed and turned throughout the night. Sleep was hard to come by and she only managed to get a couple of hours. A long cold shower did little to wake her up.

She paused at the little bakery down the street for a quadruple latte with triple shots of almond syrup to give her a jolt into wakefulness.

After Xander had stormed away the previous night, she had cried on Zach's shoulder for a while. Then she'd gotten angry that Xander's tune had changed with the video. He'd asked her about her craziest sexual experience and had been fine with the ménage when it was theoretical. With the proof of it in his hand, he'd turned around quickly.

After Xander had gone to bed, she'd stalked the

internet looking for any sign the video had been leaked. Fortunately, it was still deep underground somewhere. It would be over by the end of the day.

Before going to bed, she texted Xander asking him if he was going to stick with his commitment to the Smithsonian class. His response was a terse *yes* and nothing more. The sparse reply had been responsible for her lack of sleep. It was so cold. Unyielding. It told her nothing about his state of mind.

She was determined to show up for the classes, too, and face his angry silence. As long as they had that gig together, they would have to work together. At least she'd see him once a week for the next few weeks before she moved to LA. Perhaps their time together would chip away at his suddenly icy exterior.

Cheyenne downed the dregs of her coffee and tossed it in the trash can outside the Cannon Building, suddenly nostalgic for the time she'd spent inside. It would be coming to an end soon. Either she'd be leaving for the cooking show, or she'd be fired as part of the spin on the video being released.

As soon as she arrived at the office, she felt like everyone was staring at her. Of course it wasn't really true. The gigantic bullseye drawn on her forehead was purely her imagination.

And poor Lincoln! All the women who worked for

him were incredibly distracted by their lives at the moment—all because of this stupid Bingo game. That had been the catalyst for everything. If she hadn't been playing Bingo, she wouldn't have been tempted to go off with two men at the same time. She liked to tell herself that, anyway.

At least the Bingo game would be over today, too. She hadn't kept track with what was happening or who was winning because she no longer cared. It was weird to think how important it had seemed to her just two weeks ago.

Opal tilted her head to one side as Cheyenne met her gaze. She'd been watching her closely.

Carleen looked up from her desk as she approached. "There you are. Kenny and Dallas arrived a few minutes ago. He's in with Link already."

"Oh," Cheyenne said, turning toward Link's closed office door. "I hadn't realized."

"Kenny does what Kenny does. He likes to manage things directly. Let's go on in."

Carleen knocked on the door and pushed it open at the same time. "Cheyenne is here."

Dallas and Kenny wore the same clothes they had on the day before and their eyes were both bloodshot from lack of sleep.

"Did you figure something out?" she asked.

Dallas's smile was reassuring and put her at ease immediately.

"We've got a plan. Kenny, why don't you lay it all out. The hypnosis trick was the best thing ever."

They all sat in chairs as Kenny launched into the investigation. "Well, the lobbyist, Gordy, entered the bar and went straight to these two guys."

Kenny laid out head shots of Kyle and Shane. The names underneath were different, though. One was Mark Twilly and the other was Jonas Hemshaw. "They're both actors. It figures."

"After Gordy pointed you and Eleanor out to them, they came over to you, offering to buy both of you drinks," Kenny said.

"Yeah. How did you know that?" The hypnosis session hadn't gotten into the details after the guys had came over.

"Because we had a long visit with both Mark and Jonas last night."

"You actually found them?" Cheyenne asked, hope soaring.

"Yeah. Their photos came up on an acting agency website. Turns out they were hired to go after you."

Cheyenne looked back and forth between Kenny and Dallas. Dallas nodded confirmation.

"Well, not you specifically. Anyone from

Congressmen Pierce's office. You happened to be at the bar that night. They'd been to two other bars the night before, but hadn't been able to get the attention of other women they'd pointed out. I believe they approached Katherine O'Malley and Lizbeth Crandall Monday evening but were shot down."

"We were all at the same bar on Monday. Weird."

"At any rate, no one was interested in either of them on Monday. When they approached you on Tuesday, they were hoping that either you or Eleanor would take the bait. Both reported being completely surprised when you suggested a ménage with the two of them."

Dallas leaned forward and put his chin on his clasped hands. "By the way, Jonas actually asked me to apologize to you. He said you were really sweet and he didn't like what they were doing." Dallas let out a derisive snort. "As if. It was all I could do to not take the guy's head off. Anyway, they had set up the room so that one of them could get one of you on camera, but they knew a threesome would be even better."

"But I thought one of them looking like the congressman was key to their blackmail scheme."

"They figured out that part later. Initially, the plan was to get the congressman a black mark by sullying the women in his office. Turns out Gordy was pointing out all of you to a number of actors. They wanted to get a lot of footage with a lot of women and men to embarrass the congressman."

"This makes so little sense. Why would Gordy do that? It's a sloppy form of espionage"

"It was a stupid idea. And, according to Jonas, it wasn't really Gordy who was in charge," Kenny said.

"Who was in charge of this, then?" Cheyenne asked. If she was going to get personal justice out of this, she needed some answers.

Dallas frowned. "Well...that's where we're currently at."

Cheyenne tilted her head back. She had so wanted this to be done. Over. Finished. "Ugh. So we go after Gordy and get him to talk."

"We've got a bunch of papers ready for tonight," Lincoln said, pointing to the coffee table.

Cheyenne had almost forgotten he was in the room with them, he'd been so quiet. She followed his finger. Two sealed copy paper boxes sat on the floor. "And none of this is super important?"

Lincoln wiped at his chin. "We put in a few classified treats. There're a few pages that will get them all excited but lead them in the wrong direction. Obfuscate things for a while, anyway."

Just as Cheyenne was about to point out that she

still hadn't heard from the blackmailers, a text chimed on her phone.

**Blocked**: 9:30, Lincoln Memorial

She read it aloud.

Lincoln Pierce chortled. "I think that might be some kind of joke."

"Sick bastard," Cheyenne said.

"We need to get to Gordy before nine thirty, then. If we can get him to tell us who's handling the tech on this, we should be able to keep the video from going viral," Dallas said. "Looks like we'll be missing family dinner tonight. Dang. Mom's making sauerkraut and pork roast."

"Money," Cheyenne said, ignoring Dallas for the moment. How could he worry about dinner when so much was at stake? "Gordy will respond to money and freedom. If you can convince him he's part of something that will put him away for years and talking will help him stay out of prison..."

"Cheyenne, can you lift those boxes?" Dallas asked.

She tried, but they were too heavy. "I'll need to borrow your car. And there's no way I'm lugging those things around the memorial."

Without asking she texted back.

**Cheyenne**: No way. Too much paper. Heavy boxes. Need car to car transfer. Name a parking lot.

The return text came quickly. These people had a fucking sense of humor.

## Chapter 26

Dallas, Kenny and Cheyenne hashed out a plan over the next half hour. Lincoln excused himself for a vote. And it was a good thing he was gone, too. He probably would not approve of all their scenarios.

If all went as they hoped, the video would be history, the person or people behind it would be heading in their own personal version of hell, and Cheyenne would still be on her way to LA for *Kitchen Wars*. If it didn't, Kenny's plan B was to spin the hell out of this thing.

"What's the spin going to be?" Cheyenne asked.

Kenny leveled a gaze at her and said, "I'd rather not say in case I need to use it in the future sometime."

"You have no clue do you?" she asked, throwing a ball of wadded up paper at him.

He gave her one of his enigmatic grins that told her nothing. She would never win at poker against Kenny, that was for certain. By noon, they had most of the puzzle pieces laid out. They just had to fit them together.

Cheyenne tried to shove thoughts of Xander aside, but it was hard. She was wishing she hadn't told him about the video. If they were successful, she would have lost the man she loved over nothing. He would never have found out about the tape to begin with.

Even so, she was going to do everything exactly as planned in order to ensure that tape didn't come back to haunt her later.

Dallas and Kenny lugged the boxes of papers to Dallas' van. Cheyenne followed them out after stopping briefly by Katherine's office to let her know she'd be gone the rest of the day.

The two men worked well together. Dallas was good with people in spite of his square looking head and military gruffness. There was something genuine with him, at any rate. He was pretty much a What-You-See-Is-What-You-Get kinda guy.

Kenny had never had any dealings with Gordy before, so they decided to have Kenny talk to him first. They needed to get Gordy to confess to his part in the scheme and make him spill the beans about the person really behind this. It would take a bit more persuasion than asking politely. Cheyenne wasn't sure what form the persuasion might take and was afraid to ask.

Cheyenne called Ellis, Levin & Associates pretending to be an aide from Congressman Whitcomb's office asking for Gordy. It was no secret that Gordy had been heavily courting Whitcomb's vote on some upcoming legislation. He'd bite at the chance to meet up with anyone from his office.

"Yes, Congressman Whitcomb woud like to see him today," Cheyenne said. "The earlier the better. The Congressman will be on his boat at Central Marina."

Dallas had given her a real, honest to God, burner phone to use for the call. "Is it okay to use government property like this?"

"Look, I'm supposed to be keeping our elected officials safe. Congressman Pierce is being blackmailed through you, so this is, technically speaking, a part of my mission. Besides, the accounting is so fucking insane no one is going to miss a few phones."

"All right. So what do we do now? Wait for Gordy to call?"

"We go set our trap while we wait."

Kenny reappeared from wherever he had been. "I've got the space. We're good to go."

Dallas drove while Kenny gave directions. They

ended up at parking a short walk from the marina where Congressman Whitcomb's yacht was moored.

"How did you swing this?" Dallas asked as they boarded. The crew was expecting them.

"Let's just say the congressman is grateful for some work I did last year."

Cheyenne had never been on a boat like this. She'd heard others in the office talk about some pretty wild parties taking place on them, but she'd never gone to any. About twenty sailboats fluffed along the Potomac. Their sails filled with wind Cheyenne didn't even notice as they moved back and forth over the water. Xander had promised to take her sailing, and now? She could only hope that time would bring him around.

Cheyenne, Dallas, and Kenny sat on the deck and waited for Gordy's call to come in. They expected it would only take a few hours, and Congressman Whitcomb's crew had been instructed to treat them like royal guests. The table was laid out with salads and charcuterie and a couple of good wines.

"Don't drink too much, we need our wits about us," Dallas said as he poured them each a glass.

Cheyenne eyed the bottle and estimated each glass was worth about two hundred bucks. She sipped at hers and let the rich flavors cross her palate. It was perfection. She noted the label, automatically adding it to a long list of fine wines in her head. After they had eaten, they set up the stateroom with the gear from Dallas' van. Miniature microphones and recording equipment would pick up the gentlest of breaths and every spoken word.

They didn't need to change Kenny's wardrobe for his part in all this. Cheyenne slipped into a crew uniform and balled her hair up under a hat.

"You meld into the background nicely," Dallas said. He squeezed her shoulders with his hands. "You've got this."

It took longer than they thought it might, but Gordy finally called and they could spring their trap.

"Yes," Cheyenne breathed into the phone, going for an older, smoker's voice to disguise her voice. She hadn't spoken to Gordy more than a dozen times, but she had to play it safe. "Congressman Whitcomb has had a change of heart. But he's not ready to be open about it. Come to his yacht. You can chat in private. You know where it is?"

She hung up when he confirmed. "He'll be here in half an hour. Let's get into place."

They chose the office library on the boat for their upcoming drama. A large wooden desk took up a good portion of the room. Kenny would sit in the leather swivel chair behind the desk. He'd invite Gordy to sit down in one of the two chairs across from the desk for a simple conversation.

Part of her hoped Gordy was willing to talk without any violence. Another part of her wanted to hit him until all the anger and pain over this entire situation was gone. The thing was, she wasn't sure if it would really help. Cheyenne doubted Gordy would think to check his surroundings for hidden mikes before talking, but she and Dallas made sure the microphones were well camouflaged anyway. They were small, but not invisible.

Dallas holed up in the small bathroom off the side of the room. They'd set up the recording equipment in on the counter with room to spare. The door to the bathroom was completely camouflaged within the rich oak paneling and art work along the walls. A small bell designed to look like an old ship's ringer was actually the release for the door, but looked like another piece of nautical ephemera. When the door was shut, there was no way to see it was even there.

Kenny settled into the large chair behind the desk and spun away from the door. "I'll let him come in and surprise him. Cheyenne, you sure you're okay at the door?"

"Yeah. I look like staff, he won't even acknowledge me."

Cheyenne found a position where she could hear and see without being noticed. The whites of the crew uniform were like magic people erasers. Sure enough,

Cheyenne was completely invisible to Gordy as he boarded the ship.

The crew had been briefed on their little operation and played their parts beautifully. Ivan, the steward, showed Gordy to the library, pushed the door open and officially announced Gordy to the room. It was a nice bit of drama.

"Thank you, Ivan," Kenny said, his back still to the door.

Cheyenne followed them in, passing Gordy with a tray of lemonade and iced tea and setting it on the desk.

"Drinks, sir," she said.

"Thank you, Diana," Kenny said as he spun around to face Gordy.

Cheyenne scooted past Gordy a second time. He wasn't even looking at her. Instead of leaving, she stood at the door. He didn't even look to make sure she'd left.

"You're not Congressman Whitcomb. What the hell is going on here? Who the fuck are you?"

"Who I am is not of consequence."

"I was led to believe the congressman wanted to see me directly." He modulated his voice down immediately, matching Kenny's even timbre. He was playing a game here, too.

"The congressman is aware of some of your...shall we call them extracurricular activities? He is not amused. Congressman Pierce is a close colleague and a friend."

Gordy didn't say anything.

"Come now. You don't need to be coy with me, Carpenter. You might not have been the one behind the scheme, but you made it happen."

"I don't know what you're talking about," Gordy said. His voice had gone up a notch with tension.

"Ah. A little loyalty is fine. But here's the thing. I'd like to know who you actually work for."

Gordy feigned ignorance again.

"Oh, come on. I know you didn't do this on your own. You hired the actors. You directed the ugly bits, but you weren't the one who figured out the technical details. Who's backing it?"

"Again. I have no idea what you're talking about."

Kenny leaned forward and placed his chin on his hand. He drew his finger across the blotter on the desk, making an invisible line.

"Okay. So here's the deal, Gordo Boyo. You can stop the lame ass faking here and face the facts. You and your acting buddies are facing blackmail, kidnapping and rape charges."

Cheyenne almost jumped in to deny this last bit. She had gone with them willingly. Rape wasn't fair. Probably not kidnapping either. She'd consented to everything—everything except the actual video. Kenny was probably bluffing though, so she bit her tongue and held her ground. Gordy still hadn't made any indication he knew she was even in the room.

"Add in the video taping without permission? In a situation like this? Privacy laws and the hotel you were in? It was in Maryland, not DC. That state requires all parties give consent when taping. I can guarantee you Ms. LeFleur is fully willing to testify to that she did not give consent for the video. And your little actor friends? They signed up to play a part. They are very happy to make a deal to save their asses."

Gordy froze.

"Ah. I see I have your attention now." Kenny sat back, his fingers steepled in front of his chest. "The illegal video is worth five years and a quarter million in fines alone. How's your bank account looking these days? You ready to make a deal here?"

"Am I under arrest? Are you with some special agency or something?" Gordy licked his lips and swiveled his head to look around the room.

He looked right through Cheyenne as if she weren't even there. Servants were invisible to guys like him.

"Do you want to be? We could make that happen. If you want."

"You're not police, are you? You can't arrest me if you wanted to. Fuck this."

Gordy spun around only to find Cheyenne blocking the doorway. His eyes widened when she flipped her cap off and shook out her hair to reveal herself.

"Cheyenne? Jesus. What the fuck?" Gordy stumbled back toward Kenny, turning white as he saw her. "What are you doing here?"

Cheyenne poked a finger into Gordy's chest. His shoulders slumped and he lowered his head in surrender. "You owe me, Gordy, you sleazy son of a bitch."

He lifted his face to hers. "I'm sorry, Cheyenne. It wasn't anything personal. You were there. That's all."

She slapped him as hard as she could, surprising herself. "As if it were fine to victimize some other woman?"

"You went willingly enough, and you sure seemed to be having a great time on the video," he said, leering at her. "How much does it cost to get me a piece of that action?"

At that, Dallas sprung out of the bathroom. The sheer bulk of her brother was enough to make most men cower. Gordy was like any other regular guy who worked out a couple times a week. He was no match for Dallas.

Gordy held up his hands and staggered backward toward Kenny. "Whoa, dude. Who the fuck are you?"

"I'm Cheyenne's big brother." He rolled up his sleeves slowly. "You fucking asshole."

"Dallas, calm down. I can take care of this guy," Cheyenne said. "Gordy was about to apologize to me and tell us exactly who he's working for, weren't you?"

"Yeah, sure. Like I said. I was just kidding." Little drops of sweat had formed along Gordy's brow, and he held his hands in front of him, his fingers wide in supplication. "Really, no disrespect intended."

Cheyenne brushed his comments aside with a wave of her hand.

"It's not Ellis, Levin & Associates, is it?" Cheyenne said more than asked. "You all have questionable tactics, but Ellis, Levin & Associates wouldn't stoop to blackmail porn. This is personal. You are working for someone who truly hates Lincoln Pierce on the side." With each word, Cheyenne poked her finger at Gordy's chest as she figured it out.

Dallas hovered behind her. There was no mistaking his great big physical bulky threat.

Gordy licked at his lips as he looked back and forth between her and Dallas. His hand flew to his head and he tugged at his hair. "Fuck. Fuck. Fuck. I'll talk, but only if you make sure I get a deal," Gordy said. "No fucking way am I going to prison."

Just as she had suspected, Gordy was out for Gordy and no one else. Cheyenne put her face close to his. "You fuck us over here, and I will make you wish you were in prison. Got that?"

Dallas flipped one of the chairs near the desk around and waved at it as if he were a maitre'd at a restaurant. Cheyenne didn't like the idea of Gordy getting off with some sort of plea deal, but if it meant taking down the real mastermind behind this whole thing she'd get over it.

Gordy dropped into the chair, shoulders slumping and dropped his head into his hands.

Cheyenne kicked at his shoe. "Talk. Now."

"*D*id you get that all on tape?" Cheyenne asked as they made their way through the throngs of unsuspecting people on the pier. Tourists gaped at the views along the Potomac, completely unaware of the political intrigue happening right in front of them.

"No tape involved," Dallas said, "but yeah, we got it."

"You know what I meant."

After the initial confrontation, Cheyenne had asked Kenny and Dallas to get the details from Gordy. It was early evening by the time Kenny and Dallas had finished grilling Gordy. He was almost cooperative by the time they were done. *"Grateful for the opportunity to clear things up," he'd said.*

He balked when they told him he would be staying

on the boat until the next morning. He pleaded with them to let him go, but he eventually handed over his phone and slumped in the chair. Ivan locked him in the stateroom.

"Yep, it's all here," Dallas said, holding up a thumb drive as the three of them walked back to the van.

"That wasn't really very exciting," Cheyenne said. "I was expecting you to break his legs or something."

"I would have if you'd let me, but, hey, we usually ask somewhat politely to get going. You'd be surprised at how easy it can be at times. We escalate to mild threats if being nice doesn't work. This guy broke easier than most. A couple years in prison would be the end of him. He's not completely stupid."

"It was just...sort of anti-climatic?"

"Yeah, well, that's my life. I just try to make it seem more exciting than it really is."

"It makes me feel better knowing that, actually. That you're not really running around doing crazy things like James Bond."

"Yeah, the thing is, I *am* the modern James Bond. It's all with the tech these days." Dallas held up his arms and flexed his muscles. "These babies are just for show. The real shit goes down in here," he pointed to his head with both index fingers, "inside my head."

Cheyenne swatted him back-handed. "We should all cower in fear."

"I suspect Ivan overheard everything, but he's Whitcomb's man and won't divulge anything. He'll release Gordy after I call him. When the rest is all done."

"You must have called in a pretty big chip with Whitcomb," Dallas said.

Kenny shrugged noncommittally but said nothing.

"On to part two of the plan?" Cheyenne asked. "I'll drop you guys off at Kenny's and take Dallas' van."

"I don't like you meeting these guys alone," Dallas said. "Promise me you'll take Xander with you, okay?"

Cheyenne hadn't told Dallas that Xander had stormed out on her last night with the thumb drive intact. She didn't think Xander would do anything with it; certainly, she trusted him not to upload the video onto the internet. She was wishing she'd destroyed it and never said anything to Xander. This plan was working and she'd lost Xander for nothing.

"Absolutely. I'll call Xander as soon as I drop you off." The lie came too easily to her, but she couldn't meet Dallas in the eye. He looked so obviously relieved that she couldn't recant now.

"Excellent. You shouldn't worry too much. Whoever they send to get the papers is going to be pretty low level. We'll be dealing with the big Kahuna on our end."

"I can't quite believe Senator Markle is behind all of this. He has such a squeaky clean reputation."

"He's made no secret of his disagreement over policy, though," Kenny said. "It's public record how much he's tangled with Pierce."

"I get that, but there are a dozen other people who have been overtly nasty to Pierce. Markle is not the obvious choice I'd have made," she said.

"That's one reason I'm glad you chose to let us do this my way, Cheyenne," Dallas said. "I honestly don't think we'd ever get enough evidence to convict him or prove he's involved. We might end up having to be satisfied with just destroying all traces of the video."

"I'm okay with that, I guess," Cheyenne said. "I'd rather not have to be testifying at a trial about all of this and having the video part of every news broadcast as a result."

"I might be able to use the information in delightfully subversive ways in the future, Cheyenne," Kenny said. "If Markle ever comes to me to fix something...I could have fun with that."

"Remind me not to get on your bad side," Cheyenne said. She drove them back through town as Kenny guided her to his office.

Dallas turned to her before getting out of the van. "You got the kit all figured out?"

Cheyenne glanced back at the bag in the back of

the van that held a wire tap for her to wear during the drop off. Dallas had shown her how to tape it to her skin and hide it in clothing while they'd waited for Gordy to call. "Yes, sir."

He placed a warm hand on her arm and squeezed. "Go home. Take an hour nap. You look like you need some sleep. Xander can make sure the wires are well-concealed, okay?"

"You really think I need to wire myself?" she asked.

"Probably not, but if we don't set you up, we'll always regret it if something interesting or useful is said, right?"

"Okay. Fine. You boys get to do all the dangerous bits. I'm kinda okay with that."

Dallas squeezed her arm again before releasing it. "Nap. Change. Take care."

She waited until Dallas and Kenny had disappeared into the building before driving away. Her fingers gripped the wheel tightly the entire way to her apartment. No one was home when she got there. Friday night was big for restaurant workers and they'd all be gone until the wee hours of the morning.

She googled the address for the parking garage they'd given her in Arlington and looked at the street view. It was hard to believe this squat, boring parking garage was the exact same one Deep Throat had chosen. Was it irony or humor that had guided the decision to meet there? The area had been gentrified a bit since Nixon had been taken down, but the parking garage was the same ugly old building. It would take about forty minutes to get there from her apartment. She would give herself an hour in case traffic changed.

Cheyenne set her alarm for an hour, took off all her clothes, and climbed into bed. That would still give her another two hours to shower, set up the tap and get to the drop site. The events of the day had worn her out, and she fell into a fast hard sleep.

CHEYENNE WOKE, but not to her alarm, but instead to a loud pounding on the door.

She tossed on a robe and wiped at her face before looking through the peephole. Xander stood in the hallway, both hands on his hips eyes focused on the door. He pounded again, making her jump back. She took a deep breath, as she opened the door, hope fluttering crazily inside her.

"I was sleeping," she said.

Xander rushed past her and spun around. He held out his hand offering up the thumb drive. "I couldn't watch it."

She reached out to take it from him. As her fingers

grazed his palm, an electric shock jolted through them and the thumb drive clattered to the floor. She left her hand where it was, her fingers lightly touching his still-outstretched hand.

"Why not?" she asked.

His fingers wrapped around her hand and wrist. He swallowed and looked up at the ceiling before looking at her again. "I didn't want to. Didn't need to."

He was here, in front of her now, did she need any further explanation? She rushed into his arms, burying her face against his neck.

"I thought you'd never want to see me again," she said.

His arms engulfed her and he held her close, his lips caressing her neck, her ears. "I was overwhelmed, that's all. That issue with my student last year? It made me reevaluate my life. And then it took me a while to figure out how this videotape fit into things. I don't expect this to make sense. But I get that you didn't consent to the video. You're the victim here. I was reacting to how I was used in the past."

"I get that. Really, I do."

"So, everything is out on the table? You don't have any other reason to not get close to me? I'm back. Here for you. Now and always," he said.

"I can't think of anything else." She'd gone through the list she and Nia had prepared. Nia had won their little bet, and Cheyenne couldn't be happier. "I'm all yours, Xander."

Xander led her lead her into her bedroom.

After shutting the door behind them, Xander reached for her, his hands sliding into her hair and guiding her face toward his.

His lips touched hers gently at first. A quick peck. She opened her lips just a bit in invitation. His tongue darted into her mouth and swirled around hers.

Xander ran his hands along her back and cupped her ass in his hands. Cheyenne slid her hands between them and unbuttoned his shirt, tugging it out of his pants. She ran her hands along the thick hair on his chest, kissing his neck.

He shoved her flimsy robe off her shoulders to reveal her nakedness.

They worked quickly then, tearing off the rest of his clothing one piece at a time. Cheyenne stepped back to look at him once he was naked. This time, she didn't hold back.

She wrapped her fingers around his cock and guided him to the bed. "I need you, Xander," she said.

She fell backward onto the sheets and spread her legs to him. "I need you inside me, now. No more fore-play, no more kissing."

Xander produced a condom in record time and slipped it on. "Yes, ma'am. I am more than happy to oblige," he said, his Southern accent kicking in with a charming lilt.

"Just fuck me, Xander. Fuck me like there's no tomorrow."

He took her at her word and entered her in one quick movement. She wrapped her legs around him and held him inside her, immobile as she took his full measure.

Just as she had imagined, he was a perfect fit. She shifted her hips upward and put her feet on either side of him so she could meet him thrust for thrust. He paused, dropping to his elbows and flattening his body against hers. The weight of him against the length of her body crushing her into the bed grounded her as he claimed her physically as his.

His fingers danced against her face. "Jaani, you are so beautiful."

Cheyenne pushed upward with her hips. "Please."

Xander kissed her forehead. Her nose. Her lips. Her chin. Her neck. "When I'm ready."

Cheyenne groaned and ran her hands along his back, settling into the tease. She squeezed her pussy around his cock as his teeth grazed her earlobe, tugging at it.

"I love you, Cheyenne," he said. "I didn't know I was going to fall this hard, but I can't ever let you go. Never again."

"You have me. I'm not going anywhere...well...not forever, anyway."

What was wrong with her? Why couldn't she just say it back? She loved him. There was no doubt in her mind, and he needed to know it. She had to tell him. She practiced it inside her head, *I love you Xander. I love you. I love you. I love you.* No more holding back. No more lies. He wasn't going to run from her now.

"Xander?" she said, tentatively.

"Yes, Jaani?" he asked, meeting her eyes.

The warmth and opened of his gaze gave her courage. After all they had been through, there was no way he'd reject her now. "I love you, too, Xander. Saying it aloud makes it so real. It scares me."

"My sweet, sweet Jaani." He kissed her nose.

He was so heavy against her, it was all she could do to push her hips upward, begging him again to get moving. She needed to feel the length of him moving inside her. To have him take her fully and completely.

Xander kissed her one more time and shifted his weight to his arms, lifting himself mostly off her while remaining inside. He pulled almost all the way out and paused.

She lifted her head so she could see the length between their bodies, barely connected at one point now. Cheyenne watched as he inched his way fully inside her once again and threw her head back against the mattress, thrusting her hips upward until there was no space between them.

"Xander..." she said, trying to encompass more than just his name in it. Unable to admit she loved him out loud and hoping her body conveyed her need to him more loudly than she was able to. "Take me, please. Hard. Fast. I need you."

"As you wish, my love," Xander nipped at her nose before thrusting into her, hard and fast, holding nothing back now.

They rocked the bed with each movement, the headboard beating a constant and steady rhythm against the wall.

The rest of the world drifted away as Cheyenne was carried away by the sublime sensations between her legs. With each thrust, Xander slid his cock along her clit and then plunged deep inside her to hit her g-spot. Their eyes locked onto each other and she saw nothing but Xander. Felt nothing but Xander. Became one with Xander.

The moment came and she bucked underneath him, her body spasming out of control with an intense orgasm. She locked her arms around his neck and held on for dear life as he continued driving into her as she came. And came. And came.

Finally, the delightful painful orgasm ebbed into

generalized tingling as he groaned with his own orgasm.

He rested on top of her, his arms on either side holding up most of his weight. "My beautiful, beautiful Jaani."

He rolled off her and gathered her against him, spooning her from behind, resting.

Cheyenne wiggled her bottom against his returning erection. She'd told him there was nothing left on the table. In the heat of the moment, she'd forgotten all about her nine thirty parking garage date.

"Xander?" she asked, tentatively.

"Cheyenne?"

"So, I know I said I didn't have any more secrets to tell you, but..."

He laughed into her neck. "But? Out with it, Jaani..."

"I have to put a wire tap on and go meet someone in the Watergate Garage thing."

He laughed into her ear. "Is that all? It just slipped your mind?"

She rolled over so she could get a better read on him. His eyes twinkled with amusement.

"Yeah. So, the blackmailer? I agreed to give them some papers, and my brother helped me set up the meeting to hand them over. Link put together a bunch of stuff that will occupy them for a while without revealing any major secrets. While I'm at the garage handing over the papers, Dallas and Kenny, this fixer guy, are going to be taking over the technical side and shutting down the video."

Xander wiped at his face, and the amusement in his eyes disappeared. "And you were planning on going to this garage alone and unarmed?"

"Yes? I guess I was. I was afraid to call you and ask. Everyone else is at work…" Her voice trailed off. "I couldn't bring myself to tell Dallas that you freaked out last night and left me."

Xander gathered her against him, spooning again, kissing the back of her neck.

"This is all cloak and dagger crazy. But you are not going alone. What time do we need to be there?"

"We have another hour and a half before we need to leave."

"Good."

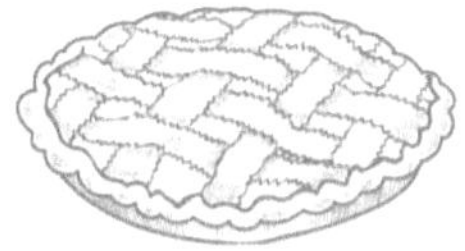

## Chapter 28

"Don't you think that's overkill?" Xander asked as Cheyenne checked herself out in the mirror. "I only have the jeans and shirt I came in. There's no way I can match you in stealth mode."

Cheyenne wore black pants and a black turtle-neck, the very definition of subversive chic. "Yeah, there's something hilarious about it anyway."

Xander had helped tape the wire up to her neck and hidden it in the folds of the fabric. He had some definite ideas about how to do it.

"I can't see anything, so that's good. Dallas said you need the wire?"

"He insisted on it, though I got the feeling it's a just-in-case sort of thing." She spun around to face him and folded the collar on his button-down evenly against his neck. "Is it wrong that I am kind of excited about all this?"

His hands snaked around to cup her bottom. "Oh, really? What part of it excites you, exactly?"

Cheyenne wiggled against his grip. "The intrigue. I don't like being the focus of the video, but I am kind of thinking the whole drop-off thing is exciting. I wasn't the only one who laughed when they said it had to be at the same garage they used during Watergate for the meeting. It's sort of scary, but I don't feel like we are in any real danger."

"I don't think you should be so flippant about it, honestly. But we have our directions. What's the back-up plan?"

Back-up plan? Was she supposed to have one? Dallas had been confident in what he'd told her to do; wouldn't he have helped her figure out one if she needed one? "There isn't one. All we are supposed to do is take the van to the garage. Meet up with whoever is there, hand them the boxes of documents, then leave. Do you think we need a back-up plan?"

"Did Dallas suggest anything? What were his exact directions?"

Xander clearly trusted Dallas' judgment as much as she did. That boded well for their future relationship. Alberto and Dallas had never gotten along all that well.

"I'm supposed to drive to the garage, go to the bottom floor and wait for the pick-up. I am supposed to get there early, park in a way that I can drive out straight, and wait for whoever shows up to show up."

"And then?"

"And then nothing. Let them go on their way."

Xander's lips tightened into a thin line. "It sounds easy."

"I know, right? But, the weird thing is, when we interrogated Gordy earlier, I was expecting Dallas to get the water-board out or something horrible like that to make him talk. All it took for Gordy to spill everything was threatening him with jail time."

"Some people break easy."

Cheyenne bobbed her head from side to side. "And, I should add, Dallas popped out of the bathroom he was hiding in and pumped himself up a little bit."

"Your brother is one scary dude. I wouldn't want to go up against him."

"Good thing you won't have to," Cheyenne said, kissing him lightly on the nose. "You ready to do this thing?"

"Almost," Xander said. "I still don't like the idea of being parked in a garage. I haven't been there, but that place is famous. It's old school. Dark. Closed in."

"The only thing I can think of is to have you follow

me over and park outside. That way, if we need to abandon the van, we can use your car."

"I don't like leaving you alone for a minute, but it does give us another way out. I'll lead us over and try to park on the street outside the garage. You can follow me and pick me up on the way inside the garage."

"Honestly? If Dallas really thought this was going to go south, he would probably insist on getting one of his work buddies to go in my stead. Or with me. He wouldn't let me do this if he thought I was in any danger."

"Is Dallas too close to the situation? I mean, if it were my sister, I'm not sure I would let her go at this alone."

"I promised him I would bring you."

"And it's a good thing I showed up, isn't it? Would you have called me if I hadn't?"

Cheyenne looked away. "No. I would have gone alone. I think. Does it matter now that you are here?"

"Reckless woman."

"That's me."

Dallas' van drove like a truck, but she somehow managed to control the damn thing. Cheyenne followed Xander to the garage and around the block three times before he slipped his Tesla into a space just outside a door leading from the garage.

"That's as close as we're going to get to the emergency exit," Xander said as he jumped into the passenger seat next to her.

Cheyenne maneuvered the van around the garage and to the bottom floor as planned. It was after work hours, and it was mostly empty. There were plenty of spaces, but nothing that made it easy to drive through so she'd be easily facing out. After a bit of work she got the van into position near a side emergency exit door.

"Help me get the boxes to the side door. I can't get the back doors open with the van parked this way."

Xander shoved the boxes over for her. "I'll tell you what. If your boss ever runs for president, I'm voting for him."

"Yeah. He's a good man to do all this for me. Anyone else, and they might have just told me I was out of luck."

"There's got to be some self-preservation going on, but yeah. The fact he didn't just throw you under the bus in all this is pretty cool."

A screech of tires from above announced the arrival of whoever it was they'd be meeting. Cheyenne patted at the fabric on her neck.

"Can't see anything," Xander assured her. "Just don't touch it again or you will draw attention to it."

Cheyenne looked at Xander sideways. "You sure seem like you know what you're doing," she said.

"I watch a lot of movies," he said, but he didn't meet her eyes.

They stood side-by-side as the other car made its way down the ramps to them. It was a mini-van with two men inside. There was nothing odd about them. Neither had giant scars across their faces or looked like a stereotypical bad guy from a movie. Both were beach-blond surfer dudes. They wore jeans and t-shirts. As they hopped out of the van, one of them even smiled at her as if they were casual acquaintances. The smiling dude wore a Nirvana t-shirt. The other wore a shirt with an image of a marijuana leaf on it and a more deadened expression. Either there wasn't much going on inside or he was high. They could be twins but for their expressions.

"You got a couple boxes for us?" Smiling Dude asked.

"Right here," Cheyenne said, sliding the door open.

They lifted the boxes over without talking. When they were done, Smiling Dude wiped his hands on his pants and clapped them together. "Looks like that's it. Hey, I'm really sorry about this next bit, but Senator Markle was pretty clear we need to not be followed."

Cheyenne's heart rate shot up a notch or two.

Senator Markle's name was now recorded for a second time. Gordy had sworn he was the force behind the entire operation. Smiling Dude had freely offered the name, and they were in Virginia where taping only required one person's consent. Cheyenne's wire had captured something valuable, after all. Having this guy's slip had confirmed Gordy's information from earlier and given them solid evidence Markle was involved in the blackmail scheme. Part of her wished they would use it in a court of law so everyone could see what a scumbag Markle really was, but she'd have to live with the hope the information could be used to hurt him later.

The information also confirmed that Kenny and Dallas were breaking into the right place. Senator Markle wasn't stupid enough to try this from his home. But, his chief IT toady, Phillip Swanson, was running the tech from a separate office in Maryland. According to Gordy, the senator was involved in several similar operations to discredit other threats to his own presidential bid, but kept himself removed from the details.

Smiling Dude reached around to his back. His t-shirt had been hiding a gun tucked into the back of his waistband. He smiled widely, showing his bright white teeth. This time, the smile did not reach his eyes. They were vacant. Hard and cold. Suddenly, all the excitement of this little adventure disappeared, and

Cheyenne's insides turned to liquid. It was all she could do to hold it together and not pee her pants or worse.

"What's the gun for?" she asked, her voice quivering like a tiny bird. "Is that a silencer? What the hell?"

Xander stepped in front of her, putting himself between her and the gun, his hands up in the air. "No need for violence. You have the documents. Just leave."

Smiling Dude laughed and shook his head, waiving the gun in a circle. "No, man. I'm not gonna shoot you. Just relax. Jeez. Do I look like a guy who would actually shoot *people*?" He turned to his friend. "Have you ever seen me shoot anyone?"

"No, brah. You'd never hurt anyone," he said, speaking for the first time. His words were slow and deliberate. "Seriously, dude is vegan. He doesn't even eat animals. Not even honey. Wouldn't hurt a fly." His pupils were rounded and fully black, almost filling out his irises, and it had nothing to do with the lighting in the garage. He was high as a kite.

Smiling Dude turned the gun toward Dallas' van and shot the tire closest to him. "We don't want to be followed. That's all." He circled the van, shooting all four tires. The first was mostly deflated by the time he'd finished.

Cheyenne didn't point out that the Smiling Shooting Dude had just mentioned his boss' name, and she wasn't about to tell them they'd got it on record.

Xander put one arm behind him to draw Cheyenne close toward him. Together, they inched away from the other two and the van. "Okay. Okay. We're not going to do anything but wait for you to leave."

"Good deal," Smiling Dude said. The twins jumped into their van and squealed away.

Xander grabbed her hand and they raced for the stairs. "Let's go."

"Are we going to follow them?" Cheyenne asked. "Is there a point?"

"If they go directly to Senator Markle, we can maybe get some photos of them handing things over. Proof he's behind all this."

"I'm not sure that photos of guys handing boxes over to the senator will prove much of anything, but we could try."

They made it to street level just as the van was pulling out of the parking garage. Xander and Cheyenne held back half a second to see which way they needed to go before running to Xander's Tesla. She was barely buckled in before Xander had them flying through traffic. The van was waiting calmly at a stop light two blocks ahead of them. Xander closed in the distance with ease.

It didn't even look like they were worried about being followed as they made their way back into DC and up to Chevy Chase. Cheyenne relaxed into the seat as Xander drove and texted Dallas to let him know they had handed over the boxes.

> **Cheyenne**: Also, they shot the tires on your van.
> We left it in the garage and are following in
> Xander's car.
> **Dallas**: Shit. Don't follow. Go home.

"Dallas said we shouldn't follow. Maybe it's not so safe. He did have a gun."

Xander's grip on the wheel tightened. "They have no clue we're here. We're safe."

Cheyenne re-read Dallas' text and sucked in her lower lip. Her brother was the security expert. Xander was an archeologist. A professor. Not exactly someone with a lot of experience with bad guys. But Dallas wasn't here, and Xander was.

> **Cheyenne**: Just confirming where they are taking
> documents. Staying a safe distance away.

"Doesn't it seem kind of weird that they would

take the documents straight to Senator Markle? I mean, if he's got the tech side at a different location, why not have the documents go somewhere else, too?"

Xander backed off the van as they turned onto Bradley Lane, a tree-line street with almost no other traffic. Suddenly, they were a single car following another car and conspicuous. The van turned into a driveway. Xander barely slowed down as they passed, but there was too much greenery to see anything other than the driveway and a general shape of a large house tucked away.

Cheyenne snapped a photo of the address. "I am pretty sure this is the senator's home."

"I'll circle back around," Xander said as he zipped up the street and pulled a u-turn.

"Pull over, I can sneak up to the fence and see if I can look through the hedge."

Xander stopped just past the driveway and Cheyenne jumped from the car. It was mostly dark out, but the street lights gave good illumination. She wasn't going to be hidden no matter what she did, so she ran to the fence and found a convenient hole in the greenery.

The Dude Twins were carrying the boxes in through a side door as Senator Markle held it open for them. Cheyenne slid the camera up into the view and snapped a few photos. Xander was probably right, though. There was nothing that could link those boxes up with her being blackmailed other than her own testimony. Legally, anyway, these photos would be useless, but Dallas or Kenny might still have a use for them in a less than legal way.

"Should we head over to where Dallas and Kenny are?"

"Probably. Let me see what Dallas says." Cheyenne texted Dallas the photos and asked what to do next.

> **Dallas**: Go home. Boing your boyfriend. Be done with this.
>
> **Cheyenne**: Hell no. I want to see the end of this.
>
> **Dallas**: We're done. Nothing to see. Go home.

"I'm pretty sure I know what pissed looks like on you," Xander said.

"He's telling me to go home."

"Sounds like a plan," Xander said.

Cheyenne shifted in her seat. How did she explain her need to see the end of all this in person? She needed something more tangible. Memorable. She needed to be a part of the destruction, whatever form that might take.

"I want to take a sledgehammer to something," she said. It was the best image she could come up with.

"Okay. Something physical," Xander said. "I get that. This whole digitized world makes it so unreal in many ways."

"Exactly. The thumb drive was just a copy. How many are out there? How will I know they are all gone?"

Xander squeezed her hand and left it on top of hers, steering with his left. "You might never know for sure. Would it help if we went over there anyway? To what's his name? Swanson?"

"Yes, please. Dallas wants me to go home and forget about it all, I just can't do that without..." she held up a fist into the air. In the olden days, there would have been actual film or tape that she could snip into little pieces. Now, she'd have to find some other symbolic form of destruction.

Swanson's office was only a few miles away from Markle's home. The converted town-house's dilapidated exterior gave it a false sense of poverty—like a mask. The row of old buildings it was attached to was in even worse repair. What better way to disguise hundreds of thousands of dollars worth of computer equipment?

The sign outside said "computer repairs" and the windows were filled with ancient bricks of computers. An old-style monitor sat center stage, its long-dead screen filled with a vinyl image of an old video game. Parts to various game systems and cartridges were spread around the base, giving the front window of the 'shop' a vague old-school and out-of-touch sensibility.

Xander drove them past the building and around the back. The rest of the block was filled with other shops, all closed for the evening, and his Tesla parked out in front would draw unwanted attention to them. In the back alleyway, a bicycle was locked to a thick pipe running along the wall next to the door.

After another trip around the block, they parked down the street in the parking for a bar not far away from Swanson's office.

"I think that bike must be Swanson's," Cheyenne said. "It makes sense for him to be there in order to upload the files or turn on the website or whatever it is he has to do."

"Theoretically, Markle has called him off because you delivered the goods."

"There's nothing to keep Swanson from taking the footage and just selling it or making money off it himself. I mean, as a pure porn tape."

Xander blinked a few times as if he were digesting this bit of information for the first time. "It's *really* that graphic?"

"You *really* didn't watch it?"

"No. But, you know what? Having the real you in my life? That's all that really matters. A movie? A photo? It's nothing but dots on a screen. It's a past you."

Cheyenne's face warmed at the words. "Nothing like that will happen ever again, Xander. I don't need any man in my life but you, let alone all of that."

"Let's do what we can to make sure this never gets out, then. But that bike? It's probably Swanson's."

"No way could a geek guy like Swanson overtake Dallas. Even with a gun or something," Cheyenne said.

"You never know. Just because someone comes across as meek or whatever, doesn't mean they aren't hiding something."

Cheyenne looked closely at Xander for some hidden meaning in his words. Was there some double entendre there? Was this professor of hers more than he seemed? He did seem awfully sure of himself. Before she could get a complete read on him, he was out of the car and opening her door.

"Shall we?" He held out his hand for her as if they were about to jump onto a dance floor.

They pretended to be interested in the bar down the street from Swanson's building while looking for any sign of life within the small shop. Dallas had still not responded to her text.

"Let's try walking in," Cheyenne said.

"You mean, just go up to the door and try it?"

"Yep." Cheyenne strode across the street and tried the front door to the shop. It was locked.

"Around back?"

"Sure."

The bicycle was still attached to the pipe with a combination lock.

"I think Swanson is inside, waiting for confirmation from Markle," she said.

Just as she reached out to open the door from the alleyway, there was a shout from inside.

"That's Dallas," Cheyenne said, choking on her words. She stepped back, shaken and torn about what to do next.

"I couldn't make out what he was saying, could you?" Xander asked.

"Not exactly, but he was sounding like Dallas the big-bad-bully-man. He can be terrifying when he wants to be."

Cheyenne tugged at the door, and it opened quietly. Unlike the façade of the building, the back entry was modern. Right behind the main door was another door with a card key reader that had obviously been hacked. Bits of wires and bobs of things Cheyenne couldn't identify hung from it. The door was ajar by three inches, not nearly enough for her to get a good look inside.

Xander put an arm in front of her and held his finger to his lips, putting himself between her and whatever was in front of them. He pushed the door open the rest of the way. Directly to the left was a shelf. It was filled with various computer parts, but orderly and neatly labeled. Past that was a black curtain, and beyond that were voices.

Cheyenne tried to press past Xander to get as close to the curtain as possible, but he held her back and tilted his head toward the curtain indicating they should listen first. Dallas, Kenny, and someone she didn't recognize were talking.

Dallas' voice was clear and loud now. "That's it for copies? Backups?"

*Copies? Backups? Worse, 'that's it'?* Did that mean Dallas had gotten Swanson to talk about the back ups and copies he'd already made? She couldn't hear the answer because it was garbled, sniveling grunts. Dallas must have scared the hell out of Swanson. Cheyenne had absolutely no remorse for the jerk who'd helped engineer all this.

"We're in," Kenny said in a sing song voice, "finally."

Xander pushed the curtain to one side and entered first, blocking her from view to begin with. Cheyenne looked around him, partly grateful he was watching out for her, partly annoyed she couldn't really see.

Dallas leaned against a table, bulging arms crossed over each other casually as if he were having a casual conversation. Swanson had practically dissolved into the chair where he sat. His entire body oozed submission and cowardice. His face, probably a rather pasty white normally, had gone splotchy red. He wiped at the snot dribbling from his nose.

Xander stepped to the side and brought her around, his arm lightly over her shoulder.

Dallas didn't turn to look at her, but his eyes met hers briefly. "I told you to go home. What are you doing here?"

"There was no stopping her. She needed to see it. Feel it," Xander said.

Dallas and Xander exchanged a look that said way more than words could. The two men she trusted more than anyone else were either bonding or colluding, and she couldn't tell which. Something was going on, and yet...what?

Kenny poked his head around from behind where Swanson sat. "We're nearly there. We had some issues getting in, but it was helpful that Swanson here actually showed up. He's been most helpful."

Swanson dropped his head to look at his feet.

"Dude was told to drop it, scrub the video as promised. Came in to make some copies to distribute on his own. You know, just for kicks," Dallas said. Twice in one day, Cheyenne was getting to see her brother in his professional capacity. It was a little disturbing. But man, did he get things done.

This was the guy who had physically done all this? Put together the video? Designed the bribery website?

Cheyenne want to punch Swanson upside the head, to take a baseball bat and whack at him until he was unconscious and bloody, until he looked as battered as she had felt when first viewing the video. She stepped forward, her hand clenching into a fist. Xander grabbed her hand and held her close before she could get a good swing in.

"I take it you persuaded him to be helpful?" Xander asked.

"Nothing was going to go on the net, I promise. I just wanted it for me. And a few friends. It's quality footage, you know?" Swanson was in tears, half sobbing and choking on is own words.

Xander released Cheyenne and grabbed Swanson by the front of his overly worn t-shirt. "You son of a bitch. You knew how that video was made, and yet you were going to keep it?"

Swanson's eyes widened into huge saucers of blue as he recognized Cheyenne. "Wait. You're her? Shit." His fear focused on Xander now.

Dallas relaxed against the table, but didn't move to interfere with whatever Xander had in mind.

Xander's fingers tightened around the fabric, pulling Swanson in closer. The younger man gaped back and forth between Cheyenne and Xander and Dallas. Cheyenne almost felt sorry for him. Being caught between a super-pissed older brother and a super-pissed lover after putting together a blackmail porn tape was probably the worse thing that had ever happened to him.

"I swear. I don't have any copies. I was waiting until I got the word to destroy the video."

"And who's running this thing?"

Swanson shook his head harder back and forth, the whites of his eyes stark against his red-rimmed eyes. "Oh, no. No way. Beat me up. Kill me now. Cause if I tell you and word gets out, I'm dead anyway."

"Yeah. You're done in this town forever. You'll be lucky if you can get a tech repair job at your local office supply," Kenny said, standing up. "Okay, I've got my guy working on things remotely. Got all the access codes, server lists, yada, yada, yada... He's scrubbing everything from there."

Swanson was breathing hard and fast now, hyperventilating. Xander shoved him back into his chair and pushed his head between his knees. "Breathe, you stupid fool. How pathetic."

"He's just a tool," Cheyenne said. "A pitiful, lonely tool. The real villain here is Markle."

Swanson's head shot up then. "I didn't say anything. You didn't hear that from me." He dropped his head into his hands. "Oh god, oh god, oh god. I am so royally fucked."

"Indeed. But only so many can say how they

fucked themselves over," Kenny said. "You got yourself into this mess all on your own."

"All right, everyone out," Dallas said. "This whole thing is ridiculous and out of hand. Kenny, you good?"

"I need three more minutes."

"And you don't need Swanson for anything else?" Dallas asked.

"Nope. You can get rid of him," Kenny said.

At that, Swanson brought his arms up around his head and neck and collapsed into a tight self-protecting ball of blubber on the floor.

"Ah, for fuck's sake. Get the fuck off the ground, you fucking sack of garbage," Dallas said, nudging him in the back with his foot. "I'm not going to kill you, you fucking idiot."

Swanson peeked at Dallas from between his fingers.

"As much as I'd like to ram a gun down your throat, you're not worth the effort. Now, get the fuck out of Dodge. You are done here. Put a thousand miles between us, or you'll never work again. Got it?"

Swanson's jaw opened and shut without sound a couple of times, but he nodded and rolled onto his knees. He crawled away from them toward the curtain and the back door before finally standing and running away.

Dallas rolled his eyes and wiped at his face as the man disappeared.

"Kenny? He's out of here. We need to get this place clear so I can do my thing."

"Your thing?" Cheyenne asked.

Dallas tilted his toward the door. "Time for you and Xander to be going. I'll check in with you later."

"And that's a wrap, folks," Kenny said as he jumped up from the console where he'd been working. "It's cleaned and wiped. Time to burn this shit down."

"You mean it's over?" Cheyenne asked. "You've gotten rid of every copy?"

"As far as I can tell, yes. And if the little shit was telling the truth, he hadn't actually made any other copies than the one on the thumb drive they sent you. The original footage...all eight hours of it...is gone as well."

Cheyenne saw the opening credits to *Kitchen Wars* flash in front of her. Images of her with Tiffany, Chelsea and Zach all in their whites and checkers looking like a winning team went from fuzzy to more clear and certain. The threat was gone. She wasn't going to mess up their chances before they were even in the competition.

"Let's get moving, then," Dallas said. This time, he held his arms out wide to shepherd her and Xander out of the room and building.

"No," Cheyenne said. "This isn't real enough. I need to feel it, Dallas. I need to...break something."

Dallas scrubbed at his face with his hands for a moment. "Okay. Tell you what." He looked around the room and picked up a metal stool. "Try crashing this into the computers. Break a monitor with it."

She turned the stool over and grabbed it by the bottom part of the legs as handles.

Kenny pointed to a monitor and said, "This is the one they used to review the footage. You were in living color and nearly life size."

Cheyenne hefted the chair and swung it around. She yelled as she brought the arc of it down onto the computer. The glass front cracked with a satisfying smash. The crystalline pattern that formed across it was almost pretty. Cheyenne pulled it back and did a side swing, putting all her weight into it a second time. The monitor flew backward into the wall with a satisfying thunk.

"This box had stuff on it," Kenny said, pointing to a tower with blinking lights and funky looking disc drives.

"Stuff" was vague, but Cheyenne didn't care. She cranked up the stool for another round of fun. She slammed the chair into the plastic. The crunch and tinkle of breakage from within was music to her ears. Dallas pointed out another computer, Kenny another monitor. The guys sat back, cheering her along as she worked off her anger one blow at a time. And so it went until Cheyenne could no longer lift the stool to hit anything. Various bits of broken computers and dangling wires, shreds of machinery littered every surface.

Sweat rolled off Cheyenne's forehead and her arms ached. She'd be lucky to lift them over her head tomorrow. "That was fucking awesome."

Xander helped her unlock her fingers' tight grip around the stool legs and massaged them out for her.

"Remind me to not ever anger you, Jaani."

His soothing voice was like a balm. It helped bring her heart rate back into normal ranges.

"Let's get outside, and I will let you push the detonator button to finish this all off," Dallas said.

"Wait, you are going to blow this building up?" Cheyenne asked. "What about the buildings it's attached to? The people around here?"

Dallas held up his hands. "It's not a bomb, not like you're thinking." He walked a circuit around the room and pointed out a dozen devices around the perimeter Cheyenne had completely missed before. Each had a tiny antenna and was attached to a gooey gray putty. "This is a special compound. Sort of like c-4. Moldable. Uses a detonator. All I have to do is send the signal over and *poof,* this building goes up. It's owned by...dun, dun, dun..."

Dallas held out his hand toward Cheyenne waiting for the answer.

"Senator Markle?"

"Score!"

"But the neighbors?" Cheyenne asked.

"It's vacant. And, before you get too worried, the damage here will be quite extensive, but it burns hot and fast to destroy all the evidence. And the fire department will be here before it reaches the other buildings. It hitting Markle in the pocket book is a nice bonus."

"Won't it be ruled an arson?"

"Yep. Probably will put the blame on Swanson, but, frankly, I don't really care."

"Should we wipe my prints off the chair? What about other things I've touched?"

"Nah. The investigation into this is going to be swept under a rug pretty quickly."

"Dallas, how do you know that?" He gave her a look that annoyed her as a kid and annoyed her now—it was a Cheshire Cat grin squared. He always managed to make himself look smug and superior while being ultra sneaky. "Dallasssssss..."

Without answering, Dallas swept his arms in a huge gesture to get them all moving out of the building. They walked the block away to where Dallas and Kenny had parked. He handed Cheyenne the detonator radio switch.

"All I do is push the button?"

He nodded.

Xander stood behind her, his hands on her shoulders.

She held up the detonator and pushed the red button. It was nothing like in the movies. There was a whumphing sound, and a few seconds later, the glass in the building broke and shattered. But that was it for the first minute or so. Then, smoke licked out of the bottom floor, followed soon by visible flames dancing along the window frames and upward along the outside of the building.

Sirens in the distance shook Cheyenne from the spectacle. "Did you call them ahead of time, Dallas?"

"Didn't really want to take a chance with the other buildings, now did we? But, that's definitely our cue to get out of here," Dallas said holding his hand out to Xander. "Thanks for joining in on the fun, man. It's been great working with you again. You two should go home and get some sleep."

"No problem," Xander said.

*Again?* Cheyenne was too stunned to speak. What was Dallas talking about.

Xander took Dallas' offered hand, but Dallas pulled him into a man hug, slapping him on the back.

By the time they were back to Xander's car, the first fire truck rounded the corner and people streamed out of the bar on the corner across the street to see what the commotion was about. Xander sped away from the scene without anyone stopping him. Cheyenne watched the growing conflagration in the passenger side mirror until they turned the corner and it disappeared from view.

## Chapter 30

"My place or yours?" Cheyenne asked.

"How about *ours*?"

Cheyenne swallowed hard. "Ours?"

"Why not move in with me until you go? That way we can spend as much time together as possible before you leave."

"Are you sure about that? Maybe we should wait until after I'm off the show."

"That will take months."

"Could be a week or two if we were to lose in the first few rounds of the competition."

"You're not going to lose. There's no way. Your team is solid. I predict you will make it to the quarter finals at the very least."

"What? You aren't predicting we will win

outright?" Cheyenne put on her best shocked and hurt look.

"I don't want to jinx it by being too honest."

"I'll have to think about moving in. We have lots of test cooking and practicing to do together before the show, and I need to be at my place for that."

"My place *for now*, then. At the very least, I want to be alone with you for the rest of the night and well into tomorrow."

Cheyenne sat back comfortably into the seat of the car, her eyes on Xander the entire ride home. He was so calm. So certain. She ran a finger along his jaw, letting the coarseness of his five o'clock shadow tickle against her skin.

"What did you have in mind?"

"It's not even midnight," he said. "I want to take you home, undress you, and kiss every inch of your beautiful body."

"Keep going," she said, already warming to the idea.

"So many things...but we have time. We have a few weeks and then, once you are back in town, we will have forever."

"Forever..." she repeated the word slowly, let it roll around on her tongue to see how it fit, how it tasted.

"Yes, forever. The last few hours have been terrifying and exciting, and there was a moment, when the madman with the gun was waving it around, I thought we were both going to die, and all I knew was that I didn't want to lose you. Not to death, not to indecision, not to petty worries. Everything else popped into perspective. The video? It was nothing in comparison to the possibility of losing you forever."

*Perspective.* Nia was always using that word with her.

"I almost peed my pants when he pulled out the gun. I was scared but also thought it was too unreal to actually be happening. It was more like...it was happening to someone else and I was watching a movie," Cheyenne said.

"When he shot the tire on the van, I thought... that's it. He's just messing with us and we are next."

"He told us he wasn't going to shoot us."

"I was more skeptical than you. And then, that asshole, Swanson? I wanted to rip him into pieces. And then I realized he's just some schmuck who will never ever have a chance to be with a real woman like you. The closest he will ever get is a brief digital image. A glimpse. And you know what? I realized I didn't care because I have you. Or at least, I think I do. In real life. And, as long as that is real, that is all that matters."

"So, if a copy of that thing surfaces in twenty years, you won't be upset?"

Xander laughed. "I might be turned on by it in twenty years."

Cheyenne backhanded a lazy slap against his shoulder. "Maybe I should hold on to that thumb drive after all."

By the time they arrived at Xander's apartment, Cheyenne's arms were stiffening up from her bashing frenzy.

"Let's turn this into an opportunity," Xander said. "Let's take a nice hot bath. I'll give you some deep massage. That and some ibuprofen will do the trick."

As soon as they were inside, he turned on the hot water to fill the bath. He handed her a couple pain killers and then undressed her tenderly. The wire was still taped to her body, and he removed the tape with sure, decisive movements.

His tub was deeper than standard baths and just wide enough for her to slip in between his legs.

Xander's magical fingers glanced up her arms and slowly worked their way deep into the knots that had gathered and bunched in her neck, shoulders and back.

By the time he'd worked through all of the kinks, Cheyenne was limp as a rag doll—relaxed and ready for anything. The tension of the last few days was gone. Everything looked perfect and bright in her future. She had Xander, in spite of all the obstacles she had placed before them. In a few months, if they won the competition, she'd be well on her way to running her own restaurant.

"Penny for your thoughts?" Xander asked, his voice buzzing lightly against her ear.

She lolled her head backwards onto his shoulder. Water rippled around them, a little dripping over the edge of the tub and splashing onto the tiled floor. "This is perfect."

Xander slid his oiled hands around to cup her breasts. "Mmmm...hmmm...agreed." He captured each nipple between thumb and forefinger and pulled gently before letting them plop back into place.

Cheyenne's nipples hardened as her breasts bobbed gently in the water. "Do that again."

Xander nuzzled at her open neck and did as she asked. This time, he twisted the nipples a little before letting go, squeezing and releasing with a little more force than before.

"Mmm. Again."

"How hard?"

"More," she said.

He laughed into her neck, grazing it with the stubble on his chin. "Like this?"

He pinched a little harder, twisted a little further. Cheyenne groaned into the air, tilting her head back and arching her hips upward. He let go of one of her breasts to slide his hand down along her slick stomach and down to her pussy.

He curled two fingers into her, slowly fucking her, one finger along each side of her clit and then inside her with each stroke.

"That's nice," she said, pushing her hips into his hand, eager for more.

Xander rubbed his face against her neck, giving her the full roughness of his fresh beard. She tilted her head away to give him even more access to her neck, and he nipped at her skin with his teeth while pulling her against him. His erect cock pressed against her back, ready and willing.

Cheyenne's breath caught in her throat for a moment. "Xander," she groaned, wiggling against him. He spun her around until they were facing each other and moved them to the middle of the tub so she could sit on top of him with her legs wrapped around him.

He paused, holding her away from him before he entered her. "Are you sure?" He motioned to his bare cock.

She sucked in her lower lip. "Are you sure?" she asked. "I've been pretty careful, but I don't have any recent results."

"I'm willing to chance it. I want to feel you completely around me, if that's okay with you," he said.

"Please. Yes, please." She hadn't had a man without a condom on in four years.

She guided herself onto him, lowering herself one inch at a time until he was fully inside her. He grasped her at the waist using the water to help him lift her up and down, ensuring her clit found purchase with each and every motion. Water swirled around them, making little waves that lapped at their skin and splashing around them.

Cheyenne grasped the rim of the tub and took over the motion, moving faster and faster as she grew close to her climax. She clung onto Xander, wrapping her arms and legs around him, holding him deep inside her as the orgasm finally hit her, just the tiny movement of her hips grinding her against him as the orgasm played itself out. She pressed into him and arched her back as she howled with the exquisite pain of it.

When she opened his eyes, he was staring at her, a little smile on his lips.

"Jaani," he said, "I will never tire of watching you come. Your enjoyment is so genuine."

Cheyenne rode out the last of the spasms filling her body, his hard and erect cock still filling her up. "My turn to watch you."

Xander lifted his hips so that she could get onto her knees without them losing full contact. He leaned back against the curve of the tub and held onto the rim.

Cheyenne grasped his forearms for balance and rode him hard and fast. She wanted him to lose control, to come inside her while bucking crazily underneath her. The water had its own rhythm, and once she caught onto it, she moved up and down his cock with the help of the water rising and falling with her, some of it sloshing over the sides and splattering on the floor. She focused on nothing but bringing him pleasure, her initial needs already sated.

Cheyenne locked her eyes on his while their bodies slammed into each other, buoyed and jostled both by the water. She didn't expect a second orgasm, so when it came, it surprised her. She refused to break her rhythm and rocked her way through it while bringing Xander over the edge with her. He bucked up into her, coming hard and only breaking eye contact in the intensity of the moment.

They slowed their pace to revel in their still pulsing bodies, her squeezing against him, milking him for everything he would give her.

Slowly, finally, they stilled and the water calmed along with them.

Cheyenne curled into him, leaning her forehead against his shoulder, both breathing hard. It wasn't until she shivered from the coolness of the water that they moved again. Standing into a hot shower, they rinsed off the oil from the bath, their hands exploring each other's bodies—still so new to each other, delighting in learning each crevice and dimple.

Dried and collapsing onto his bed, Cheyenne burrowed her face against his chest, inhaling his clean scent deeply, memorizing the nuances and uniqueness that was Xander. At length she rolled on top of him, straddling his chest.

His eyes opened and he smiled languidly up at her. "More?"

She grasped his wrists and held them above his head. Leaning over, she kissed his nose and said, "Yes, but first? You have to tell me the truth about you and Dallas. What are you hiding from me, Jaani? It's your turn to come clean."

Xander closed his eyes, but he didn't fight her or try to get out from under her. Cheyenne got the sense he was thinking very carefully about what he was going to say. After a long moment, he breathed out and opened his eyes again, meeting hers.

"How did you figure it out?" he asked.

"Dallas. He said something as we were leaving tonight. About how great it was to work with you *again*. It took me a while to figure out what he could possibly have meant. But you were so casual about taping the wire to me, and you did it without hesitating. And then, when the guy pulled out the gun, you were right there in front of me. But you were so chill.

Later, you made sure I didn't get in the way when we went into Swanson's office. And there was something about the way Dallas reacted when he first saw you in my apartment. The way he asked you your name, as if he wasn't sure he'd heard it right. It's because he didn't know you were Alexander Moore, he knew you as someone else."

"I thought we covered better than that."

"You did. Up until tonight. Dallas slipped."

"Yeah, that was a little weird, but I don't think he slipped up. I think he did it intentionally. I was hoping you hadn't noticed because I wasn't sure how you would react to it."

"Well, I did. So spill it. I don't need all the details, I get how some of that stuff works. Just general context."

"What do you know about Dallas' time in Afghanistan?"

"Not much. Just that it was rough. He came home changed, but has gotten more like his old self over the last couple years. He's a lot older than I am."

"We worked together on a couple of missions. I worked for...well. It doesn't matter, really. I was undercover. Using a different name. Serving the US with your brother. I'm afraid that's all I can tell you. Other than, he saved my butt at least once, and we have a great respect for each other."

"Fair enough." Cheyenne could live with the vagueness. She was used to Dallas' occasional stone-silences, how he would suddenly stop talking and look far off into the distance. Cheyenne released his wrists. "And I need one more thing from you."

Xander rested his hands on her thighs lightly. "If I can..."

"Are you still working undercover? Are you really a professor and an archeologist?"

Xander laughed lightly. "Actually, I am Alexander Moore. That is my real name, though Dallas didn't know that until the other night. And, yes, I am an archeologist. Have been for almost ten years now. Nothing more. That was another life ago."

"So, you're done with all that?"

"Yes, Jaani...I'm done with all that."

"There's no more secrets between us?"

"Nothing of consequence," he said, moving his hands to cup her breasts, his thumbs circling her nipples into hard nubs.

"Good," she said, leaning in to kiss him. "Now then... I'm ready for more Moore."

## Chapter 31

*Five weeks later*

Cheyenne wiped the last pot dry and handed it to Dallas. They'd finished their family meal and were on kitchen duty as usual.

"Wine, Sky?" Cheyenne asked, taking a peak at the tiny baby bump on her sister's slight frame.

"I can sip at some," she said. "The doctor said a glass every now and again wouldn't hurt the baby."

"Really? I thought any alcohol was bad. If you end up carrying my baby for me, we'll have to talk about that," Cheyenne said.

"Cheyenne, I have been through this before, trust me. A few sips of wine is not a problem. And, you need to know, if I end up as a surrogate for you and

Xander, I will still probably want my bacon on Sunday mornings."

They'd all had a good natured discussion during dinner about the American obsession with bacon. The kids had lots of questions for Xander when they learned he didn't eat it.

Cheyenne handed Dallas his beer and poured herself and her sister half a glass of wine left over from dinner. It had been a fairly crazy few weeks, and it was the first time Cheyenne had made it to a family dinner since the explosive end to the video. She and Xander were heading out to LA the following day in a week long road trip. They wanted to spend as much time together before the competition as they could.

Sky settled into the kitchen booth and clasped her hands in front of her. "Now, I have a couple more questions, just to wrap up all the deets in my head."

Dallas and Cheyenne had given Sky the basics while they washed dishes. A few of the technical bits still boggled Cheyenne. Swanson had found out about the selfie she had taken with Shane and Kyle or, actually Mark and Jonas. Dallas had explained how Swanson had managed to take over her phone without her noticing to remove the photo from it as well as to block all those texts. She still didn't know how it had worked or how Dallas had magically fixed it because all the words he had used in explaining it to her had zipped past her head in a blur. It was as if she was a Charlie Brown character listening to an adult. But, whatever. It was over.

"I get that you didn't want the video to get out, but wasn't there a way to do that and get justice? It seems a shame the lot of them aren't going to be punished," Sky said.

"There's a difference between going to jail and being punished," Dallas said lifting his beer in emphasis.

"I got a great deal of satisfaction from bashing the hell out of the computer equipment in Swanson's office. Knowing the video is dead is enough for now."

"But, don't people have a right to know about Markle? That he paid Gordy to orchestrate this whole thing? What about the actors and Swanson? They should all be in jail," Sky said.

"Honestly, I don't know what the long term outcome is going to be," Dallas said. "More stuff went down at the Vegas meeting. That fucker Gordy..." His voice trailed off and he shook his head. "Anyway... We're building a substantial and real case against Markle, so let's just say he'll be a special project of mine for a while to come."

"We?" Cheyenne asked.

"Me and Kenny. Who, by the way, is tearing his hair out over Zach. What's up with that, anyway?"

"Zach can't stop talking about him. Kenny this. Kenny that. But Zach refuses to go out with him until after we get back from the competition."

Dallas tilted his head up to the ceiling. "Oh, that makes so much more sense now. Okay. Now I get it."

Sky turned to Cheyenne. "And you, I hope you tear up that bucket list of yours. It's gotten you into too much trouble."

"No way," Cheyenne said. "There are still a few fun things left on it that I need to do." Cheyenne looked toward the door between the kitchen and the family room where the rest of the family, including Xander, were watching the traditional Friday night movie. "The best part is most of the things on that list can be done with another person."

"Xander is quite the catch, Cheyenne. He's adorable, and I love his nickname for you," Sky said. "And the way he says it? It's like he's breathing out love every time."

"It's going to be a difficult three months, but we're totally dedicated to each other."

The last few weeks had been amazing.

Cheyenne had decided to stay in her own apartment so she could practice with Zach, Chelsea, and Tiffany. They'd watched every episode of *Kitchen Wars* and recreated most of the challenges. In addition, they'd combed through other cooking competitions for other tricks and tips. While the team challenge made the show unique, cooking techniques were pretty universal.

In the time she wasn't cooking with her team, she was with Xander. They went to all the Smithsonian Museums, various gardens around town, and out to a few plays and concerts. And they had sex. Lots and lots of sex. Xander joked that he had to make sure she had her fill of him to last her through their three-month long separation.

And, the previous evening, Xander had taken her to the Central Marina and onto a sail boat for the first time. It was a small sailboat that only took one person to navigate, and he'd given her a primer on the sails. Within a few hours, Cheyenne was feeling like she could almost sail around the Potomac by herself.

They had brought a picnic hamper onto the boat with them for dinner. By the time they'd had their fill of Zach's homemade baguette, an excellent brie, and sublime olives, the pinks and golden rays of the setting sun filled the sky and reflected along the Potomac. They cuddled against each other as the boat glided over the smooth water. Happy laughter and gentle shouts from other boats drifted toward them, but in a distant, unobtrusive way.

Cheyenne had been sitting with her back to Xander, leaning against his chest, his legs around hers when he produced a ring from out of nowhere. It was an antique with a great deal of charm to it. A small diamond was set around carved gold petal-shaped cutouts. The diamond was suspended in the gold and lay flat in the recess. Decorative scrolls were cut into the sides of the ring and the metal had a patina from use and wear.

"I don't want you going off to LA without this," he said. "I love you even more than ever, my sweet beautiful Jaani. Please say you will marry me."

"Yes, Xander. Of course I'll marry you," she said turning his hand as he held the ring. Little sparks of sky reflecting made it magical.

"It was my grandmother's, and I thought the diamond being low like that would be safe for you to wear in the kitchen. It's called a Belcher set and won't catch on things. She wore it for sixty-two years."

Cheyenne hoped to wear it for as long. She turned around onto her knees to face him. "It's lovely. Put it on?" She spread her fingers wide as he slipped the ring on her finger and she leaned into him for a kiss.

They'd spent the night on the boat, making love under the light of the moon and in rhythm to the lapping of the waves against the hull. It had been the perfect evening.

"You'll have plenty of time to settle in together

once you're done with the show," Dallas said, jostling Cheyenne from her reverie.

"There's a tiny part of me that doesn't want to go, but I know it will be so worth it all if we win."

Sky raised her glass of wine for a toast. "Here's wishing you the best of luck Cheyenne. I'm going to miss you, you know."

Cheyenne leaned in to hug Sky.

"Hey, I'm going to miss you as much as she is," Dallas said, pulling both of them up out of their seats and into his arms.

"You guys are going to make me cry," Cheyenne said.

"Any room in there for me?" Xander asked from the door. "Movie's over, and I hate being left out of group hugs."

Dallas opened the circle to him and the four fell into a group hug. Cheyenne was surrounded with the best kinds of love. She sought Xander's eyes as the group swayed back and forth together. They twinkled with his special humor.

The door burst open and the rest of the family streamed in and joined in on the giant hug filling up the kitchen. Cheyenne couldn't ask for a better family or fiancé. Even if she didn't win the competition, she was winning in life. And that was all that really mattered.

*The DC Knights series can be read in any order, but we hope you don't miss any of them!*

**New to the Game—D.C. Knights Book 1**

Chloe's the new intern, but she jumps into the game both feet first.

**Playing For Keeps—D.C. Knights Book 2**

Katherine thinks she's got things figured out until a sexy scientist tangos his way into her heart.

**All In—D.C. Knights Book 3**

Madeline has no problem playing games until she meets Ewan a man who knows how to treat her like a woman.

**Fair and Square—D.C. Knights Book 4**

Lizbeth doesn't have time for games, but she ends up in the midst of a political game no one in Congressman Pierce's office saw coming.

**Only Bluffing—D.C. Knights Book 5**

Eleanor Winslow and Daniel Prado are from different worlds. Will their love overcome dark histories and ancient legacies?

**Game On—D.C. Knights Book 6**

Cheyenne LeFleur lives on the wild side. Will Alexander Moore be able to handle her history, or will he reject her like so many before him?

**For the Win—D.C. Knights Book 7** The final chapter in this series. Congressman Lincoln Pierce deserves love, too. Can he find it while maintaining his principles?

**Also by Juno Chase:**

**ARTIFACT of BETRAYAL: an exciting romantic suspense novel**

If you had to choose between saving your life or the love of your life, *who would you choose?*

Claire Townsend has it all, a great job, her own shop in Brooklyn, until one night when she loses everything. With thirteen days to pay off a dangerous loan shark, she decides to partake in a black-market smuggling operation to save her own neck.

Bruno Canul is an archeologist who works as a consultant with the FBI. He chases a suspect to Belize only to find the ex-love-of-his-life as part of the crew. He can't tell if he should trust Claire or if she's joined forces with the smuggler.

Afraid her choices will get Bruno killed, Claire tries to resist falling back in love with him. If she goes through with the smuggling scheme, she can pay off her loan, but she'd lose Bruno's love and trust *forever*. If she stands up for their love, she's a dead woman.

This adventurous romantic suspense is sure to keep you on the edge of your seat as Claire and Bruno find love in the jungle and ancient Mayan ruins of Belize.

## About Juno Chase

Who said chivalry is dead? They were totally wrong! We love, love, love hot guys who are modern day knights and heroes but also know how to heat things up between the sheets.

Juno Chase is the nom de plume of two married moms who love reading and writing happy stories. We wanted to see these modern day knights celebrated in romance, so here we are. We're not a big group of people writing—there is just the two of us. We both spend lots of time reading and writing in each story to bring you the most complete, hot, and exciting stories possible.

Thank you so much for reading *New to the Game*, we hope you enjoyed reading it as much as we did writing it. If you sign up for our newsletter, you will be the first to know whenever we have a new book available.

*Follow Juno Chase on your favorite social Media. We'd love to hear from you!*

www.Junochase.com
juno@junochase.com

Acknowledgments

We'd like to thank a few people who helped us get this book into your lovely hands, dear readers. We are part of an amazing writing group who has listened to our ideas, helped us with plotting, and given us some straight feedback. We couldn't have done this without your energy and help-—you ladies rock! Thank you for all your reading time and thoughtful suggestions to help make the D.C. Knights series a reality.

To our intrepid beta readers. Thank you for taking the time to read and give us honest criticism. Especially to Dawn who has faithfully read everything we've handed her and keeps asking for more!

And to our families—our fabulous husbands and children who have supported us in so many different ways and picked up the pieces as needed. We love you!

www.ingramcontent.com/pod-product-compliance
Lightning Source LLC
Chambersburg PA
CBHW032156180726
48284CB00001B/62